PRAISE FOR KELLY HARMS

The Overdue Life of Amy Byler

"Librarians and booklovers will fall for Amy, and Harms writes a great light read full of tears, laughter, and charming, relatable characters."

—*Library Journal* (starred review)

"In the easygoing, character-driven style of Liane Moriarty and Barbara Davis, this story of an underappreciated single mom with more freedom than she's entirely comfortable with mixes the self-assured highs with the guiltiest lows of modern motherhood. Harms's warm and witty novel will tickle fans of *Where'd You Go, Bernadette* and *Eleanor Oliphant Is Completely Fine.*"

—*Booklist*

"A laugh-out-loud funny, pitch-perfect novel that will have readers rooting for this unlikely, relatable, and totally lovable heroine, *The Overdue Life of Amy Byler* is the ultimate escape—and will leave moms everywhere questioning whether it isn't time for a #momspringa of their own."

—*New York Journal of Books*

"Filled with love, self-discovery, and plot twists."

—*Madison Magazine*

"Kelly Harms tackles modern single motherhood with flair, swoons, and the most perfect date ever written. In *The Overdue Life of Amy Byler*, readers will connect with the titular character's unexpected journey of freedom and self-discovery, all told with Harms's signature humor . . . I'm a fan for life!"

—Amy E. Reichert, author of *The Optimist's Guide to Letting Go* and *The Coincidence of Coconut Cake*

"*The Overdue Life of Amy Byler* is a charming, relatable, and entertaining look at parenthood, divorce, dating, and everything in between. No one cuts right to the heart of life—in all its hilarity and heartbreak— quite like Kelly Harms. This is easily one of my favorite books of the year!"

—Kristy Woodson Harvey, author of *Slightly South of Simple*

"Amy Byler's life isn't easy—what with an absentee husband suddenly showing up and reclaiming some getting-to-know-you time with their two teenage kids. But what follows is pure wonder. Kelly Harms brings the mom-makeover story to a whole new level, with twists and turns and dialogue that is so funny you have to put down the book and simply allow yourself to laugh. It's well written, it's original, and I fell in love with Amy and all her well-meaning friends on her journey to find out who she really is. So much fun!"

—Maddie Dawson, *Washington Post* and Amazon Charts bestselling author of *Matchmaking for Beginners*

"Amy Byler's husband ditched her and their kids three years ago, so when he shows up, full of regret, we can forgive her for being less than welcoming. Still, she could use a break—and a life. What follows is so engaging I had to clear my calendar. Harms dances on the knife edge between snort-your-coffee humor and bull's-eye insights, often in the same sentence. As a card-carrying curmudgeon, I resist such tactics, but here I never felt played. Instead, I was swept up in Amy's everymom dilemma, her quest for a full life without sinking into the swamp of selfishness. Whip smart and honest to the core, *The Overdue Life of Amy Byler* is a thoughtful, nimble charmer. Did I mention the hot librarian?"

—Sonja Yoerg, #1 Amazon bestselling author of *True Places*

The Good Luck Girls of Shipwreck Lane

"A perfect recipe of clever, quirky, poignant, and fun makes this a delightful debut."

—*Kirkus Reviews*

"Set in small-town Maine, this first novel is a story of rebuilding, recovery, and renewal. Harms has created two incredibly likable heroines, allowing the strengths of one woman to bolster the weaknesses of the other. While the central conflict of the story appears to be resolved fairly early, a succession of plot twists keeps the reader intrigued and invested. In the manner of Mary Kay Andrews and Jennifer Weiner, Harms's novel is emotionally tender, touching, and witty. Great for book clubs."

—*Booklist*

"Spunky leading ladies that you can take to the beach."

—*Fitness* magazine

"The story is funny and heartbreaking throughout."
—Melissa Amster, Chick Lit Central

"Another perfect summer diversion is *The Good Luck Girls of Shipwreck Lane*. Kelly Harms writes with love about a trio of women desperate for a change and smart enough to recognize it may not be exactly what they planned. Delicious."

—Angela Matano, *Campus Circle*

"The friction between the Janines, along with a few romantic foibles and a lot of delicious meals, results in a sweetly funny and unpredictable story that's ultimately about making a home where you find it."

—*Capital Times*

"Kelly Harms's debut is a delicious concoction of reality and fairy tale—the ideal summer book! You'll feel lucky for having read it. And after meeting her, I guarantee you will want a great-aunt Midge of your very own."

—*New York Times* bestselling author Sarah Addison Allen

"Warmhearted and funny, *The Good Luck Girls of Shipwreck Lane* pulls you in with quirky yet relatable characters, intriguing relationships, and the promise of second chances. Harms's debut is as refreshingly delightful as a bowl of her character Janey's chilled pea soup with mint on a hot summer day."

—Meg Donohue, bestselling author of *How to Eat a Cupcake: A Novel*

"Funny, original, and delightfully quirky, Kelly Harms's *The Good Luck Girls of Shipwreck Lane* shows us that sometimes, all we need to make it through one of life's rough patches is a change of scenery and a home-cooked meal."

—Molly Shapiro, author of *Point, Click, Love: A Novel*

"The characters are so well drawn that they practically leap from the page, charming dysfunction and all! A poignant, hilarious debut that's filled with heart, soul, insight, and laugh-out-loud moments. It'll make you rethink the meaning of what makes a family—and if you're anything like me, it'll make you want to pick up and move to 1516 Shipwreck Lane immediately! I'm such a fan of this utterly charming novel."

—Kristin Harmel, author of *Italian for Beginners* and *The Sweetness of Forgetting*

"Clever and memorable and original."

—Samantha Wilde, author of *I'll Take What She Has*

"Janey and Nean each have a common name and uncommon hard luck, and when they suddenly have in common a sweepstakes house, their lives begin to change in ways neither of them could have imagined. Their quirky wit will win you over, even as they fumble through their crazy new life. *The Good Luck Girls of Shipwreck Lane* is alive with warmth and wit; I enjoyed it right through to the satisfying end."

—Kristina Riggle, author of *Real Life & Liars*, *The Life You've Imagined*, *Things We Didn't Say*, and *Keepsake*

"Kelly Harms's *The Good Luck Girls of Shipwreck Lane* is a delightful book bursting with good humor, fast action, and delicious food. Aunt Midge is a pure joy, and I loved Harms's surprising, spirited, and generous slant on what it takes to make a family."

—Nancy Thayer, *New York Times* bestselling author of *Summer Breeze*

The Matchmakers of Minnow Bay

"Kelly Harms writes with such tender insight about change, saying goodbye to her beloved yet troubled city life, and hurtling into the delicious unknown. Her characters sparkle; I loved Lily and wished I could have coffee with her in the enchanted town of Minnow Bay."

—Luanne Rice, *New York Times* bestselling author

"The temperature in Minnow Bay, Wisconsin, may be cold, but its people are anything but. Kelly Harms has created a world so real and so inviting that you absolutely will not want to leave. *The Matchmakers of Minnow Bay* proves that a little small-town meddling never hurt anyone and that, sometimes, it takes a village to fall in love. Kelly Harms has done it again!"

—Kristy Woodson Harvey, author of *Dear Carolina* and *Lies and Other Acts of Love*

"*The Matchmakers of Minnow Bay* is a glorious read, full of heart and humor. Lily is the kind of character you'll root for to the end, and the delightful residents of Minnow Bay will keep you chuckling with each turn of the page. Kelly Harms is a talented author with a knack for writing a story you'll want to read again and again."

—Darien Gee/Mia King

"In *The Matchmakers of Minnow Bay*, Kelly Harms weaves together a small town and big dreams into a delightful and heartfelt tapestry of friendship, love, and getting what you deserve in the way you least expect. I was hooked from page one, then laughed out loud and teared up while reading—exactly what I want from romantic women's fiction. Kelly Harms is the real deal."

—Amy Nathan

"In *The Matchmakers of Minnow Bay*, Lily Stewart is Shopaholic's Becky Bloomwood meets Capote's Holly Golightly. This charming tale is filled to the brim with eccentric characters, uproarious predicaments, and a charming (if chilly!) setting. Kelly Harms has created the most lovable character in Lily, a starving artist with a penchant for disaster and a completely unbreakable spirit. One for the beach chair!"

—Kate Moretti, *New York Times* bestselling author of
The Vanishing Year

"Filled with witty dialogue and an unforgettable cast of characters, *The Matchmakers of Minnow Bay* is a complete charmer. I rooted for Lily from the first page and didn't want to leave the magical town of Minnow Bay. Kelly Harms delivers another heartwarming novel that lifts the spirit."

—Anita Hughes

"*The Matchmakers of Minnow Bay* is the perfect feel-good read. An irresistible premise, a charming—though forgetful—heroine, an emotionally involving love story, lovely writing . . . it all adds up to cozy hours in a fictional place you'll wish you could visit. Don't miss this delightful novel!"

—Susan Wiggs

"Sometimes you read a book that hits all the right notes: funny, charismatic, romantic, and empowering. *The Matchmakers of Minnow Bay* is that book. Kelly Harms's enchanting writing lured me into the quiet yet complicated world of Minnow Bay, and I never wanted to leave. I loved it in every way!"

—Amy E. Reichert

"Delightful, and sure to captivate readers and gain new fans for author Kelly Harms. With sparkling dialogue and a winning heroine who finds her big-girl panties amid the disaster zone her life has become and heads in a new direction, finding love along the way, it had me turning the pages into the night."

—Eileen Goudge

"I loved this book! Fresh and devastatingly funny, *The Matchmakers of Minnow Bay* is romantic comedy at its very best. The talented Kelly Harms is one to watch."

—Colleen Oakley, author of *Before I Go*

"*The Matchmakers of Minnow Bay* thoroughly entertains as it explores friendship, flings, and finally finding yourself. Harms tells the story in a funny, fresh voice ideal for this charming coming-into-her-age novel."

—Christie Ridgway, *USA Today* bestselling author of the Beach House No. 9 and Cabin Fever series

THE
BRIGHT
SIDE
OF GOING
DARK

OTHER BOOKS BY KELLY HARMS

The Overdue Life of Amy Byler

The Matchmakers of Minnow Bay

The Good Luck Girls of Shipwreck Lane

THE BRIGHT SIDE OF GOING DARK

KELLY HARMS

LAKE UNION
PUBLISHING

Text copyright © 2020 by Kelly Harms
All rights reserved.

Published by Lake Union Publishing, Seattle
www.apub.com

Amazon, the Amazon logo, and Lake Union Publishing are trademarks of Amazon.com, Inc., or its affiliates.

ISBN-13: 9781542020916 (hardcover)
ISBN-10: 1542020913 (hardcover)

ISBN-13: 9781542014113 (paperback)
ISBN-10: 1542014115 (paperback)

Cover design by David Drummond

Printed in the United States of America

First edition

To all the book influencers who help me find new books and help my books find new readers. Please don't throw your phones off a cliff.

MIA

When it happens, I don't exactly know what I'm doing. I'm angry; I know that. Angry at a lot of people.

Like, half a million people.

And I'm scared. I'm in danger of being exposed as a fraud. And I *am* a fraud. I know that suddenly, as clearly as I know the mountains are tall and the lake is cold. I've lied about something important, to so many people. And for what?

I'm standing in front of a cliff. I'm ten paces from the edge. I could stop what I'm doing and freeze in position and wait for someone to come and talk me back into reason.

But I'm not going to.

I pick up my phone. Look at it as I do five to six hundred times every day. The previews on my lock screen are infuriating. I don't want to talk to any of these people. They're either strangers or virtual strangers. They all believe a version of me that is not true. They all want something from me, a piece of me, but not the real me, to make them feel less invisible, less tired and sad or bored and aimless. I don't want to answer any of these messages or return any of these calls. I have to. I have to chisel away at each of them, thumb through miles of scrolling, catch up on days of missed messages, posts, and photos. Hit Like and Like and Like some more.

Only I don't.

My mom likes to point out that if you take the entire history of humanity and squeeze it onto a football field, the amount of time we've had mobile phones is less than the breadth of a human hair.

A human hair.

My own hair is slicked back from sweat, and there's mud in my ponytail, and some of the shorter layers around my face have gotten loose and are stuck to my cheeks. I reach up and feel the grime; it feels human and real and so different from the patented polymer that covers my phone and has protected it from every storm so that nothing real can touch it, so that it is always at the ready, always at my fingertips, no matter where I am.

And I know: This is not real. Nothing I've been doing for the last five years is real. It's all been zeros and ones, "likes" instead of likes, "friends" instead of friends, "followers" when there is nowhere to lead. I want rid of it. I want to be free of it, not just for twenty-four hours, not just for a week, but forever.

I stop right at the edge of the mountainside, where the park-service railing rises up to catch me before I plummet over. I can't think about what I am going to do, not even for another second. If I do, the brilliant engineering that all these app developers and tech engineers have put into place will win out again. I will put another token of my life into the slot machine. I have to act.

I clutch my hand tightly around my phone and wind up.

When I let go, the phone sails through the air, over the cliff edge, out of sight, down, down, and then I hear it hit.

It makes a small crunch. And then a nice echo.

And just like that, with no way to tell anyone about it, my real life finally begins.

PART I
PAIGE CLICKS

MIA

Hey loves, hiking thru the gorgeous woods in one of #Colorado's amazing #stateparks. Tucker says hi! Check out this view. (No not talking about myself for once, I swear!) I defy you to stand in the soaring Rockies without your heart soaring a little too. QOTD: What makes your spirits soar? How can you get more of it into your everyday life? <3 you! xoxo Mia

From where I stand, I can see mountains in every direction. Over to the left they are tallest, they stretch, they seem to grow every time I look back, they cast shadows, they tower. To my right they topple, fall down, tumble like hair over Rapunzel's back: rivers of rock and shrubbery and, probably, if I could see better without all these tears in my eyes, actual waterways. In front of me is a bench, and I sit on it, and from it, when I let my head tip all the way back, back, back, in a position that every yoga teacher knows is unhealthy, I can read the sign above me upside down.

Kelly Harms

What Tucker said when he found out I could read upside down: "You're amazing. Is there anything you can't do? How did I get so lucky?"

What Tucker texted when I asked him why he was late to this park bench where I am craning my neck and probably ruining the C1 through C4 vertebrae: I don't think we should do this. "This" being our wedding.

My brain flips the letters on the sign around for me, so I don't see them as upside down. It reads:

WELCOME TO LANGE STATE PARK

There is a trail map worn thin from fingers tracing it and a Plexiglas registration-form holder and the words *Elevation 8890*, which I would have cropped out of the photo of me and Tucker—if Tucker thought we should do this, which he doesn't—because 8,990 feet above sea level isn't particularly impressive in Colorado, and those who realize that will know we hiked not at all but just drove here, parked in the parking lot, posed for several photographs, and then drove back to the hotel where we are staying.

Where I am staying. Where I am staying alone, I realize.

I have been staying alone since I got to Colorado. It's hard to be an internet celebrity alone, but I have been doing it because Tucker had to travel for work last week and needed a chance to decompress between work and our wedding. I, too, would have liked to decompress, but my followers won't have it. They need updates every day, multiple times a day. They need something to like. For some reason, it has to be me.

Tripods are all well and good, but they are slow and unwieldy, and I bought a cheap remote, so it takes three clicks to get a picture. Three

6

clicks while I am frozen in a certain spot, with a certain look on my face, with my body tilted one way or another, or sometimes in an asana, a yoga pose like warrior two or half moon—one of the positions that photograph well. Not warrior one or crow pose. Though I have been doing yoga for years and have been an internet celebrity for many of those years, I have yet to do crow pose without making an expression that is best described as "gastrointestinal-distress face."

"Hey, are you using that bench?"

I bring my head up slowly, slowly, slowly, until it's back on top of my shoulders. Sure enough, my neck hurts. In front of me is a guy wearing one of those enormous climbing backpacks, but his mat isn't loaded up into it yet. I have worn that kind of backpack before, when I did some climbing during hashtag outdoor matters month hashtag sponsored by hashtag Outfitters Inc. and hashtag Mountainhigh Climbing Gym, and I know it is heavy and unwieldy. I stand up from the bench. "Here you go."

"Thanks," he says, then adds, "I won't be long."

I look at him. He is too doughy to be a climber, I think, then remind myself to stop with my assumptions. He is pretty good at getting his gear loaded, compared to me, who had to wave Tucker over and get him to do it and then take my picture after it was done. I smile at Mr. Doughy and say, "I haven't seen any other climbers out today," which is true, and well informed, considering I have been waiting near this bench for Tucker for an hour now.

He shrugs. "Guides never come here. Takes too long to hike out to the routes. And they're high rated—I mean, they're steep."

I nod but also wonder if I should stay a few more hours, just so I can call 911 when I hear his body hit the ground. "You're climbing alone?" I ask. I sit back down on the bench because thinking about climbing has made me tired.

"My girlfriend's out there already," he says, scooching away from me.

I want to clarify. I wasn't flirting. I want to tell him that my fiancé is on his way here to take the prerehearsal dinner photos with me because we are getting married in two days.

But we aren't. Tucker just texted me to say that we aren't.

I start to cry.

The climber looks horrified. "I'm sorry—I didn't mean to say it like that. I just meant . . ."

I wave him off. He doesn't need to know. "It's not about you," I say, and it comes out a bit bitchy, which is fine—I don't know this guy. But the thought that I've been mean to a stranger makes me feel awful, until my mind helpfully turns it back around on him. He could have been nicer, after all. I wasn't asking him to marry me, was I?

I turn to leave. It's well past time I leave. I should have left hours ago. I should have never come.

But first, the photos. Even at my worst, there have to be photos.

Carefully, I take my pointer fingers and wipe straight lines under my lower lashes to clear away the tears without smearing my mascara. I am mindful not to open my mouth while I do this—the universal impulse to open one's mouth when touching one's lashes was caught on film one time, and I learned never to do it again. I looked like a drowning fish.

"Can you take my picture?" I ask the climber. "Just a quick snapshot." I inhale and pivot and lower my chin and widen my eyes into a facsimile of a secret smile. He just needs to get me and some mountainscape in the frame. Beyond that, well, I will edit the crap out of it anyway, like I do all of these pictures. Like we all do.

Maybe not all of us. The climber looks perplexed. "Well . . . ok," he says after a second and takes my phone. He points and clicks and hands it back to me without looking. I exhale and let my shoulders slump and flatten my mouth into a line and take the phone back, my real, heartachey, deflated self reappearing as I do. "Thank you," I say, meaning it. "Have a good climb."

"You too," he says, even though I am obviously not climbing. The only climbing I'm doing today is into a bottle of bourbon. But then maybe, just going from the look on my face, that's exactly the climb he's talking about.

PAIGE

"I don't mean to shock anyone, but the FRS just gave this penis a name."

My cube farm breaks out in laughter. I'm laughing, too, but also I'm curious. What is it about the penis in question that made our facial recognition software think it was a person, and which person did it think it was? Knowing my company, it will turn out to be someone for whom this mistake is wildly offensive, like Gandhi. Or Pat Nixon.

"I want to see the penis," I say.

"Of course you do, Paige," says Peter Mason, the original penis announcer. "It's the only way you're getting a look, eh?"

No one laughs. Not because my colleagues think it was unfunny or untrue, but because we have just last week had the fear of God put into us during the latest sexual harassment web seminar, and perhaps with the exception of Peter, who is a moron, we all very badly want to keep our jobs, which, though miserable, are wildly lucrative. We, the staff of the Pictey Standards Enforcement and Quality Assurance Team, are some of the best-paid people in the entire Pictey corporate group and certainly the only people I know who can work forty hours a week, enjoy flexible scheduling, stable workflow, and large corporate benefits, and still make mid–six figures a year.

There are forty of us, never all in the same place at the same time, and we get paid by the flag. When a Pictey user (or, as our overlords call them, a "Pictigin") sees a picture that wrinkles their tender noses, they right-click it, and it is flagged, and it goes into some proprietary software to see if it's, say, a Confederate flag or just a folded Union Jack, a nipple or just duck lips. If the program can't tell, and it often cannot tell, it shows one of us the photo. And we, in our infinite wisdom, decide if it's obscene, dangerous, inflammatory, cyberbullying, or any of the other ways humans are awful to each other, or if it's just innocent stupidity. We see a lot of penises.

The penis that is now up on my screen is actually quite great. I mean, it's hideously ugly, as all male genitalia is, but it's also very friendly looking, and I totally see the face. The skin is pale, and the hat part is being held into a sort of smiley face position. "Did it tell you who it matched to?" I ask over my cubicle.

My IM opens, and I see the face of a too-tanned white woman with her hair pulled back in a bun and a kind of large, creeping smile. Her eyes are closed. *She doesn't look like the penis,* I type back. *The penis looks like her.*

My words get thumbs-upped, and I close out the windows and go back to my screen, because in this job, time is money. The photo that pops up is a woman breastfeeding a child. I hit *Y*. Next is an extreme close-up of an ear. I hit *Y*. Next is a hairy scrotum. I hit *N*. Next is a bachelorette with a penis painted on her cheek. I pause, two, three seconds, then hit *Y*.

Generally I like this kind of work. We can do up to twenty hours a week of nothing but photo screening. I think, if not for the health needs of my eyeballs, I could do all twenty in one day. But I don't. I split the time up, thirty minutes in every hour, to spell me through the much murkier work I must also do fifteen hours of weekly to keep my job: context review. This work is awful. It's god awful, and that is why we are paid so incredibly well.

I'd say about one in ten thousand photos I screen is truly upsetting, rather than just a body part or a racial slur, any response to which has long been deadened inside me. But with the cruelty potential of the written word, humans hit a far higher batting average, and the computers are much worse about screening the monsters out. The n-word, for example, is so contextually dependent that I often need to read whole paragraphs before I know whether it's empowering or racist, and the c-word is the same. And then there are the stranger phrases we have to check, like *Ann Coulter*, which is used as a truly vile derogative at least 30 percent of the time. Teens tend to use a few key phrases when driving each other to suicide, including, subtly, the word *suicide* itself, and the sheer number of times I have no-screened the word *suicide* makes me think that all teenage girls do anymore is tell each other to kill themselves, day in, day out, rain or shine. Which is ironic because in my experience one doesn't need a ton of extra encouragement during the teen years. But still, we have to screen it, because what if someone comes to our website to talk about suicide prevention awareness or a loss in the family or needs an overstatement for a terrible career choice?

Fatty is one of the easier ones, I suppose, though I don't much like it. *Fatty* plus *fish* and plus *acids* is okayed for us by sentiment analysis software. *Fatty* plus *tuna* and *fatty* plus *breasts* are a smidge harder because they could absolutely mean legitimate things—or be repulsive insults. And *fatty* followed by nearly any other word in the English language, as well as used to end a sentence, is probably an insult, but insults are allowed when aimed at certain parts of the population. For example, on Pictey, everyone is allowed to call the president a fatty. He is indeed a fatty, but I still don't think it's very helpful to say so in the public discourse. I myself am a fatty, and I don't really like reading the word two thousand times a week, but then, thanks to the word *fatty*, I'm a very rich fatty. One who can afford lots of fatty plus tuna at the best sushi restaurants in the valley.

You can't call a young person a fatty on pictey.com. As a result, lots of teens call each other tubs of lard and sacks of lard and just generally any sort of containers of rendered hog fat. They get flagged by users, and I read them, and I decide if Sandra Langingham of South Bend, Indiana, should have to see such personal attacks on her Pictey feed for the rest of time eternal.

My decision is always no.

Pictey is available for download in the Apple store and on Google Play in 168 nations. One time, we tried to list 168 nations on our whiteboard in the office, and all forty of us put together couldn't do it, though I did make an admirable contribution by knowing all the former Soviet countries in clockwise order. (Everyone always forgets Moldova.)

In each of the Pictey nations there is an office like this one. In each office like this one there are between one and eighty people who are native speakers who do what I do, all day long, though only those of us in England, Scandinavia, Japan, Dubai, and the States get paid so well. In Australia they make half as much, or so we're told, and in Russia they make next to nothing, though we infer that's because they have nothing to do because the state prescreens everything anyway. In Nepal we have an office of just six people, and they make a dime for every dollar I do. A dime! But according to interoffice talk, there is no cyberbullying in Nepal. Not yet, at least. If I could do this job without reading any more cyberbullying, I would take a pay cut. A modest pay cut.

It's a strange, strange business I'm in.

When I was a child, I did not tell my then-married mother and father I wanted to be an online standards and quality enforcer when

I grew up. I did not tell them I wanted to sit in a big open-concept office all day with excellently comfortable ergonomic chairs and look at pictures of scrotums and duck lips. I did not say, *I hope I work a job where I get free therapy included each week as a matter of personal safety.*

I wanted to be a mail carrier.

My Pomodoro timer dings. I am done with screening for today. The flag I was on, something loquacious from the comments thread of a major influencer, just hovers on my screen. I log out over the top of it, unconcerned, because we've been taught how to walk away unconcerned, and my manager and quasi therapist checks that I do regularly. I start whizzing through the Emotional Safety Questionnaire. Yes, I am calm. No, there is nothing I need to talk about from today's flags. Yes, I am ready to leave the work behind for the day and be present in the rest of my life. The prompts come up in a different order each day, with slight variations to the phrasing time and again so we are forced to really read them all rather than click through by memory. If you get one wrong, you have to schedule a therapy call for either right then or the next morning before you can start working again, so it's worth taking the time to do it right. And by that I mean to lie. I have answered truthfully a couple of times and learned that it's better to just lie and then go have a nice half a Valium tablet than it is to go through the online-therapy rigmarole.

After all, the Valium is analog.

I click on the last question. No, my heart is not racing. I put my thumb on the USB fingerprint reader for confirmation. It turns green. ESQ completed, I can now do anything in the world that I like for the rest of the day, which is long, since my shift is done by four p.m. I can take a walk, go for a hike, or sit in a chic bar with a martini and write my memoirs. Anything I want.

I go to the employee lounge with my satchel.

I set up the espresso machine. I make an Americano and put it down on the little spin-out table attached to the comfiest chair in the place, the one with the stretched vinyl seat in almost the exact shape of my own, ah, seat.

I take out my laptop. Sit down with my coffee. Take in and let out a deep breath of relief. When I'm in the right mind-set, I open up my laptop.

I open up pictey.com.

MIA

Sometimes I can't believe it's only been three months since Tucker and I decided to #tietheknot. In that time I've been bride-ing hard and loving every second. Here's a throwback post of the engagement. Best surprise ever. #blessed

Now we're thisclose to the day and I'm just over the moon. Will be posting the #weddingdress from #vintagegown dot com soon and you guys will be blown away—I hope? Let me know which dress you think I picked from the try-ons last month! Link to the dress posts in comments. xoxo Mia

Lucky for me, we were having a private ceremony: Tucker, me, our parents, the justice of the peace. That means I won't have to spend the next twenty-four hours calling cousins I barely know and telling them to turn their cars around because Tucker doesn't think we should do this.

Slightly unluckier, I have taken large sums of sponsorship money to post every detail of the wedding, start to finish, on my Pictey feed, to be viewed by some large percentage of my five hundred thousand followers.

If I told my sponsors that Tucker and I aren't getting married, I would be out of cash. Actually, I'd need to go into debt. Let's be honest—I'm never seeing any of my wedding deposits ever again.

If I told my followers that Tucker doesn't think we should do this, they would kill him. I think I'm probably exaggerating about this, but I'm not sure enough to put it to the test. My followers need me to be happy. They care about me in a time-consuming sort of way that I think they should probably care about their own daughters, sisters, friends. But they put it all on me. They talk to me, and each other, every day, and because there are too many to keep track of, they become in my mind this single amalgam of a person, full of problems and sorrows and self-inflicted wounds, and they are counting on me to do things right every single day, several times a day. To keep them happy, I must do things *perfectly*.

And I don't want to let them down. I owe them so much. After all, look at what they've given me.

A few years ago, when everyone was pretty bored with Instagram, and only book clubs were still using Facebook, and Twitter had become a political quagmire, I went on a date with a guy who had just gotten hired by a social start-up and was feeling pretty great about himself. The start-up was called Pictey, and absolutely no one was using it. I had an Instagram account that I used to show my college friends my life and keep in touch with theirs, and I half-heartedly posted promotional stuff for my yoga studio. Just me in poses, generally, because I had no marketing budget and didn't know what else to do to try to get yogis into my classes.

I didn't see the harm in double posting from my Instagram feed on the start-up, partly just because the guy didn't ask me out on a second date and I wanted him to know what I could do with my legs.

On Instagram, I had about a thousand followers and followed at least five thousand people. My feed was a jumble, and I'd go days without posting only to post ten times in one day later. I was not winning social media, to say the least. I sometimes posted quotes from the Dalai Lama or Pema Chödrön superimposed over pictures of flowers.

By my current standards, my feed was the pits.

But Pictey had started with computer programmers, and computer programmers were, back then, mostly "bros" of the highest level. They were guys hired by the company and guys who had applied to work at the company but not gotten the job and guys who read *Wired* and guys who did yoga to meet girls. So my Pictey posts, which were just exactly the same content as what went to die on Instagram, got a lot of likes, or as many as you can get when you're on a platform that has fewer than ten thousand users. I liked the likes. Everyone likes likes, right? So I posted more on Pictey. Then I posted some new things on there. I tried different hashtags. I posted about Pictey on Instagram. Some of my followers came from Instagram and followed me there. And then I started posting about Mike.

Mike was very photogenic.

Things picked up fast.

Year one, Pictey grew to two hundred thousand users. Twenty thousand of them were following me. I was, by Pictey standards, a star.

Looking back on that time, it was the beginning of something huge, for sure, but also the only year social media was just plain fun. In that first year, my yoga studio began to bustle. I hired staff, raised prices enough that I covered the rent, and dropped my own offerings to three classes a week. Instead of putting their mats as far away from the stage as humanly possible, my students crowded my low platform, mats practically touching, and jostled for the closest positions.

I taught workshops, and people came. I made new online friends and got together with them IRL. My world got really big, and my circle got really strong. I really was hashtag blessed.

Also that year, I was approached by a "monetization expert" who told me to create "passive income streams" and join a speakers' bureau. I loved speaking. I loved sharing what I'd learned in the process of "growing" my reach, and I loved carrying Mike out at the end of the talk, to thunderous applause. Mike loved thunderous applause.

After my speeches, I sat in the back of the little library halls and meditation clubs and signed people's yoga mats and sold my college friend's handmade upcycled practice jerseys, collected when high schools dumped their old ones. She—Lynnsey was her name—sliced the upper back into thirds and braided it into a racer back. Then she sewed new seams in the sides and turned it into a chic yoga top, then screen printed it with my studio logo, which at the time was still a line drawing of a blunt-nosed, three-legged pooch in downward-facing-dog position. Those shirts had to go when the studio sold a couple of years later, but then, just a glimpse of that studio logo would make me swell with pride.

Around one hundred thousand followers, I started getting meaningful press. I wasn't speaking at yoga-teacher trainings and garden clubs anymore. I was speaking at women's expos, in big convention centers, with headsets and sound crews. Lynnsey couldn't keep up with the orders anymore, and she didn't want to do all the things she needed to do to scale up—work with new material, use an offshore factory, outsource production. In the end she told me to go on without her. At the advice of my monetization expert, I gave up on my "too cutesy logo" and started selling a fifteen-dollar @Mia&Mike water bottle with much higher profit margins. Even now, with every reusable water bottle sold, I donate a disposable water bottle to the Red Cross. Sometimes the environmental upshot of this makes my head spin.

Then I got to 250,000 followers on Pictey, and as fast as I was growing, Pictey was growing faster. My "space," as Pictey's director of growth and change calls it, was getting crowded. Newer, younger girls were posting newer, bendier yoga poses, on silks in the air, on trampolines, from bungee cords, doing things I didn't even care to attempt.

And it didn't matter, because by then I was ready to outgrow my space. I wasn't limited to yoga talk or meditation links or gut-flora-replenishing smoothies. My followers wanted *anything* I cared to post, as long as Mike was somehow involved. And the word on the street was to post as often as you could, twice a day, three times. Four! Yoga posts were fine, but I hardly had time for that anymore. In desperation I took pictures of my lattes and my new mascara wand and my trips and a new meditation app. But most of all, I posted about Mike.

And that was when I started charging for endorsements.

Before, companies would send me their special kind of yoga chalk or new totally unnecessary prop or luxe cashmere blanket, and if I liked the thing, I'd post it, and if I didn't, I'd give it away to my followers.

But things changed on social media. I was being a chump, I was told by other, more experienced influencers. Endorsing a blanket for the cost of a blanket! Outrageous. From then on, if I didn't get paid, I didn't post it. The high-end espresso machine you saw on my feed came with a thousand bucks for the trouble of unpacking it. The fair-trade earrings I wore in a single picture cost two hundred dollars to my viewers but made me two thousand. And the biggest-ticket items, the brands who wrote the big checks, got to be in a picture with Mike.

Mike loved to be in pictures. He would wag his tail and arf, because he never, ever barked, and sometimes he would sort of hop straight up with all three legs straight, which to this day I never could figure out the biomechanics of. I always told a company that if their product was shown with an in-air photo of Mike, they could expect it to go viral. And I was always right.

From then on, I hardly ever had time to speak or teach classes. I got paid to put my name on things, to post about things, to show pictures of things, to write captions, to re-Pict, to do just about anything except the reason I'd started it all in the first place. I sold my yoga studio and spent most of the money on photo equipment. I bought a place in a neighborhood I didn't exactly love for the pure reason that it was very photogenic. I stopped eating carbs. I started coloring my hair. I carried my tripod with me everywhere.

And then, at one of the darkest, loneliest moments in my life, I fell for Tucker. Maybe Tucker was, just a little, just at first, a way to keep my career moving forward when it seemed like it would be easiest to just stop. Maybe Tucker knew that himself, a little bit, in his own way. Because when we first met, on an online date I had posted about just ten minutes before I'd walked into the bar, he knew exactly who I was and what I did. If he had wanted no part of that, he could have turned around and walked out the door back then. But he didn't. He did the opposite. In fact, the first thing he said to me, the very first sentence out of his mouth, was this:

"Did you know I'm an excellent photographer?"

———

Back at the inn where my wedding was to be held, I unpack a plastic bag full of gluten-free garbage foods and a very good bottle of bourbon. I will have to multitask tonight—run my Pictey feed while eating my feelings. It's not a first, let's just say. Life with Tucker has had its ups and downs, especially over the last few months, when he has begun to suggest that Pictey has become too important in my life and I have become too concerned with my brand. To this I say, So what? Of course I'm concerned with my brand. It's my job! He should be more concerned with my brand, since it's his brand by proxy. I mean, his username is @TuckerlovesMia! His income as a photographer pays for only half of his current lifestyle with me. He wanted to trade on my name, my followers, and my reach, but he somehow also wanted me to be more "authentic" and "in the moment." "Where in my brand statement did I ever write 'in the moment'?" I asked him. Answer: I didn't.

I suppose this is the last big letdown Tucker will put me through, and I should be glad of that. But I'm not there yet. I know from experience that I can survive loss, as long as I keep myself intensely distracted. I know I will survive this just the same.

Only I don't want to do it in public.

But public is how I live my entire life now. I open my Pictey feed and start scrolling my newest comments. There are hundreds.

A large majority of them are just what I think of as longhand likes. Instead of only clicking the heart button, lots of users also write something nice to me like *Love it!* or *Great photo!* I'm not sure what motivates people to make the effort, but I'm greatly appreciative that they do, because I depend on these messages to bring my engagement numbers up in the Pictey algorithms and make my post more visible to others. If a follower writes more than this, if she writes something very personal or asks a question, I try to respond back within a couple of days. It's usually little more than a (hopefully) appropriate emoji, but sometimes I do get engaged in the conversation.

Today is going to be one of those days for sure. On my post about hiking there's a thread extolling the virtues of the Rockies that I cannot pass up, as well as a thread about favorite restaurants in the area. My followers don't know exactly where I am, but I did say we would be getting married near the Arapaho National Forest, thinking it was a large enough area that no one would be able to successfully stalk me even if they tried, and their suggestions are indeed covering an area that would take almost three hours to drive. Some little piece of my brain that doesn't want to think too hard about my canceled wedding right now takes careful note of the cafés and art galleries near the inn. That part of my brain is whispering, *Go on, Mia; go get some good new sponsors.*

But then I find another thread, one much more worrying. It's from a follower I think I've heard from before, though I can't remember in what context. That's not unusual—some of my followers comment on every single post, talk to each other in the comment threads, and even strike up friendships offline. Once a group of four women who met on my feed started their own yoga retreat together and sent me a photo in my DMs. I loved that. That feels so long ago.

This user, @thatJessica17, is not planning a yoga retreat. In fact, from what she's written, it almost sounds like she's planning a suicide. I note with relief that a few other followers have already written her some encouraging words, and I hope she takes heart in them. I watch the comments grow as they share hard times in their lives and post hotline numbers and talk about recovering from depression. I have been low before, terribly, terribly low, but I know the difference between that and unmanaged clinical depression, which is a life-threatening disease that can't be fixed by a fun new boyfriend. I don't dare weigh in about something I've never personally experienced myself, so I flounder for words and try a few overly cheerful replies, only to delete them before hitting enter. Still, I hit refresh over and over again and feel grateful for my followers, who seem to be so much stronger than me. They don't seem to hesitate before telling stories of their worst days. They don't issue sunny platitudes either. They are vulnerable and raw, and they are the ones who should really have a hundred thousand likes on their posts.

But they aren't the ones. The OP wanted to hear from me. She wanted to hear from @Mia&Mike. I pour a second finger of bourbon and position my thumbs over the keyboard and type the best advice I can think of to give her.

> @thatJessica17, I will be honest, I haven't personally ever had thoughts of suicide. I'm so sorry if you're going through that. I think the other commenters here can give you much more support on that issue than I can. I will only say, I beg you, try to find a friend right now. It doesn't even have to be a human friend. In the past I found a lot of strength

in Mike that helped me get through my hardest days. Maybe what you need right now is a Mike of your own, who will lick your tears when you cry and snuggle up when you need a hug. xoxo Mia

I look at my glass. It's empty, and the slurry of strong drink, nuptial remorse, and talk of my best friend has left me teary eyed. I set my phone to ring with Pictey notifications so I will see when @thatJessica17 writes me back, then drop my phone and switch on the TV and try to distract myself from my disappointment with baked taro chips and *Veep* reruns. It works, up to a point, and I lose the rest of the night in a sort of numb haze. But I don't forget that post, and when she hasn't written me back within a couple of hours, I decide it can't hurt to err on the side of caution. I find the original thread and call it up, read it again. It's probably nothing, I tell myself.

But just in case, I long-click on the comment. A small menu drops down. The prompt asks me: *Would you like to flag this comment?* I think a long time, shrug, and then click "Yes."

PAIGE

The day after the penis-face incident, I come into my office and sit down at my workstation, and my computer screen is off.

It's quite unexpected. Who would turn off a computer screen? Who turns off computer screens at all anymore? I think of my father, a professor of statistics who works from home in the summer. When he still lived with my mother, he would call me into his otherwise off-limits office every summer day at three thirty and announce joyfully, "It's quitting time!" Then he blew canned air into his keyboard, shut off his monitor, and pushed in his desk chair, like a janitorial team might be coming in at any moment to vacuum and he wouldn't want to inconvenience them.

Assuming my dad, who now lives in Washington State, wasn't here in the office messing with my workstation, that means someone else from his generation was. That means Karrin, I suppose. She is the only older person within ten miles of the Pictey offices, and she isn't very old, in point of fact. She still has half a life ahead of her, if she isn't a smoker. She is just old for a start-up, old for the company, and I am sure we feel like children to her. She certainly treats us like children.

With a sigh, I stand up, head to the lounge. I don't want to be summoned to Karrin's office by an act so passive as a turned-off monitor, but at the same time I am not quite sure what else to do with myself. I know she's been at the station, or someone has, and I know from experience that this only happens after an escalation. Karrin doesn't know how to do remote work. She has this understanding of a computer as a thing, a box, with stuff inside. If she wants to see what I was working on yesterday before I logged out, then she comes to my computer, wakes it up, enters her high-clearance password, and runs an applet that shows her every single moment of my day in fast-forward.

Never mind that this function works via any computer in the office, or any secure company laptop, of which she has at least two sitting in a corner in her office. This is Karrin.

Karrin wasn't hired for her intelligence. Or rather, she was, but I don't subscribe to the notion of what she has as actual intelligence. They call it EQ, of course, but no repeatable study shows there's any concrete way to test EQ. Depending on who is administering any given test, a scholar will get a different result. I therefore conclude that EQ is not a real thing.

The metric I find most accurate for intelligence is a coding-challenge site that ranks the fifty top-scoring coders hourly. I do very well by this standard. I was in the top fifty for six weeks, and I am also a woman, which makes me very desirable to companies who are trying to create some semblance of gender balance. Pictey recruited me and said I could pick where I worked within the company. They did not expect me to pick Safety and Standards, where I barely code at all. They underestimated my desire to be left alone.

I have reason to believe Karrin would not be able to complete even the log-in for a coding-challenge site. Her job title is *resiliency manager*, and she is supposed to save us from drinking ourselves to death, which a few Safety and Standards people attempted to do before she arrived. Since she's been here, there haven't been any more rehab emergencies, and Karrin feels personally responsible for this. I put it down to the fact that they gave us all a 6 percent raise, three more paid vacation days, and access to the company travel agency.

Karrin likes to "listen" to us. We have to go into her office once a month or so and tell her the most disturbing things we saw, then take her "prescription for self-care." My prescription for self-care is the same as it has been since I was in my late teens: high doses of SSRIs, mood stabilizers, and benzodiazepines as needed. Karrin's is a piece of notebook paper with some instructions on it. Instructions like: *Take time to breathe.* I told her I am fortunate in that I can breathe while doing other things. She laughed, as though I were kidding.

Largely, I find Karrin to be an impediment to getting my job done in a prompt fashion and a danger to the future of my career. She doesn't exactly understand how all the proprietary software we need works and is always pestering the higher-ups to get them to write in trigger warnings before each potentially upsetting flag. I tell her what they tell her, but less patiently: You can't have a computer warn you about something until it knows what it is, and if the computer always knew what it was looking at, we wouldn't have jobs, now, would we?

Karrin is in the lounge.

I turn around and start to head back to my computer, but it's too late. "Paige! Terrific. Just the woman I was hoping to see," she calls, uncomfortably loudly. I keep walking while considering what I know about Karrin. She values the odious "people skills." She won't talk to me about an escalation in public, grab my arm to keep up with me, or shout through the office that I need to report to her at once. She would view any of those behaviors as "disrespectful." So I am now free to go back to my workstation, turn my monitor on, *ugh*, and start going through flags.

But when I sit down, I start to wonder what she wanted. Was there an escalation? Did I in fact err? Nothing of import strikes me from yesterday's flags. In fact, it's been a very quiet week at Pictey, if only behind the scenes. From the user interface, things are more exciting. A few of our biggest stars have things going on this week that they're either live-ing or posting hourly about. There is going to be traffic in droves, and I'm going to make a fortune on daily-flag bonuses if I come in this weekend. In particular, my half sister's favorite influencer, @Mia&Mike, and her much less famous fiancé, @TuckerlovesMia, are getting married on Pictey this weekend. The lead-up has been everything you'd expect from a woman who makes a living taking pictures of herself: vapid, commercial, and exceptionally good looking.

There will be *so* many flags.

To my knowledge, this is Pictey's first major wedding. It is also the first wedding that I've been invited to in years, if you count running Safety and Standards during the event as an invitation, which I absolutely do.

I turn on my monitor. In the log-in field I type a 7, the first user ID number for management, and the autocomplete fills in Karrin's user ID. I'd know it anywhere. Curses.

I think back to last night again. What if there hasn't been an escalation? What if I missed a question on last night's Emotional Safety Questionnaire, and now I have to do a remote therapy session, or worse, an online mental health workshop, before I can get back to my work? What if I can't work this weekend? I have no plans to visit my father. What on earth would I do with myself instead?

I stand up and walk through the office. A few sets of eyes follow me, I think. I suspect people in this office will look at anything they see and think *Y* or *N*. I try to ignore their eyes. Karrin's office is set into a corner right by the bathrooms. I could be going to the bathroom, for all they know. What's unusual about using the bathroom? I almost go, just to sell it. But I can't even wait the length of a pee to know what's going on.

"Fine," I say as I walk into Karrin's office. "You win."

Karrin is on the phone, the kind that plugs into the wall. Her use of the phone is so annoying. I feel for her fellow middle managers, who probably had to get an office phone just so she could call them with it. Her desktop computer, with its convenient keyboard, is just two inches away from her. She could be DMing them. She could be Zooming them. She could be in Slack. Why does she always insist on the intrusive, overpersonal telephone?

"Right, well, it looks like we're ready to do this," she says to the phone. I knock on the doorjamb and gesture to her to hang up the receiver.

"Ok," she says, while giving me a little palm up, sideways wave, which I think means *come in, sit down.* I do these things. "Right, right. I hear you," she says, though I am sitting here waiting and it is me she should be hearing. "I can absolutely see what you are saying," she adds.

I roll my eyes and cross my arms, because she is supposed to be an expert on body language. She notices and gives me a little grimace I don't care to translate. "I appreciate your time," she says, and I hope it's me she's addressing. "We'll circle back later so I can get right on the first steps," she goes on. To the phone, I'm fairly sure. "Goodbye. Yep. Thanks."

"You see," I say when she finally sets the phone in its cradle. "If you don't call them, then you don't get stuck on the phone with them." I have tried to explain this to her before.

"I just love a good conversation," she says to me. "And for me, it's easier to understand someone's meaning and express my own meaning with my voice. It's more personal, you know. If I could just get up and go to Howard's office, I would, but that would require a plane ticket."

"Why were you talking to Howard?" I ask. Howard is our COO. He is at the top of the flowchart for Safety and Standards, and he seems like a brilliant man. I am a little disappointed to learn he uses the telephone too.

"Same reason I'm talking to you," says Karrin. "An escalation that was of note."

"You mean a flag," I tell her.

"Yes."

"An escalation is what happens if you miss a flag. Did I miss a flag?"

"You did not."

"I could have missed one. I handle a lot of flags. All day. Every day," I say.

"And whenever I ask you how that makes you feel, you share your desire to leave my office," she replies with a smile. "So I won't ask you that today. Instead, I'll ask if there was anything memorable about yesterday's flags."

I think back. "There was a penis that the facial recognition software thought was a person. Not exciting. There was a big multiaccount attack on a twelve-year-old that met my standards for cyberbullying. I wiped that and issued four decency warnings. There was some child pornography that got by the computer. I did all the FBI reports for that," I say. I hate child pornography, which comes with so much extra paperwork. "There was a coded conversation about cross-state sales of bump stocks. At first I thought they were talking about cocaine, actually. It came clear in a few seconds. Drug dealers are actually smarter than gun dealers, it seems."

"Sounds like a fairly normal day," she says. "Anything else?"

I search my mind. "No. The regular flags. Nipples, threats, some fake news."

Karrin pauses a moment. "I have something I need you to see," she says, and she hands me a piece of paper.

"You can show me computer screens," I tell her, annoyed. "You don't have to print everything out."

"Sometimes it helps me," she says.

"Whatever," I say and take the paper. It's a flag dated yesterday. I don't recognize it, but that's not unusual. It's from the thread of a popular influencer—@Mia&Mike, in fact—and as I look at it more closely, I see that it's in a foggy area we call *possible ideation*. Possible ideation—the mention of a plan to commit suicide in a post—is my coding nightmare. Even with the best sentiment software we have, there is simply no way to automatically discern the difference between what shrinks describe as a "cry for help" and an empty threat.

I should know.

"It's a possible ideation," I say to Karrin. "Item seven, part b. 'If a possible ideation occurs on a celebrity page, the posting user's comment will be deleted and the user will automatically receive suicide-deterrence resources via their original sign-in email.'"

"Paige," she says quietly. "Look again."

I read it again. This time I notice the user ID. @thatJessica17. Unlike in our flagging software, on this printout there's a small thumbnail photo of the user. I recognize it at once.

"Is this . . . does this account belong to Jessica Odanz?" I say, confused. My half sister is the happiest person I know. She's currently finishing her last year at CU Boulder. She's on the dean's list, for goodness' sake. This post—asking the influencer if she ever felt so bad she wished she were dead—it doesn't even sound like her. It sounds more like me. The old me.

Karrin frowns. "I'm sorry to say it is. She attempted suicide last night. But she's alive—" she tells me right away. I sag in relief. *She's alive,* I tell myself. *No need to start panicking. Above all, do not start panicking.*

"How did I miss this?" I ask. My voice sounds tight and high.

"You must have logged out right in the middle of this flag. Consie got it next, and she's overactive on possible ideations, thank goodness. She pinged your sister, got no answer, and called 911."

My heart seems to freeze up. "Please tell me my sister wasn't using a VPN," I say. A virtual private network can be used to connect to proxy servers, making it impossible to find where someone's logging on from. Meaning 911 wouldn't be able to find my sister.

"Just a plain old IP from her dorm room."

I experience a moment's relief, but only a moment's. I think of a breathing technique I read about years ago. Breathe in four, hold four, breathe out four, hold four. Karrin picks up a yellow pad upon which she's scribbled some notes. As she reads them aloud, I get stuck on a hold and don't remember to breathe out.

"First responders found Jessica unresponsive after serious blood loss. She was rushed to Billman Adventist Hospital and has been admitted. Again, Paige, I'm so sorry to share this upsetting news with you."

I stare blankly at the desk between me and Karrin. The mess of papers, the yellow pad, that stupid telephone. The latest *Diagnostic and Statistical Manual of Mental Disorders* lies open on the floor. I wonder, for a strange out-of-body moment, how it would categorize me. I suppose it describes me to a T: Rising heart rate. Tightened breathing. Sudden feelings of detachment.

"I hardly know her anymore," I find myself saying, my voice growing more pinched with every word. "I only see her once a year. Over the holidays."

"Even so, this must be a shock," Karrin says. I try another relaxation technique, making note of the physical objects I see in the room. Lamp. Desk. Chair. Suicide note.

"What's a shock," I say stupidly, "is that Consie's overactive imagination actually did some good for once." Consie calls 911 in some municipality at least once a week. The dispatchers always tell her they prefer that she is too careful, rather than the opposite. But I've seen the statistics. Very few completed suicides begin with a post on social media.

Attempts, on the other hand . . .

"She didn't really mean it," I continue to bluster, my voice getting higher by the second. "It must have been a stunt for attention." I don't actually believe what I am saying, but I can't seem to make myself stop. "I'll start looking at ideations harder. I know I should have caught this. But you know how it is," I tell her. "So many people use them to try to manipulate internet personalities. And then there are the careerists," I add, referring to the people who threaten suicide every time they need attention. "And the shock artists."

"It's hard to tell which is which," she agrees. "To be clear, no one believes this is your fault. No one blames you. We've trained everyone in S and S to leave their work behind when the day is over. That means you did the right thing."

"I read it, though," I tell her. I am breathing in now more than I am breathing out. I need to take a benzo. Right away. I start rustling around in my boxy black handbag. "I read it, and I missed it."

"It's just a bad coincidence," says Karrin. "I mean, what are the odds that you'd get that flag?"

"There are forty people in this office," I say, fishing around in my purse more. "So around one in forty, give or take." I find the bottle and pop it open with one hand, still concealed by the leather bag. But it's empty. Right. I put in for a refill, but my doctor wanted me to come in first. Bureaucrat.

Karrin pauses. "We need more staff," she says, apropos of nothing. "How are forty people supposed to handle four million users?"

I don't have the calm necessary to answer this. If Karrin doesn't know by now that the code handles 99 percent of all daily flags, she'll never know. Instead, I fall back on distraction. *Solve a technical problem,* I tell myself. *Write some mental code.* I wonder if there's a way to rank these flags based on the users generating them. Demographic risk levels, number of similar posts . . . maybe I could write something that would give ideation flags a danger score of one through ten. "For next time—" I begin.

"Regarding next time," she says. The words come out very slowly, like the beginning of bad news.

"You're not firing me over this," I tell her, and what I could deny before is now obviously becoming full-blown panic. "That doesn't make sense. I didn't do anything wrong."

"I'm not firing you at all," Karrin says. "Paige, don't be silly. You do great work! We love having you as part of the team. That's why it's so important to keep you in the best kind of emotional health possible. And a way to achieve good mental health is through support and connection. That means when you have a family emergency, we want to support you."

For some reason, the words *family emergency* upset me more. It is because they've been used in this context before. "You did support me," I try to tell her. "Or Consie did. She saved my sister's life. Problem solved." Problem not solved. Why didn't I go in for more Xanax? Why didn't I find another doctor?

"And we're proud of that. But there's more we can do for you. I was thinking of giving you some extra vacation," she says. "So you can go see your family."

The penny drops.

"No, no no no no. You can't do this to me."

"Give you extra time off of work?" she says curiously.

"I don't want time off of work," I tell her. On this I am adamant.

"Don't you want to be with your family?" she asks.

"They're not my family," I say on a hard exhale. "I mean, they are, but we're not close." My breathing has a hiccup now. I feel like air isn't getting into my lungs. I try to breathe in four counts, but I can't, and I start to cough, and my coughing seems to echo in my body like I'm the inside of a cave.

Karrin replies, but I stop hearing. I squeeze my eyes shut and see the comment. The comment that made me think, *Oh, just another suicide threat*, and *What is wrong with these people?* and *Why am I even seeing this?* And then I see my sister's username and her pretty little profile pic and her real-life face and hear her always-bouncing laugh, teasing me about my clothes every year since she was eleven in sparkling sneakers and I was home from grad school in all-weather sandals with socks.

My racing mind recalls how rarely I see Jessica, how I never call or visit her at school, even though I know what life can be like with our mom and know the genetic brain chemistry that we very likely share. And I am certain that Karrin is wrong. She said no one blames me for logging off midflag, for ignoring my own sister's cry for help.

But someone blames me, after all. I blame me.

"Paige? Paige, are you ok? Are you experiencing distress?"

"I feel fine," I say. But I don't. My hands are sweaty. I put them to my face. I seem to be dying. That's what's happening. I'm back in my mom's house, I'm shaking and crying, I'm hiding and coughing and choking down pills. I'm falling off the chair and onto the floor, and I'm thinking, *The pain will be over soon*, and then I'm in that awful place, between the bridge and the water, and I'm trying to gag myself, trying to make myself throw up, but it's too late, and then I'm back in Karrin's office, trying to stand up, to get out of here as quickly as possible. And as I stand up, I feel my legs crumple, and I think, so dissociated that it is like I'm watching myself from a great height, I think: *This cannot be.*

I am rock solid, I think. I am untouchable. The version of myself that could get shaken so easily is long gone. Snuffed out through a careful combination of practice and psychopharmacology. And still, no matter what I tell myself, it's still happening. Here I go, down a path I've been before and I thought I'd never go down again, to a place where everything feels too much and is too loud and too scary and too dangerous.

I hear Karrin call my name again. But I can't respond. The edges of my vision tighten in like a close-up . . . the Vaseline is smeared over the lens . . . the lights go dim, and then I feel the floor come up to me and meet me hard. The room becomes a blur of shapes. I'm not dead, but I'm not alive either. I'm breathing, and somewhere, someone is calling out for help. I try to make sense of the blur, of the noise, but my eyes close, and the room is black. And then, with the loud sound of ringing in my ears, I'm out.

MIA

Thanks for all your responses, my friends! I love hearing from you, and your comments on my newest shade of lipstick are sooooo sweet. And guess what? Our friends at EverydayGlam are so thrilled you like the MatteGlam Everyday Lip Barrier and Color in One from the last post that they've given me a #couponcode to share! Who wants 25% off all lip products until Saturday? Which, PS: IS MY WEDDING DAY (in case I haven't mentioned it four hundred times). I ordered two more shades that will be perfect for the honeymoon. Any guesses to which colors? #HappyShopping xoxo Mia

My mom lives in a hippie fairyland.

Generally, we keep a safe distance from each other, my mother and I. She's lovely, and it's nothing personal; it's just that everything she does is crazy and wrong. She doesn't understand me, either, so the feeling is mutual. She doesn't know exactly what it is I do and seems to operate under the impression that I'm mostly unemployed. If she would *just* look at her phone once or twice, she would get it. But she stubbornly refuses to look, and she was born in a time without internet, so she will never, ever get it.

That said, she's very nice. My dad bailed early—he now lives in a Nova Scotia fishing village following his own strange drumbeat—and she never once complained about it. She was a loving, hardworking single mother, and she raised my brother and me to know the value of hard work and have self-esteem and so on and so forth. Growing up, she worked a third shift at the hospital so she could be there for us after school, on sick days, when I got my period during volleyball practice. And still, twenty years after she rushed clean underwear and a maxi pad to the high school gym and passed them to me hidden in a two-disc *Best of Dolly Parton* jewel case, whenever something terrible happens, just like anyone else, I want my mommy.

I call her. I call her landline, it should be said, because though she has the latest cell phone technology and a cell contract, both paid for by me, it's a reasonable guess that said phone is in a drawer somewhere, with the tech watch and the Pro tablet and all the other attempts I've made to bring her into this century.

She's not home, of course. The phone rings and rings. And of course, a ridiculous answering machine—an actual machine—picks up, and it's one of her favorite radio stars whose voice starts playing, because she once, maybe fifteen years ago, won an NPR quiz show, and the prize was the voice of Carl Kasell answering her phone. Yet another argument she makes against switching to mobile.

I do not leave a message, because I will not stoop to her level, even in this, my time of need. Instead I drive to the pretty little B and B where I've been staying in the Copperidge Ski area. This, the Inn Evergreen, was to be our wedding headquarters, and I have already told the friendly guy who runs it that I've been jilted and the 50 percent deposit is all he's getting this weekend. He was pretty amicable, considering the financial blow. He said, "Shit happens," with a sort of sad smile, and "How ya holding up?" Then he told me since we had prepaid one room for Tucker's parents, one room for my mom, and a room apiece for our officiant and videographer, plus the room that was to be our honeymoon suite, I was welcome to stay put through the rest of the weekend. So I have a place to put my head down from now until Sunday night, when I'm going back to Los Angeles, which is where I live but also, regrettably, where Tucker lives, four blocks away from me.

When I get to my room, everything I need is there, and the room's been made up. Last night's bourbon, taro-chip, and coconut-ice-dessert weepfest has been cleared away, and there are fresh garden roses in a large vase on the nightstand. They are yellow, fuchsia, ballet slipper pink, and peach. A mountain sunset in a vase. It's as pretty as it's going to get, I suppose.

I guess I'd better do the dress photos.

I get out a long white garment bag from the pretty wardrobe on the far wall, think better of it, hang the bag back up, and clear out all the clothes hanging next to it that are anything but white, silvery, or gray. It's still too plain, so I hang up the long satin pink bed sash, doubled over on a hanger to look like it might be a scarf. *There.* I put my wedding heels on the floor of the wardrobe, toes out. I slide everything to one half of the clothes rod and close the opposite door, because the wardrobe really is that pretty, and open the other half wide. It would be nice, I reflect, if there were a mirror on the inside door of the wardrobe, but since there isn't, I take the square mirror that is hung above the vanity off the wall and lean it against the side of the wardrobe "casually." I stand back and look, and it's really close, to my surprise. Sometimes these shots can take me hours. Selfies are so much faster.

But selfies don't pay for canceled weddings.

The garden roses are mostly bright, so I pick out the palest ones and put them in a water glass I find in the bathroom and set them on the floor. No, inside the wardrobe. Nope—I take them out of the water glass and balance one rose on top of the mirror. That's it, and I adjust the curtains and take pictures, adjust the lights and take pictures, change angles, squat down, stand up on the bed, snap snap snap. I cannot have too many choices. After all, this will have to be the shot I post to announce the cancellation. It needs to be pretty and soft, the dress sheathed in the closet, the graceful acceptance writ large.

But. Per my sponsorship contract, I need to do a full-length dress photo, wedding or no. I was thinking of one of those classic dress-on-the-bed pictures, but the duvet is white and the dress is antique lace, so it may not show up. Maybe better to put the dress on? But no, I cannot do that, not today. I'm holding it together so delicately as it is. And sure enough, when I have the dress out of the bag and have it draped across the pretty four-poster and see how charmingly the subtle sepia aging of the vintage dress stands out from the white lining, see the strapless lace from bust to toe in a slim sheath with just the tiniest kick in the front and an extra foot of train in the back, see the perfect little off-the-shoulder straps I requested at the last minute, I feel a few tears get loose.

Enough, I tell myself. I cried enough last night. Tucker is just a guy. He's just some guy who takes gorgeous photos and loved me for a while and doesn't love me anymore. I am done crying over it. Tucker and I dated for nine months. There are plenty of other Tuckers in this world. At twenty-nine I can find another one and still do all the things I wanted to do. I'll have to move faster, but come on. There are five hundred thousand people who want to look at pictures of me *every damn day*. The odds are fair.

Anyway, I tell myself, I'm not crying over Tucker. I'm crying over the dress. It is so pretty, and it cannot be reused. For one thing, I've posted myself shopping for it, posted myself getting fitted, posted shots of lace being hand-tailored, even posted the strapless bra I will be wearing underneath it, sponsored by a high-end French lingerie line to the tune of a cool three grand, plus a full trousseau.

I wonder if I will have to pay that back.

A chill of panic runs through me. The dress itself is a sponsorship for an online vintage wedding shop. The tailoring was free in exchange for a mention of the alteration shop in at least three posts. The hashtag-sponsored cake is probably sitting in a cooler waiting to be frosted. Even the florist is doing my bouquet for free. Am I going to go belly up in this fiasco? Anger sponsors? Or worse . . . *lose followers*?

I feel shaky. I try to breathe deeply and walk myself through some positive thoughts, but they won't take root. My fans, what will they say? Will they rally around me in sympathy? If I am sympathetic or, more accurately, pathetic, will they still buy what I am selling? Or will they turn on me, as Tucker did, and find someone new to follow? Someone whose life is more perfect, more seamless, more like it's supposed to be on Facebook and Instagram and Pictey and everywhere that is only somewhere on your phone?

If they do, what will be left of me?

I style the dress. I add the necklace of tiny gold filigree and the stylized veil, puff up the bed pillows, tinker with the lighting. The room's gas fireplace, just inside the shot, is turned on, turned off, cropped out. The roses are added, moved three inches one way, two the other, until everything is absolutely, completely perfect. And when all these things are in their perfect place, I take the shot. On the screen of my DSLR, it comes together and looks almost magical.

Or maybe the better word is *unreal*.

But that doesn't matter. I upload it, do a quickie edit, post on Pictey, tag all the sponsors, add my favorite wedding hashtags, and add a throwaway caption: *Can't hardly wait!* And then, heart in throat, knowing that Tucker will see this and praying he will understand my plight and play along, I push "Post." My phone makes a whoosh that gives me goose bumps. Whoosh goes my sanity. Whoosh goes reality. And in its place, something else. Something perfect. And perfectly false.

PAIGE

The ability to actually anxious oneself unconscious is a rare one, I realize, but I've never had to work at it. The first time I did it was in high school, and after that I think something short-circuited in my brain and decided it was better to black out during a panic attack than to stay awake for it, and from what I've read from others about panic attacks, my brain may be right. I keep thinking next time I feel it coming on I will have the good sense to lie down on the floor, but so far no luck. So when I wake up, I'm disoriented and have a headache from hitting the floor. Karrin's office floor, I remember, but I'm not in Karrin's office now. I'm in my bedroom, in my apartment. I have no idea how I got here, but my head is really throbbing, so I should check my pupils before I do anything else.

I struggle to my feet, stagger out of the bedroom, and put myself in front of the bathroom mirror so I can look into my own eyes. I don't know exactly what pupils are supposed to look like when you have a concussion. Whirly? Should I look for tweety birds flying around my head? I lean in closer to the mirror.

"No concussion," says a voice, and I jump a foot.

"Sorry to startle you." It's Karrin. "I must have been in the kitchen when you woke up. How are you feeling?"

"Fine, thank you," I tell her. "Did you bring me home?"

"Not at first," she says. "First you went to the Pictey clinic. I was pretty sure I knew a panic attack when I saw one, but I wanted that noggin checked out. The good news is it's perfectly fine. The bad news is it was in fact a panic attack."

I sigh. These idiotic panic attacks. They are so, so, well, *beneath* me. They're a poor use of time and resources. They solve nothing and make most situations worse. They seem to be resistant to daily medication, so I have become perhaps a bit too reliant on antianxiety pills to keep them at bay, and even then, I've found them to be a bit too slow to do any good in the moment of crisis.

"What time is it?"

"Seven p.m.," she says.

"Still Friday?"

She nods. "You woke up briefly in the clinic. They gave you a very mild sedative, and I brought you home. Do you remember?"

I nod. "Vaguely. Yes. It's coming back to me now."

Karrin hands me a cup of tea. "I assume this is your first panic attack, Paige?"

I nod, because mine is one of those rare jobs where stable mental health is a formalized prerequisite.

She arches an eyebrow. "You don't seem terribly surprised."

I look up from my tea. "Panic attacks are seen in as many as three percent of the adult female population. Women my age are more likely to have a panic attack than successfully convert to veganism."

She nods. "Interesting comparison. But you can see how such a diagnosis might change the conversation, vis-à-vis our department at Pictey," she says gently. I narrow my eyes at her. "But we can talk about that later."

We can talk about that never, I think. I've had panic disorder since I was a young teen, and it's never kept me from doing quality work at my company.

"You took me by surprise," I say. "The news of my sister's attempt was upsetting. Speaking of which, I'd prefer to be alone right now. To reflect and . . . process."

Karrin nods. "Totally understood. I've written my number down, on that notepad"—she gestures toward the table—"and a prescription is there if you feel another attack coming on."

"Thank you," I tell her.

"And don't rush back. We won't expect you at the office for a while. Maybe two weeks?"

I open up my mouth to protest. But I think twice. Now that my panic attacks are on the record, my options may be to take a long leave or never come back at all.

My shoulders sag, but I say, "Yeah, that's fine." It doesn't feel fine, but what else can I say? "If something comes up, I can always call . . ." My voice trails off as I try to imagine who I would call. "The staff psychologist," I finish.

"And maybe you can go visit your sister," she suggests. "It could really help you process those feelings that overwhelmed you earlier."

"Sure," I say, though I have no intention whatsoever of going to Colorado. My mom lives in a large suburb east of Denver. I have deemed the entire state off limits to be on the safe side. "Maybe," I add, as I shovel Karrin out my door.

—

When I am alone again, I get out my work laptop and my personal laptop and put them on the desk next to my desktop monitor. I pour the tea down the drain—even modest caffeine is contraindicated in many cases of anxiety—and pour myself a nice glass of milk instead. Then I wake up my big computer and get back on Pictey.

My sister and I have different last names. Mine is Miller. Hers is Odanz. As far as I know, she lives somewhere in Boulder. She is in college there, as a communications major, of all things. I fear that major leads to a career in PR, or worse, writing.

It takes me almost twenty minutes to find anything new related to my sister, so thoroughly has the Pictey team been erasing things. The flagged comment I dropped is long gone, obviously, and my sister's account is hidden, but from tags to it I find a few of her friends' accounts, and they are totally normal, vapid college-girl accounts. I note with disdain the typical foolishness—pictures that will make it hard for them to get jobs in the public sector while also revealing their exact location at all times.

But one of them is even more clueless and tasteless than her friends. *RIP JESSICA* reads this girl's latest post. There's a picture of my sister and two other girls hugging and laughing.

I feel anger surge up in me, or some feeling I vaguely recall as being anger. I realize I was hoping, for my sister's sake, that her attempt was going to be a well-kept secret and she wouldn't have to answer questions about it or be stared at or otherwise ever revisit this horrible moment in her life. It seems like a simple dignity to pretend an attempt never happened. But that's not the world we live in anymore. There's no more "Grandma's memorial" or "ankle sprains" to hide behind. Now there are emojis that look like funeral sprays and the general understanding that anyone under the age of thirty who goes dark on social is probably dead.

A thought bubbles up in my mind. *Is* she dead? The only person who told me otherwise is Karrin. My breath catches. I reach for the new prescription—Valium, I see, which will do me just fine—take a pill, and begin my square breathing immediately. This soon after an attack, proactivity is the name of the game. And what I have to do now, I cannot do without extra help. I take off my glasses, rub the bridge of my nose, and then tell my phone to call Mom.

"Yello!" True to form, my mom does not sound like someone sitting vigil by her daughter's hospital bed. She sounds like someone on the way to mixed doubles.

"Hi, Mom," I say to her.

"Paige! My goodness. To what do I owe this pleasant surprise?"

I look blankly forward and will the Valium to work faster. "I'm calling about Jessica."

"What about her?" she singsongs.

"Mom, don't make me go fishing through hospital records to get a look at her chart. I just want to know how she is."

My mom's voice drops an octave. "She's fine," she says. "Not that you care."

"The very fact of this phone call is evidence that I care," I say, staying as placid as possible. "In fact, I am deeply concerned."

"She says you haven't talked to her since Christmas."

"She hasn't talked to me since Christmas either," I say.

"She's busy! She has so much going on, with college and dating and friends. You're the older sister. You're supposed to manage these things."

"I have an actual job," I point out.

"That's all you have," my mom says quickly. "Anyway, she's just under a lot of stress, and she needs to rest for a week or two."

"I heard she tried to kill herself," I say.

"Oh, no no no." Mom tsks. "Where did you hear that rumor? It was just a fall in the shower, when she was shaving. Poor thing couldn't find her safety razor."

I translate this from Mother to Reality. "She slit her wrists?" I ask.

I can hear my mom's frown through the phone. "I just told you what happened. You and your imagination."

"I'm already past the firewall at Billman Adventist," I warn her. "It just gets more illegal from here. And embarrassing," I add.

My mom inhales audibly through the phone. "It's all such a mystery. She's a very happy girl. She always has been. She's never needed a single pill in her life. I can't sort out exactly what happened, but somehow she ended up in the ER around nine last night with cuts all over her arms." I hear emotion cracking through my mom's voice, but I refuse to acknowledge it. She's a far better actor than I am a lie detector. "They gave her blood and admitted her. She's doing fine now. Just needs to stay awhile to get back on her feet."

"She's going to be ok?" I ask.

"She'll be fine. Just don't overreact. We don't have to make this into something more than it is."

"It's big, Mom. Don't you realize it's big?"

"I'll say to you now what I said to you then. Moments like these can be anything you want them to be. Make it into some big drama, and it can define you for the rest of your life. Or you can say *oops!* and put it into a little box and just get on with it. No one has to know. Jessica is going to be fine. We never have to think about it again."

"Mom—" I start, but she makes a little "ooh!" into the phone.

"My dentist is calling, hon. Let's talk another time."

"But I—"

"Kisses!"

My mom disconnects.

I let my head sink until it's resting on my hand and listen to the phone going off. My poor sister. Our mother may stick to the "fall in the shower" line for the rest of her life, but I know what happened. The flag came in yesterday around four p.m. Most likely it was flagged by the influencer, or one of the influencer's fans. It's also possible Jessica might have been the flagger. Maybe she really was making a cry for help. Whether it was her or not, she would have been refreshing the feed from then on, waiting to see if the influencer, or the unseen mechanisms behind Pictey—namely, me—would reach out and try to give her some kind of hand up. She would have waited hours. Specifically, she waited five hours, waited for me to do my job.

And when I didn't, she tried to kill herself, exactly as I did when I was in her shoes, almost twenty years ago.

MIA

#WeddingDay is here at last! Even though I've only known Tucker for 9 months now, and we are about to start the rest of our lives together, our story still feels like a true romance. And like every good story, it has a beginning, middle, and end. Beginning: we meet, and you, my friends, were there! Middle: we both fall hard, and you were there! End: my last morning as a single woman . . . and yep, you guys are here for me now too. How do you say goodbye to one stage of your life? What helps you move on to the next? Any advice for me as I get ready to say #iDo? Don't worry, plenty more wedding posts coming, but I've got so much to do, it might be a while . . . xoxo Mia

On Saturday, the morning of my wedding, I wake up in a puddle. Grief, ice cream, potato chip crumbs, and wine seem to be gathering where I lie, which, fortunately, is the luxe soaker bathtub of my en suite. Last night, at some point between pinot grigio bottles one and two, I decided that, as an internet fraud and future nobody, I was not deserving of a fancy bed. Drunk-person logic is weird. Maybe I just anticipated spilling my wine, which I did, like, thrice. I took my pillow and several towels and the duvet into the tub to continue my pity party. I know there was a pint of melting organic vanilla bean full-carb premium ice cream with crumbled potato chips on top, and then the rest is kind of a weepy blur.

Now, looking around the honeymoon suite of the inn, I realize I can't stay here a moment longer. It's too bright, too promising, too much of a lie. I pack up a night's worth of stuff and drive to my mother's house, about twenty minutes toward Dillon. If I'm going to fake my own wedding to five hundred thousand people, then Mom is literally the only human in the world I can count on to support me, because she has a complete disdain for social media, phones, and tech in general and thinks of it all as a house of cards anyway. Plus, she keeps a healthy supply of good wine lying around.

When I arrive and stand on my mom's long wooden porch, trying to decide between knocking and walking right in, the door flies open of its own accord. "About time!" says my mother. "I expected you yesterday."

I step inside, trying not to show my instant Mom-induced fatigue. "How did you know?" I say obligingly.

Mom gives me a quick hug hello, notes aloud that she thinks I'm losing muscle tone, and then gestures to a little table mounted near the front door. It has legs that swing out from the wall and support a fold-down top. On it, next to a familiar family photo turning yellow with age, is a small altar with my framed senior photo, arms crossed, back against a tree, hair resplendent, outfit unfortunate. And then various candles and beads and a deck of Goddess cards.

"Mom," I say. "You can't be doing my cards all the time. It's intrusive. And also a waste of your time."

"You're here, aren't you?" she replies, which is not, I notice, an acknowledgment of my request. "I bet you're hungry too. I can warm up a can of soup."

"What did the cards say?" I can't stop myself from asking.

"That you'd be injured and need nursing. Maybe something with a broken arm."

I roll my eyes. "Look at me." I wave my arms in front of her. "Nothing broken, no bleeding whatsoever. Right as rain."

She narrows her eyes at me and actually takes me by each hand, running her fingers over mine, as if I'm trying to cover up a splintered wrist or shattered ulna. Finding no actual damage, she flips over my right hand and looks at my palm. Her cool finger on my life line is soothing, and I'm a bit disappointed when she stops suddenly and drops my hand. "Well," she says. "That's a relief. Watch out for falling objects in the next few days, ok? I know those thumbs of yours are basically the only part you need for your work."

"Which is?" I goad, as I slip out of my ballet flats and ease my bare feet onto her cool, smooth floor.

Mom turns from me and starts moving away, which is her tell. "You know, computer stuff. Cyberspace," she adds dismissively.

I laugh, because I have to. I've explained to my mother what I do for a living dozens of times, and she's not dumb. She's just got a powerful sense of denial and a blind spot around the internet, which she uses only sparingly and then with great protest. "I think this is the visit where I get you a computer," I threaten.

"Oh, honey, no. I have a computer, and I never use it." She's referring to an ancient first-gen iPad I gave her years ago, which has a detachable keyboard.

"That's not a computer, Mom. And nothing will work on it anymore anyway. The apps stopped updating years ago."

"You can do crosswords on it," she says.

"Do you?"

"No. It will show you the answers if you push a button, and I can never seem to resist pushing the button. Besides, I like reading the *Post*." That's evident by the stack of unfolded *Posts* by the side door.

"When you die and I have to throw out five thousand old newspapers, I'm going to wish you read your news online like everyone else."

"But that's not my problem," she says gaily. "I'll be dead!"

"You know," I say, as I sit down and take a banana from her fruit bowl, "if you had a computer, you'd know exactly what I do every day. You could see every detail of my life."

"I already know every detail of your life, and I find it boring. You stare at a screen all day looking for meaningful validation where there can be none, and you have a boyfriend who could be making beautiful art but instead does the same thing you do, for an audience of ones and zeros."

Ladies and gentleman, meet my mother, Marla Bell.

"Why do I ever come here?" I ask her. I try to make it sound loving. I get close.

"For my cooking. Want that can of soup?"

I shake my head. "Too high in sodium. Let's go to Vail," I say. I don't want to go back to the ski resort, where I was supposed to be married today. But I do want a decent gluten-free, carbohydrate-free meal to stop the bloat.

"Can't," she says. "I'm on call."

My mom was a nurse in her younger incarnation, and it's safe to assume she was a wonderful one. She is both doting and bossy at the same time. But she doesn't like the medical system these days, and after she did her thirty years and started her pension, she became a doula—a birth coach. Everywhere she goes, she brings with her the tools of the trade: lotions and oils and teas, warm packs, cool packs, soft socks, massage tools, nursing aids, a portable stereo and calming music, that sort of thing. When she's on call, she doesn't go anywhere outside a certain radius so she can be there for her patients in twenty minutes flat. You'd think a good mobile phone would help with that. But no.

"Who is it?" I ask.

"N," she says. She only tells me the initial of any given patient's first name and takes their confidentiality very seriously. But I do know that N is a first-time mom with an overinvolved mother who wants her to get an epidural the minute the first contraction comes. N would just like to have room to make her own choices. *I feel you, N.* "She's twelve days over now," my mother adds.

"Oof," I say, because though I have never been pregnant, my mom has described in great detail the work that goes into cooking a baby. "Ok, I'll scramble some eggs. You do have eggs, don't you?" Since about six years ago, my mother does not, as a rule, stock groceries or apply heat to anything that requires a flame.

"I don't even have soup," she admits. "But! My neighbor has chickens. He keeps the eggs in a cooler on the sunporch. You can just pop in and grab a dozen. They're a great deal too."

"I don't have any cash," I tell her.

"It's fine," she says. "I have a subscription. I got the chicken-feet package."

I press my lips together. This new life my mother has carved out for herself postretirement is in so many ways the opposite of what I have in LA. I have read, and possibly even posted, about the benefits of offal for health and the environment, but in LA that translates to buying wildly expensive little pots of pâté at Whole Foods. Absently, I wonder what my mom plans to do with all her chicken feet but decide not to ask her. Instead I say warily, "Would you like me to pick up some chicken feet, too, while I'm there?"

She laughs. "Of course not. He doesn't just keep chicken parts lying around, does he? What kind of farmer would do that?" I raise my brows. What kind of farmer lives in the foothills of the Rockies and sells subscriptions to chicken feet? "Besides, I'm coming with you. Otherwise he'll think you're a random thief. He might shoot you."

"I don't think you can shoot people on your sunporch if you sell groceries from it."

"You don't know this guy. He's very edgy," says my mom with a grin, and now I am worried about *her*.

"All right, then," I say. We get our shoes on, me in my flats, Mom in wellies. She looks askance at my choice of footwear. "I'm here to get married, Mom," I say to her unspoken accusation. "Not to muck out a barn."

She sighs and says nothing, and we walk out toward the road. The air is fresh, as it always is, but a bit cooler than yesterday. There's a scent of campfire in the air, as well as that ionized charge that happens when snowcaps are melting thousands of feet above you. The sky is as blue as a painting.

"You're not getting married, though, are you?" she says softly, after we've been walking a minute or two.

She catches me by surprise. Instead of answering, I say, "Mom, don't be so creepy."

"If you're asking how I know, it's because you have none of the happy anticipation you should have. And you're not on your phone. You've only glanced at it twice since you came in. The only reason you'd be avoiding your phone on the morning of your wedding is if you don't want to have to tell the bad news to your zillions of acolytes."

Well, she has me there. "Ok," I say. "I'm not getting married."

"Well, shit."

"It's ok. I mean, I don't know if it's ok or not. I feel crushed."

"Seems fair. It's a blow."

"And sad."

"I'd worry if you weren't sad."

"And ashamed," I add. "And foolish. But I don't feel . . ." I can't think of the right word.

"Heartbroken?" she asks.

"Right. I don't feel soul-deep longing for Tucker or anything." I pause, considering how to say what I want to say. "You know how when Andy left us, we only wanted to talk to him about our grief, and that just made things a thousand times worse?" It's been almost six years since my brother, Andy, died, and it still pains me to say his name, even after all this time.

Mom just nods.

"Well. I don't feel that way about this. I don't want to talk through my feelings with Tucker. I don't miss him. I even feel a tiny little sense of relief." I stop walking. "Is it this house?" I ask her, because we have finally come to the first driveway after my mom's.

She shakes her head. "Two more," she says, and we keep walking up, gaining altitude and proximity to the modest hill that dead-ends this road, a beautiful, easy three-hour summit called Mount Wyler.

"Part of the relief is probably just shock," says Mom. "Heartbreak will be coming," she warns. "Then you'll feel awful."

I nod reluctantly, but I wish there was something more encouraging she could say. "Yeah, you're probably right. But part of the relief is just straight-up relief. I didn't want to be dumped two days before the wedding, and it's embarrassing, and I'm staring down a career crisis as a result. And yet I wasn't one hundred percent sure I wanted to actually marry Tucker, and if he's a runner, isn't it better he should run now?" I ask.

"My logical little girl," my mother says and puts her arm around my shoulder. "Yes. It is better. But did you love him?"

"I think maybe I did," I say, my throat just a bit thicker than before. "He was funny and talented. He was handsome. When I looked at our life together, thought of our future, it looked beautiful."

My mother pulls a face. "I'm sure it did," is all she says, and there's more to be said, I can tell, but I don't want to hear it. When I don't ask, she says, "Why don't you stay with me for a while? I'll get groceries. There are fresh sheets on the bed."

"Mom, I can't stay with you. You know that. You don't have Wi-Fi."

"What do you need Wi-Fi for? You need a Jane Austen marathon and unlimited cookies and bubble baths. Not Wi-Fi."

I sigh, exasperated. "I have to post, Mom. I post like ten or twenty times a day. The cell service out here is unreliable, and I need tons of data."

"Oh, well, I can help you there. I have piles of data on how excessive screen time reduces your attention span, harms your ability to process complicated sets of information, increases anxiety, reduces exercise—"

"*Roaming* data," I say. "And no, don't just spout more pro-Luddite statistics to me while you walk around in circles. This is my livelihood, my job, and I have to do it. And it's going to be especially hard this weekend, because I have to somehow tell everyone I'm not posting the wedding and make it look like everything is hunky dory when it totally isn't."

"Forget 'everyone,'" she says. "They aren't even real people."

"They *are* real people, Mom! Hundreds of thousands of real people. They have feelings and needs and hopes. Most of all, they have expectations." And right now I'm suffocating under them.

"Fine, but I refuse to accept that they are the true source of your livelihood. I've seen you speak. I've been to your classes. Those are the things that bring you *alive*."

I sigh. Those are the small parts of my working life that bring me joy. But they aren't the real work. "Pictey is why anyone wants to hear me speak or take my classes. If I don't post, the fans go away. If the fans go away, there's no one to teach or speak to."

My mom shakes her head stubbornly. "I think you're wrong about that," she insists. "If I were you, I'd take this as a great opportunity for freedom from the obligations of these so-called followers. Maybe they'd all go find something better to do than to comment endlessly on your pictures and fawn over your impractical footwear." Now her gloves are off. It took, what, thirty minutes since my arrival? "You'd be doing everyone involved an enormous favor. What do phone addictions bring? Stress. Depression. Bad sleep. Poor concentration. Second screening!" She's worked herself into another of her antitech lathers. "If

I were you, I'd hike right up to the top of Mount Wyler and toss that phone off the cliff."

We are standing in front of the right house now, a house that has a little wooden sign hanging under the mailbox that reads FRESH EGGS. The sign, however, is utterly unnecessary, because there's also a six-foot junk art sculpture of a chicken in the front yard. "Subtle," I say, both to my mom, the phone hater, and the giant metal chicken. Neither replies. But my phone buzzes, and I take it out. There's service up here. Not an opportunity to be missed.

"Well, seeing as you're busy," she says, annoyed, "I'll go get some eggs. Need anything else?"

"Like chicken feet?" I ask as I work my thumbs over the keypad. "Pass."

"Snob," says my mom, who is, in fact, quite a snob herself, but about the funniest things. Like my career. "You stay here and think about what I said."

I finish my comments and likes and then pause a moment and think, *How did I get here?* How is it that I was in Los Angeles planning a full-glamour Rocky Mountains wedding two days ago, and now I'm standing on my mom's rural route staring at a giant chicken made of old garden implements? Does my life really need to be quite this *whimsical?* What is even so great about whimsy, anyway? What about building your dreams and capitalizing on opportunity and inspiring thousands and having it all? Is that so much to ask?

The chicken shrugs. I wipe my watery eyes, look again, and see that right behind the chicken, in a picture window of the pretty white ranch my mom is currently taking eggs from, is a girl, a young girl, maybe eleven or twelve. She looks out at me, watching me stare into space, and lifts one arm in a quiet little wave. The girl has long light-brown hair and full cheeks and wears an orange hair bow and a flouncy coral tunic over the top of purple leggings. Everything is two sizes too small and unflattering and clashes. In other words, she looks exactly like I do in 90 percent of my mom's photos from that age. I raise my arm in a wave, but what I really want to do is rush to her, take her aside, tell her how to avoid all the pain that is coming for someone like her: an unself-conscious, unprepared, plain-looking, chubby girl about to enter ado-lescence. I think of my brother, what he did for me in those awkward years. If I could just smuggle her some magazines, a razor, deodorant in a feminine scent, an on-trend outfit . . . I come to my senses and shake my head. Life would come for her some other way instead.

"So," says my mom, startling me out of my phone coma. She is holding a small brown paper bag and hands it to me. "Are we throwing that phone off the cliff?" she asks.

"Of course not," I say. I see a tub of herbed chèvre on top of a dozen eggs in the bag. It's dairy, which isn't good for my diet, but at least it's goat milk. I can make an exception. After all, it's not like it's my wed-ding day. "But I'm not throwing you, either, so that's something," I add with a smile.

"I'll bring you around one of these days," my mom says cheerfully. "Until then, I suppose you want a photo with the chicken."

I start. I didn't even think of that. That's so weird. I always need visual content. Always. How could I have seen this chicken and *not* have snapped it? I blink and hand my mother my phone in camera mode so she just has to point and shoot. "Thanks. That would be great," I say and then go crouch by the bird, elbows on knees, to make it look bigger. "Hold the phone up higher," I say. "Higher. Like you're going for an aerial."

Then, when I realize the angle she's at, I make her move to the side. "You'll catch glare from the window that way," is what I tell her. But the truth is I just don't want the girl to accidentally show up in the photo. There's no way I'm exposing her to the trolls that lurk around my feed waiting to find flaws in the tiniest places, find the cracks in my facade.

These are the people who, as my mom would say, have too much time and too many opinions. They point out when my hair needs a touch-up color, when I have gained an ounce, when I have toes curled where they should be flat in some esoteric asana only they would know.

My mom gets a few more pics, and then I stand up, take one last look at the window. The girl is gone, and I am relieved. The trolls are a part of my everyday life, whether I like it or not. But there's no possible way I'd let them into hers.

PAIGE

I was twelve years old when Jessica was born.

By twelve I knew I had problems. By fourteen, I was starting to suspect that the problems were not entirely of my own creation. By sixteen, I was suicidal. But at twelve, Jessica was born, and my entire life suddenly seemed to make sense.

My mom was not a perfect mom. She was very interested in appearing to be a perfect mom, and perfect in general, which meant long hours working on her figure and "image," as well as lots of benign and not-so-benign neglect, punctuated by hours of abject terror when we were out in public and she was paying attention to every move I made.

My father, a statistics professor at Boulder, seemed perfect, but now that I am an adult I know that perhaps that was a bit of an oversimplification. In many ways, though, he did right by me. He hired an affectionate nanny for me when I was small, even though my mother stayed home from work, so I was not in danger of developing any attachment disorders. He had me tested for autism spectrum disorders, since he was on the spectrum himself, even though my mother was adamantly against it. When I did not have Asperger's like he did, he pretended not to be disappointed. During my parents' long-overdue divorce, he did not cause any drawn-out public feuds, and he did not "make me choose" between my parents.

On the other hand, after a few years sharing custody, he left me with my mom and stepdad and moved to Washington for a job. There was a period of resentment after that.

That ended when Jessica came along. Though I had already started to develop some of the markers of the depression and anxiety disorders that both of my parents' DNA is laden with, her birth made me feel like I had been left with my mom for a reason. That reason was a beautiful, giggly baby. Her first smile was at three weeks, and while I know now that statistically this is unlikely and that smile was probably gas, I also remember vividly how it felt to receive it. After that I would do anything for that smile.

I performed well on school exams, so it made almost no difference in my GPA when I stopped going to the library after school to do my homework and started racing home instead to play with the baby. Absolutely no one protested when I moved her crib into my room to help with midnight bottles and changes. As she and I both got older, I developed an authoritarian way about me around her and began sending home the nanny when I got home from school, and the two of us would toddle to the neighborhood park every day and play on the swings. On weekends we walked to the bakery. I gave Jessica everything she wanted the moment she wanted it, and she loved me. How she loved me.

And my mother loved us both for it. There was no question that Jessica was the answer to all of our prayers. She was beautiful where I was plain, she was vivacious where I was sullen, she was adored by all who met her where I had only been adored by my father and him alone. Mothering her, as I did then, was the highlight of every day. Mom beamed when she saw us together. She took us around everywhere and said, within hearing, "Paige has been *invaluable*," and people started to ask her if I could come over and babysit their own children on Friday and Saturday nights. I would agree but insist on bringing Jessica along, and no one ever seemed to mind. After all, Jessica would play with their kids and laugh and laugh and befriend every child in the neighborhood, and by the time she was four, she began carrying her own doll around everywhere and "babysitting" it, saying when she grew up she wanted to be just like me.

Then, that same year, there was a catastrophe. It was implosive, and our family would never be the same afterward, and yet to anyone else in the world, it was probably impossible to notice. It happened at the neighborhood bistro, where Mom had taken Jessica and me to lunch one day. It was a school day, but some woman Mom knew from college back East was in town. Mom wanted her to meet her "amazing daughters."

We had gone together to a nail spa and gotten our "tips and toes" done. We sat with Mom in the salon, drying our nails while she got a blowout. I read a *Highlights* magazine to Jessica, gingerly turning the pages with the pads of my fingers to preserve the perfect sheen of the polish. She laughed and laughed at the "That's Silly" page. It was a line drawing of an ice cream parlor full of patrons, but everything in it was slightly awry. There was a penguin instead of a human serving ice cream. In her baby voice, Jessica would point at something and say, "You don't eat ice cream, Octopus! That's silly!"

Leaving the salon, I felt absolutely beautiful. Jessica already skipped everywhere, but her bounce was extra high. She pointed to a car painted a garish shade of pink and said, "That's silly!" I buckled Jessica into her car seat, and she said quietly, "Thank you, Mama Paige," and I put my finger to my lips, hoping it would remind her, *Don't say that when Mom is around*. I winked at her, and she nodded. I thought we understood each other.

We sat in a square around a four-person table at the café. Mom had given me some advance instruction on behavior and dressed me up—I was not in my usual baggy jeans with a college tee on top but wearing a knee-length dress with tiny little flowers on it. Jessica was wearing a dress with the same print but in a much more flouncy style. Mom was wearing shorts in the same print and a white button-down shirt tied in a knot at the waist. I remember she whispered as we walked in the door, "Girls, think *effortless*."

But as we were eating with Mom's college friend, a woman who was slightly thinner than my mom and had slightly higher breasts and was wearing an engagement ring just the tiniest bit larger than Mom's was, Jessica leaned over to me and said in a voice that probably felt sneaky to a four-year-old but was blaring to everyone else, "I have to go potty."

My mom started to push back from the table, as though she were used to such requests. I froze. I felt what was going to happen before it did. I tried to shake my head at Jessica. But fate was written. She said to my mom loudly, "I DON'T WANT TO GO WITH YOU! I WANT TO GO WITH MAMA PAIGE."

My mom just laughed. "Sister Paige," she corrected gently, and she put her hand on Jessica's forehead and smoothed away some of her bouncy blonde hair from her eyes. She turned to her college friend and said, "How lucky am I that they bonded like this? I am just so blessed." And then she turned to me, where I was still frozen. "Better hurry along, Paige, honey. We don't want an accident."

And it was over. I took Jessica to the bathroom. We came back to the table. Mom told Jessica to come and sit on Mommy's lap. A cab driver came in the front door, and Mom told me he was here to take me to school. She wasn't going to let me miss math class, was she? Not when it was my favorite hour of the day.

I went to school in that expensive pink-and-purple dress, and the kids all made fun of me, because it was so different from my usual garb, and when you were as unpopular as I was, you certainly couldn't be allowed to win for trying. When I got home, my mom introduced me to Jessica's new nanny, a stern woman with a thick French accent whose job it would be to give Jessica the gift of a second language. In a move that can only, in retrospect, be called Machiavellian, Mom signed me up for swimming lessons at the public pool, and since I had never set foot in the water before, I was made to parade in my swimsuit past all the experienced swimmers my own age to the shallow end of the pool to join a class of six-year-olds with nose plugs and unicorn floaties. Jessica and I started passing like two ships in the night. She was moved into her own bedroom and was allowed to decorate it to her liking, which made her giggle and laugh and dance. She started speaking pidgin French.

If she missed me, I couldn't tell. As for me, perhaps it was well past time for me to realize I was not this child's mother. At sixteen I probably should have been texting and driving or drinking and driving or doing something else equally dangerous to try to differentiate myself from my parents.

Maybe that is why, to make up for lost time, I took a large collection of my mother's Ambien and tried to put myself to sleep.

Jessica was only four years old that day. I don't remember her coming to the hospital during that time, and it's exactly as it should be. The universal family opinion was that, though the family record with mental health was not great, Jessica was a happy kid who had been spared the whole mess.

And so far as I know, that opinion prevailed all this time.

That means right now people in that family are having all kinds of feelings. Doubt. Guilt. Recrimination. Anger. I remember each one cycling through my father when I was recovering from my own suicide attempt. I imagine Jessica, who is alive because of a cautious stranger named Consuela, is on the receiving end of all that and more. I imagine she is feeling deserted, lost, and maybe a little relieved but still very, very ashamed. Maybe she is feeling thwarted. Maybe she is feeling furious.

Think how furious she would feel if she knew there is one other person in the entire world who knows what it is like to be her, and that person is cowering in her apartment two states away rather than showing her frightened, panicky face and explaining why she didn't teach her little sister how she learned to survive this too big, too crowded, too noisy world.

My phone pings, and I decide to "compartmentalize" this line of thinking immediately. Until someone forces me to do otherwise, I will try to keep my distance.

That is, after all, the entire secret to my success.

I cross the little apartment to get my phone.

Last night in my searching, I created a Pictey notification for any time @Mia&Mike puts up a new post. My thought was that maybe I could keep a loose eye on the comments, see when my sister resurfaced on them, and know that she'd made it through to the other side.

The downside to this plan is that now I'm subjected to a lock screen notification that reads,

> @Mia&Mike put up a new post! Will you be the first
> to comment?

No, Pictey overlords, I will not. But I will look at it, thanks to your very effective use-reinforcement engineering. I swipe to the post.

It's a picture of a gorgeous chuppah covered in fresh blooms, a flower-covered podium, a couple of white chairs with more flowers, and a path of rose petals leading to the middle of the scene. In the background I see a clearing on a mountainside, a riot of wildflowers, a clear sky. The caption reads:

> #Apologies. Deepest heartfelt apologies are due
> today.
>
> Have you ever promised something deeply from
> your heart, only to learn that to deliver that prom-
> ise would betray someone you love?
>
> I find myself in that dilemma now, dear readers,
> because I've promised you total access to my

wedding day, but I find I just can't give it to you after all. Tucker has bravely shared that he needs the events of this day to be just between us, and I'm going to honor that need, even though it means I will only be posting a few wedding pictures today. #ToughChoices Please forgive me! This photo, taken first thing this morning, is beyond the beyond for my wedding wishes. Those peonies! I can't wait to walk into that fairy-tale dream of a scene and say #iDo. And by the time you see this, I will be doing exactly that.

Now, I'm sincerely hoping Tucker's going to agree to post many more photos down the line, so please stay tuned. And don't be angry with him, my friends. Not everyone wants to put down their yoga mat in front of the whole class, even if they have a gorgeous half-moon pose and excellent form. Some people want to roll out in back, where they might feel more private, more authentic even. That's how they #honor themselves. That's what we're all about here. Today, honor yourselves. Let me know how it goes. xoxo Mia

PS: thanks to the amazing Wild Bloomery for the stunning peony display, the abundance of perfectly pink roses, and the bouquets, which I'll show off in another post soon. #Sponsored #WildBloomery

I put down my phone and wish I could throw it across the room. What a self-centered, navel-gazing, cliché-abusing joke of a human being. If I had a bottle of whiskey, I think I'd drink some right now, because whiskey is what angry people drink on TV. How can Mia Bell do this to Pictey? After all the ways they've prepped for traffic today and all the algorithms made just for people like her. It's all utter nonsense. What the hell even is half-moon pose?

This woman has Picted every single moment, instant, beat of a heart on Pictey for as long as I've worked there, and she has never, ever turned off the camera. For goodness' sake, she even posted on the day she buried her damn dog. It nearly crashed our servers.

Why would this attention whore—it's a distasteful term, but what else can she be?—marry someone who wants to stand in the back of the yoga class? Whatever the hell that means. Why wouldn't she just say, *Dear affianced, get your butt up here and support this because this is who I am and I already told half a million people this damn wedding was going to be online?* And why would he have rolled with the whole thing until the wedding day? His username is @TuckerlovesMia. What exactly did he think he was getting into here?

I almost go to the comments and post exactly that. I know I'll get at least ten thousand likes if I do. But then I stop myself. Something isn't right about this. Something is just off. I look at the caption again. What is nagging at me?

I sit up. Turn up the brightness on the phone screen. Huh. That's it. I turn it back down and look again. There's something missing. It's the lighting. There's a #nofilters certification, and the pic doesn't look tampered with. It's not that. It's that there're no shadows. The shadows from the chuppah are straight down, and the same with the chairs and podium. And they're short too. Maybe a tenth of the height of the actual chairs. *This photo, taken first thing in the morning,* she wrote. But if it was taken in the morning, where are the shadows and the bluish, pinkish light of the early hours? This photo looks like it was taken ten minutes ago.

I grab the pic, drag it to my laptop, and crack into the photo tagging to try to find the file metadata. It's there; it's all there. Of course it is. These influencers never scrub their metadata, even though if they don't want to be stabbed by a stalker, they really should.

But today she should have scrubbed it for a different reason. Because the photo shows exactly the moment it was taken. Not at nine a.m. or even ten, but at 12:11:48 p.m. on this very day. Roughly thirty minutes ago, and twelve minutes *after* her wedding was to have started. Further, the GPS shows the post was from the sparsely populated foothills near County Highway AB. Which is, according to Google Maps, an hour drive from the Arapaho and Roosevelt National Forests, where the whole thing was supposed to go down.

This picture isn't from her wedding. It's not even from the same zip code.

In other words, this entire post is one big fat whopping BS lie.

MIA

#Bouquet shots! I mean, how stunning is this? I know banana-leaf wraps are practical, but the way the florist instead wove together the long stalks of prairie grass to make the ultradetailed hilt of the bouquet is #tooperfect and celebrates the natural beauty of this place. The calla lilies are sourced from an organic farm in Chile where workers are all paid a living wage and treated with equity. Thank you to #WildBloomery again for this stunning display.

Oops! Gotta run! They're calling me for our portrait. Sooooo wish you could see it . . . soon I hope! xoxo Mia

Because I believe in the power of a good fait accompli, I put up three wedding-related Pictey posts to my feed *before* I call Tucker.

When he picks up, he is frantic.

"Mia? Mia, are you ok?" he asks me, and it's such an idiotic question I just laugh. "You got my message, right?"

"What message?" I ask. "Oh, you mean the text ending our engagement without explanation? Yes, I got it."

"You didn't reply," he says glumly. "And then I saw your post last night, and I wasn't sure what was going on."

"Generally I don't text back to utter morons," I say and too late remember that I sort of need a favor here.

"You're hurt," he says.

"Of course I'm hurt! What did you think I'd be? Thrilled?"

"I thought you'd be relieved, honestly. We'd let this fantasy go on far too long."

"It wasn't a fantasy to me," I say. I'm not sure how much truth is in that. Maybe it wasn't so much a fantasy happening on my end as a willful ignoring. "I thought we were getting married. I thought we were going to buy a house and have kids and build a life together."

"Build a lifestyle brand, more like," Tucker says.

"What do you mean by that?" I snap, favor utterly forgotten.

"Mia, come on. Really? You made me sign a prenup. *You* were going to buy a house that I would be living in by your grace."

"That's not how it would be," I say. "I tried to explain this to you. It's not my fault you came in with debt and I came in with savings!"

"The prenup was beneath me. I should never have agreed to it."

"So you want me to just share everything with you half and half?" I ask, feeling stupid as I do. But let's face it: some part of me worried he might be just a tiny bit more interested in my followers than in me.

"Yes, I do! Well, I did. That's marriage," he says bitterly. "Sharing."

"Tucker, if the roles were reversed, if you were the influencer with so much unrealized income, no one would blink when I signed a prenup. You're just bent out of shape because I stand to make so much more money than you do."

He laughs. "Of course you would think that," he says. I don't know what that's supposed to mean. What else could I think, when he frets over getting the best of me in a divorce before we're even married?

"Well, I don't want to be used for my success, and if that's so crazy, I'm sorry," I say. "I thought it was me you wanted, not all the perks." Maybe not *thought* so much as *hoped*, I admit to myself.

There is silence on the phone, and I don't know what it means, so I decide it must be meaningless. Finally Tucker says quietly, "Are you doing ok?"

I could think of all the ways I don't feel ok, but what good would that do me? Instead, in this space in the conversation, I am able to find my way back to what I need from Tucker, now that he's failed me so spectacularly. "I have some obligations," I begin. "I made a commitment to some sponsors regarding this wedding. Actually, *we* made a commitment."

"I know," he says. "And I'm truly sorry."

I blink away something moist in my eyes. I have had time for crying. This is not that time. "I need your help," I say. "I need to find a way to smooth this situation over and soft sell it to my followers. I'm counting on the income, you see. The deposits have been so expensive . . . I'm thinking I might need to . . ." I let my voice fall away from the rest of *that* sentence.

"You're faking our wedding," he says flatly.

"I think it would be more like just glossing over it," I say, because I have to hear trolls call me a fake ten times a day, and it just hits a little too close to home right now. "I'd post some scenery, the flowers, that kind of stuff, from my mom's house, where it's private. And then I'd post about other things for a couple weeks, use the archives a bit, do some callouts and sharable posts, and then announce a separation later, some Sunday afternoon when no one is at their desks, and try to just slide in that we've gone our separate ways."

Tucker pauses. "Blowing up the wedding in a live feed today would draw more traffic," he says, like we're talking about other people's lives. Sadly, I've already thought of that.

"It would be bad for you, Tucker," I say plainly. "You'd need security for a while, probably. I'd be worried."

"You could say it was mutual," he says.

"It wouldn't fly, not with all my planning posts so fresh in their memories." Not to mention the fact that as soon as he looks on Pictey, he'll realize I already started the process. "Besides, if we blow it up, we might be in breach of sponsorship contracts. What kind of bakery wants to be affiliated with a doomed wedding?"

"You didn't cancel the cake?" he says.

"Did you?" I reply.

Tucker sighs. "All that is your thing, Mia, not mine."

I press my lips together. If Pictey and the @Mia&Mike brand and the wedding are "my thing," then what, exactly, does he think he's entitled to outside the prenup? I try to stay with the breath, which is what I'm always telling my followers to do in tough moments. It turns out I'm panting, and staying with the breath is only making things worse. I've been giving bad advice. No surprise there.

"Will you go along?" I plead. "I'll drive traffic to you."

Tucker coughs. "I don't want traffic. I'm quitting Pictey."

"What? You're a photographer! What are you going to do if not Pictey?"

There's a silence on the line, and then he says, in that awful why-do-I-have-to-explain-this-to-you way, "I'm going to do a show. In a gallery. A real gallery, an actual building, with walls and stuff. I'm going to be an artist."

I throw my hands up and almost fling my phone across the room by accident. "You *are* an artist, Tucker. Your photos are in front of half a million people every day!"

"That's not art," he says.

"Right, because it makes people happy, it's beautiful to look at, and you can make a living doing it, so it can't possibly be art," I sneer.

He ignores me. "I want half the endorsement income from the wedding," he says. "It's as much mine as yours."

"You realize that if you'd just kept your promise and married me, you would have gotten all that anyway, right? Not to mention the honeymoon endorsements that were scheduled for next month, which we can kiss goodbye." Not to mention the honeymoon itself, a trip to Paris, chosen by him because it was "the most photogenic city." I exhale deeply. Try to take in one long, slow inhale. It turns into a gulp. "Sure, fine, half the cake, flowers, and the chuppah. But don't close your Pictey account until I have a chance to walk back the wedding. It'll be fishy if you just disappear."

"I don't want to be on there anymore, Mia," he tells me. "It's stifling my creative voice."

Was he always this tiresome? I ask myself. "It will only be a couple of weeks," I tell him. "A month at the longest."

"No."

I think for a minute. I know this man. What will make him change his mind? "I'll cut you in on half the dress as well." This means I'll break even from the wedding deposit on the inn and the other things I can't recover but not have a penny in liquid cash left over. I'll be back to start. But it's worth it.

"How much did you get for the dress?" he asks, and I know, no matter what he says about being an artist, that he is going to say yes for the money.

I tell him. "Is that enough?" I add.

"Yeah," he says eagerly. "That's enough."

"Well then," I say. "Congratulations. You're the real winner in this, aren't you?"

"I didn't mean to hurt you, Mia," he says. "I didn't even know this *would* hurt you. Isn't this just a learning experience or a growth opportunity? Isn't this the gift of failure?"

These are my words, taken from my posts over the years. "The gift of failure" is one of my key mission messages in my upcoming e-class, something I developed after being lectured, by Tucker and others, that I needed something called a passive income stream.

I want to gift him in the face right now with a nice big heavy box of failure, one with lots of pointy edges. And then push him into a rushing passive-income stream.

"Thanks," I say. "Thanks for the gift of failure. I really appreciate it."

"You weren't so sarcastic when we first met," he tells me. "You used to believe in everything you were selling."

I swallow hard, because this is true. But when we first met, I was mourning Mike, and I was clinging to earnestness and optimism to usher myself through. Now I've hit some kind of tipping point where my phone is buzzing thousands of times a day, people are criticizing me in think pieces just to get clicks, and my followers are bringing me problems I can't possibly solve. I've needed armor to get through my days. I thought Tucker, who would spend days in a funk after one bad troll attack, could understand that.

"I believed in you," I say softly. "I thought you already were an artist." His photos are beautiful. When I was in one of his best, it felt like immortality. "What did I know?"

"You knew I was changing. You knew I wanted more. And still, you were forcing me to shrink my dreams down to your size," he says, and maybe that's true. Maybe I didn't care that he was losing interest in the enterprise. After all, he seemed to enjoy spending the money that came out of it just fine.

The thought gives me a shudder. Am I the coldhearted lifestyle zealot he thinks I am? And if so, why did he ever propose to me? Who, exactly, was using whom?

I sink down on the back stair, seeing the fields of wildflowers that climb up the hills as nothing more than a blur of green and blue and brown and then seeing them sharpen and then finally seeing them as what they are, a beautiful picture. A beautiful sentence made of color and carbon, in the beautiful story that is supposed to be my life. "My dreams are big," I say to him. "My dreams go beyond your wildest imagination."

And he replies, "If your dreams can be faked for an audience, then just exactly how grand can they be?"

PAIGE

The weekend has been hell, has been worse than most weekends, because I can't pick up hours remotely or do staff trainings to fill the long drooping hours between lunch and dinner. I try to stay off Pictey but can't; I try to leave off from searching for new information on my sister and fail; I try taking walks and reading, and I even uncrust my one bottle of nail polish and try painting my toenails. It is tedious and pointless, and I throw the polish away after four toes. This, I think, would be the optimal time to use recreational drugs, but I don't, and I wouldn't know how to start.

My apartment, all five hundred square feet of it, starts to shrink in on me. The television, which I enjoy so much after dark, taunts me during the day, when I am too agitated to focus on just one screen at a time. I very much like going to the movies, but the movie I want to see is in its opening weekend, and those crowds are too much for me at the very best of times. I feel the unnatural, shame-ridden luxury of being bored, and I hate it. There must be a hundred things I *need* to do—when was my last oil change, I wonder?—but absolutely zero things I either must do or would like to do.

Through a combination of boredom eating and internet abyss diving, I make it to Sunday night, but when I wake up Monday, there's absolutely no question what I must now do—I must go get my job back. I do not want two more weeks, or even two more days, like the last two. What I will do is talk to Karrin about a new piece of code I'd like to try out to catch what I am now thinking of as the habitual threateners, users who cry suicide on a celebrity post once a week. Basically, if we can run a screen on those at the time of the flag, we'll know we aren't looking at that when we do our ideation review. I have some doubts about this idea's real viability, just as I am suspicious of any programmer who says they can use AI alone to screen for clinical depression, but Karrin might love it. It might be the thing that gets me back to my desk early. It's worth a try.

But I underestimate not just Karrin's discernment but also Pictey's desire to back her up. My swipe card doesn't work on the front door of our office. I have to piggy in with Sumeta, and she clearly knows I'm on leave because she raises her immaculate eyebrows when I slip into the building behind her. "Are you supposed to be here?" she asks, and I say, "Yes." But I don't get on the elevator with her, opting instead for the stairs and a way out of that particular conversation. When I come out of the stairwell, I am stuck again; there is another, more specific card-entry door at the entrance to our office suite. This was created so that only Pictey Safety and Standards personnel with nondisclosure agreements ten miles long come within a mile of the work we do here.

My ID also is deactivated at these doors, but Karrin is apparently expecting me, because she's standing by the door and opens it for me.

"Good morning, Paige," she says warmly. "Would you like to join me in my office?"

I would not. I would like to go to my computer and do some flags. I think if I weeded out a few private parts and some skinhead propaganda this morning, I would be able to gain my equilibrium. But I can't possibly say that to her. "That would be great. I've got something on my mind."

"I'm sure you do," she says.

"Did you . . . did you know I was coming?" I can't help but ask.

She smiles weakly. "I put your badge on the no-fly list," she says, referring to the code Pictey gives people who have been fired or have been judged unstable at a mental health screening. "Not because you're a danger to anyone," she adds quickly, "but because I wanted to know when you came by. Forewarned and all that." Her smile is surprisingly casual. "My job, remember, is to support you. Sometimes we don't make choices that align with our best interests. Sometimes we might even be harming ourselves, despite our best intentions."

I roll my eyes. "I'm not harming anyone. I'm just trying to figure out what went wrong, is all."

Karrin sighs. "Let's talk in my office." Her eyes slide side to side, as if she's looking for someone who might have heard me suggest something went wrong in our perfect little department.

I follow her back in there and feel strangely disoriented. Has it only been since Friday that I learned about Jessica? Since then I have tried and failed not to dig deeper into my sister's online life. I have found baby pictures my mom uploaded years ago, seen a video of her first tap recital, made a series of informed guesses about her teen years, taken a virtual tour of the Airbnb she stayed in last year, and read all her online reviews. Including a rave for something called the Magic Hair Wand with the headline *Bibbity-Bobbity-DO!*

I have not yet figured out how to call her and say hello.

As soon as I sit down, Karrin starts in. "I just want to stress, not just from a legal perspective but also a psychological one, that Pictey didn't do anything wrong in this situation, and neither did you. Your sister's cry for help was not your responsibility. That she posted it on our platform is a sad bit of fate. And there are hundreds of different ways that post could have been interpreted. The flag you saw—I've looked at it from every angle—was inconclusive at best, and the way we work here allows for redundancy and safeguards, and yet, even if we somehow caught every moment of desperation on our little corner of the internet, even if we dispatched emergency services at every instance, it wouldn't be enough for some people. We cannot stop someone from taking his or her own life. No one can, if the person is determined. And the larger fact must stay with you: Suicide is a cocktail of events, health conditions, and personal situations. It is not the result of any one incident. It's one of society's great sadnesses, but it's certainly not fair to lay it at the feet of some coding on a mobile app."

I nod to all of this, because I have had this conversation with myself several times in the last three days.

And yet I am still sure I could have made things different.

"It's not that I don't accept all those things to be true," I start. "I'm just interested in shifting the odds."

Karrin leans back. "That's awesome of you," she says. "Just super awesome. The trouble is you can't do that *right now*."

"Why not? How would it hurt for me to sit at my desk and play around with some code?" I ask.

"It could hurt you, Paige. You had a blackout from panic three days ago, and now you seem to be exhibiting survivor's guilt. You need time to process all that before you leap right back into the fray."

"That's not the real reason," I say. "If you were just worried about survivor's guilt, you wouldn't even have told me about the suicide. There's no possible way I would have found out. There must be a lawsuit."

She pauses. Starts to say something, then stops herself.

"But my sister's not dead," I say. "Doesn't that limit the damages?"

Karrin says absolutely nothing but is watching me carefully.

"It's a class action," I say.

Karrin puts her hands on her desk, softly, slowly, like she's sinking into a chord of a piano nocturne. "Paige," she starts. "You've shared that you're not close with your mother's family. We don't want to . . . add fuel to that fire."

I roll my eyes. "My mom won't join a class like that. She won't even tell a soul this happened. She'd never want it to come out in public." When it was me, she never even used the words *attempted suicide*, even after the neighbors started blabbing. She called it "Paige's little accident." If she called it anything at all.

Karrin shakes her head. "I cannot comment, Paige, even if I wanted to. And I don't want to—because my mission here is straightforward: I'm here to support and protect our team. That means I want to help you process these events in a healthy way. And being here, in this office, thinking up these ideas you're having, is unsupportive of your best health. You need to go home, lose yourself in books and movies, and, if you feel ready, spend time with your extended family. Regroup. Touch base with what your values are and make decisions about whether you want to come back here or if it's time to move on to another department. You excel at coding, and there's hardly any coding in this office anymore. Maybe you'll be happier somewhere else."

My eyes stretch wide open. "I thought I wasn't getting fired!"

"Of course not. You're getting opportunities, though. If you want them."

I narrow my eyes. "I don't. I want to come back to Safety and Standards. Now." I say this because I don't know what else to do with myself. I've been doing this for years. I don't know if I remember how to do anything else.

"You have time to think it over."

I put my head on Karrin's desk. I don't care if she sees how annoyed I am or how disappointed. It's only Karrin, after all.

With my face down, dark all around, I think of one of the many studies Pictey has run to find out how to make sure people want to keep coming back to our platform again and again and again. One of the findings of this initiative was that we must, under all circumstances, preserve the equanimity of the influencers. People like @Mia&Mike

are the reason millions of users open Pictey ten times a day, every time they sit down to pee or eat or wait in line at the DMV. Mia Bell must be kept happy at all times.

A single normal user's happiness, however, is inconsequential to the future of the platform. Like, for example, that of my sister.

"I have to look at my phone," I tell Karrin. I pull it out and open Pictey and look again at @Mia&Mike's feed. To my surprise there are several new posts since yesterday. There are photos of her wedding flowers, the cake, the pretty canopy of wood wrapped in peonies from five new angles. In one, Mia, decked out in a lacy white wedding gown, is hugging a woman who is so similar to her that she must be her mother or older sister. I don't read the captions, not right that second. Like the post on Saturday, there is something screwy about them all, and the pics are more like phone snapshots than the perfectly exposed art photos she normally shares.

I close my eyes and search deep into my memory, trying to figure out what my subconscious is trying to tell me, but nothing clicks. When I open my eyes again, I momentarily see the lovely foothills in the background, the sun dancing on the wildflower-covered hills, and wish, not for the first time, that I were not Paige Miller, Pictey screener and abandoner of her half sister in her time of need, but instead Mia Bell, vapid but beautiful lifestyle guru and internet celebrity, gallivanting up and down the Rockies in the high June sun, surrounded by wildflowers and hothouse peonies and loving family.

"Ok," I say at last. "I'll go away for a while, if I can have my job back after two weeks. Ok?"

Karrin nods. "Two weeks. You come on back, and we'll do some behavioral screening, and if everything checks out—and I'm sure it will by then—you can get back to your regular routine."

"Ok," I say again and begin to gather myself up to leave.

"Paige?" asks Karrin. "May I ask where you're headed?"

Back to my apartment, I think. Back to stalking my sister and living vicariously through a total stranger and maybe just getting the damn oil change whether I need it or not.

God, even I have to admit that sounds awful.

Instead I hold up my phone screen, showing her one of Mia's pictures of the mountains and sun and flowers. "Here," I say. "I'm going here."

She smiles. "That looks perfect. I'm sure your sister will be so glad you came."

"Maybe," I say. "But even if she's not, I'll still regroup, like you said to do. Read books and go on walks or whatever."

"Whatever you feel is best," says Karrin, sliding over yet another NDA for me to sign. "Within our lawyer's parameters."

MIA

Hey #squad, I wish I had time to write more, but let me just say that yesterday was my dream come true and today is all about hanging with family, especially my mom who keeps me #grounded at all times. Who keeps you grounded? If you can't answer that question, what can you do to build that relationship? Hint: That relationship may be with yourself. I am reposting a favorite guided #meditation I did earlier this year to walk you through some grounding visualizations in case that's what your soul needs right this moment. Thank you for all the love and well-wishes, my friends. I can't imagine this without you. xoxo Mia

By Sunday lunch I've got all the sponsored posts ready. I post the flowers, the cake, the dress, the chuppah, the makeup, the shoes, and even some things that weren't sponsored, like the inn, just because I like the guy who runs it. I get my mom to dress up and take some posed pictures with me. I use the tripod and get more, just me, the mountains, just Mom. Hippie though she is, she is uncommonly beautiful, like me but better, because I need mascara and highlighters and shading and airbrushing to be picture ready, and she needs only a shapeless silk dress and a barrette to hold her shoulder-length silvery hair away from her striking face. Her skin stays a pretty olive from April to November, and her lips are rosy brown without lipstick. Though she irritates me on so many, many levels, this is one thing I find endearing about her, this ease and success on film. It makes for a kind of balance between us, a way for us to relate.

"Let me see," she says when we're done. I show her, and she smiles, pleased with herself. "I guess I could use a lip filler, if I were the kind of person to get lip filler," she says, but she is angling for compliments.

"Don't you dare, Mom," I oblige. "Leave the Juvéderm to us mortals." I do not tell her I've actually already used an injectable, just under my nose, where something thin and crepey was beginning to reach toward my lips. She wouldn't like knowing.

But after I schedule the coming week's photos, dredge up some repeats to repost, shoot a few videos, cull the last three hours' worth of trolls, and do a quick and selective set of responses to my comments, my mood starts to sink again. It's time for me to check out of the B and B and go back to LA, and then it will be time to get back to the business of being me and to start a new work project: Operation Unmarry, in which I will have to tell my followers the wedding was a mistake and that we are going to annul it and get on with our lives, beg them to be kind to Tucker, say it was my fault, and Venmo Tucker a large amount of money. And then after that, the personal project: get over Tucker and get on with my life.

On the plus side, underdog Mia is on-brand. The @Mia&Mike ethos has been, at times, about picking up the pieces after a loss. After all, though I was a rising Pictey star when Mike was still with me, it was his passing that turned my followers into true devotees. When cancer came for my three-legged best friend too soon, it was my followers on Pictey that kept me from taking the short trip from grief to despair.

In real life, the statute of limitations for socially acceptable sorrow was far too short. The "real" people in my life forgot about him over the course of minutes. They'd ask me why my nose was so red, and I'd say that my dog had cancer and it was terminal, and they'd say, "Oh, your dog was so cute! That is so sad. Do you think you could sub for me at the six forty-five tomorrow morning? I'm going out tonight."

Then later, when it was time to help him across the rainbow bridge, people would say, "Oh, I thought he was already gone. So sorry. Do you think you could mention my store on your feed, by any chance?" At night I'd go home, and he wouldn't be there, not to greet me, not to sit directly on top of me and render it impossible to reach the remote, and not to crawl into the crook of my legs, where my knees bent when I slept on my side. Sometimes I'd wake up in the middle of the night, disoriented, and find I'd cried myself to sleep on his dog bed.

It was my Pictey followers that gave me the comfort I needed. When I lay in my dark apartment and wept for Mike, they didn't ask me what was wrong. They asked for more memorial photos, more video, more memories. I was surrounded by thousands of people who missed him too. Who had lost pets of their own and had taken as long as they needed to get through it. Who encouraged me to do the same when it came to my very best friend. Knowing how loved Mike was, knowing I wasn't mourning by myself, made all the difference in the world. It carried me through.

And it will carry me through again. I don't care what it sounds like—losing my dog was a thousand times more painful than losing my fiancé. The love I had for that man was people love, with fights and recriminations and always the possibility of betrayal, the chance of our shining attraction softening into something dim and dull. With Mike, there was no possibility of betrayal. He was devoted to me, absolutely trustworthy, a walking, woofing heart and two bright eyes the color of agate. His entire guiding principle, sunup to sundown, was simply this: *How can I make everyone feel loved today?* And he was so good at it.

———

Mike and I had this burgundy love seat. It was more like one of those chair-and-a-half things; I must have gotten it secondhand. It now seems so utterly unlike me, more like something you'd find at Mom's house. It was plush and sloppy and low; it never looked anything but rumpled. I kept a blanket on it because the fabric upholstery acted like Velcro to Mike's hair, of which there was a lot, only some small portion of it actually on his body at any given time. The blanket was old, a college keeper my mom had given me on move-in day. It had a silky edge on it, and Mike licked that edge a lot when he first came home; the vet said it was anxiety, the same thing that made him pick at his stump and eat the baseboards of that old apartment whenever I went off to work.

Two weeks into our cohabitation, I looked around the tattered moldings and half-gnawed chair legs and told Mike, fine, he could come with me to the yoga studio. But, I added, there was to be no shedding there, and I said it clearly and firmly, and I think he must have believed me. I brought him into the back room, made him a nest in an always-open kennel with prized toys and a white noise machine. I put an air purifier in the studio and ran the HEPA vac nightly, and no one seemed bothered. Mike's anxiety abated quickly, and in time, he ventured into the studio and began sitting on the platform with me during classes. He would often try to nap on my yoga mat while I was in downward-facing dog, and he'd be surprised when I moved into chaturanga, a modified sort of push-up hovering directly over him. He'd roll over just in case I wanted to somehow pet his tummy with my elbows. He'd breathe his hot puppy breath into my face.

Still, no one complained. In fact, more people started coming.

Mike noticed. He knew the students were there for him. He started sitting next to me during the opening. During the class proper, he puttered through the lines of mats, almost as though he were my assistant, ready to call my attention to a potentially unsafe back position in a twist or an especially beautiful triangle pose. His nails, however short I kept them, clicked slightly on the cork floors as he moved. When my students were in an inversion, he craned his head to one side from the back of the studio and seemed to smile at them. They all smiled back.

At the end of each class, I'd bring the students into a resting pose, flat on their backs, for quiet mindfulness. Mike seemed to notice this transition right away, and he didn't like to be out on the floor when it happened. By the third or fourth class, he had learned to come back to the podium with me several cues before I started this portion of class, and his breathing was very loud by then from all his exertions. My students came to sigh with pleasure when they started hearing his panting over my headset, because they knew the hardest parts of class were almost over. Like magic, their bodies loosened and gave their all for five more minutes, knowing that after that, I would let them rest.

Mike and I taught hundreds of classes together. I put his name on the schedule next to mine, with a little note for allergy sufferers about how I would wet dust before and after the class and run allergen filters throughout. The sheer number of filters we went through probably wouldn't have been worth it to some people. But to me it wasn't an option to teach without him anymore. He and I had become an us. Mia and Mike. I haven't taught a single live class since I went back to being just me.

Mom turns to me now, on the bed of the inn where we both are propped up side by side.

"Honey, we need to pack." Her words are softer than usual and kind. While she is not exactly sympathetic about Tucker jilting me, she seems to understand that the next weeks and months are going to be hard.

"I don't want to go," I tell her, and she nods.

"I know. But you can't stay here," she says.

I tip my head back on the headboard. "I made a mess of things," I say.

"Oh, you did not. You must have done something very right, to dodge a bullet like this."

"Not all marriages are bullets," I tell her.

"Of course not. But this one must have been. Or things would have been very different right now."

She's right about that, of course. I think back to the conversation with Tucker. I don't want to spend my life with anyone who sees me as a fraud. I don't care how right he may have been.

"When I go home to LA," I tell her, "I have to tell everyone. I have to find a way to explain all this to so many people. What on earth am I going to tell my followers?"

My mom tsks. "You don't have to tell them anything. You don't owe these people. They're total strangers! You could quit the whole thing tomorrow, and no one would blame you."

"Mom!" I say. "They would blame me. They'd be outraged. They'd be betrayed. They'd turn on me. They'd be hurt."

"You give your little picture messages a lot of credit, missy," says my mom.

"You don't understand, Mom." I'm not sure why I think she ever will, but I can't seem to stop trying. "My followers count on me. Together we create community. I give them something they care about. I post about important values and start conversations about what matters most."

My mom rolls her eyes. "Mia. Come on. You post pictures of wedding dresses on a website. You give people a distraction from their real lives and a false sense of familiarity that stands between them and having true connection, true community. Your impossible-to-live-up-to images make people think there's no point in even trying to enjoy the messy real lives they have been given."

I jut my chin out, maybe to look stronger than I am, or maybe to try to keep some tears in. I swallow. "Do you really mean these things when you say them to me," I ask her, "or are you just trying to keep me humble?"

Mom pivots on the bed so she is sitting in what I call sukhasana and she calls crisscross applesauce, facing me. She takes my hands in hers. "What I say, I mean. But mostly I am sad when you live your entire life on a tiny screen. You're a wonderful yoga teacher, or you used to be, and when I hear you speak about losing your brother or Mike, I get chills. You have a gift. Deep down, I think you are just looking for a way to share that gift." She sighs heavily. "I only wish you found a more productive way to share it. If you were a photographer, a visual artist of some kind, I'd say, *Great! Post your pictures online.* But you're, what, an 'influencer'? Is that what you dreamed of being when you were eight years old? No! When you were eight years old you wanted to be a teacher."

"I am a teacher," I say. I think of the conversation that circled around that sad message a few days back. Sure, Pictey took it all down, but I saw the connections forming. Maybe somehow my followers did some good that day for someone who was feeling lost. Isn't that something worth doing?

My mom lowers her voice. "When I look at your account, and I do sometimes look, I don't see you, my beautiful girl. I see Mia Ampersand Mike TM. I see cheaply filtered phone pictures and staging and faking."

I cringe. There is that word again. My throat feels constricted, and my eyes are getting hot.

She seems not to notice. "And look at how you reacted to this setback. You didn't create truth or beauty or honest community. You faked it."

I cough. "So you're not criticizing me," I say dryly, but inside I'm spinning out. First Tucker, and then my own mom. If people have so much trouble with my choices, why am I just hearing about it now?

But then, am I just hearing about it now? My mom has never made any secret of how she feels about online celebrity. It's just that I've never much minded. After all, I make a living, I have nice things mailed to me every day, and I am so lucky that it's hard to even keep a level head most of the time. And then there are the followers. No matter how people might see my tribe, I care about them; I believe in them. I want them to have what I have.

Except maybe not right now.

"All this talk," I say, refusing to cry, "it's just talk. You might be right. This might be all glass castles or a house of cards or any number of other architectural metaphors. But it is what it is. My career. My purpose. I need to keep it going, and I don't know how to face it tomorrow."

"Don't," says my mom. "Just don't. Come home with me. Hike up the flat side of Mount Wyler. Take a picture from the top and post it and tell your followers you're ok and all is well and you'll see them when you see them. Then throw that damn phone into a canyon and live offline for a little while. See what life is like when you're looking at it directly and not through a tiny screen." She pauses. "Take some time to remember what your dreams really are."

I shake my head. "I could never do that," I say. "I'd leave people in the lurch. I would disappoint everyone. I'd lose ground in my crowded marketing space."

But even as I protest, something in me has started singing. A tuning fork of recognition is vibrating in my soul. It's singing in perfect pitch: *Do it.*

"I could never do that," I say again, but now it's feeling less true. "It would be bad for my career. It would set me back years."

My mom stands up from the bed and pulls me up with her. "Would it?" she asks, and there's a twinkle in her eye. "Or would it catapult you forward?"

PAIGE

It's nearly a three-day drive from the outskirts of the valley to the top of the Denver metropolitan area. I get my oil changed after all. They check my tire pressure and put wiper fluid in and do all those things I know how to do technically but have never actually done myself, even though my dad tried to teach me how to be a good car owner. When I get back in my car afterward, I feel like it's had a magical protection spell put on it and will now safely get me anywhere I want to go.

And it does. It takes me through the most desolate country I've ever seen, the middle of Nevada, and to Salt Lake City, where I have some truly fantastic mole and then spend the night on the east side in a two-star chain motel. When I pay the bill there, I think of all the money I've saved up simply by not having a life. No restaurant meals, no drinks out, no need for entertaining space in my apartment or spending money on travel. When I last looked at my cash savings, there were six figures in there, just sitting, ignored. I realize there could be a metaphor here about my remaining youth, but I staunchly refuse to acknowledge it.

I could, I tell myself, stay in a fancy resort and then linger over breakfast in bed complete with a 20 percent convenience fee before tip. But I don't want to. I want to pay sixty-five dollars for the night, eat a partially frozen poppy seed muffin from the lobby, and get on with things. Besides, the area I'm headed to in Colorado will not be cheap.

The interesting thing about driving through the West, besides the sweeping landscapes and complete lack of meaningful radio, is that when one drives for eight hours a day, one cannot, even if one pulls to the side of the road for safety, use one's phone. There is no service for hours at a time, and on the first day I start to visualize all the terrible things that might happen to a person driving without cell coverage in the desert in a ten-year-old car.

But after a bit of that nonsense, I stop at a filling station and load up the tank and buy two gallons of water and some protein bars and press on, giving myself a stern word about the pioneers and Lewis and Clark and so forth. While I gas up, I check my phone, but nothing loads. Still. So that's it. I didn't download any of my podcasts or audiobooks or music. I planned to stream everything. How tech centric of me. Now it's just me and the radio. No one can reach me—not that anyone would want to—and nothing can invade my car bubble. No googling, no scrolling, no pinging, no nothing.

For a time, it almost feels liberating.

That time passes. While I understand the facts on technology dependence and appreciate that Steve Jobs was deeply concerned about how the iPhone would affect future generations, I happen to like the internet, and I don't care who knows it. I like constant access to my public radio station. I like buying my groceries online. I like buying my *everything* online, really. I'm perfectly good at reading a map, but I prefer not to have to while driving at seventy-five miles per hour. When I feel myself craving the news, I want it to be from the last ten minutes, not from the night before.

Alas, there is only the *USA Today* national edition rack I pass en route to a gas station bathroom for hints on what's happening in the world. The headline reads, *South Dakota: The State of the Nation?* I buy a copy on my way back to the car and scan the headlines before I start driving again. It says nothing about what I want to know: Is my sister doing ok? Will she be glad to see me or mystified at my sudden appearance?

These questions dog me as I drive and drive and drive. The only thing that helps is that no matter which oldies-station range I'm in, the DJ will play the "Golden Slumbers" medley at least once an hour.

Finally, on the third day of driving, I take out my phone at a Dunkin' parking lot and see that I'm back in a solid service area. I have the usual nonsense notifications and get a chance to see what likely fraud influencer @Mia&Mike has posted, as the line for doughnuts crawls forward. The entire time I've been on the road, she's only posted more of the same generic, meaningless phone-camera photos, most of them sponsored. Her latest post is the biggest insult to her fan base of all, a throwback photo, which is just a nice way of saying a rerun. The whole post is a rerun. All she's added to the caption is, *Still as true today as it was before . . . am I right?*

No. You are not right, lady, I think, as I open my map application and hover my finger over the destination bar. There are a few places I can choose from.

The first, the most obvious, is my mother's house. Lodging there is free, and further, she is my mother. To get there, I need to circle around Denver for about an hour to the east. Traffic being what it is, the app warns me to plan for an hour and a half just in case.

The second, also a reasonable plan, is to go straight to my sister's hospital and stay in a motel nearby. It's closer and in a more appealing area. It's the ostensible purpose of my long drive. The time of arrival would give me decent odds that I wouldn't run into my mom right away, or perhaps at all, especially if I just visit Jessica, spend the night, and then turn around and drive home. That's probably what I should do.

But then there's the other option. The one I've been nursing since Wyoming. This destination would serve so many purposes, not least of which is giving me another night's sleep before I have to figure out what to say to my sister. Additionally, it's likely that going there would answer some questions that have been weighing heavily on my mind ever since my sister's original cry for help on Pictey. And going there wouldn't really be stalking, because I know from the metadata that my quarry isn't there anymore. So I wouldn't have to worry about running into her, taking her by the shoulders, and accusing her fake life of misinforming my sister's very real one.

I certainly wouldn't want to do that.

Thus decided, I instruct my phone to navigate me to the Inn Evergreen, the site of about 80 percent of Mia's prewedding geo tags. It's an hour from my sister's hospital and a good two from my mother's house. It's got an advertised vacancy and high-speed wireless. It also boasts of local restaurants and entertainments in walking distance and a variety of spa-brand toiletries and linens. What more could I want from my lodgings?

Besides, I can be sure it will be an appealing night's stay. After all, I've seen many, many recent photos of the place.

MIA

Darlings, will you forgive me if I take a few days offline? I know you will. Thank you for being the most wonderful followers a girl could have. Be kind to one another. I'll see you soon, with comment replies and posts and all the good stuff I love sharing with YOU. xoxo Mia #missyoualready

In the end it is just like my mom says. On the morning I run out of prescheduled posts, while Mom goes out to escort a new life into the world, I hike to the top of the little minimountain, 10,500 feet above sea level, that rises up behind my mother's neighborhood. It's a fold, like the rest of these amazing Rocky Mountains, but the horst is one sided, so it has a flatter side and a steeper side. The steeper side is fun for climbing, or so I'm told. On foot, it's suicide.

The gradual hike up the flatter side is mostly shaded, with periods of trail that open up to wildflowers and then close up again into towering trees. Halfway up is a mountain pond, not big, and the creeks that feed it are low trickles of snowmelt. As I hike, I try to take it all in, but really I am listening to a podcast feed that is new to me, because they've invited me to speak in a few weeks. The thrust of the podcast is general lifestyle, with sort of an antisitting/prostanding perspective, and I'm going on to talk about my own audio series, several guided twenty-minute yoga classes for encouraging different states of mind. I had such fun with that one. There are a lot of cool studies out that show how even a tiny amount of exercise and deep breathing can change how your brain works and encourage creativity.

That said, this podcast does not encourage creativity. It discourages people from listening, by scolding us constantly about the dangers of sitting, which is not just the new smoking but the new smoking while taking antibiotics and using a nonergonomic mouse. I hit pause, round a corner, tell my phone to remind me to buy an ergonomic mouse, and then look on GPS to see how far I still have to go till I reach the summit.

I have no intention of throwing my phone over the edge of Mount Wyler, and my mom knows full well that's true. But I am going to take a picture of the scene and post a "bear with me" kind of message, then go dark for a few days, maybe a week. It's not great for my empire, so to speak, but it's not the worst thing I could do either. A week off social media sounds downright healthy, really.

I'm making good time. It takes about three hours up unless you cut the switchbacks, and I hate doing that. For one, it's harder work. For another, if you want a steep climb, don't hike Mount Wyler. A trail is cut already here, and that is where a hiker should stay, in my less-than-humble opinion. But I am alone in this; there's a hiker-made trail on the short side of the looping trail that draws a straighter line up the mountain. It's probably better cardio, I have to admit. Never mind; I have no place to be.

Because Wyler is a foothill among giants, the view from the top is mostly of taller mountains. But I love it up here; there's no denying it. Mom moved to the mountains from my childhood bungalow in Denver, and I've made the hike a tradition of my visits ever since. I usually pack a lentil salad, which is slightly naughty if one believes in the danger of legumes, as I maybe do. My mom had some chèvre left over, and I put it in this time, so it's totally naughty. Dairy and legumes. Gasp. I get to the top, sit in the full sun on my jacket, take out my earbuds, eat my lentils. I think to myself, *Mia, feel the sun.* It's like a bath of light. I feel like a solar panel, charging, charging. A week off social media. Every time I think it, the tuning fork effect starts again. My soul whispers, *YES.* My heart skips an actual beat. It will be pure bliss.

After my meal, I hike down a few hundred feet to the west, where a photo vista with a sturdy pipe safety railing is built right at the edge of the steep side, just inches from where the gradual peak descends into a sheer cliff formed by millennia of rockslides and schisms. From there, I take as many photos as I can bear, plus some selfies. The landscapes work best, so I pick my favorite of those, turn up some of the warmth and increase exposure ever so slightly, darken the blue of the sky so it looks more stark against the higher peaks, and then post it. The caption is simple and to the point. Going dark now, my dear friends. Just indulging in a bit of #metime before leaping back into real life. Please keep the light on for me—I'll be back soon! xo Mia #selfcare

The reception here isn't amazing, but it posts, slowly, slowly, and after I see a few likes come in that confirm it's live, I turn off Pictey, really turn it off, going so far as to delete the app on my phone. Then I delete several other social apps. Basically, if it pings in the next ten minutes, I delete it.

There. When I'm ready to come back, it will take only seconds to reload everything I just deleted, but for now I have created some space for myself. I can spend the week crying over Tucker, I can spend it hiking every day, I can spend it watching Vimeo or binging on Netflix or just catching up on the zillion emails I never can get through. Whatever feels good, I'll do it, and *no one will be watching*.

In relief, I drop my phone on the soft ground and turn to the view, leaning myself against the strong, reassuring railing, and let some of the thin, sharp air fill the lowest recesses of my lungs. I think of the loving-kindness meditation I only remember when I'm already feeling good, and I take myself through it slowly. I move through the blessings: from myself to someone dear (today it has to be my mom, even though she is annoying) to someone neutral (the innkeeper) to someone who I feel negative about. Tucker, of course. By the time I've blessed him with prayers of health, happiness, and safety and asked *May all be happy*, I feel it, the tug of happiness I sent out, pulling back at me, as it always does. My eyes are softer now; they seem to see better, and my lungs are used to the altitude. For the first time I notice some of the sounds of the mountain: a stream below, wind, wingbeats. I feel almost alarmed that I have this luxury, the luxury of sending wishes of well-being to the man who has hurt me, the luxury of standing on this mountain on a weekday on an impromptu vacation, the luxury of a mother who suggested such a thing and will put me up while I do it. And the luxury of the mountain alone, I add, because it is so, so easy to have some perspective when you're alone in a place like this.

And then I realize I am not alone.

I hear footfalls. I spin and see a guy, a panting guy. A runner. But he's not exactly runner shaped, I notice as he comes closer. He's broad and tall, not the wiry type at all, no kind of ultramarathoner. He's not wearing compression tights, he's not in a race jersey, and he's not wearing special shoes with pockets for every toe to help him achieve a more natural stride. He's just a guy, in shorts, regular athletic shoes, and a T-shirt with zero wicking power, from the damp look of it. He's dressed way too normally to be dashing up the side of a mountain in top gear. And from the way he's breathing, I start to wonder if I'm going to be doing CPR on the poor guy when and if he makes it to where I am.

But he doesn't make it here. He comes through to the clearing, spots me, and freezes, like he's discovered the yeti. He doesn't actually freeze, I guess. He stops moving forward and doesn't move back, but he keeps jogging in place, like he's at a stoplight, but I am the stoplight.

I will myself to turn green. "Hello," I say casually.

He keeps staring and jogging, bounce bounce bounce.

"Am I . . . in your way?" I ask, because I know you can't actually be in someone's way on a mountaintop, but I'm not sure *he* knows this.

The question wakes him up, which is a relief, because if he doesn't answer me by now, we are seriously in weirdo territory, and I would hate meeting a weirdo at the top of Mount Wyler. It would ruin it for me. He stops jogging, then says, "Sorry," and then starts walking toward me, and he is smiling warmly now, looking less shocked. If he is a weirdo, at least he is a handsome weirdo. "You took me by surprise," he says. "I've been doing this run for a long time and never seen you up here before. You must be from out of town," he adds.

I nod. "I am," I say. But then I think of the upcoming week. "And I'm not. My mom lives on County AB." I point straight downward, like if you were to bore into the rock face, my mother would be standing there at the bottom. "I'm visiting."

This elicits a nice smile from him, and for a second I swear I can actually hear my eyes telling my brain, *Holy crap, this guy is cute when he smiles,* and my brain saying back, *Shut up and look away,* and as usual I heed my brain. This is no time for cute smiles.

"Well," he says, breath starting to recover, "that's a relief. I had this moment where I thought maybe word had gotten out about this trail. It's categorized as a county natural area, not a county park, so it doesn't come up in any route apps. I hate to be greedy, but I like it that way."

"But someone else has found it," I say. "There are shortcuts stomped down on the switchbacks."

He shakes his head, smiling. "It's the muleys."

"The muleys!" I say. Mule deer. "Well, that's a better explanation." I notice the guy is already breathing normally, and it's clear that while he's largely built, he's fit too. Switchbacks or no, there's some serious elevation on this run. Unless he only ran the last fifteen feet. But then, if that were the case, I would have seen or heard him below me on one of the switchbacks on the way up.

"You run all the way up here?" I end up asking, even though I'm pretty sure of the answer.

"I run up, yep. I run up, but full disclosure, I walk down. My knees hate the descent. And I love my knees."

"I'm sure you do," I say, then frown at myself, because it sounds like I'm judging his legs somehow, and of course I'm not doing that, though ok, now I am, and the legs are good, strong and bulky, with a dusting of hair two shades lighter than the brown on his head, as well as a slight tan. I fish around for how to categorize them, and dammit, the words *tree trunks* pop into my head.

"We need knees for so many things," he says.

Is he talking about sex? Do we need knees for sex?

"Sitting," he goes on. "Deep knee bends," he adds.

I breathe out. "The Charleston!" I say, and I'm so impressed with myself for coming up with something witty after my brain went on such a sexcapade that I actually *do* the Charleston right there, and that gets me enough of a laugh that I can get grounded again and am able to interact more normally. "Do you live close by?" I ask.

"On route AB, just like your mom," he says. County Highway AB is the road that meanders from the outskirts of Copperidge, goes downhill a bit, and then winds up into the hills, getting smaller and smaller, until the road is only a lane and a half. Set on either side are modest little homes like my mom's, and developers have yet to fill in the gaps with mansions and chalets, because there's not much depth between the road and the rock to build in, and there are still so many better places to plop a zillionaire.

"My name's Dewey," he tells me.

"Mia," I say. "My mom is Marla Bell. She lives in the little white ranch with the big porch."

"Love that porch," he says. "Your mom's a nice lady. A nice lady with a nice porch."

"She is," I admit. "And I love the porch too." It's too folksy the way she has it, but I always imagine it without the rocking chair with the heart-shaped back and the wicker porch swing with chintz pillows, and it holds so much promise when I do. Maybe it's Hollywood's doing, but I think porches like that are for first kisses and fond reunions. To my knowledge, neither thing has happened on that porch, but maybe it would if Mom would just let me paint the floorboards blue and the railing white. That and some tulips . . .

"I didn't realize she had a daughter," he says.

"I don't visit much. Once a year." That makes me sound neglectful. "She likes to come to me. And we travel together."

"I'm glad you're here this time. It's nice to have company on my run."

I take him in. Sweaty. Rectangular. Strong and broad. He has a mess of thick brown hair and a beard that looks hot. If I were a man, I'd shave my beard during the summer and grow it in the winter. I wonder why he hasn't shaved. I wonder if he has a chin or if that chiseled shape is just a facial-hair illusion. Something inside me is telling me not to look him too hard in the eyes, but I already know they are hooded and bright—maybe not brown, maybe hazel, blue, green. Maybe just really light brown.

"It's so pretty up here," I say. I wonder why I'm finding someone attractive right now. It must be the meditation, the air, and the breakup. Oh, duh! Of course it's the breakup. This is what always happens to me after a romantic disappointment. I have a natural instinct to get under one guy to get over another, so to speak. It's not the worst idea.

"The funny thing about this bump is that it looks so small out here," says Dewey. "It looks like nothing set against the bigger mountains. But if you put this same bump in, say, Kansas, just this little hill, Mount Wyler, we'd never miss it, but it would make Kansas a wonderful place."

I laugh. "How do we know Kansas isn't a wonderful place already?"

Dewey shakes his head. "There are wonderful places *in* Kansas, but Kansas itself is not my favorite state. Yet. When I figure out how to move this mountain there, Kansas will become heaven on earth."

"Isn't Kansas the state that teaches creationism in science class?"

"I think it is," he says with an emphatic nod.

"I don't think we should give them a mountain. It's much too old to make sense there."

"You're being greedy," he says.

"I think we should offer them the mountain for changing their textbooks. How could they say no? They could ski on it, hike up it; they could put up gondolas for scenic tours. And think about property values! I personally would want to move to Kansas if they had this mountain."

Dewey laughs. "Where do you live now?" he asks.

"Los Angeles," I say. "I have a town house in Mar Vista." I'm not sure why I volunteer this information so early. Until I realize I used the singular pronoun. Jeez. What's wrong with me? I'm basically lying down in front of this guy naked. Did he miss it? *Please let him miss it.*

"Just you?" he says. Oh, come on!

"And my dog," I add. I don't know why I say that. Mike has been dead for almost a year now. But Mike would have loved this guy. He was very goofy. "What about you?" I ask, then cringe. I want to stop saying such ridiculously obvious things.

"No dog," he says. "One kid."

"That's nice," I say. "Well, you should get a dog. The dog could run up the mountain with you every day and keep you company." *Oh my god, Mia, what did I say about not talking!*

"Do you run with your dog?"

"No," I say. "He only has three legs." Mike was thrown out of a moving car when he was younger, before he came to live with me. I got him a little set of boots for his other feet, plus a bow tie. He loved the attention he got in his bow tie.

"Oh," he says. "Poor fella. I'm sure he's still a great pal, even if he's not a running buddy."

I decide I should stop talking about Mike as though he is still alive. It's disrespectful. "Yes," I say, "the best," and I try to say it in a way that makes it clear that I want to talk about something else.

He picks it up. "We're having a coyote problem right now," he says. "Around my house. Has your mom said anything?"

I frown. I don't have anything to say about coyotes. "No, I'm sorry," I say.

I must go glassy thinking about this, because Dewey turns around on me. "I'm heading back down," he says. "I've got to keep moving; I get cramps in my hammy otherwise."

Oof. The word *hammy* breaks the spell. Why did he have to say *hammy*? Or maybe it's good, because I can't even *fantasize* about sex with someone who says *hammy*. I'm safe now. "I'll walk you down," I say without thinking.

"Great," he replies. "If you can keep up."

For a second I can't tell if he's joking. Then he turns on the smile again. *Hammy,* I whisper to myself. I grab up my raincoat and my empty salad container and my water bottle and gallop after him. And in the end, I kind of do have to race to keep up with his long legs. But talking the whole way down is easy, and I get home feeling loftier than I thought I could this soon after being jilted. In fact, I'm feeling so lofty it's not until I get to my mother's house that I realize I left my phone at the top of the mountain.

PAIGE

Here is what I know, or think I know, about Mia Bell:

She is a yoga instructor, and after college she started a yoga studio in Southern California, which she sold to Hastings Management Group in 2018.

She has been on Pictey since it was still in beta.

She started her social-influencing career with yoga and yoga-lifestyle posts, often featuring her late dog, Mike, a three-legged bulldog mix often photographed in a red-and-white-dotted bow tie.

She now distributes a lifestyle email once a week, does speaking events, and, most of all, endorses crap no one needs on her Pictey feed.

She recently announced her marriage to a mildly talented photographer going by the username @TuckerlovesMia. (@PaigeMiller feels nauseous.)

And she just posted a message saying she was taking some time away from her feed, for no reason whatsoever.

I am checked into the Inn Evergreen, and it is indeed beautiful. I am shown to a room that is done up in what I will call "expensive chalet," where I collapse on the bed before the owner of the place has even shown me how to work the gas fireplace. He takes the hint, but before leaving he mentions cookie time in an hour. I do not miss such an important detail as this. After the hour passes, I toss aside my phone, march from my pretty bedroom to the dining room, and hover uncomfortably near a little table by a tall shuttered window. There are a few other guests there, and I try to get excited about eating cookies while milling about with strangers.

But it turns out cookie time is a seated occasion. The innkeeper shows me to a little table like I'm at a restaurant, asks me about coffee and milk, and then says cheerfully, "Chocolate, hazelnut, or both?"

I say both, and then when he brings in a saucer piled with soft, warm cookies, I begin to understand the reason people love B and Bs so much.

When I am polishing off the last of the hazelnut rounds, but before I start on the chocolate chip, I ask the innkeeper if he does many weddings, and he says, "Ah, you thinking about a wedding?"

The question surprises me. Dating, love, and marriage are things other people do. Masochists, specifically. I make some awkward noises. *Uhhh* and *ahhh* and *umm*.

"I only ask because we just had a cancellation," he says, then makes a tsk sound with his mouth. "That poor woman. It was a mess—she had put down her deposit and all, but it threw me out of whack, and I had pangs of guilt keeping the money in her worst moment. I want my guests to be happy, you know. I'm thinking I might change my wedding policy."

All my light bulbs start going on. "But the bride, she was ok, right? You saw her?"

"Oh yes. Totally fine. I mean, well, it was hard to tell. I think she was putting on a brave face. Obviously this wasn't how she meant things to go. And it was only a small event, she said, just immediate family and the officiant, but she had booked all four rooms here so everyone could be together. So it was like, *Sorry about your wedding, but thanks for the massive deposit.*"

I try to think of what a normal nonstalker would say to that. I think of what my roommate Michelle from college might say. With three kids, a balding husband, and a big cheerful house full of throw cushions that say *Live, Laugh, Love*, she is highly normal. Of course, no one in their right mind would jilt her.

So I say, "You know, if that happened to me, I'd probably get all my girlfriends in here and just binge on Häagen-Dazs and the wedding champagne and feel sorry for myself for the entire weekend." This is so far from the truth. If, in some alternate universe, I dated, and then if I met someone, and then if he actually wanted to marry me, and then if he jilted me at the altar, I would have a panic attack, spend a night in the hospital, get my meds adjusted, and remind myself never to date again.

"You'd think, right?" says the innkeeper. "But not this woman. She went up there alone and locked the door and didn't move for a day or two, not that I could tell. Except for breakfast. I brought up her breakfast—she'd made all these specialty diet requests, so I couldn't use her food for anything else anyway. No dairy, no gluten, no grains, Lord a'mighty. Of course, maybe she's onto something; she was the size of a toothpick," he goes on, patting his not-insignificant tummy. "But still, life is for living. What was I saying?"

I smile warmly. Or I try to. "The bride, you were saying she locked herself in her room."

"Right. And then one day she must have come out while I was gone, and then she came back with her mom, and by then she was all business. Like nothing happened. No tears, no nonsense. Packed herself up and away. Even took a selfie on her way out. I mean, good for her, but still, whoa."

"Yeah," I say. "Whoa."

"Well, all I can say is that I wish you a happier stay here at Inn Evergreen. Oh! And I smudged the rooms, so don't worry about bad energy."

I make a note to myself to look up smudging when I get upstairs. "Thank you?" I say. And then, as I eat my final cookie, I whisper to myself, like the late-night-TV stalker I seem to be, "You were right, Paige. You were right."

———

So Mia did not get married. The post about Tucker not wanting to post about their wedding was utter bunk, and the truth is he jilted her. I am so excited by this information at first that I spend some considerable time forgetting that Mia is an actual person with actual feelings. But even so! I knew something was up, and It Was! I'm an internet-celebrity myth buster. I have no use for the information, and I still don't know the woman from Adam's off ox (biblical, of course, but also touching on the wise idea of placing an unfamiliar [off] ox farthest from you in a yoke, if you're ever in a multiple-ox situation). Even so, I am vindicated! I have proof that internet celebrity is indeed, as we all knew, utter tripe, that no one's life could possibly be as beautiful and happy and perfect as hers is supposed to look. Mia Bell's entire wedding was a publicity stunt! I want to shout it from the rooftops. I want to go on Pictey and post the news and bring the whole thing crumbling down . . .

Except I also don't. I think of the thousands of Jessicas who love this woman, and I cannot decide which would make them feel better—knowing that her perfect life is impossible or believing that it could be attainable somehow.

In the end, it's not my decision to make. By the time night falls, Mia's feed seems to be bringing itself down. All she said was that she wasn't going to post for a while, and her comments blew up. Half the feed says some version of *take your time; enjoy your new husband.* The other half ranges from mild disappointment—*awwww, we will miss you, Mia*—to straight-up entitlement: *Marriage ruins everything* and *I'm going to need someone new to follow.*

Most surprising are the trolls. I didn't know @Mia&Mike had trolls, but that may be because she has earned a Pictey Gold Button, which is a special dashboard widget given to Pictey superstars who drive a tenth of a percent or more of daily traffic. Basically it gives them the ability to hide—not delete but hide from public view—any upsetting or offensive comments, even if they aren't caught in a flag. Pictey quietly monitors the use of the Gold Button, and if someone goes too nuts with it, we reduce its efficacy, but otherwise the mind-set is, to hell with free speech: if an inappropriate comment doesn't have to cross our desk in Safety and Standards, so much the better.

I didn't realize Mia had a Gold Button, because she lets all kinds of truly critical comments build up in her feed. People ask her about the environmental impact of every move she makes, complain fervently when she links to a brand page, and just generally hate everything she does with her hair. But when I read the first for-real troll comment, I realize that they're in a different league. It says, *About time you stop selling hope to the fat fucks out there with nothing going on in their lives. Maybe then they'll get off their asses and lose some weight.*

I feel a chill. It's the chill of the sheer meanness, the artless yet multidimensional cruelty that this one purportedly human commenter has been able to dump into the world in just a few lines. Cruelty that, while actually random, feels deeply personal. Am I not, in this stranger's eyes, a fat fuck with nothing going on in my life?

I flag the comment. It's despicable and unnecessary. Then I read each of the posts under it, the indignant followers who don't know, or do know but can't leave it anyway, that a troll's only desire is for attention. The loyal followers rush to Mia's side, saying her life is not public property, saying that there are professors and doctors and artists in the comments feed showing that her fans have lots going on in their lives, that her lifestyle promotes health and well-being, that her followers are a community of support and kindness, that fat shaming is no better than racism or homophobia, and on and on. Eloquently they rush to her defense, they spend thousands of words on carefully crafted responses, they try to drown the troll in logic.

But trolls float like an unflushable poo. When you comment on a comment on Pictey, the original comment crawls to the top of the feed for "relevance." By the time I've finished reading everything from the morning's post and hit refresh, the troll's post is the very first one under the original caption.

It makes me furious. Sure, Mia is a liar and a hack. But also, look at all these nice people spinning their wheels, being insulted for no reason. With Mia gone, there's no one to stand up for them. There's no Gold Button.

But of course, I realize, there is. I get out my work laptop, caution to the wind, log in to the Pictey Support general user account, pull up the flag I just made for the troll, and Gold Button the hell out of that asshole myself.

MIA

I start missing my phone around ten minutes after I get down the hill. That, naturally, is also when the skies open up and it starts pouring rain. I am not used to rainstorms. I don't have a raincoat or quick-drying pants, but my mom does. I climb into her rain gear and put on a Rockies cap I find on the coatrack, even though she would sooner wear a sombrero than anything affiliated with pro sports, and some tech-wool socks. I don't think I could make it down the wet rock-and-mud path safely in galoshes, so I leave hers there and gratefully lace back into her hiking shoes, which are utterly no nonsense and thankfully just a half size too big for me. When I glance at myself in the hall mirror, my blonde hair threaded through the cap's back, my clothes and shoes just incrementally out of style but utterly weatherproof, I smile. I look like a real Coloradan.

And wouldn't that be nice? If I could live in Colorado and hike up mountains every day and run my "brand" from these views instead of from my third-floor two-bedroom with a view of another third-floor two-bedroom?

But that's stupid. I need to be close to the airport to do the speaking gigs, and I need to be close to all that Los Angeles offers to do everything else. Besides, I'd get tired of this little tangle of towns and ski resorts eventually. Unlike Dewey, I don't think I could run up the same mountain every week without going insane.

But today I get to summit it twice! Whee! I decide to try to run up it, since I'm drowning in this rain anyway. I get a third of the way up when the lightning starts, and I realize I am not safe. Further, I am not in good enough shape to get to the top running, so I'm going to have to walk, increasing the amount of time in which I might get caught in a mudslide or hit by lightning.

But. I need my phone. What else can I do?

I am embarrassed to admit that even after the thunder and lightning are undeniable, I still keep climbing for ten minutes before I come to my senses. I'm on a wooded slope, and I'm miles from shelter. I need to turn around. The phone is waterproof, and the case is one of those rugged monsters that you can set on fire or take down into the Mariana Trench. It will, in other words, survive. I will also survive if I go home until tomorrow and take cover. I tell myself these facts over and over again as I carefully jog my way back down the hill. When I get inside, I'm up to 30 percent relieved I wasn't hit by lightning and only 70 percent panicked about being offline.

My mom has a phone! I go looking for her—she's in the basement moving cardboard boxes up off the floor. "This is a real gully washer," she tells me in lieu of hello. "Whoa, you look like a drowned rat. Did you get caught out in it?" She tilts her head. "Is that Andy's hat?"

I purse my lips and then shrug. "I was hiking," I say, then grab a box and lift it onto a wooden pallet in case the basement floods. "Hey, um, you know that phone I bought you?"

"Sure I do. You want it back?" She looks totally unsurprised. We keep loading boxes.

"Could I borrow it for a few days?"

"Absolutely. I can get it tomorrow or Sunday."

"Sunday? It's not in the house?"

"Oh, hon. What would I do with it? I have the red one and the one on the wall. That's two phones already, for one person." The red one is a flip phone from the age of the dinosaurs. Remember when phones, not cases, came in rainbow colors?

"Mom, you need a real phone, for emergencies."

"That's what the red one is for."

"But you have to keep it with you all the time so it's there when you need it."

"I keep it in the car so it's always charged up! Honestly, what kind of emergency am I having outside of home or the car?"

"What if a baby came?"

"I keep my red phone with me when I'm on call," she says. "I'm not on call right now."

"What if you were taking a walk or went on a bike ride?"

She rolls her eyes. "Honey, people didn't have cell phones for millennia. And they have been hiking the Rockies since God was in short pants. Life goes on."

I give up. "Whatever," I say. "I just need to borrow the phone I got you. I dropped mine on my hike, and it's too wet to go find it."

"Oh shoot. I gave that extra phone to Aunt JoLynn."

When I was born, Aunt JoLynn was neither my aunt nor JoLynn. She used to be my mom's college friend Joe, but she transitioned years and years ago. Now she manages a senior-care facility in Golden and is always scrounging up used handheld devices and outfitting them with adaptive functions for her clientele. They love the changeable size of the text and icons, the backlighting, the high headphone volumes. "Mom," I say. "That's not some ten-year-old iPad. That was new! And expensive!"

"It's just on loan. You can go get it anytime. Though I will warn you, she actually is using it herself. She gave her old phone to a sweet old lady who likes to watch unboxing videos at an otherwise deafening volume. I gave her those fancy blueface headphones too."

"Oh, Mom." This is my mother. This is why she thinks phones are stupid. She thinks they just stream constant unboxing videos into, what, *blueface* headphones? I sigh. She smiles. She well knows I won't take away Aunt JoLynn's phone. She needs it more than either me or my mom. And the thought of the senior woman with the unboxing habit makes me strangely happy. It makes me want to send the care center something that comes in an elaborate package that she can unbox herself—or better still, a subscription gift that comes every month. I reach for my phone to make a note of this idea, but it's not in my pocket. It's on the top of Mount Wyler. How does anyone remember anything without a phone?

I sigh again. I'll have to dust off my mom's modem to get online later tonight, but that's not good for much—if she needs to connect, she still plugs her modem into a phone jack. It'll take ten minutes just to download my email. I shake my head. My mother is crazy.

"Why is all this stuff on the floor?" I ask, because I am making no headway on the phone conversation anyway. Usually her basement is sort of orderly, boxes on shelves, labeled. *Mia's crap. Marla's junk.* Those boxes are all still shelved as usual, but these on the floor are new to me, closed tight with clear plastic packing tape. They're mostly reused wine boxes. I look around and find no kind of labels on them.

Mom gives a sad sigh. "These things, they were your brother's."

"They were?" My voice gets quieter. Six years after the accident, we still speak in hushed tones whenever Andy comes up. We probably always will. "Where did they come from?"

"His apartment. I forgot all about it after he died. His landlord packed this stuff up and took it home and called me to come get it, and I forgot that too. And she never pestered me about it, just kept them in her own basement. Sweet woman. But she passed a few months ago. Her kids looked me up."

"Oh man," I say. I don't want to see Andy's stuff from the apartment. I couldn't even go into his apartment, after. We got anything important back years ago from his friends. The rest is probably flannel shirts and Bed Bath & Beyond coupons. "Oh, I remember her," I say, thinking of the landlord. A doting woman with great-grandkids and a pocketful of lollipops. "Just old age? Nothing tragic?"

"Old age," says my mom. "Ninety-five this year."

"I should send a card."

"I'll give you the address. She lived about a block from Andy."

"Do we have to open the boxes?" I ask. I don't want to see Andy's old clothes. His socks that always had holes in the second toe area because it was longer than his big toe. Mine is the same way. I thought it was hideous. He thought it was hilarious and was forever buying me flip-flops and daring me to wear them in public. "You can't hide your shame!" he would say with an evil laugh. "Don't even try!"

"You don't have to open anything," my mom says with a frown. "I will, when I'm ready. There might be something good. Photos, maybe. I never thought we got back enough photos. But whatever it is, I need to get them off the floor. We got a ton of rain this spring, and the ground is already saturated. I'm sure it's coming in by the evening."

"Does it flood down here every time it rains?" I ask. I don't think that's good for a house, but what do I know—I live on the third floor.

"Nope, just special situations. Don't worry; I'm not going to float away. At worst I get an inch."

I grab the last box. Is there a photo in here I haven't seen before? In those first six months after he died, I looked at every photo of Andy so many times I started to create imaginary memories around things I had nothing to do with. Did I go with him to Mesa Verde? Or was that a Scout trip? I cannot be sure anymore. "Well, even so," I say, glad to talk about anything besides that, "I'll order some shelves for this stuff." I reach for my phone to place the order. Again I'm out of luck. I'm going to have to start writing things down. On pieces of paper.

"That would be great," says Mom. "Even after I do sort through it, I don't think I'll be able to throw any of it away just yet. You know."

I do know. We had to go through his closet and drawers here at home, and that was bad enough. Andy didn't keep much, but what he kept was meaningful. Not every birthday card I ever gave him, but like, the first one I picked out myself—a sparkly blue card that played "When You Wish upon a Star" when you opened it. And the one where I wrote twenty-five reasons he was the best brother ever for his twenty-fifth birthday.

He never had a twenty-sixth birthday.

"It might not be photos," I warn. "He never really remembered to take photos of anything."

My mom nods. "Probably not," she says sadly. "Probably it's all nothing."

I try to issue some kind of comforting smile. "Let's finish here and go upstairs and have a beer."

My mom looks at me like I've proposed we take a rocket to Mars. "You mean actual beer?"

"For you. Not for me," I say. "For me I mean white wine. Beer has gluten."

She laughs. "Right. And gluten makes you fat," she says with raised eyebrows.

"Well, it does."

"Does tequila make you fat?" she asks.

"Margaritas, yes. Tequila by itself, no."

"Well, the rain's not stopping, and moving Andy's boxes makes me want tequila," she tells me. "How about a shot of Cuervo with a white wine chaser? Sounds gross to me, but whatever. God forbid you gain an ounce."

"Sounds like a deal," I say, and I try to forget about Andy for the rest of the night. But without my phone to pull me out of my thoughts, it is impossible. All night long I am crawling the walls. After my mom goes to bed, I sneak downstairs with packing tape and scissors. I open each box of Andy's, rifle through the contents, and tape them back up so Mom won't know.

I find no photos. Nothing personal at all. Just long-outdated papers, textbooks from college, worn-out socks, a pair of swim trunks with the tags still on. In the last box I find a navy T-shirt of his, from an Arcade Fire tour, being used as a protective wrap for a lamp I swear I've never seen before. The shirt is dusty and smells of nothing, certainly not of Andy, not his neutral mix of dude sweat and Irish Spring. Even so, I shake it off and put it on over my pajama camisole and go up to bed. Though I don't remember seeing him in it, it is soft from multiple washings, and the neckband is loose. He wore it, maybe to play basketball. He might have played a pickup game after work in this shirt.

I would have been in LA already, back then, still trying to get my yoga studio off the ground. But as I fall asleep tonight, I imagine I was there, in Denver, at the gym, waiting for him to finish so we could go out for dinner and catch up. In my half-asleep, half-waking state, I imagine that he comes over and gives me a stinky hug and says, *I'm gross. Let me run home for a quick shower and then meet you at that place by my house?* But then, instead of him getting T-boned on the way to his apartment at six thirty p.m. by some guy who had spent the day holding down a barstool, I would tell Andy, *You smell fine to me. I heard there's a good place around the corner. Why don't we just walk?*

PAIGE

Once I start, I can't stop. I keep my laptop logged in, spending half the night monitoring Mia's feed. I also pace around the room, read a few pages of a book so boring I've had it unread for almost an entire year, flip on the TV in the background, get stir crazy, go for a walk, enjoy the mountain views, come back, and hit refresh. By the time the feed has a thousand comments, I've zapped eight trolls, who have suggested, among other things, that Mia needs to get laid by force and that she is a waste of usable organs and that she is actually a Russian hacker catfishing the entire @Mia&Mike fan base. I almost leave that one because it amuses me. But it seems like if I'm sort of half hacking Mia's account, I should at least be consistent about it. I fall asleep next to my laptop, wake up around seven, and start it up again.

Around breakfast, I'm about thirty pages into my boring book and three trolls down and getting hungry. I realize this is a bed-and-breakfast, but I don't think I'm going to get breakfast delivered to my bed, so I take a shower, pull on my clothes, and grab my computer and charger. I figure I can take my laptop down to breakfast and just keep refreshing.

But when I get down to the dining room and seat myself where I had my cookies, the innkeeper looks from me to my laptop and says, "Oh, no. No way."

"Am I late?" I ask.

"Late to the revolution, my dear," he replies. "Here at Inn Evergreen we don't dine while gazing into our screens. We chat. We mingle. We read a book."

I blink at him. "I'm from California," I say. "Can I use my laptop?"

He looks back, and I can tell he's totally considering it. He should be! This is a ridiculous rule. But when he speaks, he says, "I'd really prefer guests not work in the dining room."

"I'm not working," I assure him. "I would need a more secure connection to do any meaningful work here."

Again it takes him a long time to answer. Finally he says to me, "Paige, may I call you Paige?"

"As opposed to what?" I ask.

"Ms. Miller," he supplies smoothly.

I think it over. "I prefer that," I say at last. I wonder if I could ask Karrin to call me Ms. Miller at work. It would be reasonable, since I'm of generally higher usefulness than she is and have longer tenure.

"Ms. Miller, would you consider dining in the kitchen today? I can make you comfortable there, and you'll be able to use your computer without affecting my general policy."

I blink. "I don't care where I eat," I say. "Though I am hungry."

He actually claps his hands. "Terrific. Let me show you the way."

As the innkeeper gallantly escorts me to the neighboring kitchen, I pass the other diners in varying stages of their repast. I do notice none of them even have their phones on the table, much less a computer, much less a twenty-inch SmartThink Pro. Colorado is a very interesting place.

"Here we are," he says when we get to the kitchen. I take it in, and it's an assault to my senses after the clean, upscale lines of the hotel proper. There is fruit wallpaper on two walls and bright-yellow paint on the others. The two wall ovens are avocado green. Above the cabinets on the bulkheads are floating shelves positively teeming with ugly salt and pepper shakers. A little tube TV plays a network morning show in the corner.

"I can turn that off," he says when he notices me looking at it. "It's all commercials anyway."

I shake my head. "Leave it on," I say. "I haven't seen any commercials in years." Hardly anyone my age has cable anymore, and all the streaming platforms have a premium ad-free option. I'm not a huge football watcher, but I know a lot of the Pictey staff watch the Super Bowl just for the nostalgia of thirty-second spots.

"Well, ok. If you're sure."

I nod. "Is it ok if I sit here?" I ask, picking a hideous vinyl stool at the Formica island.

"You wouldn't prefer the table?" he asks.

The table is a different color of Formica, and the chairs are rattan and look frail. I don't like frail chairs, in general. "This is good for me," I say. "I am glad you invited me in. I prefer this to the dining room."

The man laughs heartily. "Perfect, then," he says. "Welcome to my happy place."

I look him over. He's exceedingly friendly. I can't remember the last time someone invited me to their sanctum, and this guy hardly even knows me.

Maybe that's why he's doing the inviting.

"Now, I'm sorry about my dining room policy," he starts saying to himself as he fills several mugs with coffee. "Workaholics welcome at the Evergreen, I always say. But even workaholics need a moment off. You know, a lot of B and Bs don't even have decent Wi-Fi, but I think if you're traveling for work, an inn is so much more cozy than some Marriott, not that the business-travel vendors seem to believe me." He gestures toward me with two mugs in each hand, as though I am a business-travel vendor. Then he is through the door to the dining room. I get my laptop out.

"So what line of work are you in?" he asks when he returns a split second later. I jump.

"Ms. Miller?"

I swivel toward him. I haven't even unlocked my screen, so I don't have to tell him anything. "I work in IT," I tell him. "In the valley." How's that for vague?

"Ah, of course. I did IT before this. But as I always say, it wasn't my cup of I-Tea."

I look at him.

"By the way. You can call me Cary. Like Gary, but better."

This, I know how to respond to. "Cary," I say. "Nice to meet you."

"And you. Would you like some coffee?"

"No. Thank you. I will have the milk you put in it instead," I tell him. "And breakfast. I would like breakfast."

"Breakfast you shall have, madame! How do crepes sound to you?" He puts a nice tall glass of milk in front of me.

"Very nice, thank you," I say. Then I think of what else I might say. "I really liked the cookies. Also, it's beautiful here," I say. "And sunny."

"Are you here for work?" he asks, producing a pair of plates and some nice napkins and going to the stove top.

"Not really," I say. "Actually, I'm trying to take some time off."

He tips his head to my laptop. "How's that going?" he asks.

"Poorly," I say, and that's the most honest thing I've said to anyone, including myself, about the circumstances that brought me to Colorado.

"Hey, I feel you. Idleness doesn't come naturally to some people. I got into this line of work because I wanted to work all the time but not feel like I'm working."

"I don't mind feeling like I'm working," I say. Never mind that I'm on administrative leave, so how I feel about it is largely moot. "I don't like the feeling that I should be doing something besides work."

"And what, pray tell, should you be doing?"

I take a drink of my milk and shrug in lieu of answering. Then I turn to my laptop. There are no new troll comments. Or @Mia&Mike posts, for that matter. All is quiet in the Pictey world, which is too bad, because it means I have no excuse to avoid my sister. I surf around a bit, aimlessly. My eyes drift to the TV—it's a commercial for hearing aids—and then to Cary, who is half cooking, half looking at me curiously. I look at him back. He has a nice face, comforting, well-placed wrinkles, and a large undisguised bald spot on the top of his head. He is wearing a floral apron. The salt and pepper shakers he is using at the moment are shaped like the front and rear halves of a pig. He seems to have no beef with my stare and eventually slides me a plate of spinach crepes with a smile and takes two more plates out to the dining room. I eat quietly while he's gone. The crepes are delicious.

"Let me ask you a question, Cary," I say the minute he walks back in. Cary is much older than me, and he used to work in IT. He may be a qualified person to talk to about my situation, or as close as I'm going to get. "Let's say that you had failed to avert someone's suicide attempt while carrying out your job, which, in some small part, involves averting such things wherever possible. And then further, let's say that the attempter was, by modest odds, your half sister." I tilt my head. "What would you do in this situation?"

To his credit, he doesn't make a fuss. "This," he says, "is why I don't work in IT anymore."

"That would be throwing the baby out with the bathwater," I say to him. "My job is very fast paced and autonomous. And quite competitive too," I add happily.

"Right, well then. We'll scratch *Quit and become an innkeeper* off your list. What about this half sister? Have you spoken with her?"

I frown.

"Ah. Bad blood?" he asks.

"She's fine," I say quickly. "I mean, she's not fine. She tried to die from blood loss. Gruesome. But otherwise she's very nice and generally thoughtful. She buys me a sweater each Christmas from a brick-and-mortar retailer. Is the salt in the pig's butt or the head?" I ask as he seasons another plate of food.

"The butt. I don't actually keep pepper in the head. It's sweet paprika. It's that special something. I grind pepper fresh." He lifts a small one-handed grinder. "See?"

"These crepes are very good," I say.

"Would you like some more? I'm about to do crepes suzette."

"Yes, please," I say. I stand by while he takes another couple of plates out to diners, comes back, carries out a mug of coffee, and then returns to the kitchen.

"So your sister," he says and starts violently whisking some crepe batter. "How exactly did you make her attempt suicide?"

"It's possible that I should have warned her that she would become affected by severe depression at some point," I say. "There were many reasons to assume that. It's further likely that, having shared the same mother, I should have realized I would be the only person to talk to her about her family history of poor mental health." I pause. "And it's also possible that she posted a cry for help on a social media site, and I was in a position to intercept said cry but didn't."

"And where does this sister live?" he asks.

"About two hours from here. But her hospital is much closer. Last I checked she was in stable condition."

"I see," says Cary. "So she's not very close to Silicon Valley, where you live."

"Not in proximity, no," I say.

"And you were there, not here, at the time of the suicide attempt?" I nod.

"It's possible that your culpability in this incident is being over-stated," he tells me.

I consider this. "That's possible," I admit.

"But on the other hand, how would you rate your response to the incident? On a scale of one to five, with five being 'very helpful' and one being 'not helpful at all'?"

"Well . . ." I think about what I've done thus far. Researched my sister clandestinely, driven to the general area of her hospital, and then imposed myself on a stranger's comment threads. Also, eaten very good crepes. "I think a one. Maybe a two, depending on how you feel about the role of unrealistic expectations on the mental health of young women."

"Interesting," says Cary. He plates some more crepes with butter and lemon and takes them to the dining room. When he comes back, he gives me my own plate.

"Let me ask you another question," I say, after I have chewed my first mouthful. "Last one, I promise. Would you want to be an internet celebrity? I mean, if you could just instantly wave a wand."

"How do you know I'm not?" he says with a smile. "But right, I'm totally not. And I would definitely want to be! I'd get free stuff all the time and get thousands of likes on my posts, and my inn would be super popular; I could charge double what I charge now."

"Yes, but you'd give up your privacy and integrity," I say.

Cary shrugs. "Eh. Who of us really has any privacy anymore in this digital age? And it's better than being a real celebrity, because you don't actually have to do anything or have a talent. You just make some repeatable sentences and take some cool pictures here and there. No starving yourself for a role or killing yourself at football practice or writing the great American novel."

"Hm," I say. "So you think celebrity is a positive pursuit?"

"Not positive. Neutral. Human. When you post on social media, when anyone posts, celebrity or not, aren't you just looking for likes? Isn't that what it's all about? Feeling liked?"

I reluctantly nod.

"Well, who wouldn't want that writ large?" He gives a little shrug. "And I have relatively high self-esteem, not that you'd know that from what I just said."

"I believe you," I say quickly. "You need self-esteem to invite anyone into a kitchen like this." The words fall out before I think about what I'm saying, and I immediately feel my cheeks redden. *Why, Paige? Why do you have to say things like that?* This is why no one ever wants to hang out with me.

But thankfully, Cary just laughs. "Truer words," he says. "But you dig it. And when you bring your sister by," he adds, "she's welcome back here too."

MIA

Nomophobia is the fear of being without your phone. Some people say it's not a phobia but an anxiety disorder. Some people say it's fear not of being without your phone, per se, but of being without an internet connection and a tool to access it. As in: you could have a tablet or a laptop and Wi-Fi, and you'd be fine.

Occasionally, by accident, I forget my phone at my house when I run to the grocery store or do another small errand. When I first realize I don't have it, I feel something like low-grade panic. I pull over and empty my vast purse onto my passenger seat, and when I don't find it that way, I try to get a Bluetooth connection from my phone to my car, in case it's fallen out of my bag and made its way into the phone-size cracks between a seat and the door. When I'm 100 percent positive I don't have the thing, I usually go on back home. I keep my grocery list on it, for one thing. For another, something could happen to my car, and I don't want to be stranded. If I'm just out picking up toilet paper or coffee beans, I get what I came for and go home as quickly as possible. While I drive home, I try to think about where I left the phone, visualize it, and then when I walk into the house and see it right where I thought it would be, I feel like I've slipped into a warm bath in a candlelit room. It's such a relief.

My laptop, I quickly realize, can only connect to the internet via Wi-Fi. There is no plug for Ethernet, or anything else for that matter.

So much for elegant design. My mom has an ancient computer that she keeps in the third bedroom always plugged into the modem. It's not the brand I'm used to, so I fumble with it a little at five a.m. when I give up on pretending I don't *need* to know what's going on online. My mom's password is probably *password*, or *hello*, but I try those things and her birthday and don't get on, so I try to figure out how to log in as a guest. While I am doing this, I think, *I'll just look up instructions on my phone*, realize for the four millionth time that I don't have my phone, and sigh.

Finally I get the guest log-in screen and go onto a web browser that hasn't been updated in ten years to get my email and DMs. There are four hundred new messages. I don't want to answer any of them. I scan the list of emails and see the one that matters most, from my Pictey friend Heidi, who lets me guest at her studio whenever I feel like teaching. She writes, Whoa, girl, saw your latest post. You ok? Loop me in, please?

Quickly I type back, Totally fine, do not worry about me. Because what else can I say? I scan the other emails. There is nothing of even moderate import, not if I want to stay off Pictey. There are a lot of DMs from followers—I generally answer as many as I can each day, then batch send the rest an autoreply and a link to a free video yoga class, but there's no way I can do that on this pony express–paced internet connection.

I'm just going to have to let them go for a while. I mean, I did say I was going dark. If anything's truly important, I'll see it when I get back on my phone.

The rest of the real email is just miscellaneous stuff. Project updates, PR outreach, endorsement requests, invoices sent and received. I handle most of it in ten minutes. This is a relatively small part of my work, a part I don't much mind. Even so, I make an out-of-office message, giving myself two weeks instead of one so I have time to get up to speed when I come back. In it, I write that I won't be checking email, though of course that's a lie. Whenever I see that phrase in someone else's out-of-office reply, I get a good chuckle out of it. There is nowhere on God's green earth where someone won't check their emails at least a couple of times in a week, except possibly a monastery. Until someone tells me they're at a monastery for their spring vacation, I will know it's not that they aren't checking email; it's that they wish they weren't.

My mom comes in the room about then. She's wearing tech pants and a red flannel shirt buttoned up to the neck. She looks ridiculous. "What are you dressed for?" I ask her. "A lumberjacking competition?"

"A hike, my dear. You said you left your phone on top of Mount Wyler, right?"

"You're coming with me?"

"Absolutely. We may need to look around a bit, and more eyes are better."

"But you think phones are the devil, Mom," I say, a bit surprised.

"But you don't," she says. "And you've been twitching like an electroshock therapy patient since you lost the damn thing. Go get dressed. The sooner we get up there, the sooner you can stop with your DTs."

"Ah, Mom. You have such a way of doing something nice and being mean about it. Give me ten minutes," I say, turning back to the computer and starting to log out of everything.

"You know . . . ," she says, the ellipsis practically audible. "You could always leave your phone up there. Just use my computer whenever you need to get online."

I furrow my brow. "Mom, it's one thing to take a break from my Pictey account. It's not the same as dumping my phone. I need that phone about a hundred and fifty times a day. I've got my messaging, my passwords, my credit cards, my medical charts, my grocery lists, my recipes, my phone book, my address list, my camera, my *everything* on that phone. Honestly, I'm not even entirely sure I could find my way from the Target back to your house without the phone. What if I need to buy a toothbrush or some—" I realize I'm about to say *dog treats*.

Target sells Mike's favorite dog treats. I cut myself off and say instead, "Toothpaste."

"You just go up 70," she says.

"Easy for you to say," I reply. "And if I got there, how would I pay?"

"You'd just use a credit card. Remember those?"

"But my credit card info is in the Target app."

"They'll take money in any form."

"But I would miss out on my bonus points."

"Oh dear," she says sarcastically. "You wouldn't be self-reporting your every purchase to an international conglomerate in exchange for a few pennies' discount here and there? Tsk tsk."

There's no point in talking to her. I just need to get back my phone.

"I'll go suit up and meet you on the trail, ok?" I say, because my mom is kind of a slow walker.

"Ok. See you there."

In about ten minutes I'm dressed in cute sky-blue hiking pants and a drapey athletic tee over a floral sports bra. I could be an REI model, if one on the older side. I grab Andy's hat and hustle out the door, noticing for the first time that my mom doesn't even have a smart lock on her door—of course, she'd need Wi-Fi to use that—so there's no way to lock up behind me. I guess I just leave the door open for anyone to stroll in? Well, luckily this is nowhere. To rob a place you have to find it first, I figure.

I expect to catch up to Mom around halfway to the foot of the mountain, but I don't see a glimpse of her until I'm within view of the mountain spur on the trail, and I quickly see she's not alone. She's with someone a foot taller than her and in possession of that thick brown unruly hair and tanklike build I recognize from yesterday. Dewey. It has to be. Quickly I do the calculation: Mia plus Dewey equals good. Mia plus Dewey plus Mom equals x, where x is unsolved but probably a negative number. Hm. "Mom, did you pick up a stray?" I call ahead of me loudly, because I'm terrified if I sneak up on them, they'll be talking about me.

"There you are, slowpoke!" she says. "Dewey says you guys met yesterday on the hill."

"We did," I agree. "He escorted me down before the rain came."

"Dewey's my egg guy," Mom says.

I look at him in surprise. He seems somehow too butch to be an egg guy. Where the hell did I get that idea? "Those were delicious eggs," I say instead. "What kind of chickens do you have?"

He starts saying names of chickens. I don't listen because I wouldn't know a bantam from a golden retriever. I really shouldn't have asked, but knowing where your eggs come from is definitely on-brand for @Mia&Mike, and maybe I should get some photos if he'll let me. I can take the breed names down later, when I have the feathery faces to go with the names.

"Those little blue ones are my favorite," says my mom. "Almost too pretty to eat."

"Ameraucanas," he says with a smile. "Those girls are so lovable."

When he says that, it stirs a memory. "You have a girl," I say. "A daughter?"

Dewey nods. "I do. Nine years old going on forty-five," he says.

Nine. I think back to the egg house. The girl in the window. "What's her name?" I ask.

"Azalea," he says. "Lea, I call her."

"Lea," I repeat. Lea, the girl who looked so unprepared for the world.

My mom interrupts. "I'd like to borrow that daughter of yours," she declares. "I don't necessarily buy into the 'woman's touch' idea, but there's something to having a grandmotherly presence in a young woman's life."

"You mean, a presence besides her actual grandmother?" Dewey asks with a smile.

"I thought you said she was in Florida," my mom replies blithely. "I'm right here." Mom gestures to me. "And I raise great kids," she says. I am startled to hear her say something nice about me. "Though childless."

I purse my lips and look up out of the corner of my eye. There is nothing polite I can say right now.

"Strong argument," Dewey replies. If he's noticed me making faces, he pretends not to. "What would your grandmotherly presence involve, exactly?"

"Backwoods camping?" she suggests. "White-water rafting?"

Both Dewey and I laugh. "She doesn't mess around, does she?" he asks me.

"No time for baking cookies and fixing braids," I say. "Does Lea own a good pair of waders?"

"I'll be honest—Lea's not as outdoorsy as I would have expected. She's got a homebody streak. Mostly likes to hang out with the chickens. Makes me worry sometimes. I want her to have social opportunities, enjoy the mountains, you know."

I nod. To my mind, *homebody* would be the worst insult someone could level at me. My work depends on me being *out there*. All the time. That's what makes people love me. "I'm sure she'll do great when she finds her thing," I say, because what else can I say? "Ah, did Mom tell you where we're heading?" I ask him.

"Back up the bump, I guess?" he says. "She asked me to come with. And I may as well. It's a gorgeous day for walking."

I give my mom a look, and she pretends not to see it. "It's going to be more of a brisk hustle," I tell him. "I left my phone up there yesterday." *Because you caught me by surprise,* I think. "I'm at a loss without it."

Dewey makes a worried face. "In all that rain?" he says.

"It's in a BadgerBox," I say. "It'll be fine. It would survive a mudslide and a forest fire, if it came to that. And I know exactly where I put it. So don't feel like you have to tag along."

Mom coughs. "Someone's overconfident."

I can tell my mom is hoping I don't find my phone. I suspect nothing could make her happier than me floundering around techless for a while. "It'll be fine," I say again.

"I'll come anyway," says Dewey. "Shall we?" He gestures up to the trailhead, and we start off.

On the walk, my mom asks him more questions about chickens and his daughter. Apparently she's been down lately because one of the hens she especially likes was nabbed by a coyote. I try to pay attention, but my mind wanders off. Embarrassingly, I'm thinking about the phone. I'm thinking about how good it will feel to unlock it and see my notifications, what a huge relief I'll feel.

Then I realize it may have lost its charge, if it was looking for a signal or pinging me all night. *Ugh,* I think. I'll have to get it back down the hill and plug it in before I can even start to get up to speed.

And what will happen when I do? I keep ruminating while we're hiking, as the grade gets steeper and we all get a bit winded, even my mom, who is fit as a fiddle. When I do get my phone back, plug it in, charge it up, what exactly am I expecting to see? Calls from Tucker, I am willing to bet. Either to argue with me more or to apologize more. A text or two from my bank about my low balance. Scads of notifications from social apps—only I deleted my social apps yesterday, I remember.

Outside of the big platforms, what exactly do I do with my phone? I wonder. I mean, isn't most of what I do with it liking, posting, commenting, tweeting, snapping? All on apps I deleted for the week.

When I finally do get it back, will I turn it on and see . . . nothing?

I hike faster. I need to get to the top of that mountain and prove to myself that I'm a person, with friends, not just contacts, not just followers or "Friends" with a trademark symbol behind the word. Without Tucker, who has been my closest confidant since Mike, and a few colleagues who I emailed this morning, is there anyone else I honestly know in real life who will even notice I'm offline? Other influencers, maybe? But personal friends? I think of Lynnsey and other IRL people I knew from before my star rose. We can go weeks without texting. Months, probably.

"Mom," I say. "Dewey. I think I'm going to hike up ahead."

"Are we really that slow?" asks Dewey, though I have noticed him taking shorter, lazier strides to keep from outpacing my mother.

"We're not," says my mom. "It's just that she's addicted to that damn thing. She's like a junkie running to her dealer."

"Not her fault. Phones are engineered to do this to people," he says. "It's part of the inner workings. Like a slot machine, only with your human attention, not quarters."

I walk faster. This has been my mother's favorite subject since I became an influencer, and I've heard it all ad nauseam.

"Maybe," I hear my mom saying as I gain distance, "but like a slot machine, it's up to you if you use it."

To my surprise, Dewey doesn't agree. "If you had a slot machine in your pocket since you were eight years old, you might feel differently."

I smile to myself as I keep lengthening my stride. That Dewey's not a bad guy. I appreciate anyone who can give my mom a little pushback.

And because it's not me she's arguing with, she listens to reason. "Maybe so," I hear, still farther behind. They must be slowing down as I speed up. "Maybe the engineering these systems do is enough to make us all gambling addicts." There's a space in the conversation. But then she speaks again. "But even still, I wish my daughter fought it a little. Instead she's just become part of the problem."

I break into a jog. I gain more ground, and when I'm out of sight, I find myself cutting the switchbacks, treading up the deer trails, just as I disdained yesterday. Risking my ankles and the ecosystem to get to the top faster. I need to see that phone, see that there's even just one meaningful message on it. A connection. A genuine benefit to the buzzing, tracking, pinging slot machine I cannot seem to stop feeding with my attention. If there is . . . I can ignore everything Mom says, go back to LA, get back to work, get that tuning fork of *YES* out of my head.

If there isn't . . .

What if there isn't? What if my phone is just full of messages from Tucker asking about when he's going to get the first check and telling me I'm a fraud and asking if my dropping off Pictey for forty-eight hours is going to hurt his revenues? What if it's nothing but strangers haranguing me to get back on there and do my duty, post my outfit, say something re-Pictable, recommend my favorite coffee grinder? What if it's just the empty Pictey prompt and the blinking cursor and me trying to live a lie for a few more days or weeks or years?

Some combination of dread and yesterday's tequila gurgles in my stomach. I'm running hard now, crashing through the deer trail, messing up their scents and the foliage and the intricate underground life of the forest that exists off the man-made trails. I feel a stick against my leg and see I've torn the hem of my hiking pants on some kind of wildberry thorn, and a rip is moving up my ankle. I am thirty feet from the top. I've been running full out for a long time. I stop, pant for a minute, think of my mother's words. *I wish my daughter fought it a little.*

That goddamned phone. Look at me. Carelessly, thoughtlessly careering up a slope with one of the most beautiful vistas in America, not seeing a thing because all I can think about is what packets of data might be on one three-by-five-inch screen.

Instead she's just become part of the problem.

I burst into a run again. I am at the top of the viewing spot now, right where I set down my phone yesterday after my out-of-office post. It's right there, muddy, but there. I lean down, breathing hard, and wipe off the screen to wake it up.

It shows a list of notifications. Calls from my pharmacy, my dry cleaner, and Tucker. Spam callers. A reminder that my period is two days away. An update that something I ordered online once three years ago is on sale. My screen time update: I used my phone an average of six hours a day last week. And most recently, a text from Tucker that says Hey—signing off may not be the best move . . . call or DM asap?

My blood boils. He was ready to close his account without a word, but when I take off a night—just one night—he's in a hot panic. What does he know about the best move? The best move would have been to marry me on the day he said he would or, better still, to never have proposed at all. I look one more time at my phone. Not one meaningful text, email, DM, notification, banner, alert, ping, or share. It's been almost twenty-four hours, and all the billions of buzzes that normally keep me jumping every three minutes amount to exactly nothing when I ignore them. Just absolutely *nothing*.

I hear a growl of fury and realize it just came out of me.

Then I hear footsteps. Mom and Dewey, I imagine. I don't care. They're probably starting to draw near on the switches. They'd love what I'm about to do—or at least Mom would. So much so that I almost wait so she can witness it. But I can't wait, in the end, because I'm terrified. The hold this tiny device has over me is too much. If I don't get it out of my hands right now, I may never be able to.

So I wind up. The phone seems to be screaming. It's vibrating even now, another notification—another "call me" from Tucker. *I will not call you, Tucker. I will never call you again.*

I scream now, a full-on scream, like Xena the warrior princess getting ready to run forward with a spear and stab the bejesus out of someone. It's a battle cry. That's exactly what it is.

Then I wind up and thrust my arm forward, just like Mom showed me how to do in slow-pitch. Follow through with the wrist. Watch the arc.

It's a good throw. My cell phone flies off with a beautiful, graceful trajectory, a toy airplane made of silicon and glass. Then the descent begins. I realize what I've done. I open my eyes wide in disbelief. I see the phone fall out of sight over the edge of the cliff.

I hear it hit with a sickening crunch.

So that's it, then, I think. That's that. I've just thrown my phone over the edge of a mountain.

That was really weird of me.

Weirder still, I feel . . .

Amazing.

PAIGE

Search for: @Mia&Mike

NO NEW POSTS

Click HERE to see the feed.

Click HERE to find similar accounts you might enjoy.

Obviously after the crepes are gone, I know what I must do. I call to be sure my sister is still in the hospital. She is. I don't know why—suicide watch? Healing from her wounds? But no matter: I'm not squeamish. Because of what I did back then, my dad hates emergency rooms and has told me not to take him to one when he's too old to decide for himself. This means, I suppose, that he'll die in the back of my car in the hospital parking lot.

Luckily, I don't remember any of that night. I only remember waking up and getting medicine and feeling somewhat better but exhausted. Very, very tired. I remember my dad was there, and my mom came, too, and they were cool but polite to each other. I remember Dad saying, as I moved in and out of sleep, that maybe I should move in with him. I remember my mom asking how it would look on my college applications if I dropped out of all my obligations at my current school. I remember thinking, *Do I have to put my suicide attempt on my college applications?*

Now, I park on a huge ramp and go to the front desk of the glossy hospital and ask for Jessica Odanz. No one asks me why I'm asking for her. There is no metal detector, no bag search for contraband. They just give me her room number and directions to a bank of elevators.

I find this all very annoying. I could be a madman, a reporter, or, worse, a lawyer. And I had such a great cover story all ready to go. I think I look like a guidance counselor. I only wear flat shoes, and I have a frumpiness I can't really shake, not that I've tried that hard. I don't have a school ID, but it seems like something a person would forget when she rushed to the hospital to see her suicidal student. Anyway, it's all moot. No one asks. I go up to room 632—it takes three elevators for some reason, which can't be efficient—and start wandering around in the hall.

I don't really have a plan for next steps. My guidance counselor ruse is as far as I got. I suppose I need to just go in and talk to Jessica. I need to let her know she's not alone and that whatever she's feeling right now is understandable. Survivable. I need to say: *I know that place you're in, between the bridge and the water. You jumped, you meant to jump, but as you fell, you were overcome with regret, because just as it is human to want the kind of pain that brought you to this bridge to stop, it is also human to flinch when you see death rushing your way.*

I need to say all those things without telling her I was falling once too.

I start trying to think up good lies about why I know she's here. Things that will make her apt to open up to me. The thought of someone opening up to me is almost laughable, but once, a long time ago, she trusted me. What if I could be the person she trusts again?

Before I can think of how to say any of this, a nurse comes barreling out of her room, talking on a little *Star Trek*–style chest-pocket-mounted communicator, and she nearly smacks right into me. "Jessica, you have a visitor!" she hollers back into the room. "She's decent," she tells me. "Go on in." And what can I do but walk in the door?

The first thing I notice about my sister is that she is much prettier this year than she was even the Christmas before. She has a new sharpness to her eyes, a sharpness she is leveling at me right now. She also has greasy blonde hair pulled back in a ponytail and a hospital gown, so she's not at her best. But there's a bit of life about her I wasn't expecting, not in someone who just tried to off herself.

"Well, well, well," she says. Her voice doesn't sound shaky or angst ridden. But it's not manic either. I remember, when I was her, wondering how I should act in order to make the people around me most comfortable. Happy to be alive? Sad to be depressed? By that point, though, I was so numb most every emotion had to be faked. "I wasn't expecting you to waltz in here."

"Neither was I!" I say with more emphasis than I intended. Well, she knows I'm a homebody. She won't take offense. "You look quite hale and hearty," I tell her. "Are you sure you shouldn't be home by now?"

"I definitely shouldn't," she says. Then she holds up her arms.

So it was the retro wrist-slashing thing. Her arms are swathed in bandages up to the elbows. I try not to show my upset, but it is just empirically upsetting. She is so, so young. I know she's almost twenty-two, not really a child. But she's sure as hell not old enough to do what she did.

Jessica watches my face for a moment. Then she says, "I fell through a plate glass window."

"No, you didn't," I blurt.

She looks down. "Who told you?"

"Mom," I lie. "She just called me on Tuesday. I drove here to see you. It took me three days."

"Am I supposed to believe that?" she asks.

"Definitely not," I admit. "I mean, the drive did take three days, but the rest would be very strange. Mom would never call me about something like this."

"Was it my dad?"

"I don't think he even has my phone number," I say. "I found out on my own. The charting software around here needs to be updated." This is true, if not pertinent.

"So you hacked the hospital?" she asks. Jessica knows I can get around computers with some level of competence.

I shrug. It's believable, I think.

"Why, though? If no one called you and you didn't know I was here."

"Maybe I just have an alert set for all hospitals near your university," I say.

She shakes her head. "That doesn't make sense, Paige. Are you tracking my cell phone or something?"

"No," I say. "Though that's not a bad idea. I might look into that in the future."

She makes a face and shakes her head. "Then how?"

I give up. "I found out at Pictey," I say. "Though I think I should clearly state that I am not here in any official capacity. I don't want to be fired for misrepresenting my work to you."

"You work for Pictey?" she asks. "That's the start-up you told us about?"

"That's the one," I say.

"It's hardly a start-up," she says.

"Well, it was. At one time."

"Every company was a start-up at some time. Now it's a huge corporation. And don't you have some fancy job there too? Mom tells everyone you're very successful."

"I work in Safety and Standards."

"What does that mean?" she asks.

"If you flag something, I review it to see if it's ok."

There's a moment of quiet. Jessica shifts uncomfortably in her bed.

"So what, did someone flag me?"

"Yes. Or you flagged you. That happens too. The point is, your flag came across my desk, the night you . . . you know." I grit my teeth, waiting for the onslaught of anger or disappointment or maybe hurt that should accompany my confession.

But all she says is, "What?"

I level a look at her. "Have you been on Pictey since you . . . you know?"

"I don't know!" she says. "I don't know what you're talking about."

"Since you tried to do yourself in," I say, and too late I realize how inappropriate that was. "Since you got hurt, I mean."

My beautiful sister cracks a beautiful smile. "No, the first one was right," she says. She takes a breath. "Ok. Yes. I know what you're talking about now. Mia Bell's feed. I posted a sort of pathetic comment on her feed." She narrows her eyes at me. "What does that have to do with you?"

"I was the one who should have gotten you help when I saw it. I should have called emergency services and escalated the situation and saved your life," I tell her. "But I didn't, because I didn't know it was you, and it was time for me to go home for the day. And I'm very, very sorry about that."

"Oh! So you think . . ." Her voice trails off. "Paige, no. Just no. I wasn't posting on Pictey to get flagged, and I certainly didn't know you worked there until five minutes ago. I mean, I don't know why I posted there exactly, but it wasn't to get attention from a sister in another state I only see once a year. I just wanted to see, I don't know, if I was the only one, I guess?"

I think of what I should have told her long ago, before things got this far. Now would be the perfect time to fill her in. I could tell her about my challenges with Mom, my own depression, my anxiety, my attempt. I could put myself in a tailspin and end up facedown on the floor.

Instead I say, "You're not the only one. You're not even in a very exclusive club. Statistically speaking, someone in the world tries to kill themselves every two seconds."

Paige raises an eyebrow. "Is that what you came here to tell me?"

"I came to apologize for missing your flag. And to see how you're doing," I say. "How are you doing?"

"Apology unnecessary," she says dismissively. I try to believe her. "And as for how I'm doing . . ." She shrugs, then gestures around the room.

"I think you're saying you're not doing as well as you could be," I carefully interpret.

"Yeah, maybe. Though really this is about as good as I can hope for. I'm on suicide watch. There's no glass in the room. They took away the cord that works the call button."

"Let me see your phone," I tell her.

"No," she says quickly.

"Where are Mom and your dad?" I ask.

"At work."

"Oh," I say. I guess that makes sense. She has been in here for a week. How long did I have to stay? Three days? A week? Either way, Mom only came that first day. People have to work. "Well, if you give me your phone, I might be able to help you feel a little better."

"You don't have to make me feel better. I'm already feeling better. I'm getting the help I need. Or I will be."

This is good news, empirically speaking, but it puts me at a loss. "But Jessica, I need to help you. I feel very poorly about your situation. I feel it's largely my fault."

"In what universe is this your fault?" she asks archly.

"Well." I try to figure out how to make her see. "I'm the person who reviewed your flag. I understand it wasn't your intention when you posted to ask for help, but I should have helped you anyway. If that post hadn't gone to a colleague who called the ambulance, I could have been responsible for your death. And besides . . ." I pause, try to tell her my truth. "I know what it's like."

Jessica blinks up at me. "What *what's* like?" she asks, almost like it's a dare. I try to answer, but panic rises up in me every time I even think the words. I can't have a panic attack in the hospital where my sister is recuperating from a suicide attempt. That would be very selfish.

"What it's like to have a lot of pressure," I say at last. "Mom. Grades. That stuff."

She looks at me for a long time. "So you drove for three days to see me?"

I nod.

"To see if I was ok and say sorry you didn't call 911 because of something I posted on the internet?"

"That's right."

"Oh, Paige. You are so weird." She reaches out her arms. "Come here."

Awkwardly, gratefully, I lean over the bed, my arms by my sides. I know in a normal hug the hugger should put one's arms behind the huggee's body, but her body is pressed up against a hospital bed, and I don't want to hit her scars. I let her wrap me up, though, and squeeze tight. It feels impossibly good.

"I can't believe you work for Pictey and never told us. That seems really weird."

"It never came up," I say truthfully. We mostly talk about the weather at Christmas. Sometimes sports.

"Well, you never brought it up," she says. "That's for sure. I love Pictey. I'm addicted."

"I don't think that's accurate," I say. "I've reviewed your daily usage times, and they seem within healthy ranges in general."

"It's an expression," she says.

"Ah."

Her shoulders slump. "You know, Paige, I almost died," she says.

"I know. I'm really sorry."

"Me too. And the worst part is, I was not going for 'almost.'"

Shivers of recognition run through me. "I know that too."

"The doctor says it was a cry for help," Jessica says. "But really I'm just very lucky. If that person at your office hadn't called 911, I would be dead."

"That's what I figured." *Between the bridge and the water.* Consuela was her net.

"Pictey kind of saved my life," she says.

I wish I could make her see it's much more nuanced than that. If she weren't being spoon-fed unrealistic expectations every time she opened her phone, if she weren't a demographic to sell to, a data mine to cull, if every ad she sees weren't so perfectly designed to meet up with her own perceived lacks, she might not have been so depressed in the first place. And if people like Mia Bell didn't make their livings telling everyone how perfect they were, maybe Jessica wouldn't feel so damn imperfect at the end of every day.

"Are you sure it doesn't make you feel worse?" I ask. "All those retouched photos and"—I search for something innocuous but come up empty—"dream weddings?"

"Nah. I know that stuff isn't real."

Now I know she's lying. If she didn't believe in Mia Bell, then why did she ask her if she ever felt like dying? "Give me your phone," I say.

"Why?"

"I want to show you that the people you follow, the influencers, aren't real."

She looks at me for a long time. "This is a weird conversation," she says at last.

"Not that weird," I say. "Though I'm not that versed in the art of conversation. We're exchanging information, though. That's pretty much my goal here. To exchange information that will aid in your recovery from an attempted suicide."

Jessica shakes her head. "No one says 'attempted suicide' here. They all say 'cry for attention.' And 'self-harming behaviors.'"

"Lipstick on a pig," I say.

"Exactly. The thing is, those euphemisms all make me feel like an idiot. Like I can't even do suicide convincingly."

"You convinced me way too much," I say. I feel all those old feelings, feelings I hate, rising in my throat.

We are both quiet.

Generally, many of my panic attacks come from experiences that touch, however gently, on the first month I came back from the hospital after I tried to kill myself with pills. That first month was awful, because I was terrified of myself. I walked through the house and saw ways to kill myself everywhere. I saw curtain cords and poultry shears and my stepdad's Gillette and the giant mahogany highboy that certainly could be pulled down atop myself with a well-placed yank. I simply could not trust myself not to do that. I thought I would do it in my sleep, if not while awake. I felt, whenever I was alone with myself, that I was locked in a room with a murderer. It took a very long time for my meds to work.

"Are they giving you proper treatment?" I ask.

Jessica nods. "Antidepressants, superstrength, and Valium, and sleeping pills at night, which seems a bit ironic."

I think about telling her Mom's sleeping pills were my weapon of choice. Instead I say, "It takes a long time for the SSRIs to work. Sometimes weeks, sometimes months."

"That's what they tell me."

"When can you go home? When you're stable?"

"When I'm stable, my parents are putting me in a loony bin."

"What?" I immediately think of *One Flew over the Cuckoo's Nest.* "Like an asylum?" When I was discharged from the hospital, I went right back to high school. I had a GPA to think of.

"There's a pamphlet over there," she says. When she points, I notice for the first time that she has an empty IV port on her left arm and wires coming out of a pocket of her gown attached to a heart monitor. I see an oxygen tube hanging down on her neck, but it's turned off. It's been fifteen years since I was in Jessica's place, but not that much in the treatment process has changed. Her vitals have been normal for three days now. Anyone else would have been sent home. She really is on suicide watch.

I get the pamphlet. *The Colorado Springs Suicidal Ideation Treatment Clinic for Young Adults.* It has a picture of a tree on it. "Well, it will keep you safe," I say. I feel inexplicably jealous.

Jessica sighs. "So you're on their side."

"I probably am. I want you to live."

"You barely know me," she says.

"Well, that's true. I only see you once a year. Maybe you're a terrible person."

"I'm not a terrible person."

"Oh," I say. "Well, either way, you still shouldn't kill yourself. Anyway, if you're truly evil, the state will take care of it eventually, at no small cost to the taxpayer."

"Jeez, Paige. You're so weird."

"I'm very average, actually. I am an outlier only in my profession—which, while difficult and taxing, is also highly competitive—and I'm a decent programmer as well. I also have an exceptional credit score. On all other fronts, I am the absolute median American Woman."

"Ok," says Jessica. She looks up at the ceiling. "So you're not weird." For the first time in this conversation, Jessica Odanz sits up.

"Hey!" I say. "Are you allowed to do that?"

"Do what?" she asks.

"I don't know. Sit up? Move?"

"Of course. I'm supposed to take walks, too, but I can't go outside, so what they really mean is I'm supposed to drag myself around the thirty-foot hall of the psych ward for ten minutes and then come back in here."

"This isn't the psych ward," I say. "This hospital doesn't appear to have a psych ward. This is general medicine. Much better. You know," I offer, trying once more to give her the benefit of my experience without actually facing down that experience, "you won't have to talk to people about this when you get home. People will be hesitant to bring it up. Everyone will be very awkward about it."

"Oh yeah?" Now, finally, she reaches over to her bedside table and grabs her phone. It's an older model, probably Mom's old phone, and the case is black glitter. She pulls down the notifications and holds the screen to face me. "You're right about the awkwardness, but not the hesitance."

The first text is a phone number with a nearby area code and the words R U dead?

The next is from someone named Ilsa P., and it says, is it true? & did u use pills or ? It goes on like this, maybe six more barely literate text messages asking about the specifics of her suicide attempt. Times have changed. When I went back home, no one knew what I'd done. My dad told my high school principal we'd had a family emergency in Asia, and that was why I was out of school for so long. I have to give him points for that—vague enough to mean basically anything, and in Asia—too big to check up on.

"At least you're popular?" I say.

She shakes her head. "I'm not popular. I'm newsworthy."

"Well, I like you," I tell her. I'm pleased to find that like her much-younger self, adult Jessica is bright and sharp and quick minded, very easy to be around.

"You're weird."

A voice comes over the intercom announcing the hour and telling me to be on my way. "Visiting hours are almost over," I repeat needlessly. "I'm coming back again soon."

"I may be in the loony bin by then."

"Really?" I ask.

"Probably not. I think it takes a while. But I'm not sure."

"Well, if you aren't here, I'll look there."

"Why?" she asks. "Don't you have to get back to your work? Which is highly competitive?"

"No. I don't. I'm only very lightly occupied at the moment."

"So you've got nothing better to do than hang out with a head case?"

"Yes. That's about it. Also, I am staying at a very nice inn."

"Well," says Jessica, and I'm happy to see the glint in her eye is as bright as it's ever been, "in that case, next time you come visit, bring a cake with a file baked into it. I want you to break me out of here."

MIA

My first instinct after the big phone toss is to go straight home, get my laptop, and drive to a coffee shop with good Wi-Fi. My second is to look up the address of such a coffee shop on my phone. My third is that *holy shit*, I just threw my phone over a mountain, and now I do not have a cell connection or a way to post on Pictey or Facebook or Instagram or even freaking *Yelp*. Yelp, for the love of all that is good in this world and the next.

And I did it on purpose.

I must be out of my mind.

Right now, right this second, anyone in the world, truly anyone, could be trying to reach me. Oprah Winfrey might be calling me right now to invite me to do yoga together. An editor from New York might be calling to offer me a book deal. A producer might want to make a movie of my life.

Which would show exactly what, I wonder. An actress sitting in her apartment scrolling and tapping and then staging photos? My life is not exactly the makings of the next *Free Solo*. And that, I remind myself, is the entire point. I'm going to go live a life worth making into a movie, now that I'm unyoked and free from the chains of technology. I'm going to celebrate the freedom and live, truly live.

To be clear: I have no idea what this involves, exactly.

I go find my mom out in her garden. She's putting in vegetable starts. "Mom."

"Oh! There you are. Hand me that thing with the leaves."

"The plant?"

"Yes. That. And before you ask, yes, I'm taking my ginkgo. I was already forgetting words when I was forty, and now whole days go by when I don't speak to anyone. Don't start calling around for memory care."

"I wasn't going to ask about that. I was going to ask you what people did before phones."

"What do you mean?" Mom replies. I note she is using her bare hands instead of a shovel to scoop a hole in the soft, freshly hoed ground.

"I mean, like, describe a day in the life of a normal adult—so not you, I should stress—living in a time before the internet."

My mom frowns at me. "Aside from not being zombies, people were exactly the same, as far as I remember. They got up, put on their pants one leg at a time, and went to work all day. Then they came home and had dinner with their families and went to bed. I suppose there was prime-time TV in there, over the air, with commercials that allowed you to get up and pee. Books, with paper pages that you manually turned. Is that what you're asking?"

I furrow my brow. "Kind of. But not exactly. Imagine my normal weekday. I wake up in the morning, grab my phone, and look at my notifications until my alarm, on my phone, goes off. Then I get up, take a shower while listening to a podcast on my phone, get dressed, and do my emails on my phone. I make the breakfast that comes up on my meal-planner app, and then I put my macronutrients into my diet app *on my phone* while I'm eating. I ask my smart speaker to play the entertainment news while I scroll what's trending on Facebook and Twitter. If I'm using the last of something, I order it on my grocery-delivery app.

"Then, after I eat, I get out my laptop. I post about my morning and the daily intention. I do ten minutes on my meditation app. I put on music via Bluetooth and spend most of the morning online responding to followers and keeping up with my social media. Maybe a break for online window-shopping. Lunch from my meal-planning app, another post, more social media, sponsor emails and Slack meetings, content generation, podcast interviews, the gym with my wearable or yoga on my fitness app, a Pictey Live, dinner with Tucker provided by a food-delivery app, a streaming show or three, one last update of my story with the day's mentions, and then bed."

My mother looks at me, appalled. "Do you need your phone to have sex too?" she asks.

"Mom. Ew. And no." I think for a moment. "But I do use it to listen to white noise when I sleep. Tucker snores."

"Another plus to being single again," says Mom. I'm glad *she's* over Tucker. Never mind how I feel. I mean, I feel ok. But I wouldn't mind the tiniest bit of fawning.

"His snoring wasn't that big a deal," I reply. I found it comfortable. I knew he was still breathing.

"So you're asking how to live a life without every move dictated by notifications and applications?"

"Well . . ." It sounds stupid when she says it. Much like everything I do.

She sets down her tray of seedlings. "You start by facing the fact that for the last however many years—I'm just going to guess six—you've been distracted and distant to the things actually going on around you in the present. You may feel euphoric at the moment, like you're free, and you are. But what comes next will be a hard transition. Now that you don't have a screen between you and the world, you stand to be very overwhelmed. Things you've buried may come up."

"I'm not overwhelmed," I tell her, bemused. "Have a little faith, Mom. I'm just at loose ends. I tried exercise and reading one of your books, but it's not what I would have picked, and my e-reader won't update without Wi-Fi. I did some yoga, but I'm used to using an app to move me through my yoga routine. I flossed, unpacked, started a load of wash, and parboiled some veggies. Now what do I do?"

Mom looks up at me and then at her (yep, analog) watch. "It's been thirty-five minutes since we got down the mountain."

"The longest thirty-five minutes of my life. Oh, stop rolling your eyes. I mean, for one thing, I'm effectively off of work as a direct result. Lots of people struggle with keeping busy when they take time off of work."

"Lots of ding-dongs. What's to struggle about? You can do whatever you want with your days now." She pauses. "Do you need to borrow some money? Is money the problem?"

"It's not the money, though that's awfully nice of you," I say, knowing I make double in sponsorships what Mom earns in a year of birth coaching. "Though . . ." I think of something I haven't done in a while. "Do you know of any local studios who might need a substitute teacher this week?"

Mom looks at me in surprise. "You can still teach yoga?"

"Of course I can. I mean, I haven't taught in person for a while. Not since Mike. But a couple times a month I upload online classes for YogaStar.com."

She frowns. "I thought maybe you'd quit." She wraps her hand around my biceps. "There used to be muscle here."

For the first time since I was a kid, I consider my biceps in terms other than svelteness. "There's a lot of pressure to be thin in LA," I admit. "When I'm at home, I keep to a pretty intense diet."

She says nothing, which is so unusual it makes me nervous. Silence falls over us. I get more nervous still.

"Hey," I ask. "Why aren't you using that trowel? It's sitting six inches from you."

"I just tilled, and the earthworms are on the move. I don't want to accidentally bisect one," she tells me.

I look at her flatly. "But you know that it won't kill the worm, right? If you hit one. It actually doubles the worm population."

"Even so, it would be sad for the worm. Plus, this way I get to feel the dirt. It feels very nice. Try it."

I kneel down to where my mom is digging and sit on my heels. "Mom, tool use is one of the few things that differentiates humans from animals."

"Actually, apes use tools too. You're not so special. Get your fingers in there. Start experiencing the world without a filter."

I grimace, but after all, I am trying things her way, aren't I? Obediently I put my hands in the slightly moist, fluffy dirt. It's dark brown, the color of fresh-ground coffee, with some sparkles in it. It feels cool and soft and sort of nice, I admit. But when I take my hands out, the undersides of my french tips are filthy. I hold them up to her, as if to say, *See?*

"Now, isn't that nice?" she says, missing the point entirely. "Don't wash too carefully before you eat next, and you'll add all those new lovely microbes into your gut."

"That's literally eating dirt, Mom. Can't I just take my probiotic?"

"This is better," she says. "The real version is always better. If you really want to quit your phone addiction and not just go rushing back to the Apple store at the first opportunity, I recommend you OD on the real-life versions of everything you previously did online."

"Like what?" I ask.

"Go to the market instead of buying supplements online. Shop around. Talk to people there. Get your nutrition through actual food."

I shrug. This sounds less than thrilling, to be honest.

She goes on. "Do yoga on the mountainside and then fall asleep in the meadow. Read a newspaper on the porch, and feel the cold pump water wash away the ink on your grubby hands afterward. Listen to one of Andy's old records while you eat lunch and notice how you start chewing in rhythm. Go to town and ask for a map of the local stores and restaurants. Read a book even if it's not what you would prefer, just to see what another genre is like. Take off your shoes and get your feet muddy down by where the frogs live. Wander around the neighborhood looking for someone to talk to. Write things down, with a nice pen, on scrap paper, and stuff the bits of ideas in your pockets so you'll meet them again at the end of the day."

I look at her in wonder. She pauses. "Everything you can do on a phone you can do better without a phone. Except the self-numbing and avoidance. Just skip those."

"Maybe I should just scoop up a handful of compost and send it right down the hatch," I say.

"I've heard worse ideas," Mom replies. She breaks up the small root ball of the new plant, something puny with broad true-green leaves, and throws a sprinkling of gray stuff into the hole she made before nesting the roots into the earth and smoothing dirt around the plant in a heap. "Ta-da!" she announces. "That will be lovely come fall."

"What is it?" I ask.

"A parsnip," she tells me, grabbing her watering can. "I only plant one each year. To me, they taste like old, stringy carrots. But they must be eaten, for character building, and besides, the greens are nice."

I think about my "must be eaten" foods, and none of them are for character; all of them are for minimal total body fat percentages. Pea protein powder, arugula-and-cacao smoothies, and gluten-free, dairy-free, sugar-free iced "dessert substitute." I might actually prefer the parsnip, but it has twenty-eight net carbs.

I wonder if, while taking some time off from being in front of the camera all the time, I might not have a carbohydrate or two. Nothing crazy. Just let my hair down a little. I can put it back up when the time comes.

—

Thirty minutes later I am sitting alone in a restaurant looking at a half-empty pizza plate and a totally empty beer glass. Now, this is some delicious character building. This is the first meal I have eaten alone without my phone in . . . ever? It was awkward at first. I went in without reading any reviews, I didn't have a chance to look at the menu ahead of time, and I couldn't figure out where to put my eyes for the first twenty minutes of dining alone. But once the pizza came . . . well, did anyone tell me how delicious pizza was? I must have known. I must have had some inkling. After all, I once posted a recipe for almond-flour-and-cauliflower pizza crust that got massive click-through. I posted that it tasted "just like the real thing!" But somewhere around college age I'd stopped eating gluten and then later most alternative breads and finally most carbs, so how the hell would I have known what the real thing tastes like? I must now amend that a cauliflower-and-almond-flour crust tastes absolutely *nothing* like the real thing, and to anyone who knows better, I sincerely apologize. I actually think I'll post an apology to carb eaters, even though it's entirely off brand. I can call it back to the lifestyle by talking about moderation. And then after that I can eat the rest of this pizza all by myself.

I grab around in my handbag for my phone. The inside of this bag is black, but my phone is not black, so why can't I ever find it? Why am I carrying three lipsticks in one bag? Do I plan on wearing lip stripes? Maybe the phone is in the zipper compartment?

Oh yeah.

I don't have my phone.

I threw my phone over the mountainside.

I drop my bag heavily onto the floor of the restaurant. No big deal. I'm taking off the filter of my life, like my mom said. I look at the half-eaten pizza. It's pretty, because the crust is thin and toasty and the cheese is fresh buffalo mozzarella, and I can see the brick oven it was cooked in right behind the table in the background. I could set the focus between the two of them, on the brass bar, which is helpfully empty at this hour.

I could get the beer glass out of the photo and maybe order a nice red wine, because there is simply no way to tie beer into my brand, moderation or no.

Except I don't want a glass of red wine. I want another beer.

And I have no camera anyway, so I might as well have one.

I love going without my phone.

This is not just the first meal I've eaten without a phone in years but also the first attractive restaurant I've not photographed in some way while eating in it. When we went out, Tucker and I, we only really went to attractive restaurants. So . . . this is kind of a thing. An achievement. An achievement I'm utterly alone in. Every other table of diners in this restaurant either is on their phones or has their phones screen up on the table, except for a mother and her teenage daughter right next to me. The two of them are just talking. My heart pulls. I got my first real phone when I turned sixteen, mostly for calling and a few labored texts. At eighteen, though, I got a phone with a camera. I got an iPhone from Andy for my college graduation.

And after that, I became an inveterate phone diner. Did I ever put my phone away when I ate with my family? Maybe once or twice with Andy. I haven't gone totally phoneless with my mom since I joined Pictey. After all, someone might have been trying to reach me.

When the server comes to check in, I intend to just order another beer, but instead I say, "Do you have time for me to ask you a question about your job?"

"Sure," she says. She's middle aged, with a friendly face and the look of someone who has nowhere to be. "I mean, assuming nobody flags me down, 'course. Fire away."

"Do you mind when people take pictures of the restaurant or the food with their phones?" I ask.

She doesn't take a beat. "But you lost your phone," she says immediately.

"Why do you say that?"

"Because you're eating without it. Alone. Look around. Everyone else is on their phone or with someone, and some people are on their phone and with someone."

"But what if I told you I didn't have a phone anymore," I say.

"I'd say, Congratulations? And that's really bizarre? I mean, don't get me wrong, I love customers without phones."

I furrow my brow. "Why?" I ask. "Do they tip better?"

"Oh my goodness, no," she says. "They're generally cheaper. But people without phones, they come in here, they look at the menu when they sit down. They order drinks when you come over to ask for their drink order. They ask you questions about what's good. They notice you when you come back to the table and say thank you when you refill their drinks. They're not, like, too busy leaving the Yelp review for the meal they just ate to pay the tab in some reasonable amount of time."

"So phone users are slower?"

"Yeah, and when they do look up from their phones, they have no sense of time. So they'll be like, 'Where's my waitress? I haven't seen her in a half hour,' and really I was there ten minutes ago and they didn't even notice me. They're in that immediate-gratification mode, and it hangs around even when they're actually interacting with real people. Plus, it's just depressing when four people come in to eat together and don't actually talk to each other. I know it's normal, but it makes me feel like an old crank."

"Don't be silly. You just want to be able to do your job," I say with a smile. But I feel awful. I recognize myself in that description as clearly as if she had done a police sketch. Tucker and I would do this dance: The phones stayed put away for five minutes. But then there'd be some question that came up in conversation that we had to google, and then he'd see he had five texts, and I'd get out my phone while waiting for him and see eight new comments. And then we'd both say, 'Let's just get caught up,' and then the server would come ask us if we were ready to order, and we wouldn't have opened our menus.

The phones would stay faceup on the table from then on. And if you can see yourself get a notification, it's not like you're not going to look to see what it is. That was date night with Tucker.

That's incredibly sad, I now realize.

"Anyway," says the server, breaking me out of my thoughts, "the official answer is we love it when our patrons post about us. So take as many pictures as you want. If you do ever get a new phone, I mean."

"Thanks," I say. "But I might not want to go back."

"I sure wish I could quit mine," she says. "Want another beer?"

I do want one. I've forgotten how flavorful and thirst quenching a good American amber can be. Who cares how it photographs? Who cares what the followers think?

For once, not me. I go ahead and say yes, I would. Better still, when it comes, I have no trouble at all enjoying it.

PAIGE

Not three blocks from expensive downtown Copperidge, on the drive between the hospital and the inn, is a whimsical, folksy coffee shop called the Sleepy Bear, in an old brick building with a bank and a restaurant on either side. The sign hanging above the entrance shows a napping bear getting a whiff of coffee aroma from a perfectly poured latte. I wonder if Jessica likes bears, or lattes. It could be a neutral subject of conversation for my next visit. I take a picture with my phone.

Inside the Sleepy Bear, there are tin ceilings and exposed brick walls, with ornately framed oil paintings hung helter-skelter. There's an old carved-wood fireplace on one side of the room and lots of small mismatched tables and chairs that are surrounded by a short little white-washed wood fence, like the diners are lambs at pasture. On the other side of the fence are the service counter, a pastry case, and a chalkboard with a list of sandwiches with people names. I order a Rick and a decaf chai tea latte and sit down at a round table for two near a plug-in for my laptop.

Then, as has become my new habit, I open Pictey and take a look at Mia's feed. No change. She must have really meant it when she said she was going offline. But the comments are going strong with or without her. I expand them and see the natives are getting really restless. The longer she is quiet, the more people seem to behave as if her life belongs to them. And maybe the trolls smell weakness, because they seem to be growing bolder, like cockroaches in a condemned apartment. I can't zap their remarks from here—my work laptop is still at the inn—so I just have to look at them in all their miserable ickiness.

I am beginning to wish I could contact this woman and let her know her feed is going down the toilet. Pictey encrypts emails and real names, and for good reason, but I think she'd want to know. That she doesn't is very perplexing to me. After years and years of carefully cultivating her online status, this is how she lets it all fall apart? What if something really is wrong with her? What if no one has noticed?

I shake my head. That's a silly thought. She's an extremely popular woman. She has many friends, I'm sure. Friends who would notice if she'd, for example, had a traumatic brain injury and needed intervention.

But then, she was just jilted, and that's probably quite upsetting to her. Perhaps she's retreating from her social support systems. Perhaps no one but me has even noticed that something is awry.

My thoughts are interrupted by the arrival of my latte in a pretty china teacup with a matching saucer. A quick look around tells me they've got a large collection of such sets, all in different patterns. I think about the work of someone behind that counter, taking various cups and saucers out of the dishwasher and matching them back together. And then the further trouble the barista went to with the latte art. It's not a heart or a clover or anything else I've seen on a thousand Picteys. It's two wings, with space between them, like an angel's. Not a children's angel but a more sophisticated antiestablishment angel, if such a thing is possible.

I look around. Taking a picture of one's latte art is a socially acceptable behavior. That said, I've always had strong feelings about people taking pictures of their food. It's so . . . pedestrian. *Yes, yes, everyone, you're eating again. Well done.*

But just look at those wings. They seem like they're made of foamy delicious feathers. I'm just going to do it. Never mind my personal thoughts about phone etiquette. At least I'm not posting it online, right? Or . . .

I look at my phone screen. The latte picture has turned out surprisingly well. You can see the pretty blue china cup and the rich depth of color under the froth. I can fuss with the editing tools a little and make it all a bit nicer still. Maybe I can put a filter on it. I think if I do that, it could pass itself off as something Mia Bell would post.

I flip back through her feed, and sure enough, there are latte-art pictures here, there, and everywhere. As our sales managers would say, my art is "totally on-brand."

I take a moment to think this impulse through. If I log in as Mia—and that should be easy enough with the state of passwords today—and post this photo on her account, and she takes it down right away and changes her password, then my curiosity will be satisfied.

Further, assuming she's still alive, my post will be unmissable. Mia will get an email from Pictey saying she's logged in from a different device, so there's no chance she'll miss it. And if she reports a breach, the IP address will be from this coffee shop, ten minutes' walk from where she was staying a few days ago. They'll think she used an unsecured hot spot while having lunch here sometime or other. It'll be of zero concern to anyone. More to the point, Mia Bell will realize her account is slowly melting down and get back to work.

Further, I reason, influencers are a key part of the Pictey business model. Recovering the attention of this major influencer will also benefit my employer.

Carefully, I consider the cons of posting on a stranger's social media feed. As far as I can see, there are none.

So. It's decided. I'll be able to call Mia's attention to her neglected feed with alacrity, and nothing will be hurt in the process. In fact, she'll only be helped. It'll save her from blowing up her entire career as an influencer.

So resolved. But there's the matter of the caption. Can I write something that sounds like her? Some Mad Libs–style combination of buzzwords and hashtags?

Better still, something coded that lets her know: someone out there notices that something's amiss.

It takes me four minutes to get into her account. Her password is *Mike*0204*. His adoption anniversary is February 4, as she's posted several times. I was only slowed down by the punctuation—most people use a period or a dollar sign or an exclamation point between key word and key date. I can't help but laugh. Even just by forcing her to change her ridiculously obvious password, I am doing her a massive favor.

From there I load the coffee picture, adjust it until it looks good enough to me, and type out my best attempt at a caption.

> Spending some time with my #betterangels today. Saw these wings and thought of the care that goes into the invisible parts of our lives, and what else is latte art if not making something previously unseen into something beautiful. And just like that, a truth lands on angel wings: What if you guys are feeling unseen?

I pause, thinking of what I want to tell Mia, exactly, through this post. I want to tell her she's blowing it, sure. But there's more than that. I want to tell her that I know something happened, something sad, and it's ok, and she doesn't have to be perfect. I want to tell her that maybe it would be better if she didn't pretend to be. Better for everyone who sees her and feels like they're doing something wrong by comparison. Better, especially, for my sister.

So I type:

> Here's what I need you to know today: You are seen. I need you to know that what's happening on this side of the camera isn't always perfect, it isn't always beautiful, it isn't always an exercise

in joy and mindfulness and #gratitude and bliss. It isn't even always as real as it could be. When you suffer, when you feel pain, when you don't feel good enough, you've got to know you're not alone. There's someone out there, maybe someone you don't even know, who sees what you're going through. xoxo Mia #SleepyBearCoffee

I look up from my typing. My, but that is a good imitation of this woman, I think. I am freakishly good at impersonating an online celebrity. Is that a skill? It's certainly eye opening.

I suppose as I've been looking into Mia Bell, I've taken more notice than I realized. I've internalized her voice. That means I've probably also internalized her perfect hair and perfect skin and perfect clothes and perfectly positive attitude too. I've internalized the idea that every single thing she does is beautiful and polished, that she's incapable of screwing things up, that there must be some reasonable explanation if she does. As much as I've been dubious of her carefully curated identity, I've still bought into her bill of goods.

And consider me, with my complete lack of "lifestyle aspiration." Last haircut two years ago, last diet much longer, clothes assembled from online batch shopping, shoes by New Balance, replaced by the same exact model every four hundred miles. If I've bought into what Mia is selling in even the smallest of ways, then it's official: No one is immune. No one can follow these so-called influencers and come out with their head on straight.

I guess they're called *influencers* for a reason. Staying sane in a Pictey world is a lost cause.

MIA

The next day, having bored myself to tears on a few of Mom's books and wandered the house aimlessly driving her nuts, I hike up to the chicken house as soon as the hour is decent. As I walk, I wonder if I'm puffy from the pizza and beer, but there's no way to check in my phone camera, and so I decide my only choice is not to care. Besides, Dewey is the size of man that could make most any woman feel dainty, and a few carbohydrates can't change that.

I knock on the door. I hear a girl shouting through the door, "If you want eggs, they're on the screen porch," so I shout back, "I'm looking for your dad."

The door opens. It's that girl, the chubby young tween I saw in the window last weekend. Azalea. Oh, how I wish I could take her shopping. "Hi," I say, trying not to be intimidated by her appraising look. "Is your dad home?"

"Yes," she says. "Do I know you?"

I look at her for a moment. Is she old enough to be on Pictey? I suppose she is. "I don't think so," I say hopefully.

"He has a gun," she says, and I realize she wasn't asking if she knew me because I'm internet famous. She was asking because she has taken me for an assailant of some kind.

"Maybe I should come back later," I say, backing away quickly. "When would be a better time?"

The girl's eyes shift, slowly, and then start to sparkle. She cracks herself up. "Dad's in the backyard adding a wire coil to the fence. We have coyotes."

I exhale in relief. "Oh, thank goodness. You had me going with that gun talk."

She giggles, pleased with herself. "We do have a gun. But not, like, for killing people who come to the front door."

"That's reassuring," I tell her. "So coyotes, then? Maybe I can help him out."

She looks at me with a raised eyebrow. "Are you a coyote expert?"

"I have watched a lot of Road Runner cartoons," I admit.

"Did you bring any Acme TNT?" she asks, and I laugh, pleased to find that Dewey is raising this goofy daughter of his with the classics.

"Meep meep," I reply. Andy and I used to watch hours of Looney Tunes on Saturdays when Mom worked a swing. He made us "cereal salad," a mix of frozen fruit, Mom's homemade muesli, and Lucky Charms. Something about this girl reminds me of my own childhood. I had a goofy sense of humor, I was just this side of roly poly, and I probably would have enjoyed a junk art metal chicken in my front yard. And I loved people but never knew what to say to them. Without Andy, I would have been desperately lonely.

Azalea smiles, but it fades. "I do wish we could just blow those coyotes up. They ate Magdelina and her sister Dolores."

"Oh dear. Were you close?"

She shrugs and tries to look casual, but I see sorrow in her eyes. "I mean, we're going to eat everyone eventually. I just hate that it was a violent end. And I guess I was kind of close to Maggie. She was a good friend."

"Well then, I'm very sorry for your loss."

"Thanks. Do you have any pets?"

"I had a dog," I tell her. "He was my best friend."

Azalea's wide eyes get somehow even sadder. "He died?"

I nod. "Cancer, not coyotes."

"My mom died of cancer too," she tells me. "It was when I was young. My dad says, 'Eff cancer.'"

"Your dad is exactly right."

"You can come through here," she says, walking me back through the house. "I'm Azalea, but you probably know that. Dad talks about me constantly. Are you Mia?"

"I am." I wonder how she knows this. Does her dad also talk about me constantly?

"You moved in with Nurse Marla?"

"I wouldn't say moved in. I'm just here for a week or two."

"Your mom is nice. She came over when I fell off the roof." I am about to ask her about that tidbit, but she isn't done talking. "Dad said you threw your phone over the edge of Mount Wyler."

"That's true. I did. Do you want me to take my shoes off?" I ask as I follow her through the tiled entry to a small living room that leads to the kitchen.

"Why'd you do that?"

"I think I was overusing it," I say honestly. "And also I was in a bit of a mood. Shoes?"

"I'd leave 'em on if I were you," she says and gestures to the kitchen. When we arrive, I see that a chicken is sitting on the kitchen table.

"Oh," I say. "There's a chicken inside your house."

"At least one," she says.

"My in-house chickens are usually of the frozen, skinless variety," I tell her. "Sorry," I say to the chicken on the table.

"It's ok. Dad has drilled into me that the girls are food. But I still always think of them as pets. This is Veronica." She gestures to the feathery dame on the table. "Maggie used to come in here, too, but . . . you know." She sighs, and my heart goes out to her. "Veronica isn't as friendly as Maggie was, but the other chickens were all jealous of her looks, so we moved her inside."

"I can see how they'd be jealous," I say. "She's very attractive. Nice . . . feathers."

"Yeah, we're not sure what it is, exactly. She looks like a regular chicken to me. Here," she says. "My dad is through that door." She points to the kitchen door, where I see a little flap at the bottom, a doggy door, only it is shaped like a small round arch. "Is that a chicken door?" I ask.

"We don't want her pooping in the house," says Azalea, matter of fact. I love this girl. I am about to ask her to introduce me to the rest of the birds when she reaches for the person doorknob. "DAD!" she shouts, before the door is even fully open. "DAD, THE PHONE LADY IS HERE!"

The phone lady. What a dubious honor. But Dewey doesn't respond. "He might have his headphones on," she says. "You can just go out there."

"Ok," I say, but I'm a bit hesitant. Am I walking directly into a chicken yard? Will there be poop everywhere and jealous chickens with inferior feathers pecking at my ankles? I take a fortifying breath of indoor air and step out into the yard, trying not to look like a city-girl cliché. "Dewey?" I say in a low voice, afraid of what, I'm not sure. Alerting the chickens?

There are a lot of chickens. The yard is huge, four times the size of my mom's, and instead of a mess of raised garden beds and small trees, it's just a mix of clover, gravel, and grass. Toward the back fence there's a row of tidy chicken coops surrounded by a chain-link run, several beehives, and a swing set—the kind that's just two plastic swings hanging on a wooden A-frame. My eyes follow the fence line, and I see Dewey, facing away, stapling loops of what I think of as prison wire on the top of the five-foot wooden fence. He's in his element, worn jeans kind of just hanging onto him somehow, dusty white T-shirt, work gloves, muscles, butt. If I had a phone, I would probably take a pic for posterity. Maybe show it to my mom. But I don't, and maybe I look a bit harder as a result. In fact, it's a full minute before I call out "Dewey!" again. This time I'm louder. The chickens don't seem overtly dangerous.

His head turns sideways, and he notices me, or notices something. He pulls off his headphones and lets them hang from his neck. Turns around. His hair is thick and messy, and his face is tan. I smile at him. "Hi there," I say.

He takes a few long strides to me. "Hey, hey!" he says, and there is excitement in his voice that seems like a promising sign. "What are you doing here? Are you low on eggs?"

"We're fine on eggs, thanks. I just came to see you," I tell him. "I'm phoneless, you know, so if I want society, I have to go a-visiting."

He smiles indulgently. "I'm happy you're here, but if you ever actually need to make a call, don't forget about landlines. I know your mom has one. She posted the number on my refrigerator."

I laugh—that does sound like my mom. "Assuming you haven't done the same back to her, how would I find your number without the internet?"

He laughs too. "The numbers to most landlines are in that large yellow book your mom is using to even out the legs of the wicker table on her front porch."

I blink for a second. A phone book. Of course. I get one and throw it away every year as a matter of course. The thought that they have a use simply never occurred to me.

"Still," says Dewey, "I am all in favor of this technology ban, if it means surprise visits. I just didn't realize you'd be sticking with it."

"What do you mean? I threw my phone over an actual cliff yesterday. What else would I do?"

He gives me a little side-eye and says, "Not to enable, but if you want a new phone, I can take you into town."

"That is the very definition of enabling," I say with a laugh. "Anyway, I have my rental car until tomorrow. So I can enable myself.

But I am actually kind of enjoying not having the digital monkey on my back."

This is partly true. But partly like saying you enjoy having allergic hives. I hear phantom text notifications and feel as though my back jeans pocket is vibrating constantly. There is a large part of me that truly believes something important is happening and I am missing it. All the time. Every second of the day. I reach for my phone over and over again. Even just a few minutes ago I wanted to find out how far in miles my mom's house is from Dewey's. Do I need that information for any reason? No. Did I want it? Yes. Is phonelessness a very repetitive exercise in not getting what you want the moment you want it?

Apparently it is.

"Can't say I blame you. It's a struggle to keep my phone boundaries, but it feels like an important thing I can do for Azalea at this moment in her life, since I'm the only one she can look to for healthy modeling. I'm already fighting a losing battle—all her friends at school have phones. In fact, I'm starting to worry that I might be actually isolating her with my no-phones-for-kids policy. But I want to give her time to go outside, play with the animals, stay a kid a bit longer, I guess. She's only nine."

I smile. "She does seem like an awfully fun kid. She and I would have been fast friends at that age. My three deepest passions were animal stickers, reading about animals, and actual animals. Specifically cats, at the time."

"Well, my daughter is my favorite person, and cats are her favorite animal. So any hypothetical friend of hers is a friend of mine."

I put this theory to the test. "Oh, good. Because I'm kind of spinning my wheels in this posttech world of mine, and I was hoping you could come out tonight and spin some wheels together."

Now a cocky smile cracks over his face. "Are you asking me on a date?"

"No," I say, flushing. Having gotten to know both Dewey and Azalea even a little, I've concluded he's probably not the sort of guy who would enjoy being someone's rebound. "I'm afraid not. But there's a good reason: I was jilted at the altar a week ago."

The smile fades; the eyebrows lift. "Oh. Well. That's shitty."

"It's for the best," I say, knowing I'll have to get good and used to saying such things whenever I decide to resurface. Not sure when that will be. "I think we were on the wrong course," I add and weigh the truth of it as I do. It feels close. Not quite there.

"Still, I can't imagine how upsetting it would be," he says.

"I'd rather not dwell," I say. Typically, when it comes to my online presence, I have a well-practiced way of avoiding anything of a too-personal nature. In real life, I just sound standoffish.

"We don't have to talk about it. Maybe instead I can take you to the 'Ridge and show you a good time. Sway you on the whole 'no date' thing."

I flush with the flattery. "Um . . . well . . ." I shop around for how to handle it. Flirt back? Warn him about my emotional state?

What would I do if I had my phone right now? I consider. Well, I wouldn't be here, for one thing. I'd be texting him from my mom's porch, while also scrolling email or watching YouTube. In texts, a million things go unsaid or misunderstood. I could pretend I didn't notice he was flirting. I could take thirty minutes to respond while I thought of the right answer. I could decide I was in too deep and go quiet and never talk to him again. I could spend the next hour cyberstalking Tucker.

But also, on text, I wouldn't see how good Dewey looks in those jeans. So then, it's a good thing I'm here in real life. "How about not downtown Copperidge," I say, thinking of the Inn Evergreen and the time I spent there wallowing in the bathtub. "How about . . ." I try to remember what other resort towns are within a short hop of here. "Let's go to the village and have dinner at Black Diamond Baron's. I've always wanted to go there, but my mom says it's too touristy for her."

Black Diamond Baron's is a restaurant packed with hungry skiers seeking calorie-laden après in the winter, but in summer, it's opened up on all sides with a large courtyard where patrons can bring their dogs. Unbidden, the memory of Mike in his wagon outside his favorite coffee shop comes up. All the wagon memories are bittersweet—it was only toward the end that he needed that much help to get around. I push the thoughts of Mike away. He's gone now. It's long past time I accepted that.

"I want to spend the night eating a massive juicy burger *and* fries," I tell Dewey, determined to keep things light, "and petting other people's dogs. I want to do all that while talking to someone fun and interesting, in real life, with no phones on the table and no notifications on my watch."

Dewey's eyes smile at the suggestion. "I love this plan," he says. "I love the little doggy menu they have."

"There's a cocktail there for dogs too," I say. "It's peanut butter and bacon bits in a stainless shot glass. The pups lick it out. It's very cute."

"Oh, that is cute," he agrees emphatically. "Let's go, and then if we see a particularly good-looking dog, we can send a bacon shot over with our compliments," suggests Dewey.

"If we see a really cute one, can we just keep the treat and see if the dog will come home with us?" I ask. But even as I speak, my heart gives a tug to remind me, as nice as a new dog might sound, I could never survive that kind of loss again.

He sighs. "Azalea would kill for a dog. But I'm not having great luck with canines and chickens at the moment," he tells me, gesturing to the fence.

I pause. "You just need the right canine. A vegetarian, maybe, or a pacifist?"

"Now, that I could get behind. Do you know any such canines?" he asks.

"I did." I remember telling him about Mike as if he were still alive and try not to be embarrassed. I had enough on my plate in that moment. I wanted to pretend this one sorrow was still ahead of me.

"The truth is," I say, "my dog recently died. I'm just very bad at talking about that." So bad, I mentally add, that this is the first time I've done it in a very long time.

"Oh dear, I'm so sorry," says Dewey. "Do you miss him all the time?" he asks.

"All the time," I admit, praying I won't cry in the face of Dewey's kindness. "He was my best friend. I tried to replace him with a guy, but look how that turned out."

Dewey shakes his head. "A two-legged jerk is no match for a three-legged dog," he says.

I smile. "What makes you think my fiancé was a jerk?" I ask.

Dewey doesn't answer but just makes a soft sound with his mouth. A sort of *hm*.

"Well," I say. "He wasn't that bad. Still, I preferred my dog."

"Will you ever get another?" he asks.

I don't know if he's talking about fiancés or dogs. Either way, the answer is the same. I shake my head. "I don't think I could bear it anytime soon. But it can't hurt to see what else is out there. Just for fun."

PAIGE

"So you want me to check you out of here?"

"Check me out? Like a library book?" asks Jessica. I am back in the hospital, back in my sister's needlessly beeping room. Last night after my visit I spent my waking hours monitoring the comments of my/Mia's post like a hawk and zapping occasional trolls. And then, thinking I may as well be hanged for a sheep as a lamb, I started commenting back to some of the most heartfelt comments. Or as Mia might put it, I was making sure everyone felt "seen." After all, lemminglike though Mia's followers may be, everyone there is somebody's Jessica.

By this morning I am starting to feel jittery. There's been no response from Mia. Nothing. Not the slightest blip. At the very least you'd think she'd have an assistant or a friend who would catch this kind of thing, but nope. I look through every possible social outlet, and she hasn't posted anywhere, and neither has anyone else on her behalf.

Is she really dead after all?

The obits yield nothing. She's not dead. At least not publicly. But my sister nearly was, so after breakfast with Cary in the kitchen and another of his fortifying pep talks, I head back to the hospital with an armload of flowers, ready to discuss her request.

"I don't mean check you out like a library book. I think you would be out of circulation if you were a library book."

"Nah," she says, reaching for the box of cookies I picked up on the way. "They don't have that kind of budget. They'd just write 'damaged' on the inside cover and put me right back out there."

"On further thought, I wonder if it's not better to leave you here," I say. "For several reasons."

Jessica grimaces around a mouthful of cookie. "I don't think so," she says. "I don't like it here, and my IV port is itchy. Two people have the flu down the hall. Mom hasn't been by for three days because she's afraid she'll get a staph infection. Dad won't take me home without Mom's agreement, so I'm in limbo."

"Really? So your father actually wants you to go back home?" My dad offered to take me home, too, back then. In retrospect I wish I'd gone with him.

"No," Jessica says sadly. "He wants to say he wants me to come home," she says, astutely, "and let Mom be the bad guy."

"Mom will not knowingly be the bad guy under penalty of death," I say. "She'll leave you here indefinitely."

"Not indefinitely. The suicide squad will pick me up as soon as they have space for me. Sometime mid–next week at the earliest."

I train my eyes on the corner of the room. I do not like the idea of my sister being in the hospital for an unnecessary week. "Perhaps," I say slowly, "I could speak with Mother about her taking you home. Perhaps she could take some time off of work to support you."

Jessica looks as skeptical as I feel. There is nothing wrong with my mom, per se. She's not abusive. She's just not especially good at saying or doing helpful things in times of trouble. Or at other times either. But, I try to tell myself, just because she's wildly self-absorbed doesn't mean she *couldn't* do the right thing. If you could only get her attention.

"Maybe she could. But she won't. And anyway, truthfully," Jessica admits, "I'm not a minor. I can leave anytime I want. I'm just scared."

The awful days rush back to me. I breathe. I think about slipping off and taking half a Xanax. I tell myself: This is not me anymore. This time things can be different.

"What are you scared of?" I force myself to ask, as if I don't know. As if I didn't live these weeks myself, live through the shame and the tiredness and the wondering why I'd survived and what it was for when I was still so very, very sad.

"Myself," she says at last. Her eyes lose focus. "Being left alone." She inhales and exhales, sets her chin, as if daring those fears to get in her way. "That's why I want you to spring me. Just until they get a bed at the loony bin."

"And what, exactly, would we do if I 'sprang' you?"

"Well, what are you doing when you're not here?" she asks.

I think of Mia's feed and how to explain the nuances of my slightly dubious recent behaviors to a young adult battling depression. "I'm working on a sort of freelance project," I say. "For a high-traffic user on Pictey."

"Are you ghost posting?" she asks.

"What is 'ghost posting'?"

"It's when an internet celebrity hires a ghostwriter to post a jillion photos a day and keep up their feed so they can lie around and binge-watch Prime Video."

I look at my much-younger, in-the-know sister in surprise. "Is this a common occurrence?" I ask.

She shrugs. "I mean, sure. Lots of them are totally open about it. Some don't point it out, but you can totally tell, because their ghost spells everything right and makes things nicer than they really are. But I don't like it when people do it. I think it's really fakey," she says.

I swallow. "More fakey than just being an internet influencer in the first place?" I ask.

Jessica looks at me like I'm crazy. "Influencers aren't fake. I mean, lots of them do all their own stuff too. They can be really inspirational and show their real lives and encourage people to be themselves. They're, like, empowerment agents."

"Like @Mia&Mike?" I ask flatly.

"Yes!" Jessica says emphatically. "Wait. That's who you're ghost posting for?"

I try to think how to answer this. Perhaps I will say nothing. Now is a good time to arrange these flowers.

"I don't believe it. She's definitely never used a ghost before." Jessica frowns. "And also . . ." Her voice drifts off.

"Yes?" I say, turning back to her, ignoring the vase.

"Well, it's an odd coincidence; that's all. You work at Pictey, and you see my post on Mia's feed and find out I've done . . . what I've done."

I nod.

"And then a week later you're working for her? I mean, how exactly did that come about?"

"I thought you were majoring in communication studies," I say to her.

"What does that have to do with anything?"

"You're just making surprisingly intelligent connections for someone whose career ambition is to go into PR."

Her face falls. "I'm not going into PR," she says. "Though I would if I could. I'm not going into anything. I'm getting kicked out of school."

I look at my sister in disbelief. "Surely you're joking."

She shakes her head sadly. "I got caught cheating in my last final."

I nearly drop to the floor in shock. "You cheated? On a communications final? What on earth, Jessica! Communication is a skill that people normally master by the time they are five years old."

She pops up in bed. "I don't know what you think communications classwork consists of exactly, but I got behind in privacy management."

"Ah," I say. "That does make sense."

She puts her hands up, bandages flapping. "What's that supposed to mean?"

"It means you posted your suicide note on a social media platform. Privacy isn't your strong suit," I say.

Jessica, who her whole life has been nothing but a one-person laugh track, laughing at board books and knock-knock jokes and teen foibles and *Saturday Night Live* sketches, many of which I don't totally understand, begins to cry. I deflate and start wondering where to put my hands.

"It's not," she says through her tears. "It's really not. Mom should have taken that class for me. My friend Jules told me that Mom told her I was in the hospital for bowel problems. I mean, *bowel problems.* She must be absolutely humiliated."

She probably is, I have to privately admit. Two daughters trying to kill themselves looks causative. But Jessica doesn't know about me and my "emergency trip to Asia."

"She shouldn't be humiliated. Empirically," I say, "people your age are highly susceptible to depression. Your odds are further multiplied. You have a familial tendency toward perfectionism, unreasonable role models, and untreated depression. Your likelihood of being sexually assaulted is one in three, your odds of finding a job that covers your expenses are thirty percent, and your generation's average student debt at graduation ranges from one to three hundred thousand dollars, depending on who you ask."

"Jesus," says Jessica, and she starts crying harder.

"I'm trying to make you feel better," I insist.

"You are terrible at it!"

I sigh. "Yes. I see that. I don't have a terribly high 'emotional intelligence quotient,'" I say, making scare quotes around the words. "That's why your leaving with me may not be such a good idea. I'm afraid I'd upset you and you'd hurt yourself again."

"It's not like that," she says. "It's like, I don't want to be dead. But I don't know how to be alive."

I nod and sit on her bedside and try to think what Karrin would do. She would wait for Jessica to go on, so I do.

"I've been very unhappy, for a very long time, and I've toughed it out and talked to my family and increased my exercise and taken Wellbutrin, and I still don't know how to feel happy that I'm alive. Mostly when I go to bed at night, I feel relieved that the day is over, and when I wake up, I wish a new day didn't have to start. It's so hard to get out of bed. It's so hard to do anything. And you have to spend the entire day faking as though you don't feel that way, when that's the only way you know how to feel anymore."

My heart squeezes in recognition.

"That's why I follow people like Mia Bell. If you look at her feed, you can tell she knows how to enjoy being alive. She is always doing fabulous things and eating fabulous meals, shopping, attending events, doing yoga workshops in the Caymans."

"It's entirely possible you could do most if not all of those things," I say.

"The trouble is I don't want to," says Jessica. "All I want to do is sleep all day and cry."

I frown. "Then isn't it good you're in the hospital, where you can do exactly that? You can sleep for a week straight, and no one will mind at all."

"That's what I've been doing for the last six months," she tells me. "Spoiler alert: It didn't make me feel better. It just got me behind on my coursework."

Ah.

"And you cheated," I supply, "because you knew Mom wouldn't speak to you for two weeks if you fell off the dean's list, which is published for anyone to see."

She nods. I sigh.

"She means well," I say. "If it matters. Things were much worse for her growing up."

"I know. And yet she still never got a B and can't imagine what it feels like."

I shrug. These things are all true. My mom is nowhere near as cruel as her own mother was, nor as neglectful as her father. She never hit us for laughing or locked us out of the house for wearing a skirt shorter than our knees. She never surrendered to her own sorrows or spent weeks in bed or stopped putting food on the table. She did better than she was raised to do. And yet it wasn't quite enough. Not for me, and not, I now realize, for my sister.

There is no answer for this dilemma that is my mother except the answer I chose after I graduated, which was to move far away from my family and turn the volume of my feelings about them down to a polite hum that I can ignore at any time. Jessica, who has a much higher EQ than I do, will never be able to do either of those things.

Could she?

"Maybe you should come stay with me," I hear myself say. Jessica's face brightens up like I've promised her the moon. "If you leave here with me, I'll need you to sign something. A pledge or something that I could trust you not to do yourself any harm. And even then I wouldn't give you much alone time. You'd still be on suicide watch in effect."

"Ok," she says.

"And then, when that place, the rehab center or whatever it is, has room for you, you'd have to go straight there."

"Ok."

"But until then, the inn is very nice and comfortable. I know a lot about antidepressants and can help you while you get used to your medications. I can keep track of your dosages and monitor your activity."

"Ok," she says again.

"Also. I'd need you to do something for me," I say. "Remember how you said you wished you could live like Mia Bell?"

"That was five minutes ago."

"So then you do remember. Well, if I'm going to be, ah, ghost posting for her," I say, trying the term out on my lips, seeing if it feels real enough, "you won't be able to sleep all day. You'll have to get up, as miserable as you may feel, and come with me while I, you know, impersonate someone happy to be alive."

She considers this for a moment. "Then . . . I'd kind of be helping you," she says. "With your work."

"Yes. That's correct. You'd be a big help. I never think to take pictures of anything I do. Plus I never actually do anything. And I'm not that familiar with her, ah, oeuvre. Having you along would be a huge help."

Jessica's blotchy, miserable, tearstained face brightens even more. "So we could have a big Mia Bell week?" she asks.

"I'm not sure what that means, so . . . maybe?"

"It means we'd go dress shopping and have pedicures and a fancy-looking lunch and then hike up a mountain and take pictures of the view and then go eat real food that also looks good on film. Like, frites standing up in a big paper-lined cone. From a real Belgian place. Or maybe we could eat Moroccan! Then we'd hear a bluegrass band at some outdoor venue and pose all goofy in adorable sun hats."

"No," I say. "We can't be in the photos," I remind her and myself. "But the rest are actually wonderful ideas." I shake my head in wonder. "It would have taken me hours to come up with any kind of itinerary, and it wouldn't have been half so good as what just sprang to your mind. You're going to be a natural at this," I tell her. "Much better than me."

She shrugs. "Believe me, Paige. It's not hard to post stuff on the internet. It's just hard to make anyone care."

MIA

I walk into my mom's kitchen the day after my nondate at Black Diamond Baron's with Dewey and find Mom loading up her birthing bag and some extra stuff. An air mattress and a sleeping bag. A nylon bag in bright yellow that I think might be a tent. I am still too buzzy with that happy feeling of a relaxed evening with someone new and awesome to realize this spells danger.

"Where are you going?" I ask her.

"Where are *we* going," she corrects. "Now that you're detached from your digital tether, we're going camping."

"What now?"

"Surely you must have heard of it, in all your Patagonia-sponsored activities."

I shake my head. "I've heard of it, but I don't care for it. I sleep in beds."

"This is Colorado, honey. You'll sleep on the ground, and you'll like it. Besides, it's part of your detox," she tells me. "What could be more offline than a place with no electricity, no bathrooms, and no cars?"

"A coffin," I say. "A lead-lined coffin would be more offline. That doesn't mean I should crawl into one."

My mother gestures grandly to the heavens. "Open yourself up to Mother Nature, my darling. Take in the lessons she has to offer. Let her stars be your backlight and her winds be your recharger."

"Oh boy," I say. "I'm gonna have to pass."

My mom drops her arms and shakes her head. "Sorry. You have to go. I already told Dewey."

"Dewey?" Last night we agreed to hang out again as soon as possible. I didn't realize he had discussed this with my mother too. "What did you tell Dewey? And when?"

"Just now. On the phone. I told him we were taking Azalea camping. She can't very well take herself, now, can she?"

"Dewey is letting you take his daughter camping?"

"I don't see why not," says Mom. "He's known me for years. You're the question mark here, and he seems willing to take the chance."

"We went out last night," I tell her. She's not one to pry, and it drives me crazy.

"Did you, now." It's not exactly a question, but I'm just going to pretend it was.

"It wasn't a date."

"Why on earth not?" she asks.

"Because I've only been single for about fifteen minutes!" I say. "Plus I'm having some kind of mother-induced nervous breakdown."

She laughs at this. "More like nervous break*through*," she quips, and she smiles with pride at herself even though I am pretty sure she's the one who bought me the Luscious Jackson EP of the same name years ago. "So if you're not dating the guy three doors up who looks like a sort of cross between a Viking and a Highlander, what exactly is your plan for him?"

"There's no plan," I tell her blithely. "I'm just savoring the offline experience. Hashtag no filter."

"I would encourage you to stop saying *hashtag* in front of polite company," she tells me. "And as for having no filter, when it comes to your romantic dalliances with my egg guy, please do consider using a filter. You're on the rebound, and this is my only reliable source of chicken feet."

"Mom, what *do* you do with the chicken feet?" I ask her.

She sighs. "I was kind of hoping you wouldn't ask."

"I'm asking," I say.

"I eat them," she says.

"Really!" I exclaim. "That's interesting. When did that start?"

"When this started," she says and points to some small wrinkles on her forehead. "I eat them for the collagen. It took some getting used to."

I break into a grin. "So you're saying you eat, what, boiled chicken feet for reasons of vanity?"

"That's right."

"*Aha!*" I cry in delight. "You do care about how you look! I'm vindicated!"

"Are you?"

"I am. You can preach about your graceful aging and plastics-free medicine cabinet and your 'Mother Nature's backlighting,' but you are, deep down, just the same as anyone else. Willing to eat variety meats to avoid wrinkles!"

"It's also very good for my gut biome," she says, utterly unfazed.

"But that's not why you do it," I say.

Mom shrugs. "When eight hundred years old you are," she paraphrases, "look this good, you will not."

I smile. But then Mom catches my eye, and we both sigh deeply, at the same time. Neither Mom nor I has any natural proclivity toward science fiction, though I do remember my mom strongly advising me to read *The Handmaid's Tale* when I first got my period. Looking back, that was a strange recommendation. Anyway. It was Andy who was into Star Wars.

He did not care that we weren't remotely interested. Every Christmas Eve he put on the first one ever, the one with Carrie Fisher wearing earmuffs made out of her own hair, and *Return of the Jedi*, where Yoda says his classic line about being old. Andy, three years my elder, told me when I was five that the emperor was Santa Claus's evil twin. That was to explain why we had to watch it at Christmas. When we were older, he talked like Yoda anytime he needed to get a laugh out of me or say something wise but not sound preachy. I remember how when I was eight or so, the three of us went to see *The Phantom Menace*, waiting in line for hours for tickets at the big mall theater. I wanted to dress as Leia, of course, and begged Andy to be Luke, not Han, his true favorite. In the end, we settled on him going as Chewbacca, and when in the last hour of waiting I started to freeze solid in my white cotton nightgown, he gave me his furry paws and knit bandolier.

Mom swallows. I ask her something I always wonder about. "How much do you miss him, these days?" I ask. "Is it getting better? On a scale of one to ten." For me it has been stuck for some time not at a ten but at a number too high for me to bear remembering him often.

She sits down wearily on the sofa, her packing forgotten. "A thousand," she tells me. "Sometimes it almost seems to be getting worse, not better. Every year new things happen that he misses out on. Or something new comes up that I could use his help with. It was hard to pick out a dress for your wedding without him. His job was to make sure I didn't look too hippie dippie at your school functions and the like. Six years, and I still can't dress myself."

My heart sinks. I try not to forget that for every memory of Andy I try to squelch, my mother lets in two. "I can help you, Mom. Or you can just wear your hippie dresses. I don't care. I'm not sixteen anymore."

"I just would prefer it if he were here." She says it with an edge. Like she's not sure if I feel the same way.

"I miss him too," I say, pretending not to care that I feel my own way of mourning Andy has always been graded on a curve. "God, how I wish he were here now. He would have no time for Tucker."

"Tucker would be persona non grata around here, that's for sure."

"Well, he still is, isn't he?" I ask.

Mom thinks about this. "If he came by, knocked on the door, I would certainly let him in. Wouldn't you?" she asks. "I'd offer him a drink and a chair. After all, exactly what has he done that was so bad?"

I try not to overreact. This is my mom. She is not known for mincing her words or suffering fools, even when her daughter is the fool in question. Growing up, when I wanted tact, I went to Andy. "Tucker did kind of hurt my feelings," I point out to Mom now. "And embarrass me. When he left me at the altar."

"Well, technically, he never made it to the altar. He gave you two days' warning. And that was for a private ceremony."

"Yes. Very private," I snap. "You, the minister, and five hundred thousand of our closest friends."

She opens her mouth to annoy me further when, thank heavens, the doorbell rings.

As she goes to answer it, I whisper, "You eat chicken feet."

She replies just a hair louder, "Millions of people eat chicken feet. Stop being so culturally insensitive." And then, last word guaranteed, she throws open the door. "Azalea!"

———

Though it is not a pretty impulse, whenever I see Azalea, I want to take her aside and fix her. Today is no different. She comes through the door in pastel-striped leggings that are too juvenile for her age and don't flatter her body shape. On top she is wearing a too-small hoodie open over a shirt from a children's theater company whose mascot is an ear of corn. She needs a training bra underneath but is instead wearing something that flattens her out and squeezes her around the stomach, some kind of too-short tank top. She will probably be tugging at it all day—she can't stop fiddling with her clothes. Probably because she is uncomfortable. How I would love to take this child shopping, but I know why I can't.

She has no idea that she's grown up so much. She has no idea she looks odd. I should not be the one to tell her.

She pulls out of an awkwardly long hug from my mom—my mom thinks we should all hug everyone for at least twenty seconds, in order to get the true stress-reduction benefits of human connection—and beams at me. "Dad said you spent last night at a dog restaurant."

"That's right," I say. "We met a lot of nice dogs."

"He said your dog had three legs."

"He did." I cough. First Andy, now Mike. These conversations make me miss being anywhere but here.

"What happened to his other leg?"

"Someone threw him out of a car and drove away." I don't tell her the car was moving. That part bugs me too much to repeat.

"Did you rescue him?"

"Yes." Without intention, my hand moves to my heart. "Well, it's more accurate to say that he rescued me."

"That's what it always says in my books!" she says. "The person rescues the dog; then the dog rescues the person."

"Your books?" I ask.

"Humane Hannah and the Haunting Hounds," she tells me. "Hannah works at a dog shelter, and she can talk to the ghosts of dogs, so she solves crimes with their help. There's, like, thirty books in the series."

My heart squeezes. I would have read that series at her age. I would have read all thirty in one summer while everyone normal was outside playing. Or camping.

"That sounds like a good series," I say.

"I brought three in my backpack," she tells me happily. "You can borrow one."

Her backpack, too, is an invitation to teasing. It's shaped like a kitten. An acrylic kitten with rainbow sparkles for fur. The eyes of the cat are hearts. It's packed to bursting and looks incredibly heavy, but she's bouncy enough with it on her shoulders. "I also packed marshmallows!"

"That's wonderful," says my mom. "But where's your sleeping bag?"

"Oh, well, I didn't bring it," she says. "When Dad and I camp, I always get scared at bedtime and go inside to sleep."

"Scared?" asks my mom, who has probably never had that emotion in her life.

"There's coyotes. You can hear them. They ate my chicken."

"Well, they won't eat you," she says. "I promise. And where we're going, there's no 'inside' to sleep in. Mia, run downstairs and get an extra sleeping bag, will you?"

I follow orders, hearing poor Azalea tell Mom she'll just sleep in the car and my mom informing her that she will do no such thing. When I come back up, the girl's face is the same color as an overbleached hotel towel.

"Mom," I say. "Azalea doesn't want to go camping."

"No," she tells Azalea, who is nodding. "Mia doesn't want to go camping. Stop poisoning the well, Mia."

"Can't we just have a girls' sleepover?" I suggest. "Make beet chips and watch movies?"

"We will not make beet chips," she says. "It is not beet season. We will eat marshmallows and sleep under the stars. You two, in the car. Enough silliness."

Knowing there's no point in arguing, I take Azalea by the arm and try to be reassuring as I load her into the car. But I am filling up with resentment for my overbearing mom. I remember how my phone used to buffer me from her. "It's not beet season?" I hear myself muttering. "When, exactly, is marshmallow season?"

Helpfully Azalea tells me, "Well, they're just sugar and horse hooves, so you can have those at any time," and shrugs.

"Blessed are the peacemakers," I tell the poor girl, before going back inside to throw a change of underwear, a small dopp kit, and two extra blankets off my bed into a paper grocery sack that will serve as my rainbow-sparkles-kitty backpack for the purposes of this adventure. Though my mother is many things, reasonable is not one of them. But then my heart softens. After all, as Andy was fond of saying, "reasonable" may be highly overrated.

PAIGE

No better place to spend a #honeymoon than @ InnEvergreen, sweet friends. Did you know they can prepare a completely gluten-free, dairy-free, grain-free, sugar-free menu for every breakfast? No need to waste a #cheatday just because I'm away from home. That's the kind of care that makes you feel like you're at home, only with no dishes! QOTD: What creature comforts make you feel most at home when you travel? For me, nothing beats having clean food to start my day. If it's your jam, there's nothing wrong with having a bagel (singular LOL) in New York City or a perfect scone in London. But if you'd rather spend your mountain time vibrant and energized, you can skip the #carbcrash at breakfast and indulge in a nice coconut smoothie and a perfect sesame-sprinkled kale and egg scramble instead. #Nourishingandflourishing

Together, Jessica and I make a safety plan. We get a terrific worksheet from www.samhsa.gov that helps us figure out who to call and how to proceed in case of emergency, as well as how to avoid danger in the coming days together. We both put hotline numbers in our phones and put each other in favorites. I have no intention of letting her out of my sight, but even so, it feels important to be prepared.

Then a nurse sends me home from the hospital, promising someone will call me when Jessica is close to being discharged and that that process will take "at least a day." I drive back to the inn and spend the first several waiting hours thinking, thinking, thinking about Mia, Jessica, and myself. Three people who are hiding from the world—one a fraud, one afraid of herself, and one, me, having largely lost interest. Until now.

There's still no response on the page from Mia. I find myself wondering what I am hoping for—to be caught or to be allowed to carry on. But for practical purposes, that doesn't matter. It's time for "Mia" to post again; her followers are so grouchy and needy, and also they are quitting her feed in droves, due to an algorithm created by designers at Pictey to make sure new users can rise up in the ranks when old ones start to go stagnant. I don't have Jessica to abet me yet, but I can do some of the things that will placate the masses—for example, I don't need help to go back to the Sleepy Bear. My latte foam is styled as a sea turtle—maybe too cutesy for Mia—so I post a picture of the stained glass above the door, with sun streaming through it, and some nice thoughts about seeing the beauty in everything. I'm pretty sure it's a paraphrase of something Mia went viral with a year or two ago, but whatever—it'll do. It *does* do. Her comments fill up, faster than last time, and her follower numbers start to bounce back to where they were before her "wedding."

I read all the comments as they come in, and some of them are really moving. A woman in Northern California talks about finding her faith in the stained glass windows of an old church after a wildfire destroyed her home, and "Mia" definitely writes back about that. People post their own stained glass photos and tag me—tag Mia, that is—and they are spectacular.

I like this back-and-forth interaction so much and am so bored waiting for Jessica's nurse to call that I post again. This time it's a few pictures from inside the inn, tagged #InnEvergreen. After all, it's so pretty here, and it might be good for Cary, who has been so nice to me. More likes flood in. My phone notifies me nonstop. I sit at "my" table in the inn's kitchen, eating two rich molasses cookies while listening happily to Cary marveling at his sudden influx of off-season reservations. And griping about how many of them are asking for dietary modifications.

Then someone bitchily posts about how it looks like Mia hasn't been outside in a week. I generally do not care for going outside, beyond my commute to work and back, but I will have to do it here in Colorado, because I've got no microwave and not enough books. First thing the next morning I walk to a bookstore and take a picture of it from the outside of the store, and then I go in, avoid the salesperson, buy a cozy mystery based on a staff-recommendation sticker, and leave without saying a single word to anyone except "No bag, please."

When I post that little adventure on the feed, the store almost immediately reposts it. They tag me, and again, by *me* I mean Mia, and the level of excitement they express at having "us" in the store is absolutely bananas. They DM me a coupon for a free book the next time I'm in, along with a sincere note of appreciation for the mention, saying they've done more online business today than in the previous month put together.

More business in one day than in an entire month. Because I walked into their store and picked out a book! After a lifetime of buying everything—books, food, tampons, houseplants—online, I wander into one store because of one snarky online comment about being a shut-in, and I change the course of a business's fiscal month.

I can't use the coupon, obviously, even though after three chapters I already want another book in the series. If someone looking like me came in with Mia's coupon, there would be questions to be answered.

Anyway, free stuff is not the point, as Mia Bell has missed so completely. The point is, independent bookstore owners seem like very nice people, and I—*Mia*—just apparently made a small businessperson's burden a tiny bit lighter.

I kind of want to do it again.

There is no sugarcoating it: at this point I get a bit delirious with power. Mark it—11:30 a.m. one June morning in Copperidge, Colorado, Paige Miller, erstwhile hater of influencer culture and internet celebrity, is corrupted. Absolutely.

MIA

Have you seen lots of sitcoms where bumbling idiots go camping, can't set up the tent, get caught in a rainstorm, and are forced to eat ice-cold hot dogs? My mom is no bumbling idiot. An hour after arrival at a remote site about two hundred yards from any service access, she's taught Azalea how to pitch the tent and set up a cook station at the edge of the picnic table under a rain sail. A waterproof, bear-proof bag is hanging from a tree limb with our food in it. A Jetboil has been produced, along with three travel mugs, and we're having hot beverages—Mom and I tea with a tipple, and Azalea, who my mom has taken to calling Izzy, a mug of hot cocoa. It's about sixty degrees up here, which is winter-coat weather in LA. But with tea and whiskey and the assortment of fleece sweater jackets my mom has produced, I am snug. We are at around ten thousand feet, and a two-mile, steep out-and-back hike tires us all, and when we return to the site, it is time to build a fire.

It is then that I realize that it is the golden hour.

The golden hour is the time just before true dusk when everything photographs well. The light is diffuse; the clouds reflect color. The last six months of my life, since Tucker and I got very serious very quickly, have been all about running around madly during the golden hour. On days when our schedule allows, I take a collapsible crate I keep in my car at all times and load it with sponsored items and props in the right colors and mixes of textures, from a collection that takes up the entire coat closet in my apartment. I pack two or three outfits as well, to be wriggled into in the back of my car as needed. Tucker shows up from wherever he's been—family portraits, pet sessions, just a happy hour with the guys—and we jump in the car and drive somewhere in time to spend the hour taking photos for my feed. He is obsessed with the golden hour and has an app that will predict its arrival on any given day. We can end up with twenty really gorgeous photos from each golden hour we catch. Or we could, I should say.

But somehow, in all that, I have never noticed what the golden hour actually looks like.

Tucker told me that the one downside with getting married in the Rockies is that the mountains ruin the golden hour. But I am looking at the golden hour right now, and there is nothing ruined about it. Sure, I vaguely understand that even at this elevation I'm not seeing the purples and oranges of the sunset, but for the first time I get where the word *golden* comes from. The mountains are reflecting the light from the waning sun on everything, bouncing it around, so that it looks like there is a fine rose gold dusting on every rock face. The clouds are high and threadlike, and they are the sweet brights of a sorbet case, mango, kumquat, passionfruit. And the snow on the caps is turning, slowly, from the palest peach to pink to violet and now, as the night grows closer, the faint periwinkle from the gown of a fairy-tale princess.

I observe all this slowly, in some kind of relaxed stupor. My mom is teaching Azalea and me how to build a fire in her even, repetitive way. She has Izzy making tipis out of twigs and log houses out of logs and bending and stooping and blowing and waving her arms. I am in a crouch just behind this, thinking of the fire, thinking of the mountains, marveling at the colors, gaping. I think of Tucker's declarations, about the golden hour, about me. I think of the way Dewey made me laugh last night, doing the voice-overs for all the dogs on the patio. There must have been twenty. I remember the color of the microbrew he ordered, how he let me have the second half of it when I realized how badly I wished I had gotten beer myself, how he, without being asked to, swapped me for my low-calorie vodka soda, took a drink of it, twisted up his face, and said, "This is what I order all the time." And then burst out laughing.

That laugh was a funny "ha ha ha" laugh, and unbidden, a vision comes to me of my lying on his stomach while he laughs. I think of how my head would bobble. It's a strange thought. I imagine Mike, now, on this imaginary couch with us. I know with some weird certainty that he would sit on Dewey's side, because Dewey is one of those guys who are always warm.

Then I feel a pressure on the front of my deltoid, and I am off balance. I startle to alertness as my mom pushes me off my haunches backward, and I roll onto my butt. "I'm revoking your merit badge, space case," she says.

"You were right," I say. "Life without my phone is overwhelming."

She and Azalea extend arms to help me up to standing. I am surprised to see the fire is roaring. The sky is almost dark, and stars are starting to come out. My private plan to sleep in the car with Azalea seems absurd now that I realize what beauty I stand to miss. I need to stay out here, stare into the flames for a few hours, and eat marshmallows.

"My daughter," she says fondly. "When will you realize? I'm always right. About everything."

I sigh, because she truly believes this, and I will probably be called to her deathbed to pronounce it if I don't just get it over with now. "You're always right, Mom," I say. "But never humble."

Azalea stands from the firepit and dusts off her leggings. She is watching me and Mom carefully. Maybe she is not sure if this is a friendly transaction or some long-standing fight—my tone is always a bit flat with my mother, even the truest sentiments spoken grudgingly. Sometimes, when she came to visit me in LA, Tucker would tell me I was too hard on Mom. But I knew that was because she liked to impersonate a frail old person around him, when in fact she is not one, despite her age. In fact, the older I get, the less she seems to age. Why is that?

I smile, first at Azalea, then at my mom, to try to put them both at ease. "How do you like camping so far, Azalea?" I ask.

"I like it!" she says. "Marla, thanks for bringing me."

"Anytime, sweetheart. It's no trouble for me. Now, when this one was little, she and her brother would give me such grief. Every time I turned around, they'd be gone, Andy ten feet up in some tree and Mia hollering at him to show her how to get up too."

Azalea looks at me. "You have a brother? I want a brother."

Mom looks at me. "You didn't tell her?"

"She's only nine, Mom," I say. "It didn't come up."

"Tell me what?" Azalea asks.

"It never comes up with you, Mia. Sometimes I worry that you'd prefer to pretend he never existed."

That's not remotely true. I prefer to pretend that he never died, that he's just somewhere offstage, and if I needed him, he could come running. But I can't say that to my mom. It would just strengthen her case that I live in a fantasy world of my own creation.

Instead I say, "It's been six years, Azalea, but Andy passed away."

"Oh," she says. "My mom died around then too. Was it cancer?"

Mom shakes her head. "A car accident. Just one of those sad things." I can hear the emotion rising in her voice, and it hurts my heart. I miss Andy terribly; I really do. But it is my mom who has come to own this grief. She was his mother. He was her only son. When her voice cracks and she pushes her lips together to stanch tears, I put my arm around her and pull her in. I wonder, What is the "appropriate" amount of time to grieve a brother? A dog? An engagement? A son? Why does it seem as though not a day has gone by in her life since Andy was here, whereas for me it's been the longest six years of my life?

"Mom," I say, and I try to turn my conversation to something gentler, to save her from tears. "I think I want the recipe for your chicken feet. Your skin really is amazing."

She smiles, even laughs a bit. Little lines appear, as if to reassure me I'm not going mad; my mom isn't reverse aging. But when they do, I realize what is making me feel old and world weary while she stays young: she is on her own timetable, unapologetically.

Of course. Speaking metaphorically, if you never download the program that everyone else is using, you never have to run updates.

I watch her work capably by the fire, her eyes glazed over, thinking no doubt of camping trips long past. My mom can do this: she can grieve, she can take as long as she needs. She never feels that push, push, push to move on.

And it's just the same with the tech. She doesn't need to know about Pictey because she didn't need to know about Instagram because she didn't need to know about Facebook or Myspace or Friendster or Napster. All that bandwidth is still free for camping, planting turnips, reading mysteries, loving her children. These are things she could carry on with if the cell towers collapsed and all the silicon in the world turned to dust.

That's her secret: if you are unwilling to reshape yourself every time the times change, you are, effectively, timeless.

PAIGE

In absolute love with this #knitting store in the mountains. Look at all the pretty piles of softness and color! Did you know you don't have to visit the Rockies to shop the store? Their online presence is utterly #nailedit and the shop is full of #fiberwork pros ready to help you start in on the meditative path of making something from a ball of yarn and a good idea. Let me know what craft unravels your stress in the comments. xo Mia @DarnyarnbarnCO

It turns out that Mia is a knitter. Scrolling and scrolling and scrolling, I learn that she started out making sweaters for Mike but hasn't posted a final product since the dog passed away. She does, however, still post pictures of yarn. Yarn and books, I can see, are both highly photogenic, as inanimate objects go.

Cary tells me there's a yarn shop in town, an independent small business that I look up online and read about. The owner had breast cancer and knitted her own cashmere bra inserts while she was waiting to be well enough for reconstruction surgery. After that she decided life was too short to work at the tax return farm where she'd been for the previous twenty-five years and opened up the Darn Yarn Barn with her best friend. Ten minutes after hearing that story, I'm dressed and out the door. I ask for a learn-to-knit kit and also buy some of the most luxe pretty woolly stuff I've ever seen, yarn the color of rain clouds with the consistency of a good fluffy cat. It's thick yarn, and I'm told it matches up with some fat wooden needles made out of gorgeous acacia wood. I buy it all—kit, needles, enough yarn for a scarf—to the tune of $170 and try not to gasp at the register. When I get home, I take a picture of it, as artfully as possible, and post it on Mia's feed. It gets eighty thousand likes in forty minutes.

I feel drunk, or perhaps this is that feeling from junior high debate club, the one I remember so clearly. The feeling . . . it has a name . . . I look in the reaches of my mind and find it: giddy. I want to run through the resort towns of the immediate area, taking photos and tagging small businesses and responding to comments until my thumbs fall off.

And I absolutely can.

When was the last time I ate dinner out in a restaurant? When was the last time I went shopping outside my computer? When was the last time I spoke to three different people in one day, much less eighty thousand? These are all, aside from the eighty-thousand-likes thing, what most people do all the time, on a regular basis. And while I realize I am not most people, I am starting to wonder exactly what I've been missing out on. And why.

My musings are shut down by a call from my mother. I don't pick up—that would be absolute insanity. Instead I let her go to voice mail, and because she is from another generation, she leaves a long and detailed message that it takes my phone a long time to transcribe. When it is finally ready, I read:

Paige, honey, I had no idea you were in the area! Jessi says you're volunteering to host her while she rests up from that nasty accident. Poor thing, what a terrible stroke of luck to fall into that glass door! Jeezaloo!

I stop reading to reflect on how I would have reacted to that bald-faced lie if I had actually picked up the call. Not well, I suspect.

Her dad and I are just so grateful. You know we're never home with work and travel, and Jessi says you're on vacation? Without you we would have had to hire a nurse, though she was covered to stay in the hospital, so that would have been fine, really. Maybe better, but did you sort of tell Jessi that she'd be happier outside the hospital? That seems like a stretch, honey. Wherever you go, there you are! And may I also add, I can't believe you vacationed an hour away from us and didn't say a word! What on earth! It's like you're avoiding me, but I'm sure it's nothing like that.

It's exactly like that.

A few ground rules for Jessi's visit: Make sure you watch what she eats. She does love to indulge her sweet tooth. We don't want her getting our metabolism the second she turns thirty, do we? And speaking of genetics, she's got a few meds to take—I'll let her talk to you about those, if she likes—no big deal, but I think one or two of them a day, and would you just see that she does take them? Oh, and call me back if you're staying in a place with an outfitted kitchen. No big deal, just some precautions with sharps we should take while she's getting back on her feet.

How has my mother talked so long about my depressed sister without admitting she is depressed, I wonder?

Right, so that's it. No kitchen access, at least not alone, and make her take her meds, and not too much dessert, and if you need anything, call me, or call her dad, though we are both so busy. We're never home! Tell her we love her!

Then my phone rings again, and it's the hospital number. I pick it up, and it's time: Jessica is finally ready to be discharged. I delete my mom's message and let it slide right out of my memory. Why bother with her nonsense? In fact, my job to help Jessica means I need to keep Mom's nonsense as far away as possible.

I grab my charger and my wallet and head to my car with a spring in my step. It's all coming together. I was sent on leave to be with my family. I came to Colorado to make some kind of amends to Jessica. I went to the hospital to try to alleviate her burden. Now, by giving her a safe place to go outside of the hospital, I've done exactly that.

And further, Jessica will be an excellent addition to my little side project.

I remind myself gently: I am not a hired ghost poster, an assistant, a stand-in, an influencer. I am not @Mia&Mike, not really.

And then, with a wicked smile, I say aloud into the empty car, "But then, at the moment, neither is anyone else. So why not me?"

MIA

That night, as my mom snores in the tent and Azalea sleeps soundly in the reclined passenger seat of my mom's car, I tend the dying fire. I've never tended a fire before, and I'm not much good at it, but neither can I seem to let it go. The picnic table has been pulled close enough that I can sit on the bench and face outward, lean toward the pile of logs and shift them with a hot dog fork. I've unzipped my old childhood sleeping bag and made it into a blanket to wrap myself up in, and I have a few inches of Fat Tire left in the can I had with dinner. Without my trying, a caption springs to mind. I'd post a 180-degree view, with the campfire in the center, and talk about doing a one-eighty in my life. I'd explain that without my tech addiction driving my every move, everything I do and feel has come into focus.

And I'd urge everyone to get off their own phones for the weekend. Just one weekend! It's only been a few days since I trekked up Mount Wyler, and that's all it's taken for me to get the soles of my feet planted back on the ground. I do mean "planted." I've heard that expression—used it, too—a hundred times. Only now, by the fire under the stars, do I consider what it means. It means that when I rock the ball and heel against the insole of my shoe, and the tread of that same shoe sways over the gravelly mix around this firepit, and the gravelly mix shifts slightly, the earth below me supports my weight. And that earth is supported by the stone below that, and by the water and the fossilized ammonites and the magma at the core. I am planted amid all that support, shooting up from the ground as surely as an evergreen.

I lean my back against the table edge and look up at the stars. They are good here—my mom was right. Always so annoyingly right. What else does she know that I haven't figured out for myself yet? I try to think of all the ways she's harassed and harangued me in the last ten years. There are many. Too many to list. Uncomfortable shoes. Funny diet. City life. Childlessness. If she only understood how that ticker tape of disapproval makes it so hard to hear the things I actually need to know.

I hear car wheels.

I turn and see blinding headlights.

I think, *I hope it's Dewey.* Then I think, *Better unpack that later and go see who's here and if they are going to kill me.*

The car stops; the lights cut; I blink away the spots left behind. The shape of the vehicle comes into focus. It's a truck. A truck with a magnet sign on the door that reads **ORGANIC EGGS** with a phone number below.

I think of hiding my smile of delight and decide, in the spirit of my one-eighty, not to.

"Hello?" whispers Dewey as he steps out of the truck. "It's Dewey. Is everyone asleep?"

I am probably outlined by the fire, but I say anyway, "Over here. It's Mia."

His boots crunch softly as he makes his way to me.

"What are you doing here?" I ask softly.

"Camping," he says. "I got the door on a new coop today, and all the girls are inside for the night. Fences are reinforced. Coyotes are gonna have to find a new restaurant."

I look at him. He's wearing those low-slung jeans again, a rolled-up flannel shirt, a lazy smile. Of all that information he's just delivered, I can only ask, "Where are you going to sleep?"

"Not between you and your mom?" he says, and now that he is close enough to the fire, I can see his smile turn into a grin.

"She snores," I say. And then, because if he's here for the night, I might as well spill it, "I think we both do."

He laughs. "I'll be in my hammock. I can get it ready for the night in about thirty seconds, and I won't wake anyone."

I look at him blankly. "You're gonna spend the night in a hammock out here?"

He shrugs. "I'm too lazy to put up a cot and too wussy to sleep on the ground. Speaking of. How'd you get my daughter to go to sleep out here?"

I shake my head woefully. "I didn't. She's in the Prius."

He laughs loudly.

"Shh!" I say. But my mom doesn't stir. "Sorry," I add. "I just don't want to wake my mom."

"That's nice of you," he says back.

Little does he know it's not entirely altruistic. Sage though my mother may be, I don't need her critiques at this particular moment in time. "Hey, since you're here," I say, "can you help me make this fire more . . . fiery?"

He looks from me to the fire. I hold out my poker for him, but he just sets it down on the table and grabs two logs instead. One, the smaller one, he uses to flip the burning logs off the center area of the fire. He stirs the little glowing coals beneath them, fans away a bit of ash, and then replaces the logs, turned upside down so the black part is up, in a tidy Lincoln Log formation. The larger log in his left hand goes across this. He puts the right-hand log back on the unburnt pile and then crouches low, gets face to face with the fire, and blows one long, slow breath of air on the coals.

The fire bursts to life. Flames leap up to knee height, and I hear hisses and pops and then that wonderful sound of a happy campfire, the crackles and fizzles and snaps. Sparks light up the two feet above the fire, and smoke begins to ascend in earnest. Gently, I feel the heat climb all over the front of my body, and I sit back down on my sleeping bag to take it all in. "Nicely done," I say. "Thank you."

"No sweat," he says. "I like playing with fire."

"Is that meant to be some kind of double entendre?" I ask.

"No. I literally like playing with fires. I like building fires. I like staring at fires. I like poking fires with sticks."

"Should I be worried about arson?"

"Not in the slightest. Or, I should say, not more than you're worried about anyone with my genome. I am pretty sure this particular trait is on the Y chromosome."

I raise my eyebrow. "You think so? A lot of things that are put down to gender just come from the culture," I say. I realize I could be my mother verbatim right now. "Anyway, my mom can build a fire like nobody's business."

"I have no doubt of that. And Azalea will be the same. She likes knowing how to do things, all kinds of things. It's a great trait for the daughter of a chicken farmer."

I've noticed that about her. She wanted to use her compass for our out-and-back hike on a clearly marked trail. She listened attentively to my mom's lecture on edible mushrooms and how to make stinging nettle tea. She turned her marshmallows over the fire like an even browning was the meaning of life. "I really like that about her," I tell him. "She's good company, if studious."

"I was like that as a kid too," he says.

"Same here. Lots of passionate hobbies, lots of science documentaries and encyclopedia browsing. I guess it went away in my teens. I got more interested in staying in my lane."

"Grown-up life is all about choosing what to let in and what to keep out. But Lea's miles from that point. I tell her, 'If you're interested, let it in. Chase it down. See what you're capable of.'"

"You sound like my mom. She's the king of nerd enablers."

Dewey makes a face. "Don't let me hear you calling Lea a nerd. She'll take it personally, and in my opinion there's nothing nerdy about being a polymath."

"What's a polymath?"

"Someone who's good at several things."

"Ah. Well, I won't. But to clarify, nerdiness is not an insult to me. I'd like to be a polymath. I'd like to be the sort of person who knows what a polymath is without being told."

"When you're a gorgeous twentysomething living *la belle vie* in Los Angeles, you might be flattered by being called a nerd. When you are an actual nerd and in the fourth grade, you might feel differently."

"Do you think I'm gorgeous?" I ask.

Dewey raises a hand up at me. "Don't even. You've already friend zoned me. I don't have to go through the motions of flattering you for flattery's sake. Besides, you know exactly how you look. You had to literally throw your phone off a cliff to stop yourself from taking selfies."

I wince. "That sounds like something my mother would have said. Were you guys talking about me?"

He smiles. "Busted. I mean, I did ask her about you. Someone new and . . . interesting . . . comes into the neighborhood, you're gonna ask."

"And she told you I'm vain?" I ask sadly.

"She told me you are some kind of internet celebrity. Or you were. I assume the phone toss means you've quit."

"I'm taking some time off," I say. "A break. To get . . . ah . . ." I think of the sensation I feel here by the fire under the stars. "Replanted."

"And how is it going?" he asks.

"Extremely well," I admit. "Better than I thought it would be. It turns out half my reasons for being a phone addict were based on absolute nonsense."

"Such as?"

"I thought it made my life so much easier," I say. "I mean, maps, navigation, online shopping, banking apps, that sort of thing."

"I like all those things," he says.

"Me too. But only when I'm actually going someplace I've never been before or buying something I actually need or automating my bills. When I'm using maps to intricately plan trips I'll never have time to take or shopping online to kill time while waiting at the pharmacy or getting notifications about ups and downs in my retirement portfolio twice a day, then I hate those things. I never realized how completely draining they were. It's much less crazy making to just be still."

Dewey smiles gently into the fire. "Sounds like the replanting is going very well," he says.

"The trouble is, at some point I have to go back to real life."

Dewey frowns. "Do you?" he asks. "Do most addicts go back to using after rehab?"

I roll my eyes. "Phone addiction isn't the same as heroin addiction."

"Of course not," he says. "Phone addiction is much less likely to kill you right away."

My shoulders sag. "I'll admit, some of my game plan has involved trying to pretend that I never have to go back."

"Do you?" he asks.

"I do. It's my job. And it's just life. Even if it's a genuine addiction—"

"Which it very well may be . . ."

"I'm beginning to see that it might be," I push on. "Even then, there aren't very many people in this world who can totally avoid digital life. It's how we file our taxes, how we order pizzas, how we learn the news and talk to our friends and play music. My friends are scattered all over the world. We would have lost touch if we couldn't use Pictey."

"So what do they think of this total-abstinence plan?" Dewey asks.

I pause. "To be honest, I have no idea if they think anything about it. Either they haven't noticed, or they have but can't reach me about it. If I had to guess," I admit, "I'd say it's the former. I haven't really made that many real-life friends since college. And I haven't seen the college friends in years. They have husbands and babies. I have work and . . .

work. And when Mike was still alive, he was the best friend a girl could ever have."

Dewey nods. "It's hard to make friends in adulthood. I met some nice dads when Lea was small, and her mom's friends would drop a line from time to time, but now Lea picks her own friends and leaves me out of it, and we've all lost touch. That's what makes it so hard to walk away from social media," he adds. "It's the only way I get to see how my old friends are, see their kids grow up."

I get that. "It's a little thread of connection that feels too precious to break. Without it, the loneliness can really get to you."

"You're not lonely, are you? Because if so, I would like to be friends with you," says Dewey.

"We're already friends," I tell him. "Aren't we? I mean, you can't complain about being friend zoned if we're not friends."

He smiles. "Ok, then you have made one real-life friend recently. And I didn't even meet you on the internet."

I smile. "You know, the trouble is, if I hadn't tossed my phone, I don't think we would be friends."

"Really? Why's that?"

I look him right in the eye. "I think I might have already slept with you."

Dewey blushes. Even in the firelight I can see how pink he is. "Ah . . ." He coughs. "Do you have any beers at this campsite of yours?"

"The blue cooler," I say, pointing to the lockable ice chest my mom has placed farthest from our tent. "Bring me one, too, would you?"

When Dewey comes back, I say, "Sorry if I embarrassed you. But you always say exactly what you mean. I like it. I thought I'd give it a try."

He opens two cans and gives me the first. "I'm all for radical honesty, as long as it passes through the three gates," he says.

I look at him, surprised. "I didn't have you down for a Buddhist."

"Buddha didn't say that all speech should be true, kind, and necessary," he says. "Or at least not anywhere official. Its origination is still unknown. But it's a decent bar for me, as long as you count dad jokes as necessary."

I laugh. "I really thought it was the Buddha. I've attributed it to him many times. And no one has ever corrected me," I add. "Who do you think did say it? Rumi?"

"Probably not," says Dewey. "I read that Rumi's vote was for more liberal expression. He says, 'Go up to the roof at night in the city of the soul. Let everyone go up to their roofs and sing their notes!'"

"'Sing loud!'" I finish for him. This is one of my favorites. In my more active yoga days, I was a big fan of a little Rumi to start out the class.

Dewey looks at me and smiles. "You surprise me not at all," he says casually. "You're just a high-fashion internet celebrity quoting Rumi while backwoods camping."

"You either," I agree. "You're just a chicken farmer single parenting a polymath and discussing the great philosophers. In a hammock."

Dewey's eyes light up. "Do you want to see my hammock?" he asks.

"God, that sounds dirty." I laugh.

"It's not. It's the opposite. Hammock sex is an impossibility."

I try not to consider that too closely. If I do, I feel like I could prove him wrong. "Fine. Show me your hammock."

Dewey fumbles around behind him on the table and procures a flashlight. "Follow me."

I tag along to his truck. He removes a small item and shows it to me. It is a tiny bag made out of parachute fabric. It's the size of a venti latte.

"What's that?"

"That's the hammock," he says. "And this is the rain fly and bug net," he adds, handing me another bag, slightly larger, but not much. "And this is my sleeping bag," he says with finality. He grabs a compression sack and leads me to a niche in the woods. "These," he says, producing two black straps, "go around those two trees." He points out two trees a good two cars' length apart. He puts the straps up, high, where I could barely reach them. Then he uses carabiners to connect one end of the tiny latte-size parachute to each tree strap. Before my eyes it unfolds all the way to the other. "Ta da!" he whispers.

"You're gonna sleep in *that*?" I ask.

"Yup. Climb in, and I'll show you how the rest goes up."

Gracelessly, I try to get myself into the hammock. This is not a beach hammock, a giant piece of flat canvas held by an iron stand. It's a floppy bit of fabric in a weave thinner than most of my panties, hanging nearly at chin height. I look for an entry point and wonder if I'll put my hand right through the delicate silk.

"Go to the middle and hop up on it backward, like a playground swing," Dewey tells me. "Then swing your legs around."

I do this. The fabric bunches up under me, and to my surprise, I do not fall on my ass. I swing my legs around, and the fabric opens up into a wide sling that cradles me head to toe and rocks gently side to side. "Oooh," I say.

"Yup," he says. "And now we bug-proof you."

I watch from my comfy repose as Dewey knots a bit of clothesline tightly from one tree strap to the other, running it just over the top of the ends of the hammock but well above where my body actually is in the middle. With a few deft moves he clips up a mosquito net that falls to the ground with weights.

"Wow," I say.

"Now, in cases of possible rain, I would add a fly," he tells me. "But the forecast is clear tonight, and I like the view."

"Me too," I say. "But my butt is cold."

"No problem," he says. He grabs his sleeping bag, which turns out to be almost double width on the bottom but normally sized on the top. Dewey crawls under the net so he is inside the little netting tent with me and snaps the sleeping bag, large side down, around the whole burrito that is my body plus hammock, leaving only my head uncovered. "And that's the works. How do you like it?"

"I love it," I tell him. "I'm up so high! I'm sleeping like a monkey! But what if I have to pee?"

"Do you?" he asks.

"Yes," I say.

"Unzip the bag halfway," he says, and I do. "Sit up. Now swing your legs back out, and then"—with this, he puts his hands around my waist—"jump."

I jump. He catches my weight and eases me to the ground. I stand there for a moment, toe to toe, his head a foot higher than mine, staring into his chest. I watch it rise and fall from the exertion of the catch. Neither of us moves.

"All right," he says, after a few long seconds. "Off you go."

I walk away, trying very hard to think friend-zone thoughts.

When I come back from a very, very, very faraway pee spot, I find myself seeing double. Directly under the first hammock, hung from the same strong trees, is a second, with a second overbag. Dewey is standing at the fire. The unburnt wood is moved off the coals to the edges of the pit, and the coals themselves are sizzling.

"Did you pee on that fire?" I ask.

Dewey smiles. "Yes. I hope that's ok. I'm getting sleepy. Time to hit the hay."

"Over there?" I ask, pointing to the bunk-hammocks.

"Yep. Do you want the top bunk or the bottom bunk?"

"Whichever," I say, surprised to find I am agreeing with this arrangement.

"The top one, then," he says. "So you can see better."

"That's really nice," I say. "Thank you." I climb into the hammock, a little less hesitantly this time. As I zip up my bag, I see Dewey standing in front of me, bending, then climbing into his own.

"If you get stiff," he calls up, "make your body diagonal in the hammock. And scooch up a bit so your head is higher than your—yes, like that."

"Are you just staring at my butt?" I ask.

"Through a seven-hundred-fill goose-down bag, yes."

"Enjoy," I say.

"I will," he replies. "How's your view?"

I look up. It's tree leaves, the undersides, branches, a few low clouds, and sky. "Amazing," I tell him. "I am up on the roof at night in the city of my soul."

"Are you going to sing your notes?" he asks.

"My heart is already singing," I tell him. "It's singing loud."

PAIGE

Another day, another #shoppingspree! You guys know most of the time when I'm at home I do a ton of shopping online. I mean, great deals, two day shipping, who's with me? But I think I might be missing out on one of the side perks of shopping, the in-person browse. Today is all about spending QT with the QT in my life, and I guess that means popping into every little store in downtown #Copperidge. Surprised how much I enjoyed the sights, flavors, and people to be found in each spot. Not surprised by how much I spent! #YOLO #dearvisalcanexplain

Do you have a favorite small retailer? Tag and share below! xo Mia

Imagine, if you will, a woman in her middle thirties, very woman shaped, a bit understyled, a bit overclothed, skin the color of fluorescent lighting. Add in her sister, who she barely knows: more than ten years younger, built for bikinis and beer ads, in a coed-chic orange cotton dress with both wrists swathed in bandages. I have a PhD in computer science. Jessica flunked out of communicating. She has my mother's eyes, round and innocent, and bright-pink lipstick painted in a bow. I also have eyes and lips. That is all we have in common.

Now we are out on the streets of downtown Copperidge, outside a high-end clothing purveyor, staring each other down.

"We need to go in there," she is telling me. "Mia would want you to. Call her if you like."

"I will not be calling Mia Bell to ask her which overpriced resort-town boutique to shop in. Don't you think she has better things to do with her time?" I ask. "Besides, I can see the price tags through the window. They are selling short-sleeved sweaters for two hundred dollars! Bad enough you have to store a garment that is only appropriate three days a year. Why would you go broke for it?"

"Ok, Paige, I'm not going to tell you how to do your job, but that sweater is exactly like something Mia would wear."

"Then she is wasting her money," I say. "Doesn't mean I have to do that."

"But you're supposed to *be* her right now," says Jessica. "Forget how you dress"—she waves at me up and down like she's trying to obscure her own vision of my outfit—"and channel the client."

I exhale aggressively. "Ok. The client. Let's see. She's a self-absorbed shopaholic and has infinite closet space, and anything she wants is given to her for free. I'm channeling."

"You sound like you don't even like her," Jessica points out.

"I don't know her," I say. Then add, "Not really."

"Well, I do. She'd go in there," says Jessica.

I sigh and get my scare quotes ready. "Since I took over, 'she' already went to a bookstore and a yarn store. 'She' has spent almost two hundred dollars being 'herself.' Can't we do things that aren't shopping?"

Jessica shakes her head. "If she were spending the week in Copperidge, she'd be spending it shopping, going to art galleries, and eating at high-end restaurants. She'd be going to hear music and drink at wine bars. She might go for a sail. She'd definitely go to the gym. Some kind of hip class unique to the location. Maybe a bike ride."

I blink at my sister. "Ok, forget Mia. We're here for you, mostly, aren't we? What do *you* want to do?"

Jessica smiles, victorious. "I want to go in there." She points at the store in question.

I roll my eyes, but at the same time I start for the entrance. If it's what Jessica wants, it's what we'll do. But I won't like it. I fear it will be one of those stores where the first thing the shopgirl tells me is that they don't sell anything in my size. I hate that. Since I have no control over other people's manners, and culture shifts around weight discrimination are going to take as long as culture shifts around everything else, I should just stop being bothered by that one of these days. Maybe today. Maybe I'll try on a nice too-small short-sleeved itchy angora sweater that I would wear exactly once. Maybe I'll stretch out the sleeves on purpose.

Jessica trots up next to me. "Ok, what we want to do is watch out for mirrors and size tags. Mia is a waif. She doesn't eat any foods that are white."

"Is that a common dietary preference?" I ask.

"It's an extremely unpleasant one," Jessica says. "I wish I could do it."

"There is a certain dissonance between those two sentences."

"You wouldn't understand. You've never worried about your weight."

"I worried about it plenty when I was younger," I tell her. "Now I have learned to trust my doctor, who assures me I'm perfectly healthy. I no longer have anything to worry about."

"That's good! But. Some people don't operate that way."

"How do some people operate?"

"They worry about what other people think. They wish they could look more perfect."

I look at Jessica, trying to understand what she would possibly change about her body. "Jessica," I say. "There is plenty of good evidence showing that dieting is a fool's game. If your general metrics indicate good health, then you simply are the size you are. Your dress size, in and of itself, is neither good nor bad, just a neutral fact."

"Where does being suicidal fall within my general health metrics?" she asks.

Hm. "I suppose your cognitive perception errors do make self-acceptance quite difficult," I admit. "The meds will improve that. Now, let's get this over with. You point out things Mia would wear, and then I will photograph them, and then we will leave."

Jessica shakes her head. "How on earth did you get this job? Just follow me."

She walks in and smiles at the salesgirl, who is in fact a man, forcing me to note a weakness in my lexicon. He is a man wearing a sports jacket with a T-shirt. I find those sorts of outfits to be very intimidating. They look like what the bad boyfriend in Hallmark movies would wear. "Hello," he says. "Welcome. Are you new to our store?"

"Yes," replies Jessica, which I believe is a mistake, because now he will continue to talk to us. "I'm not from here."

"Oh, fun!" he says. "Visiting your sister?"

I look up at him. "How did you know we were sisters?" I ask.

He looks at me, amused. "Are you kidding? You two look exactly alike."

I turn to face my sister and narrow my eyes, trying to see any similarity. Maybe this is just something he says to flatter whomever he thinks is the richer member of the party. Clearly I am the one with the money, as I have a purse, a contraption specifically designed for holding

216

money. Whereas Jessica seems to prefer to carry her girly ephemera around in a free-with-purchase makeup bag covered in sequins.

"Don't we just?" says Jessica. I ignore her social ministrations. "We need something cute to wear for tonight," she tells him.

"What's tonight?" he asks.

"Girls' night," she replies happily. "We're going to go out and indiscriminately flirt with men."

My eyebrows shoot up.

"I'm afraid that at this boutique you'll only find clothes that appeal to very discriminate men," the guy says. "But if you don't mind that, I can help you out."

What follows is a process so boring and onerous I can't even begin to describe it. It is the part where one would fast-forward if one were watching an otherwise tolerable romantic comedy. As I am subjected to it, I marvel that this place stays open. Who would possibly put themselves through such an ordeal without a suicidal sister forcing them? Imagine a small try-on room with a mirror of its own, but every time you put something on, people shout at you to come out, come out and show them! This is no way to find clothing that fits you while providing durability and comfort. Everything takes three times longer than it should due to questions like *How's my butt look in this one?* By the end I think I would be happy if I never had to consider anyone's rear again.

All that said, Jessica appears to smile through much of the process. Some studies have shown that smiling can actually cause serotonin release, and so I insist I buy her some of the ridiculous overpriced, impractical clothing she likes, to keep the smiles coming. She then insists I *also* buy some ridiculous overpriced, impractical clothing for myself. Though I cannot stress enough that what I already own is very versatile and could be worn anywhere we go this evening, and also that the job of clothes is to adequately cover one's privates and that is all, I eventually give in. I buy some stretchy jeans, which feel close enough to sweatpants, and a gauzy ecru linen sweater. The sweater cannot be worn without sufficient underpinnings due to its airy construction out of what looks like the remnants of an exhumed mummy. (I also have to buy the underpinnings, but they at least are soft.)

I note with some pride that buying clothes from this racket at least provides a living wage to their creators—everything in here turns out to be fair trade. After we've taken several pictures of everything, including the shop person, Jessica makes me go into the fitting room again and put the new clothes on to wear out of the store, as though I came in in nothing but a flour sack. Then, clad to her satisfaction, I positively demand we get on to the eating portion of being influencers.

—

Over nice sweaty glasses of mint limeade at a nearby outdoor café with a strange profusion of purse dogs, Jessica hands me her phone, and I give her mine, trying not to be neurotic about the idea of handing someone an unlocked minicomputer of mine own. We start scrolling through the new photo options for my next Mia post. I am startled to see how good they are.

"Jessica!" I exclaim around my stainless steel straw. "These are stupendous photographs. Much better than mine. How did you learn to use your camera so capably?"

"Gee, thanks," she says. "It's a class in my major. Content creation for social media."

"Content creation!" I exclaim. "That's what they call taking photos?"

"And writing posts. Yes. That's exactly what you're doing for Mia. That's what Mia does, normally. Content creation. I mean, you work for Pictey; you know this. They are in fact just content providers."

"They certainly are not. They are a social media platform. They connect the world one hashtag at a time."

"That's what you think," she says. "But how do they make money?"

"Through ad sales," I say.

"And do you need people to be connected to sell ads?"

"Certainly. You need them to come back over and over again to feel connected. Connected to their friends and their 'friends,' like Mia, who they would normally not have access to."

"But what makes them come back? The fact that Mia is there, or the fact that Mia posts constantly and you might have something new to see every time you return?"

I must stop to consider this.

"If users just wanted access to Mia, she'd never have to post again. She could just be chatting directly to friends, meeting new people privately through *their* posts, interacting one on one. But if that were enough, she never would have hired you."

I think of the speed with which her follower numbers fall between my posts. And then the quick rate of rebound after just one new picture.

"How much does she post on an average day?" I ask.

"It depends. Sometimes thirty times. Sometimes ten. And not on a schedule, so you get that random-reinforcement effect."

"Are you taking UX engineering classes too?" I ask, surprised at her understanding of random reinforcement.

"What exactly do you think a communications major is?" she asks. "Or for that matter a college degree? Everyone has to take some psych and some English and some arts and some comp sci."

"Well. I didn't realize that. I thought that was only at good schools."

"Colorado *is* a good school! Jeezaloo, Paige."

"Mom says that," I note. "Pick some photos. We need to get cracking if we're going to do thirty posts today."

"You only did three yesterday, so we don't have to do much to improve," she says. "If Mia is watching, you're already fired."

"She's not watching," I say confidently. I am starting to get an inkling of why that might be. "But I agree—we need to step it up. Thirty posts! My goodness. It takes me half an hour to write one. Mia Bell must be a very busy woman." I set down my limeade and force myself to make some eye contact with Jessica. "Jessica, I would like you to know that I'm very glad you are helping me with this, and further pleased that you are not dead, as even achieving ten posts a day would be a struggle without you."

"It's my pleasure," she says. "It's actually quite a relief to be doing this with you."

"Oh?" I ask.

"I've been in the hospital for a long time. Mostly wasting time and Mom and Dad's money because I'm too freaked out to be totally unsupervised, and trying to make friends with the nurses out of loneliness. The people who came to see me early on were obsessed with my suicide attempt and talked about nothing else. Self-care, cry for help, was it their fault, blah blah blah. No one but you came to see me later on, and you don't seem that freaked out by what I did. You're just on to the next thing now, even though you're walking through town with a girl covered in bandages."

"Actually, I was very freaked out. I needed to do a special breathing technique at one point, one that I have not used in a very long time."

"Well, you didn't let on," she says. "And you also don't seem to think I should act happy right now, or sad, or any particular way. So it's good. You're the right woman for this job."

"Whereas you," I note, "are the right person for my job. You take very representational photos with excellent use of light, and you seem to instinctively sense what Mia would do in any given situation."

"Thank you. On that note, Mia would talk about how this restaurant provides stainless steel straws with the limeade."

"Very true. Take a picture of my limeade," I tell her.

"Wrong," she says.

"Wrong?" I repeat dumbly.

"Look at the limeade," she tells me.

I look. There is a glass with a straw and a sprig of mint. A third of it is filled with pale-greenish liquid and an icy slurry. "Should it be . . . full?"

"Yes, it should."

"So I need to order a second sugary beverage just to take a picture of it, even though I have no interest in drinking it?"

"That's right."

"Excess sugar can have a detrimental effect on the human gut biome," I tell her.

Jessica shakes her head and says, "You really aren't a natural at this." When the server walks by, she catches her eye and asks what else is served with the stainless steel straw.

"Anything you like," she says. "We have as many of those straws as we have tall boys."

"In that case, will you bring us one of these rosemary gin and tonics?" she asks, pointing to an entry on the cocktail list.

"What on earth!" I exclaim.

"But use half tonic, half soda water," she adds, ignoring me. "We're watching our sugar consumption." With that she raises her eyebrows and wiggles them at me.

"No problemo," the server says. "That actually sounds like it will be really good. I'll be right back with that."

I send a sharp look at Jessica the moment the server steps toward the bar.

"What?" she asks.

"Alcohol is contraindicated in cases of severe depression," I announce. "It's going to reduce the efficacy of the medications and certainly just make you feel bad too."

"It's for you," she tells me. "Post two or three shopping pics now so you can drink the gin when it arrives."

"At this hour of the day?" I ask. "I don't think I need to be drinking."

"Maybe you don't," says Jessica. "But *I* need you to be drinking. If you're going to succeed at the internet, we need to turn down the volume on that noisy brain of yours."

MIA

My mom's landline rings the day after we get back from camping. I don't know what to do. Do I answer it? Where is it? Does it have caller ID? I follow the sound, but it's coming from the base charger of the cordless phone, not the handset. There's no display on the base. I wander around Mom's house looking for the actual phone part until it stops ringing. The machine picks up, a click, a whir, and I hear the voice of a stranger asking for me, saying she heard I was a certified yoga instructor, and could I teach a vinyasa class at her studio later today. My heart swells. I go outside to find my mom.

She's sitting in the garden but not gardening. Just sitting there. I think she might be meditating until she sees me and waves me over. I notice she's got wet eyes.

"What are you doing?"

"Listening to the bees. They sound sad."

I listen. "Really? Bees get sad?"

"I'm not sure, actually. Mostly I just said that to see if you'd believe me."

"What are you really doing?" I ask.

"Thinking about Andy."

"Happy or sad thoughts?" I ask.

"All the happy thoughts are sad," she tells me. "To be honest, I seem to be stuck in the mourning process a bit. Having you here makes me see that."

I sit down next to her, legs outstretched to avoid a row of greens, and put my arm around her shoulders. "Would you like to come do yoga with me?" I ask her. It's Mom who first taught me yoga, when I was a small child. It was a little more counterculture back then. She did it with incense burning and lots of chants.

I don't chant very much. I used to chant at the end of class—I've got a nice enough voice, and the sutras are a beautiful aspect of the yogic tradition—but people always bitched about it on Yelp. They suggested I play Coldplay at the end of class instead. So I played Coldplay.

I wonder now if that was the right choice. I wonder if I should have kept chanting and kept selling Lynnsey's handmade yoga shirts and never tried to promote my yoga studio online in the first place. I'd probably still be teaching classes of six people three times a day in that first stifling little studio and surviving on my credit cards. There was an integrity about it. But also a poverty.

Are those my only two choices? I wonder now. Playing to the masses or playing small?

I look at my mom. Her eyes are glossy and unfocused, like she's not there. I wonder how much time she spends out here sitting lost in thoughts of him. It's a worry. "Do you remember this one, Mom?" I ask. I breathe in and form the sound *Ah* and sing from below and into the note that begins the chant. Then I move through the Sanskrit syllables; my voice, which is breathy, not rich like my teacher's, rests on the note until I reach the end. "*Asatoma sadgamaya,*" I sing, letting my voice play on each of the *ah*s of *gamaya*. Then I sing the syllables again, now climbing and falling along a little melody as I learned from Mom all those years ago. Then I finish, one more repetition of the Sanskrit, ending just one tone below the one I started on. "*Asatoma sadgamaya.*"

Mom smiles. "What a beautiful voice you have. All air. No earth."

"I probably need to eat more eggplant," I say, referring to the Ayurvedic tradition that would relate to a deficiency of earthiness. A lack of groundedness. I am thinking of how it felt to sink my feet into the gravel by the firepit, my hands into the soil near the parsnips, how rooted I feel to this piece of earth right now. "But I don't feel a deficiency."

"It wasn't a criticism," she says. "It isn't all criticism, you know."

"It's mostly criticism," I say, but gently.

"Lead us from the unreal to the real," she says to me in response. That's one translation of the syllables I sang a moment ago. I suspect her perception is the real and mine the unreal.

"And from death to immortality," I finish, which is the end of the prayer that my chant began.

She leans her head on my shoulder, and I have to brace myself to keep from tipping over. I uncross my legs, bend at the knees, plant my feet on the ground, make a third leg of the stool with my back arm, and still have a hand free to rub my mother's back. She's critical, yes. But I love her. I didn't realize how sad she still was. I think of how long I've privately grieved my dog. What, then, is the appropriate amount of time for Mom to grieve her son?

"When you're here, in the Rockies, where we all spent so much time when you were kids, I miss him more," she tells me. "That's why I usually come to visit you instead."

I frown. "I planned the wedding here so we could be closer to Andy," I admit. "I didn't think it would upset you. I'm sorry."

"You know," she says, ignoring my apology, "I was married here in the mountains, just like you would have been. And then your brother was born here, because I was a hippie and I thought it would be the best place to start his life."

I nod. "And then you realized that Dad was a mistake, but before you resolved to leave him, you had an oops, and Dad didn't want

another child, and you had to move to Denver while you were pregnant and had a toddler, because that's where the jobs were," I complete.

She shakes her head. "That's not exactly true. I've said it so many
times it became our family history. But actually, it was my *asatoma*—my
unreality, my delusion, or my falseness," she translates, as well versed
in Sanskrit as she is in anything else she takes an interest in. "The truth
is, I knew Dad and I weren't going to work out, and he knew it, too,
long before you came along. But at the same time, I was the happiest I
had ever been in my life. Being Andy's mother changed me as a person.
Every day he made me smile and gave me purpose and made sense of
my life. Babies are hard, and your father didn't help much, but Andy
was an incredible little kid."

I smile. This doesn't surprise me. Andy wasn't perfect, but he was
the perfect older brother for me. He kept Mom from showing up at talent show nights in her ponchos and broomstick skirts and from packing
a lunch with hard-boiled eggs that would smell up my locker for days.
He is the one who took me by the hand the week before I started middle
school and helped me figure out what to wear, how to find my tribe,
how to let go of my stuffed-panda backpack and my bubblegum-pink
hair bows without letting go of the things that really made me who I
am. He took me along on his cross-country training runs and winked
at my new friends in the hallway and made me feel like the coolest girl
in the world when he would buy me a contraband Mountain Dew after
school.

In fact, now that I think about it, I realize that Azalea, in time, will
need an Andy of her own.

My mom goes on. "Motherhood made me so happy, in fact, that
I decided to ask your father if we could have another baby before we
went our separate ways. I knew I would be on my own, but I also knew
I wanted another child, with all my heart. So we made you on purpose.
It was your dad's final kindness to me before we parted."

My mouth falls open. "You're kidding. I wasn't an oops?"

"Not even a little bit."

"Well, but Dad didn't want me, though," I say. This is a fact of life that I've come to live with in something like comfort, like the mole on my stomach that rubs against the waistband of only one pair of pants.

"Eh. I wanted you enough for two people," Mom tells me. "But at the time, having a baby on your own on purpose was viewed as not just foolish but irresponsible. So I crafted a story that sounded more reasonable. And it became my story, in time."

Andy's words flash back to me. "Andy always said 'reasonable' was highly overrated."

My mom looks toward the sky. "See, Andy? She listened to you, always you. Never me."

"I listened to you. Sometimes to the detriment of my self-esteem," I add with a gentle smile.

"But sometimes not," my mom says unapologetically. That's fine. I wasn't angling for an apology. Besides, it's true that in our little family unit, I preferred what my brother had to say most times. With him gone, I don't always know how my mom and I are meant to fit together. That's probably why we've spent so much time apart.

"In the end," she says now, while I am listening, and listening carefully, "I told your brother the truth when he was in college. I told him our family was the way it was on purpose, and with no regrets. I told him my *sat*—my reality. And when we were camping, and his name came up, and I saw the look cross your face, the oh-no-she's-going-to-cry-again look, I realized that somehow I'd never told you, even after all this time. I let you keep on thinking that Andy was somehow different from you, that your histories were different."

Mom takes my hand. "Mia, the only difference between the two of you is that he was born in the clouds, and you were born on the ground, and he went back into the clouds, and you are still here with me."

I look into her eyes and then touch my own face in surprise. It is as if the tears I feel in my eyes are running down her face, dripping off her chin.

Sometimes when I am alone, completely alone, and my phone is on silent, and the apartment is dark, I pretend I live in a world where Andy and Mike are still here. I pretend Mike is in bed by my legs with his chin up on my knees, and Andy calls me on the phone to talk about some nice guy he just met or a jerk he has to deal with at the office. I like to imagine that these two souls know each other now, in the next world, that they look after each other and sometimes they gossip about me.

"I've always felt . . . ," I say to her, wondering why I didn't say it sooner and then knowing that until now, I've never had to. "I felt that when Andy died, something about our relationship died too. He was the one who made sense of us all together."

She nods. "That's true. But even now, he can still help us figure it out." She sits up straight and takes me by the hand that was until now resting on her back, and she presses it to her heart. "What would he say to us if he were here right now?"

I know the answer to that without even a moment's consideration, as if he were standing before me holding up cue cards and stamping his feet. "He would say, *Mia, it's reasonable to go back home and shrug off all the bad stuff and get back to work, just like you've always done. It's reasonable to ignore the cute chicken guy and his awkward daughter and your sometimes slightly annoying mom and go back to life as it was. But if that's not what you want to do . . .*" My voice trails off, my throat tight with emotion.

"*Reasonable is overrated,*" finishes my mother.

"Yes," I say, my voice wobbly.

Mom wraps me up in one of her twenty-second hugs. "You know by now how lucky you are that you didn't get married to Tucker," she tells me when she finally lets go.

I nod. I do know.

"No matter what you told everyone—and in your case it really is everyone—about your plans and your happiness and what you thought you wanted, your *sat*, your reality, was always there. Sitting in the corner. Being real. Waiting."

I think of Tucker's stupid but correct text message. As annoying as it was, it came just in the nick of time. I tried not to think about how he was wrong for me, just as I tried to distract myself from my grief over Mike, just as I pushed down all the heartbreak when we lost Andy. But those things all caught up with me. "It's better," I realize aloud, "if you just run at the truth full speed."

The truth, the sorrow, the grief, the joy.

My mom smiles and brushes a tear from my cheek. "Smarter than your mother after just a little while offline," she says. "Think of what you'll know when you're sixty-five."

I consider the last couple of weeks. I arrived here with a plan, a big plan, that would shape every moment of my future. I told everyone who would listen, which was a lot of people. When it fell through, I faked it, and when I couldn't fake it anymore, I did a disappearing act. But while I have been disappeared, I've found something in myself I didn't know I had.

And while that has been absolutely wonderful, I can't just stay in hiding for the rest of my life.

Or rather, I can, but where will that leave me?

PART II
MIA CULPAS

PAIGE

Gorgeous morning in the Rockies and I'm feeling high! Not that kind of high, LOL! (the munchies sound like my worst nightmare, amirite?) But #lifeisgood anyway—we're going to get out today and have adventures TBD, check out a few more #summercocktails, and definitely catch an act at the @DillonAmphitheater, and of course, I can't forget to talk to you guys, who make it all worthwhile. Let me know what you're looking forward to today, and if you need a boost keep coming back to the feed, because we'll be posting all the good stuff as it happens . . . xo Mia

In the end, Jessica and I achieve ninety-six posts in the next four days. We post the clothes, the shopping, the meals, the drinks, the parks, the music, and our room at the inn, which has been made up beautifully, outfitted with an extra robe and towels for my sister, and filled with garden cuttings while we were gone. When we are not posting, we are pushing the little heart button on comments, trying to respond to as many as humanly possible, and desperately losing control of the constant flood of DMs.

On Saturday, Jessica sleeps until the last call for breakfast. I get up at five a.m. to start dealing with the feed again and work on it nonstop until we go down to the dining room together. Though I am loath to give too much credit to Mia, being her is starting to feel, I have to admit, like a bit of a chore.

After I have my utterly delicious eggs with smoked trout and chives, Jessica instructs me to go upstairs and change into my "workout clothes" so she can continue eating an amount of bacon that may in fact count as a self-harming behavior. I decide not to mention it, focusing instead on the term *workout clothes*.

"All my clothes are designed for activity," I tell her. "I buy very stretchy pants."

"Yeah, I've seen 'em," says Jessica, not sounding pleased about it. "I guess what you need for today is something you can bike in that will not be too hot that you look kind of cute in."

"We are going to cycle? In the Rocky Mountains? I don't think that level of exertion is in order for either of us."

"It's a flat trail."

I look pointedly at the mountains rising up above the town outside the windows of the dining room. "How can that be?" I ask.

Jessica shrugs. "Railroad something something? Anyway, we'll take it easy. We'll have to stop constantly for photos anyway."

"Do you have a bike?" I ask her. "I do not have a bike."

"Nah, it got stolen at school."

I raise one eyebrow.

"Oh, stop it. Bikes get stolen at Berkeley too. And Harvard or Oxford or wherever you went to undergrad."

"That was also Berkeley," I say. "I don't know about bikes there. I never had one. I haven't ridden a bike since I was a kid."

"So never, then," she says.

"No," I say. "I had a childhood. Really! I had a vivid childhood and a challenging adolescence." I say no more. "I will bicycle with you, but in normal clothes. If I notice you looking fatigued, I will request that we break or even stop."

"Understood," says Jessica. "Anyway, it's good for me to exercise. It's on my resilience checklist in two places."

"What exactly is that?" I ask. "Your resilience checklist?"

"The things I am going to do to get undepressed," she tells me. "The psychiatrist at the hospital said it's my summer job."

I frown. It occurs to me that I was imagining that helping impersonate Mia Bell was her summer job.

"Very well," I say. "What are the other items on your checklist?"

She whips out her phone and opens something. "One: connection with others. That's this," she says, pointing back and forth between her and me. "Two: daily activity. Biking in this case."

"Ok," I say, seeing that her two summer jobs are not incompatible. "What else?"

"Three: time spent in nature."

I nod. "Cortisol levels. I read that study."

She shrugs. "Also nature is nice," she adds.

I shrug, having not noticed that to be true.

"Four," she continues. "Meditation or mindfulness practice."

"Oh boy," I say.

"The doctor says it works!" she tells me.

"I've seen the science. I just don't care to sit around breathing all the time," I tell her.

"Yoga counts."

I say nothing.

"Mia likes yoga," she goes on.

"Move along," I say.

"Number five: sleep. I figure I'll get plenty of that once they have a bed for me at the loony bin."

I clear my throat.

"What?" she asks.

"Well, since you asked, those things are all very time and effort consuming. Exercise is tiring; sleep isn't always up to you; nature is cold and wet and has bugs. Connection takes work and leaves you open to all kinds of hurts. And meditation is . . . well . . . dull."

She looks at me with surprise and concern. "But . . . what's the alternative? Misery and disconnection and abject failure?"

I blanch. "Of course not. After you're discharged from the center, you'll just finish your course requirements as quickly as possible at a local college and get a job promptly. Then you'll have plenty to fill your time, and money and health insurance besides."

Jessica makes a face. "But I need to learn resilience," she says. "My coursework and career come second to my mental health."

"Well, I suppose so, yes. But you needn't worry. By that time your medications will be working, and you'll feel perfectly fine," I say to her. "You won't need to be resilient anymore."

Jessica looks down. "I'm not sure that's the case for everyone," she says.

"It will be for you," I say. "The meds take tweaking, but they'll do all the work. No need for all the other stuff." After all, look at me. Right?

"What's wrong with doing both?" she asks. "The meds and the meditation?"

"It's not expedient," I say with finality. This conversation has made me feel irrationally defensive. Like my methods of coping are somehow being cast into doubt. "I'm going to go change now. Into my 'workout' clothes. Did you get some pictures of breakfast?" I ask her.

"Plenty," she calls back. "They're in your shared folder."

"Thank you," I say. "I'll be back down after I change and post."

As I walk upstairs, I mutter to myself. "Probably all pictures of bacon," I grumble. "Resilience checklists," I add. "Meditation! Why does it always have to be meditation?" It sounds like Karrin was her doctor.

Back in the room, I sit on the bed. I scroll quickly through the miles of comments for Mia. Many are nice, some are neutral, but some are complaining that it's ten a.m. mountain time and she hasn't posted in an hour. Some are trolls telling her to "get dead." Some are people saying how they wish they could afford such a nice trip or that they feel depressed about how much "Mia" can eat each day without gaining weight or that it must be nice to have stores and restaurants giving you free things all day. People! Get over yourselves!

I know the real Mia would let all these things stand, but I want to shout at them, *Stop all your whining and complaining! I paid for all those things! With money I've saved from never having an actual life!* In my mind I indulge the inner scream even further: *And I'm not even Mia, you dolts! I'm a complete stranger with a big butt, and I bulk buy underpants, and you can't tell the difference.*

Instead of typing that, I zap the worst trolls and then do my breathing exercise. In four, hold four, pause four, out four. Then I post an artful picture of Cary's dining room with the mountains out the windows and start to type the caption.

> Even on my #honeymoon, there are times when I feel overwhelmed by all the tasks ahead. I was reminded to take time out for meditation after breakfast.

I pause. A new notification pops down from the top of my screen. It says no offense but ur posts r so boring zzzzzzzzz.

No offense.

Something in me gets loose. It starts working my thumbs.

> But rather than sit and do nothing like you entitled nitwits, I'm going to try some more practical

ways of pursuing my goals, such as working harder instead of killing hours of every workday on social media, saving money instead of buying everything I see advertised on some influencer's feed, and being alone with my thoughts instead of forcing someone else to create constant sources of entertainment for me in every second of my day.

Consider this: maybe if your relationship with technology requires you to sit prone in a mindless trance for forty-five minutes per day to recover, you should just get off of social media for pity's sake and go take a nice walk!

I get hold of myself. Do another round of square breathing. Switch off my phone. Remind myself there is a reason I'm not a real influencer.

I won't actually post my little rant, as nice as it felt to type it into the prompt. It's not that I don't believe what I've written. It's just that I realize how impossible what I suggest is for most people. Most people don't want to work all the time or pinch every penny or spend hours alone with no company. They want to scroll Pictey, or whatever their internet poison is, and online shop and exchange messages endlessly back and forth with strangers, because they actually think, in that moment, that it might make them feel *better*. And probably, it often does.

I have met these people, in the comments, the DMs, the tags. I think I once even could have been one of those people. Before. But living that way—all the fear and comparison and feelings and vulnerability—was unsustainable for me, and back then they didn't know about mindfulness and resilience. They knew about Prozac. In very high doses. Doses I keep high intentionally, even years and years after my last depression, because without them, the world might still be too scary.

I think about Jessica now. I remember how frightening it felt in those early days to be drugged up to the gills and handed fistfuls of Valium and told to go home and get on with it. I couldn't sleep, but I couldn't get out of bed either. It didn't feel like anything I took was working, and I was afraid of myself, and I was ashamed of what I'd done, what I'd wanted to do. My father was terrified, my mother was disgraced, and my little sister was confused. I suppose in that time, a little Daily Activity in Nature would have helped me a great deal. A center for suicidal ideation and a resilience checklist would have meant the world.

I throw down my phone and pull on my Costco travel pants, which feature four-way multistretch and a few zippered pockets for my things. On top I wear one of my favorite shirts, a soft, well-worn cotton T-shirt with a nice scoop neck in an appealing shade of dark green. When Jessica opens the door, I pose with hands on hips. "I am cute and ready to cycle!" I tell her with as much fake enthusiasm as I can bring. I stuff my phone in one of the numerous pockets. "Let us go get some gentle healing activity in the cortisol-soothing environs of nature!"

She laughs at me, which means she can't tell I'm upset. "Yes, let's. Are you done here?"

I nod. "I'm done."

"Good. Hand over your phone, and I'll put in our destination. We need to get to the outfitters in the next twenty minutes or so to make our tour."

"It's a tour?" I ask as I obey her instructions.

"Yes," she says. "We're getting a private guided tour of the Vail Pass—both up- and downhill. Hopefully the guide has a cute butt, because we are going to be staring at it for the rest of the day."

———

I'm not sure how she predicted it, but the tour guide is a handsome fellow indeed, his skin as brown as mine is white, his eyes sparkly, and his voice a pleasant, lilting southern accent. He grew up in North Carolina, put himself through NYU as a bike messenger, and now is a biochemist in Denver. I find his short, broad frame and not-insignificant biceps to be attractive enough to reduce my earlier upset. Normally I would be satisfied to enjoy these attributes from afar, but being Mia Bell has made me bold. And besides, Jessica has given this man's employer my credit card number in exchange for guiding us through a very well-marked path the width of a golf cart with no turns or spurs and no possibility of getting lost. So that means talking to me is probably the true nature of his job.

"Why are you doing bike tours, Tim?" I ask him as soon as our bikes are fitted to our satisfaction and we are underway. "Don't they impinge on your personal time?"

"Not at all. I'd be out on my bike right now anyway, but I'd be alone. This way I have company, and I get paid for it," he tells me happily. "Plus, I'm on my second year of a postdoc."

"Ah," I say. "Well then."

"What does that mean?" asks Jessica, who can bike much faster than me and sort of drops back whenever she wants to be in our conversation, only to leave at every quiet lull.

"It means he is at or below the national poverty line," I tell her. "And he'll soon be totally unemployed."

"Not totally," he corrects. "I will still be a guide for Summit Cycles."

"I note that you have a very sunny disposition," I tell him. "Was this in evidence before you became a regular practitioner of daily activity in nature?"

He smiles. "There is no before that," he tells me. "I grew up biking outside. I never stopped. That said, I'm pretty cheery in the summer in general."

"Of course, that phenomenon is well studied as it relates to vitamin D," I tell him.

"Sure. But unless I had my D levels tested monthly throughout the year, we couldn't separate my pleasure at cycling outdoors from the benefits of the extra vitamins I make as a result."

I nod. "I do not generally go into nature," I tell him. "I live in Silicon Valley. I go into my office."

"But I suspect you are not at or below the poverty line," he notes with a smile. "Or soon to be unemployed."

"Good point," I say cheerfully. "Also, I like my job very much. It's quite rewarding."

"What is it you do?" he asks. I notice Jessica is dropping back again. Eavesdropping.

"I work at a social media start-up," I say, but just as I do, we roll out of the last bit of town, and the mountains that have appeared distant seem to rear up before me. "My goodness, what a sight!"

"That's Devil's Back," he says, pleased. The mountain is rounded, with snow over the top and lines cut into the trees for skiers.

"It's enormous."

"It's a baby compared to the others we'll pass."

"I can't help but notice we're going slightly uphill," I say, because though it's only been twenty minutes, I am starting to notice some signs of exertion, such as being exhausted. "I am not going to make it fifteen miles at this grade."

"Ah! When was the last time you rode a bike, may I ask?"

I shrug. "When I was ten, maybe? It does seem to be just like riding a bike, as they say."

"Perhaps you have never shifted gears before?" he asks.

"Conversationally, yes," I say. "On a bike, no."

"Well then. You'll be very pleased to learn how to do so. Let's start our lesson off the bike," he says.

Carefully I pull over and try to teeter off my bicycle. Not carefully enough. I fall, and the bike falls with me. We both land in a clatter. A hot flush of embarrassment creeps up my cheeks, and I think, *This is why I don't do social activity. Or outdoor activity. Or activity.*

But I'm unhurt, and Tim is just standing there with a hand out and a big grin on his face that, if possible, makes him look even more attractive. "Thank you for getting that out of the way. Until someone falls off, I spend the whole ride wondering when someone's going to fall off and how they'll handle it. It can be anxiety provoking."

I look at him with a raised brow, but he's not joking. I nod. "You're welcome," I say. I struggle to my feet, but my phone escapes one of my many pockets. When I reach down to get it, the screen wakes, and there are three hundred notifications. "My goodness!" I say. "Jessica! Did you post something new?"

She bikes back to me. "What?"

"Why did we just get three hundred comments in the last thirty minutes?" I ask her. "Did we post something new?"

"You posted at the inn, didn't you?" she asks.

"I don't think I did," I say. "I started to, but I got a bit stuck on the caption."

"Oh. Ok. Well, the natives are probably just restless. I'll go take a peek."

She takes out her phone and unlocks it. She's quiet for a second. I smile at Tim weakly. "Sorry. Show me how to shift gears," I tell him.

He starts giving me the lay of the land. One of my handlebars operates the big gear; the other is the nested one. It's very straightforward in mechanics, but I'm a bit concerned about the prospect of shifting while biking, which is apparently a key part of the technique. It seems like it'll be a bit much, as I am already pretty focused on balancing, pedaling, and steering straight ahead. I am about to suggest to Tim that he shift my bike to the most appropriate gear and then give it back to me when Jessica says loudly, "OH SHIT."

I look at her. "Oh shit?" I say stupidly.

"Um, Paige?" she asks.

"Yes," I say.

"Might you have just told everyone on the internet to get off social media 'for pity's sake'?"

I reflect. "That does sound like something I might say. *For pity's sake* is meant to sub in for *Pete's sake*, which usually refers to Saint Peter. Saint Peter is himself a substitute for the word *God* or *Christ*, which would be, to some people, blasphemy."

"You're focusing on the wrong part of that sentence," she says.

"Oh, the part about social media. I guess I might say that, too, though never in public," I add. "That would be detrimental to the success of my place of employment."

"And, um, also the health of your current client?" she says. "Because right now people are starting to threaten her well-being."

"Threatening Mia?"

"They seem to feel insulted by your last post. Did you complain about having to create constant sources of entertainment in every second of your waking day?"

"Oh, I didn't post that!" I say. "I was having a moment of frustration. I never hit post."

Jessica puts her arms out like she wants to scream. "Obviously you did," she says. "Because I can see it. Paige, did you pants post this?"

"Pants post?" I ask. "I can't even imagine what you mean."

"Did you leave that 'moment of frustration' on the screen before you put away your phone?" she asks. "Or delete it completely, like a sane person would do? So that there was no way it might accidentally get posted, through a mistaken swipe or click?"

"You don't think . . . ," I ask.

"I know," she says. "Look for yourself."

I unlock my phone.

Oh, the horror.

Comment after comment insulting me, calling me names, expressing hurt and betrayal. Making fun of one of my most used idioms.

There is a new hashtag trending. #ForPitysSake. There is a meme that starts out, *HEY NITWITS*. It seems to be in use entirely to warn people that @Mia&Mike is just using her followers for sponsorship money and fame. I roll my eyes at this. "Well, of course she is," I say to myself. "What did they think she was running, exactly? A nonprofit?"

Jessica shakes her head at me, and I can tell she's really upset. "Paige," she says. "This is bad. What you said is kind of mean. I mean, I'm a Mia follower. Is this what you think of me? That I'm an entitled nitwit who should quit the internet and go for a nice walk? And jeez, why are you taking your anger out on meditation? When did meditation ever hurt a soul?"

I put my hands to my face. "Jessica, I'm so sorry. This wasn't directed at you. For some reason I was becoming upset over the comments Mia gets every day. Not just the ones you see but all the really mean ones I have to delete every ten minutes, or so it feels. And now I realize everyone is complaining because no matter what I say, they just *want* to complain, and they think I'm some anonymous person with no feelings and no problems. Whatever I say, they compare it to their own lives and find their own lives lacking, even if I'm literally telling them to enjoy their lives!"

I sigh. "There's just so much need and sorrow and just plain whinging in every thread, no matter what we post or when or how often. Back at that café in town, you said we were creating content! But we're really creating discontent!"

I exclaim the last bit very loudly, and Tim suddenly speaks. "That's a great line," he says. "*Con*tent. Discon*tent*. Can I post that on Twitter? I'll give you credit."

I point to him, arm outstretched. "YOU SEE!?" I exclaim to Jessica, though there is absolutely no through line from what she and I are talking about and what he just said, beyond that they are both about social media.

She shakes her head, having none of my nonsense. "I can see you're upset, but you need to take this post down. You've just spread your own upset to a lot of other people. That's not the goal, is it?"

I go quiet. Here I am trying to care for my sister, and I've upset people, and probably one of the people was her. "No. Of course not. But . . . ," I begin. "The original goal was . . ." My voice drifts off. I can't quite remember what the original goal was beyond finding something to do with myself until I got reinstated at work. "The reason I started on @Mia&Mike in the first place," I admit, "was because of what you posted on her feed." I lower my voice and confess the operating assumption that has driven so much of my behavior the last couple of weeks. "There's a part of me that feels like it's the fault of people like her, *influencers*, that you were feeling the way you were. I thought once you saw what was on the other side of the curtain, their power over you would wane."

By now Tim has disappeared so completely that I wonder if we're out on our own out here. I still don't know how to shift the gears on my bike. "I'm sorry, Jessica. I'll take it down."

Her shoulders slump. "Thank you," she says, but her tone is flat, her affect low. *Is it her meds?* I wonder. But of course not, I realize. It's not always about the meds. It's the words I've said to her.

When it comes down to it, it's me, not Mia, who has made her feel poorly.

I unlock my phone again. I navigate to my Pictey app and to the post. I look at it again. My goodness. I really was in a fit when I wrote it. A fit I promptly forgot as soon as I began to do gentle activity in nature. I must be sure to thank Jessica for that suggestion, after I—

My phone bloops.

"What's that?" Jessica asks. "What's happening?"

"It's a direct message," I say. "Not a DM request but just a DM," I go on. On Pictey, only people you've approved can send you DMs.

Anyone can send a request, but you don't see what they wrote until you accept it. They go into separate mailboxes. There are very, very few people Mia has ever approved to go straight into DMs.

I go into the mailbox. Then look up in surprise.

"It's Tucker," I say.

"Tucker?" she repeats. "Why would he be DMing her when he's on a honeymoon with her?"

The shit hits the fan is one of those very young idioms that is American in origin, and likely military at that. It was only first seen in print in 1948. Its British military cousin is *things go pear shaped*, and I also enjoy its more morbid relation, *tits up*.

At this moment, on the bike trail between Copperidge and Vail, the pear-shaped shit goes tits up. I've blown up a stranger's feed and drawn the attention of her ex-fiancé. And I never told Jessica that Mia was jilted. Mia lied about it online, of course, so Jessica still doesn't know.

I open the message. It reads:

> Mia, I just saw your post. I can't believe it. I can't believe you finally said all those things. They're exactly what I wanted you to say to me when we were together. I NEEDed you to say those things. To acknowledge what a cesspool this life can be, and challenge it a little. Give a little push to the people you had such an opportunity to reach, rather than just acting like their trained seal. That was all I was asking you for.
>
> Were you listening all along, and I just didn't give you enough time to get there? I'm sorry. I'm so, so sorry. I have missed you every day since I got home. I've stalked your feed and wept every day and waited for a sign. I'm praying this is the sign. Mia,

let me see you. I'm going to the airport right now. I can be in the mountains by dinner. Your metadata says you're still in Summit County. I assume that means you're at your mom's.

Please, meet me at your mom's house, Mia.

Just give me a chance to tell you how sorry I am in person. Give me a chance to make things right.

Love,
Tucker

"Paige?" Jessica asks as I stare at my phone in shock. "What is it?"

"Jessica," I say slowly. "I believe I need to quickly bring you up to speed on a number of issues that are going to become pressing in the very near future." I look around the spot we're standing, in a man-made canyon almost as old as this state, between rises of grasses, trees, rocks, snow, blue sky, and clouds. In such a pass, you can look only forward or backward. There is no other way out.

"The first item," I tell her, deciding solidly that I will move forward, "is that we need to find Tim. To my own surprise, I don't seem to actually know how to ride a bike. Perhaps the event of my childhood was, ever so slightly, exaggerated."

MIA

The first sign that something was wrong with Mike was the peeing. He wasn't peeing, specifically. He was still wolfing down his food every morning like I'd never fed him before and going outside after, and I didn't pay too much attention to what happened when we went outside after a meal, except that I picked up what needed to be picked up.

Over time, though, I noticed he wasn't keeping the food down. Sometimes he ate too fast and barfed his breakfast up, but then he'd slow down for a few weeks after that. A little later on, though, he was back to eating and puking again, and that was when I realized I couldn't remember the last time I'd seen him pee. I offered him some water, and he drank a tiny bit, and I watched him like a hawk for a day, offering and offering, but he didn't pee. I knew right away something was wrong. His teeth and gums looked fine, and his ears were clean and healthy. His eyes were clear. His tail was wagging. I tried to tell myself it was fine. Maybe a UTI. I put some apple cider vinegar in a peanut butter Kong. He ate it but threw it up.

I offered him extra food, and he didn't eat it. His tummy felt full and hard. I canceled all my classes and pulled him up to the sofa and spent the entire day by his side, rubbing him gently, talking to him in a brave voice, trying to cover up the scent of my fear by putting a cut of beef in a pot of water on the stove and cooking it on low all day. I told him he was fine and I wasn't concerned and I'd take good care of him and we'd have an appointment with the vet as soon as they could get us in.

I took him in the very next morning. The vet's face was solemn. It was the very early stages of HSA, cancer of the blood vessels. It was in his spleen but hadn't moved to his lungs. Mike knew it was bad news. He tried to cheer me up. It only made me more frightened.

In a panic, I threw money at the problem. He would have a splenectomy and a small rest, and then he would have to start chemo. I meticulously managed his pain, knowing he would try to hide it from me. For two weeks after the surgery, I wouldn't leave him alone. Mom flew in without being asked. She watched him while I taught classes I couldn't afford to miss—the studio was in the process of being sold, and I had obligations. She fed me because I wasn't eating.

She flew home after Mike had recovered from surgery. Though he was clearly feeling better, I still brought him everywhere I went and stopped going anyplace he couldn't go. I started reading veterinary journals about canine cancers. I called a professor at the University of Minnesota who had published about a new variety of chemo. It was so promising. Because the dose was much less aggressive than it would have been in a human, the side effects were mild and manageable. Mike's three-month x-rays were good. He passed the four-month mark—the longest most dogs survive with HSA—stronger than ever. My vet never once brought up euthanasia.

I remember that four-month mark very vividly. Mike and I celebrated. I took him on a wagon walk to an off-leash park during the quietest, coolest part of the morning. We played the world's most cautious game of fetch. Mike went about marking interesting spots with tiny sprays of pee, and each one was a cause for rejoicing. We sat under the shade of a big tree near a playground, and I read a cheerful book out loud and fed him dried bits of turkey liver. I told him he was now a cancer survivor and that it was no surprise, considering all the things he had already survived in this strange world.

He wagged, as though surviving was the very point.

———

I am walking into the yoga studio to teach my first live class since Mike died when my mom manages to call me.

Considering that neither she nor I uses cellular technology at the moment, that's quite a feat. But the woman at the front desk is on the phone when I sit down opposite her to take off my shoes, and by the time one sandal is off, she's looking from me to the phone.

"Mia Bell?" she asks.

"That's right," I say warmly. "Are you Nicola? I'm excited to teach here today!"

"You have a phone call," she says, not so warmly. "Can you call them back on your own phone? I've got to keep this line empty for reservations."

I smile weakly. "I don't have a phone," I say.

She gives me side-eye that would make a honey badger shy away. *Namaste to you too, lady.* I take the phone from her hands, almost by force. "Hello?"

"Darling," says my mother. "I'm at home. Aunt JoLynn will be here at any minute."

"Ok . . . ," I say.

"There's someone who called me asking for you, and he said it's very urgent. He was really trying to exert his self-appointed masculine authority on me. I hope this person is not planning to try that crap on you."

"Mort Matthews?" I ask.

"That's the one," she says. "He wants you to call back immediately. He must have said *immediately* four times. On the off chance that he's not a total blowhard, I figured I'd better call you."

I pause. Morty Matthews is a business manager. I hire him to do all my sponsorship contracts so I don't look like the bad guy, and he barks at everyone, male or female. He's probably wondering where the hell I've gone. Too bad for him. I'm not ready to come back. "What did he say?"

"He said you know what you did and you could be in breach," she says. "The sponsors are complaining."

Nicola the Zen master clears her throat pointedly at me. "Let them complain," I say. "The contracts give me a month window for posting. I haven't broken any deals yet."

"Good for you!" says my mom. "To hell with the man!" She pauses a moment. "Can I call him back and say that?"

"You could, but I'd have to pay by the hour for it," I say. "I've got to go anyway. My class," I explain.

"I wish I could be there," she says. "But it's so hard to reschedule things with Aunt JoLynn. She's all go go go."

"There will be other classes," I say, realizing even as I speak that I want to do more classes. If I can.

"Oh! Good," Mom says excitedly. "Next time I will bring my bells. Oh! And I could brew up some chakra-balancing tea."

I imagine showing up as a sub at a new studio with my own urn full of tea. It'll make an impression. "We'll sort it out later, Mom—see ya tonight."

Nicola holds her arm out for the phone grumpily. I hand it to her and hear my mom still talking on the line. Nicola punches the talk button with relish. Immediately the phone rings again, but it's studio business, so I take off my other shoe and head to a small staff room pointed out to me with a sharp finger.

The back of the staff room is a meditation area. I pull the curtain to close it off from the rest of the room and sit cross-legged on a rolled-up woven blanket, rump higher than knees. I've done yoga every healthy day of my adult life, but I still have nerves today. I haven't advertised this class on my feed or sent an announcement to my twenty-thousand-yogi-strong email list, and the owner of the studio doesn't know who the heck I am beyond being the daughter of one of her customers. Maybe no one will come. Maybe people will prefer their regular teacher and leave on the third surya namaskara A. You can disappoint people with a class that's too easy or a class that's too hard or one that starts too easy and gets too hard. But you can't know what's too hard or too easy until you look at the miserable, bored, or panting faces of your students. And I haven't taught a class in a long time. A year, now that I think of it. I haven't done sixty full minutes of yoga in weeks. I might not be able to actually do my own class.

I sigh. I'm going to be that teacher that takes people through cat and cow and then just walks through the room in a creepy heel-toe way in an effort to be unobtrusive, only to call a cue and make the person in front of her jump. I'm going to see people looking pointedly up at the platform and thinking, *Um, if I can do it, why can't you?* and then I'm going to have to go demonstrate something and say the cues on out breaths so no one knows I'm panting.

I close my eyes, rest my hands in a peaceful asana, and start following my breath.

Crap. Morty. When I get home tonight, I do have to call him, make sure nothing really is in breach. I thought I had a pretty good grasp on what was in my pipeline, but the honeymoon stuff is gonna need to happen soon. Maybe that's where he's upset. But that's not even scheduled for another month.

Follow the breath.

I guess I can take my honeymoon by myself when I'm ready to start posting again.

Return to the breath.

When *am* I going to start posting again? How am I going to explain the absence of Tucker in the photos, if I do take the honeymoon? Should I just get a lawyer and cancel the honeymoon contract? The sponsors haven't paid me anything yet. I was looking forward to going to Paris, of course, but I was also looking forward to getting married, and that feeling has faded fast enough.

Breathing. Let the thoughts drift away down the river of my mind. In. Out.

I could cancel the contract and travel on my own dime. I could cancel the contract, go on my own dime, and switch to a flip phone. I could cancel all the contracts, switch to a flip phone with an international SIM card, go to Paris on my own dime, and bring Dewey and Azalea. We could spend the rest of the summer visiting French farms, tasting cheeses and wines, and learning about chicken rearing *au Français*. I could bring Mom too. She hasn't traveled much in her semiretirement. She could eat all kinds of unusual foods: snails and frogs and offal up the wazoo. She could dig around in the earth and fill her gut biome with all kinds of nice French germs.

And then what? I'd have to come home eventually. What would I do? Go back to the beginning and be a substitute yoga teacher for people like Nicola indefinitely? That's not what I want. I *like* being an entrepreneur. I like having enough money to pay my bills. But I haven't been happy for a long, long time. Not since my preclass meditations were accompanied by a drooly, peanut butter–breathed bulldog snoring half in and half out of my lap. That was the best feeling in the world.

That feeling is never coming back. That feeling isn't a choice anymore.

Are my choices really only Pictey or nothing?

Breathe, Mia.

Breathe.

Breathe.

PAIGE

"He's weeping every day?" says Jessica, making a sour face.

I have brought Jessica ever so slightly up to speed on the situation between Mia and Tucker. I would say we are going about thirty miles per hour, where the truth is cruising by at sixty-five and blaring its horn at me in frustration.

"Apparently so," I tell her. She knows that Tucker jilted Mia. She knows that Mia lied about the wedding. She knows that I lied about Mia's wedding, too, but she thinks it's because it was my job to lie about it. She does not know that I have no job at the moment or that I was put on leave by my company because of her suicide attempt, which upset me because of my own past suicide attempt. She doesn't know that I stalked her internet idol out of misplaced anger or that I hacked into said idol's Pictey account and am now impersonating her without her knowledge.

These are certainly details that can wait for some less pressing moment. Maybe when we both have more access to psychiatric care.

At this juncture, our work is to find Mia before Tucker does. Or find Tucker before he finds Mia. Or somehow otherwise step out in front of this untidy situation I've created, vacuum it all up with a metaphorical Dustbuster, and dispose of it carefully before returning to the valley and Pictey and normal life. I need to delete all the fraudulent posts permanently, cover my tracks more thoroughly, and then set to the business of getting Jessica admitted to the rehab center early before I screw up something truly important—my sister's emotional safety.

"Also," I say aloud, "we need to find Tim."

At that, Tim pops out from behind a copse of pines. "Pardon me, ladies," he says bashfully. "Conflict makes me uncomfortable."

"What else would it make you?" I ask him. "I would be concerned if it made you happy. Please saddle me up in this bike and then switch my gears for me, will you? We need to be quickly escorted to our car so we can get to this place." I show him a map of our destination, the geo tag for the photo of Mia and her mother. It is my best guess as to how to intercept this situation.

"Well, sure," he says. "It would be my pleasure. But I don't think you'll need to use the gears much if you turn around. It's all downhill from here."

Oh, how true that is.

We cycle, much faster this time, back to town where we first picked up our bikes. Tim continues to make nice conversation the whole way, saying interesting things about the geology of the area that I would normally be quite fascinated by, if I weren't busy trying to think my way out of this hole I've dug. Jessica, on the other hand, is not interested. At some point while I am trying to keep up with their speeds without falling off my bike, she tells Tim, "Your knowledge of rocks is probably fascinating, but I think my sister has created an internet war, and if we don't get to lightning-fast Wi-Fi soon, there may be casualties."

"Understood. Though, just to warn you, lightning-fast Wi-Fi is not really the name of the game in Copperidge," he warns her. "And where you want to go, there's not even cell service."

I look up from the trail. "Oh no?"

Tim shakes his head. "That whole side of Mount Wyler is a dead zone. Look." Concerningly, Tim lets go of both handlebars and takes his phone out of a pouch on the crossbar. While cycling at what feels like breakneck speed to me, he shows me a map of the area, with colors ranging from light pink to dark red illustrating the availability of cellular service. The area where I think Mia's mother lives is white, as in, there is next to none.

"Oh dear," I say, trying not to crash my bike. There are so many obstacles involved in locating Mia and keeping her away from Tucker in the next five hours, not least that there is no way to communicate with her and that we have no idea exactly where she's staying, nor if she's even still in the county. Then there is the fact that once we do find her, we have to somehow persuade her to leave. If Tucker finds her, we are doomed.

"What about the airport?" I ask Tim.

"The airport?" he repeats.

"The local airport. Where people would fly in, if they flew here."

He shakes his head. "Madame," he says, and I wonder if that's what he calls every woman he meets. "There are some small runways for light planes. But large commercial flights aren't coming in and out of the actual Rocky Mountains, as I'm sure you understand. Most people would fly into Denver and then drive up here." He pauses. "Well, there's a regional airport in Eagle County. Maybe your friend's paramour would fly there, on a connecting flight from Denver. It runs two shuttles per day. Ten a.m. and nine p.m."

I look at Jessica. "He said he'd be here by dinner."

"Yes," says Tim. "I heard that. And he's going to her mother's house, which I'm guessing is the destination you showed me?"

"I believe it is," I say. "You have excellent hearing," I add.

"I can also lip-read," he says. "I like spying on people."

Jessica shakes her head. "Tim. Don't say that to people you barely know," she scolds.

"Why not?" I ask. "Everyone enjoys spying in some form or other, and he's doing the courtesy of telling us not to try to tell secrets when he can see us."

Tim smiles, puts his phone away, and regains the handlebars. I note that at no point did his bicycle waver. "Paige takes my meaning," he says. "But Jessica, I appreciate your feedback as well. If it ever comes up in casual conversation again, and I sincerely doubt it will, I will say that I'm interested in people."

"It's the same thing," I say.

"It really isn't," says Jessica. "But thank you, Tim. I think that's an excellent course correction."

"Speaking of course correction, I'm wondering whether it might not be better to intercept this Tucker fellow," Tim says. "Rather than your employer. As I understand it, the post that prompted his change of heart is one you probably shouldn't have put up in the first place. It may be detrimental to your career prospects to explain to your employer what you've put out for public consumption on her behalf."

I look skyward for just a moment. There really will be no explaining what I've done when the time comes. I am embarrassed that I didn't foresee all the possible negative outcomes while in the fit of pique that started this misadventure. I suppose I thought—hoped?—Mia had quit her feed for good, considering how she was letting it die. And that Tucker was long gone, having ended their engagement just days before the wedding.

"What would we say to Tucker, though?" asks Jessica. "'Just kidding, Mia didn't post that; it wasn't a sign'?" She shakes her head. "Maybe they are meant to get back together, and this is how it happens."

"Excellent point," says Tim. "Perhaps we should turn the bikes around, continue on to Vail, and enjoy the rest of the day knowing you've had a part in the reunification of two lovers."

"I'm afraid that seems unlikely," I point out. "No matter what we've posted, quite by accident, I might add, as a result of an interesting screen-lock flaw I intend to investigate further down the line—"

"You pants posted it," interrupts Jessica. "That's not a screen-lock flaw."

"Well, whatever the case," I go on. "The fact remains that Mia isn't the one who came to the conclusion that she should 'push' her followers or whatever it is I did with that post that so appealed to her ex-fiancé. Mia is still Mia. She's still the vapid shopaholic with the New Age bent who preaches to people about self-acceptance while avoiding any foods that might change her body fat percentage from three to four. She's still the woman who posts twenty times a day about the contents of her breakfast plate, makeup bag, and coffee cup."

Jessica shakes her head. "No, she isn't," she says. "She quit."

I chance a look at my sister. Is she onto me?

"Think about it," Jessica goes on. "Before she hired you, she actually told her followers she was going on hiatus, right?" she asks. "And then it was only when there was fan pushback on that hiatus that she hired you to fill in for her. And of all the people in the world she could have hired, she picked you, who dislikes social media consumers in general and internet influencers especially."

"Maybe so, but I wouldn't tell her those things," I say, because it is true.

"But you don't have to," she says. She sounds exasperated with me, and I suppose I can't blame her for that. "It's obvious in everything you do and say. And besides," Jessica goes on, "you don't really like *anyone*, do you? Why hire a misanthrope to manage the expectations of half a million people?"

"I must interrupt here," I say. "I do like you. I also like the innkeeper, Cary, and Tim here. That's three people I like."

"Thank you," says Tim. "I like you too." He smiles his nice smile at me. His teeth are very bright against his lips. I hope I'm not fetishizing him due to innate racial bias implicit in my being raised white in our bigoted society, but the man really is quite attractive.

"Three people out of what?" asks Jessica. "Everyone you've ever met? I mean, I really want to know."

I reflect. "Well, I don't like my coworkers. They're emotional all the time, which is counterproductive in our workplace, and I'm supervised by a half wit who is obsessed with the honest expression of feelings."

"Sounds awful," says Jessica. It's sarcasm, I'm very sure.

"And my mother doesn't like me terribly much. Obviously that doesn't lead to fond appreciations."

"Obviously," says Tim.

"And you never talk to Mom's sisters," says Jessica. "Or my dad." She raises her eyebrow at me as if to say, *See?*

"There's nothing wrong with your dad," I say. "Except that he's not *my* dad, who I like very much. There's a fourth person: Dad. And I have a friend in the valley with several young kids, Michelle, who I've known since college," I exclaim. "Voilà. Two Friends, Two Family Members, and one Virtual Stranger." I gesture to Tim, wobbling on my bike. "An entire social circle."

"Am I in Friends or Family?" she asks.

"Family, of course. Cary is my other friend."

"The guy that owns the inn?" she asks. "You've known him for, like, a week."

"Long enough," I say. "I have a recurring note in my calendar to send him a birthday card every year. Our friendship is secure."

Jessica laughs at me and says, "The defense rests. No internet influencer who wanted to keep up the status quo would hire you to ghost post."

Well, I think. *That is certainly in line with my experience.*

"I tend to agree with Jessica here," says Tim. "You have an authoritarian and explicit way of speaking that doesn't appeal to just anyone."

"Thank you," I say. Tim is such a nice guy. "So your hypothesis is that Mia desired to somehow change the tone or trajectory of her internet presence," I begin.

"Which is why she hired you," supplies Jessica.

I say nothing to that, because the lie is starting to close in on me, and I don't intend to help it along. "Pressing on," I say. "You theorize that Mia wanted to change in the way that Tucker wanted her to change, and so she and Tucker should in fact be reunited? Is that the operating theory here?"

"Yes," says Jessica.

"I might further add that, in that case, perhaps it is not within the terms of your employee contract to keep them apart," says Tim. "Or the terms of your contract as a member of a society that generally values relationships and connection."

I inhale and think this through. On one hand, if we do nothing, Mia is about to find out how incredibly and completely hacked she has been, and that may cause her some distress, to put it mildly. Such distress may bring harm to my real employer, Pictey, financially, and to her followers, emotionally.

Or . . . it may cause a big public wedding, as all parties were originally promised. Hm.

Further, it is my understanding that being the bride in a big public wedding is a source of joy for many women, although to me it sounds about as much fun as doing this exact bike ride, only naked.

"There remains the fact that I posted something written out of frustration that may completely end Mia's career as an influencer," I say. "Don't I at least have the responsibility to take that down?"

"I think if you leave it up, she'll fire you," says Jessica.

"Understandably," adds Tim. "However, if you take it down, you'll also be taking down the very interesting conversation that has built up as a result of the comment. Many people have things to say on the subject of social media and mental health, it seems. They also are staunch defenders of the ancient tradition of meditation. Of all the parties in play, I'd say meditation is the real winner in this debate."

"Are you actually reading the @Mia&Mike feed right now?" I ask. "As we cycle?"

"Well, of course," he says. "Otherwise I wouldn't be able to follow this conversation. And Jessica already told me she preferred it to my discussion of the geologic time scale."

I frown at Jessica. She rolls her eyes back at me. "Well," I say, twisting slightly toward Tim again, "I suppose Mia and Tucker are more pertinent in the moment, though nowhere near as interesting or as important as something like horsts."

Jessica just laughs. "Oh, Paige. Don't ever change."

I think it may be too late. Something in me has changed. "I believe it's time I stop posting for Mia," I announce. "But I concur about letting Tucker plead his case to her directly, and damn the consequences. True love wins the day, and all that."

"Oh! Excellent! In that case, can we go to Vail?" Tim says excitedly.

"No, Tim," I say. "My crotch hurts. Also I'd like to clean up some digital fingerprints, just to avoid future issues for me—and Mia, of course."

"Understood. To the fastest Wi-Fi in the West," he announces. "To sweep it all under the rug!"

MIA

At around eight months after his diagnosis, Mike started to hide from me. I had just gotten him a new antler—his favorite thing to chew—and he took it in his mouth, and instead of chewing it on the floor right in front of me, he went to the open closet in my bedroom and put it right under his nose and lay down. I called the vet, and she bolstered his pain meds and told me this might mean it was going to soon be his time. Then his nine-month x-rays came back, and the cancer had spread. I called the vet at U of M, and she told me to get myself ready.

Every day I woke up and told myself to make it Mike's best day. The studio deal had been inked, and I was able to work from home most of the time. I could take him out in his wagon all day many days, working from a coffee shop, rejoicing in Wi-Fi and my cell phone and the freedom they allowed me. Mike could lie in the padded bed of the wagon and meet dozens of people each day and receive pets and praise for being such a good dog from everyone who passed. In the evening after work he could sit with his head in my lap and breathe loudly in unison with me as we watched TV and talked over the day. He still wagged.

When he woke me to carry him down from bed in the middle of the night so he could walk himself back into the closet to hide, I knew it was time. I went into the closet and sat down with him and promised him comfort. It was late, and the hours were long. I asked him about his wishes. I told him I wouldn't let him be in any more pain. Did he want to be buried? Cremated? What would give him the most peace? I lay down next to him and cried and vowed to him that it wouldn't hurt. Through my tears I tried to thank him. I tried to make sure he knew how grateful I was. As morning drew nearer, he lifted his head and looked me in the eyes where I lay curled around him, careful not to touch where it might hurt but unable to put any space between us. He put his nose forward a few inches until it was touching mine. "Mike," I begged him, "please don't go."

He licked my tears off my face. "Mike," I said. "Mike."

At seven a.m., I called my vet's home number and told her it was time. She drove over, and he stood up on three legs and wagged his tail when she came inside. Was it too soon? I asked her. If he was still wagging, was it too soon? She shook her head and told me, "When he is still wagging is the kindest time."

She wrapped us up on the sofa, with him shaking in my arms, and told me gently that I needed to stop crying and try to be calm. I needed to think of his favorite place and to talk to him about it in the happiest way I could. I said in a pinched, wet voice, "He's my best friend," and the vet said, "I know. He knows. Take a breath and tell him about his best day."

I looked at Mike, and he was saying with his eyes, *I trust you*. And I whispered to him, as clearly as I possibly could, "Let's go back to the old studio together. I'll teach a slow-flow class, and you'll be my special guest. You can walk on any mat you like. Everyone will stop to pet you when you come by, even if they're supposed to be in a balance pose. You can lead the ending, and everyone will come up before they even put away their props and say, 'What a good dog. What a cute good dog,' and give you lots of pets and let you lick their sweaty hands."

I took a breath, and it wobbled a bit. I sternly told myself, *Do this well, Mia. Do it bravely*. I swallowed some tears. "When the class is over," I said to him, "we'll go to the park. The one by the water, where you can put your toes in the ocean. I'll take your longer leash, and you can go out in the waves a little and let them lift you up and put you back down, over and over again. I don't have anywhere else to be. You can take as long as you like. When you're done bobbing, you can come with me into the shade, and we'll read together, and I'll let you lie down on the top of the picnic table, even if we get judgmental looks. If you roll over, I'll rub your tummy as long as you like, even if it's still wet."

I felt the vet touch my shoulder and say gently, "Ok. He's at peace now." Those words, they were the exact same ones they'd used at the hospital when Andy had let go at the end. The pain broke through then, and all the streams of my grief tangled into one.

"I love you, Mike," I told him. "You're my best friend."

"He knows," said the vet. "You both did very well."

I let my shaking body fold over his still one and gave myself over to the tears at last. I remember now that Mike's weight on my lap felt no different than it had one thousand other times we'd sat here together. But this time was the last time. Mike was gone, and I was alone.

—

The class goes ok. Fine, really. I try to stay in the moment, be present with the students, who have no idea who I am, beyond their substitute yoga teacher. They advance along at the right speeds. Someone finds a peak pose for the first time. Stuff like that used to light me up, long ago. Now I feel like my lights are on the fritz, up, down, up again. I'm aglow over a hammock, snuffed out over a mantra. At least with my phone there was a constant dim glow in front of me all the time, a translucent curtain of blue light in front of the world. I'm learning that when I was posting, I had a way to understand what was happening in my life, only a few steps removed from it actually happening. I'd post it, and when the caption was written, that was the story of the event, even if the event was just lunch. If I posted lunch, that meant I'd enjoyed lunch, and it was nourishing or comforting or refreshing or whatever it was. Now lunch is lunch. I taste it instead of telling about it. It happens when I eat it, and it's over when it's done. It doesn't live on in the feed. It doesn't garner ten thousand likes.

That's all well and good for lunch. But what about when this woman comes in and gets into bow pose the first time and doesn't hurt herself and doesn't strain and beams the whole time? How do we commemorate that? Doesn't that deserve a thousand likes? Shouldn't that achievement have a story?

Nicola comes into the studio after class. I am rolling out my IT bands, which are tight from lots of hiking and not much by way of side planks. She gestures to the roller and says, "I read that those are bad for you in *Yoga Journal*."

"Well," I say, searching for grace and wondering if it turned off with my phone, "thank you for having them in your studio anyway."

She doesn't respond, saying instead, "Are you some kind of internet celebrity? I thought you said you don't have a phone."

I shake my head. "I don't. Not at the moment. Hiking accident."

"Someone posted about you on Facebook," she says. "My phone is ringing nonstop. Can you do a second class tonight? We have a six-forty-five power flow."

I cringe. *Power flow* is often code for less yoga and more crunches. In fact, the studio I once took so much pride in now offers a power flow class, in which the students perform endless sets of "yoga burpees." Standing mountain pose, forward fold, jump back to plank, jump back to standing forward fold, mountain pose, in quick succession. I do not like teaching those classes but used to do it anyway, because the endorsement money would be the actual point.

But there's no endorsement money here, and I'm so glad of it. Today, I'm just a yoga teacher.

"I would be happy to teach an Ashtanga class instead," I say. "It's sweaty and fast."

"Sure. Whatever," says Nicola. "As long as there's music. Actual music."

Apparently my bells-and-chimes soundtrack wasn't doing it for Nicola. "Got it. Actual music," I say. "I think your students will enjoy it."

Nicola coughs. "Why are you subbing at my studio if you're so famous?"

"That's a fair question," I say. I don't answer it. "I'm going to go meet a friend now." I stand up. Dewey and I made plans to meet for a drink and a bite at the local distillery after class, but if I'm going to teach Ashtanga, I'm going to need to skip anything fermented. My body made it through the last class just fine, but the next will be hard, no matter what I do. We may have to move our meal to the sandwich shop nearby. I think of texting Dewey. I'm still not used to the logistics of life without my phone. I wonder if I ever will be.

"Can I use your phone?" I ask Nicola, with dread.

She sighs heavily. "Go ahead."

"And your phone book?" I ask.

She looks at me like I grew a third head. "You mean my computer? Yes. Fine. Help yourself."

At the front desk she logs me in and pulls up a browser. "I'll be back in five minutes. I have to go change the class name on the chalkboard," she tells me and steps outside to the front walk, where a sandwich board waits. When she's gone, I run my fingers over the keyboard, google the number of the distillery, and confuse the hell out of the woman at the desk there when I call and ask to speak with a customer. Finally Dewey picks up. I ask him to meet me at the Sleepy Bear, hang up, and look at the computer again. It's the first time I've been on the internet in more than a week. Nicola isn't back in the studio yet. I decide to check my email.

The load is insanely slow. Finally the inbox comes up, and to my shock, I have 4,200 unread messages. Four thousand two hundred emails! That is a lot even for me. I cannot for the life of me figure out what is causing this, but I don't want to know either. Even a glance at the first two subject lines freaks me out. One is Marty shouting at me in all caps, another is a sponsor re: "intentions for partnership," and the next few subject lines are just as grouchy, though I don't know the senders. My heart starts racing, and sweat beads up on the back of my neck. My throat feels tight. My stomach clenches. I log out as quickly as possible, try to shake away the very memory.

"I didn't see that," I tell myself. "That never happened." I get up and start to head to the coffee shop so I can meet Dewey and have a sandwich and pretend that I never touched that computer, wasn't even tempted.

But I did check it, and I can't unsee what I saw. Now I know what happens when I'm offline this long. Everyone is furious. Everyone wants my head.

As my mom would say, to hell with that. To hell with "everyone." I don't need them anymore. I just need my quirky mom, her neighbors up the road, a good class, a decent mountain. I am freed from the tyranny of the like button. And now that I am, I know going back online, at least as I did before, will never be a possibility.

PAIGE

We get back into town around four p.m. I steer us to the Sleepy Bear immediately. Tim takes the bikes back on our behalf, promising to return, and I find to my surprise that I hope he does. *Two friends, two family members, and one virtual stranger,* I think. Even in this strange moment where the hornet's nest has been well and truly stirred, I find myself hoping to add the virtual stranger in question to my veritable panoply of new connections.

But I've got to start cleaning up my tracks, and time is of the essence. My personal laptop is in the trunk as always, and it boots up with a happy tune, and I start taking some general anonymity precautions that I've ignored entirely up to now. I triple-check photo metadata, look up locations tagged, and congratulate myself on paying cash at almost all the places we've shopped or eaten. While Jessica is in the bathroom, I delete every single last mention of the Evergreen Inn. I know thousands of people saw those posts, but when Mia finds out what happened and reports it, Pictey probably won't do too much historical reconstruction right off the bat. They certainly won't go looking around their own company-issued laptops unless forced, because they won't want to find anything there.

They'll be mostly concerned with the very out-of-character post from this morning. And that post, happily, came from my youngest virtual private network, one that shares an IP address with a Lowe's home-improvement store in San Antonio. By way of my pants. What a ridiculous mistake.

When Jessica comes back from the bathroom, she's got an enormous grin on her face. It's the biggest expression I've seen from her since she got a pair of diamond earrings from Mom last Christmas. Two pairs, actually, because I gave her mine on the spot. My ear piercings grew over before I was twenty, and I have been giving my mom back gifts of earrings ever since.

Seeing no new earrings, I ask her what's up. She sits down too close to me and leans over to whisper, "Guess who I just saw!"

"I'm going to guess several citizens of Copperidge and a few fellow visitors."

"I saw *Mia*!" she hisses.

"What?" I ask.

"I saw Mia! She really is here in Copperidge. That means she probably will meet up with Tucker tonight!"

Oh no. "Jessica . . ." My brain starts racing. Mia is here, in the Sleepy Bear. The place isn't that big. My first instinct is to put my head down or hide behind a pillar, but then I remember: Mia doesn't know me. She doesn't know who I am. Or what I've done.

"She's nice!" Jessica says. "I knew she was, and I'm vindicated."

"You talked to her?" I ask, heart in my throat. "What did you say?"

"I told her I was a big fan," my sister says happily. The happiest I've seen her, I realize, since her attempt. My heart squeezes. "I told her I'd been following her for years, even before she got really famous."

"What did she say?" I remind myself to be calm, but I don't think I could do a breathing exercise right now even if I tried.

"She said thank you, of course. She asked me what my username is, but I said I didn't comment. I didn't want her to know I was suicidal."

"Jessica," I say, observing where the expression *cold sweat* comes from, "you're wearing a sleeveless blouse."

She looks down at her arms, then her bandaged wrists. I refreshed those bandages myself this morning, following the nursing instructions, and I'm not that good at it. Suffice it to say they are attention getting.

"Oh," she says. "Rats. Well, anyway. I was an excellent sister. I knew you probably weren't supposed to tell anyone what you were doing for her, so I acted like I didn't know about any of that."

I suck in a breath of air. Just in the nick of time; I was getting light headed. "Good," I say, calming. "That's good." I remind myself this is not life and death. Life and death is the young woman sitting next to me. At the moment, she's choosing life.

"I just told her I really loved her attitude and that it had helped me in the past, and she said thank you and she was so glad and it was the whole reason she used Pictey in the first place." Jessica's eyes start to well up. She takes my hand in hers, and the sensation is so unfamiliar that it takes me a moment to realize how good it feels. "Paige, she's so kind."

I look down at Jessica's hand. I could tell her the truth, that Mia started using Pictey for the reason everyone starts using Pictey: because it's there. But I don't.

Even with all she knows, Jessica is still enamored of her internet idol, still believing @Mia&Mike is real, still touched by even the most insincere of influencer clichés. I wish I could relieve her of all that naivete somehow. It would take away so much of the hurt life will deliver at every opportunity. But it would also take away this moment of joy.

So instead I smile at her. "You did good," I say, breathing in slowly, *one, two, three, four,* feeling the warmth of my sister's hand. "Where is she now?"

"She's gone," says Jessica. "Out the front door. She was wearing a yellow Prana hoodie and Alo moto leggings with asymmetrical mesh."

I close my eyes, partly in relief and partly to make this wardrobe update stop. "But wait, you didn't hear the best part," she adds, dropping my hand in favor of gesturing excitedly. "I made you look good to your boss!"

My chest gives a panicked thud.

"I told her I loved her latest posts," says Jessica. "I told her that her feed had only gotten better in the last week. That way she'll think you're doing an amazing job!"

"Oh, Jessica," I say. What else is there?

She thinks I'm happy. "I'm a genius, right?"

I inhale again slowly, noticing with some irony that I appear to be "focusing on my breath." "You're very smart," I say to her. I think of how many lies I told Jessica, or how many omissions I've allowed, and how she's taken each one at face value. "I hope I am not being hurtful when I say that you're too naive for the word *genius* to apply, in all likelihood. I'd have to see your actual IQ results, but I feel confident based on our time together that your score would be sub–one fifty."

She laughs at me, even after I have delivered such a terribly harsh truth. It is the sound of the old Jessica, the one I remember from long ago. A soft rolling laugh that splashes over you, like a sprinkler on a hot day, joy and surprise and freedom all combined into one.

I think of a day back then, when she was small, when she came along and made me have a reason, before life turned us into strangers. She loved an old rickety merry-go-round in an overgrown park near our home that hadn't yet been improved with safe climbing structures and pinch-proof swings. But one day I wasn't paying close attention. She laughed and laughed, and I kept spinning until I realized the platform was going too fast, and she wasn't laughing anymore. She was crying, petrified, clutching the center bar and gritting her teeth in fear. I had no idea when one kind of squeal had turned to another, but I remember the look on her face. It was a look of betrayal.

She trusted me then, and she trusts me now. Her bottomless trust is a terrible weakness or maybe a great strength, but either way, the most important thing now is that it's not snuffed out today. Not by me.

Now she turns toward me with a light in her eyes, betrayal a million miles from her mind. "I know you think I'm naive because I believe in Mia Bell. But I do believe in her, so much. I think she's a good person who is trying to figure out how to live in a world that kind of sprang up around her slowly over time. I think she's been graceful to her followers for years, in spite of the stuff you complain about after just one week of posting in her place. In spite of the mean comments and the constant demands, she just keeps posting, and her posts stay joyful and encouraging. She posts lovely things even when times are bad for her, like when she's just been pretty much left at the altar, for example, because she's trying to make the world feel like a good and happy place. She's showing people how life can be worth living."

I shake my head at her. "Even if all that is true," I say, realizing as I do that it is, that my sister is right, "you cannot deny that she is a fake."

"She's faking it right now," says Jessica. "She's in a tight spot. That's not the same thing."

I grimace in frustration, trying to reconcile these impossible truths. "What if she were a reality TV star?" I ask Jessica. "Like the Real Housewives or the Bitch Bosses. Would you love her so much then? After all, she's selling her privacy and integrity for advertising dollars. Is she really so different from any of them?"

Jessica thinks for a moment, and when she answers, she says something so smart that for a moment I really do wonder if she might be the genius and I might be the one who's been foolish all along.

"If there were a reality show about Mia," she says, "no one would watch it. Because she is the opposite of what those shows are all about. She has plenty of opportunities to create drama and pathos." My sister's eyes are as clear as the blue mountain skies this town delivers to us day in and day out. "But instead, all she creates is hope and optimism." She pauses. "Hope, optimism, and a good living selling fancy yoga pants."

MIA

Earlier today my manager called my mom's landline to yell at her.

An hour ago I had 4,200 emails.

And now I am staring at the spot where a girl I've never met came up to me covered elbow to wrist in gauze and first aid tape. And I knew, in an instant, exactly who she was.

I've thought of her more than once since I tossed my phone. When she commented, it was on the post I'd made after I'd found out Tucker was leaving me, or rather not joining me in Colorado. She said something vague, but I remember it felt dangerous, and I remember responding to her the best I could. But I also remember drinking three fingers of bourbon and crying in a bathtub that night. I remember the oppressive cocktail of rejection mixed with humiliation. I don't remember exactly what I said to her then, but I know it wasn't the same as what I'd say to her now, a couple of weeks later, since I let go of the incessant chipper fakery that was my online persona. Today I would say, *Dear Jessica, whoever you are, wherever you are, you did the right thing. You did the right thing reaching out for help, but you have to do it again; you have to find someone or something that makes you safe tonight. Someone there with you right now. Someone you can reach out and touch. Do nothing until you can talk to just one real person. Because this feed, this is not a real person.*

I would say: *There is no one alive who deserves life more than you. No celebrity or billionaire or supermodel. You've shown great honesty. So as far as I'm concerned, you're already a success.*

And then I would call 911. I don't know what I would tell them, but who cares? I would still call.

That's not how I handled it that day, and I don't know how it came to be that she and I were standing in the same coffee shop just now, but it is clear that she tried to hurt herself after our interaction, and yet somehow she still thinks I'm worth knowing. She still came up to me to thank me for something. And I took her hand, gave her a hug, and tried to tell her something—*be safe, take care,* I don't know what—but what I do remember is what she said to me as we parted. She said, "I love your latest posts. The feed has only gotten better in the last week."

And now I cannot figure out which end is up.

I walk out of the Sleepy Bear, looking for air and space and Dewey. Dewey, who makes sense, in real life, in real time. It's such a short walk from the distillery; maybe I'll head in that direction, and we'll meet in the middle. It seems suddenly urgent that I find him so I can tell him all the strange things that have happened and he can help me figure out what's going on. But the moment that I turn from the storefront of the coffee shop to walk down the sidewalk, I find myself looking into the eyes of the man I was supposed to marry.

Weirder still, the man I was supposed to marry is smiling at me and trying to give me a hug.

"Mia!" Tucker looks breathless.

"Tucker?" I say, swatting him away. "What are you doing here?"

"I went to your mom's house, but a girl walking a chicken on a leash told me you were in town teaching yoga."

Azalea, I think. I know she was planning on spending the evening with my mom hunting for frogs. Sounds like she found a toad. "What were you doing at my mom's house?" I ask, because I'm not exactly sure where else to start.

"Looking for you," he says. "Did you see my DM?"

"What DM?" I ask. "No," I say before he answers. "I haven't seen any DMs in a while," I add. "What's going on? What are you doing here? How soon can you leave?"

"I saw your posts, Mia," he says, and I see he is trying to figure out where to stand, how to reach me, though I am backing away with every step he takes. "I made a terrible mistake."

I narrow my eyes at him. "Several." I square my shoulders. The first couple of days after he dumped me, I spent a lot of time fantasizing about him coming to his senses and rushing to my side, but now that he's here, Tucker seems suddenly very tiresome. It's like I have sudden-onset PMS, if you could focus all that impatient energy at just one person, and that person is wearing stupid hipster glasses he doesn't need.

"I want to make things right," he goes on. "I am so, so sorry for what I did. I want to make it up to you. I miss you constantly, Mia. I took you for granted, and I didn't understand your timetable, and I didn't give you enough credit. I'm so sorry. Things are going to be different in the future."

"Tucker, I'm going to stop you here," I say. "I can't let you do some big apology and presentation with PowerPoint slides. There is literally no universe, none, in which I get back together with you." I pause and think about how far I've come. The time for smiling and faking it has passed.

He looks gobsmacked. "You can't mean that," he says.

"I don't want to be harsh here," I say. "But also I kind of do. Let me explain the roller coaster I've been on over you since we met less than a year ago: I have felt attracted, then in lust, then less amazed, then, though I did not acknowledge it until just now, generally stuck with you. Then, thank my lucky stars, you dumped me. Then I felt hurt, then furious, then I forgot you existed for a couple days there, and now we're hovering around annoyed indifference."

"You don't mean that. You're angry," he tries. "I know I let you down."

I shake my head. "*Angry* is too exciting a term. I am closer to moderately irritated. Irked, I would say. I have a yoga class to teach tonight, and I was planning to meet up with a friend for a quick bite first, and a few strange things have happened to me today, and you, Tucker, are the last one of those I will tolerate.

"You're uninvited and largely unwelcome, and I am not taking you back. Can we skip so much drama right now and, like, high-five and go our separate ways?"

"You're teaching yoga again?" he asks, excitement in his voice.

"I am. As you surely know, I'm taking time off work. I need to do something with purpose in my downtime."

"What do you mean, taking time off? Is that why you put up that post?"

"That's exactly why I put up that post," I say. "I wanted everyone to know I was fine and that I'd be away from my account for a while to recharge. It was pretty self-explanatory."

"Not *that* post," he says. "I'm talking about the one from this morning."

I look at him flatly. Has everyone gone around the bend?

"The one where you tell everyone to go to hell, basically."

I stare at Tucker for a long time. My brain is stumbling through a lot of thoughts, and none of them are related to one another. Marty's phone call, my email inbox, the girl with the bandages, Tucker's arrival, and now the second mention today of a recent post. These facts are colliding in my skull like pinballs, with nothing connecting or landing where it belongs. I try to figure out which piece of information is the most important. Tucker wants me back—that feels urgent but not good. I don't want to handle that one any more than I already have. So instead I say, "Can I see your phone?"

"What for?"

I don't even answer him, just hold out my hand. After a moment he places his unlocked phone into it. I open Pictey and click my own picture. My feed, that carefully cultivated mix of airbrushing, Photoshop, hashtags, and nonsense, comes up on the screen. I read.

> . . . Rather than sit and do nothing like you entitled nitwits, I'm going to try some more practical ways of pursuing my goals, such as working harder instead of killing hours of every workday on social media, saving money instead of buying everything I see advertised on some influencer's feed, and being alone with my thoughts instead of forcing someone else to create constant sources of entertainment for me in every second of my day.

> Consider this: maybe if your relationship with technology requires you to sit prone in a mindless trance for forty-five minutes per day to recover, you should just get off of social media for pity's sake and go take a nice walk!

Of all the words in the entire post, it's the last sentence, specifically *for pity's sake*, that makes me stumble the most. "For pity's sake?" I repeat, mystified. "What is this?" I ask him. "Who wrote this? You?"

Tucker looks like I hit him. "You didn't write this?" he asks.

"Did you *read* this? Of course I didn't write it. I would never talk to people that way. It's supercilious and insulting. No one on my feed has done anything to deserve this, besides the usual trolls, and the hell with them. And why would I disrespect the idea of meditation? I love meditation."

"I thought . . . ," he starts. "I thought you'd done a one-eighty. I thought you'd decided to push back against the social media machine."

"I did! I did a one-eighty; I did decide to push back," I say. "I haven't posted since just after you dumped me. All of this is . . ." I scroll and see pictures that do look like they could be mine, and I scan captions that sound exactly like me . . . "Fraud," I say. My stomach falls as the pieces of a terrible puzzle begin to slide into place. "There must be fifty bogus posts." My mind starts to reel. The first one is from the same day I threw away my phone.

Around us, a small crowd is gathering, people pretending not to look. A few with phones out. I realize my voice has gotten loud. My face is hot, my hands gripping Tucker's phone for dear life. I scroll and scroll and see how my cyberself, a persona I created so carefully and intentionally, has been online the entire time I've been off. Everything I've done to free myself from the social juggernaut has been pointless. @Mia&Mike is more real, it seems, than I've ever been.

Helplessly, I gesture to Tucker. "Tucker, we may not be close anymore, but surely you have to know I would never post this."

He deflates. "I just hoped . . ." His voice trickles away. "I don't know."

"Hoped that I'd decided to be unkind to all the people who have given me their precious time and attention?" I ask, thinking of the countless people who have told their stories, found their tribe, made their connections through the comments of my feed. "No. It was hard enough for me to step away in the first place. I felt like I had to choose between all of them and myself. And now look. I spent the last year living my life for the benefit of a social media identity that doesn't even need me to run," I say, my voice cracking. "Because it was all I had left after Mike."

Tucker's expression crumples. "You had me."

I shake my head, feeling the despair I see on his face. "But I didn't, not really. I had a guy who played the game with me, until he got far enough in his career to realize he didn't have to play the game anymore. I had a fiancé who left me in private and then extorted me for money to keep up the public charade." I see a flash of light and look to the side. There's a woman filming me on her phone. I want to shout at her, demand my privacy, but what illusion of privacy can I pretend to defend? "I had my family," I say to Tucker, thinking of Andy, somewhere, just out of sight, wishing he could just be here now, just for ten minutes, just his hand on my shoulder to tell me I am real and all this, the hacker, the ex, the feed, is not. "My mom," I correct, because as much as I've tried to forget it, Andy is gone. "But I didn't know it."

Tucker takes a step closer. I don't have the energy to step away. "I'm sorry, Mia," he says again. "I'm sorry I wasn't who you needed me to be."

"I'm sorry too," I tell him. "I used you too. When you proposed, I never should have said yes."

Now I do feel a hand on my shoulder, and for a second I think, *Could it be?* But when I turn, it isn't my brother standing there. It's Dewey. My heart floods.

"Mia," he says. "Are you ok?"

I shake my head. "I don't know," I tell him, though I am certain that having him here now can only be a good thing. "I've been hacked," I say, "and I don't know anymore where I stop and this version of me"—I wave the phone helplessly—"begins."

Dewey takes the phone from me and wraps me up in his arms, and I think, just for that tiny moment, that everything is going to be ok somehow.

But then I hear a small voice behind me, and I turn around and see the girl. The bandaged girl from before, in her high teens or low twenties if I had to guess. Jessica. Next to her is a woman, midthirties, with bike-helmet hair. The pair look like sisters, or maybe young mother and daughter. I recognize the protective stance of the older one with a twinge. It's the way my mother stood at Andy's memorial, between me and the fact of his death. They're both looking at me, the older in panic, the younger with expectation.

"I'm sorry," I say, pulling out of Dewey's arms. "What did you say?"

"I said," she calls, raising her voice so it's clear above the small crowd, the few passing cars, the wind off the mountains, "what do you mean, hacked? You weren't hacked at all. You knew exactly who was posting. You were the one who paid her to post."

PAIGE

"What do you mean, hacked?"

As we walk out of the Sleepy Bear into an unusual snarl of people on the otherwise empty sidewalk, I hear my sister speak, and I think, *This isn't good,* and then I realize this is worse than bad. This is a disaster. Mia is standing there, and Tucker, and Tim back from the bike shop, and some other guy I've never seen before, with one hand falling slowly off Mia's back, the other holding a phone and scrolling, scrolling, scrolling. Scrolling the sky down on top of my head.

"I didn't pay anyone to post anything," Mia says loudly as Jessica steps toward her. "I do all my own posts. I have never hired a ghoster in my life."

Jessica shakes her head. I reach for her arm, but she pulls it back. "I'm sorry, Mia, but you must be forgetting," she says, her voice a bit lower, even now still trying to keep what she thinks is this woman's secret. "You've been using one for a week now. You used my sister. Tell the truth. People will understand." She looks back at me with pleading in her eyes. "Paige?" she asks. I can only shake my head slowly. My voice is gone.

"But it is the truth," Mia says, to me and Jessica and anyone else within a hundred feet. "I didn't hire anyone to post for me. I've been hacked," she says, and once more for good measure: "My Pictey account has been hacked. I would never say the things the hacker posted. It's clearly someone trying to sandbag me, some troll who makes it their life purpose to torture people on the internet."

"My sister is not a troll!" Jessica cries, a wild look in her eyes. "You may not like what she posted, but you can't just sell her out like this. You're supposed to be a good person. Stand by what you did."

"I didn't *do* anything," Mia says. "I don't even know who your sister is."

I will myself to say something, to move, but I'm frozen, ice and panic mingling in my veins. "She's Paige Miller!" I hear Jessica cry. "You hired her! You must at least sign her checks!"

I force my arms to rise and grab hold of Jessica's arm again, but again she wrenches it free. "Jessica," I hear myself say, as if from a great distance. "No, Jessica. Leave her be."

Mia rounds on me. "Are you her sister?" she demands. "Are you Paige Miller?"

I don't know where to look. Not at Jessica, to be sure, but not at Mia either. I breathe in, hold it, breathe out. "Yes," I say at last. "That is my name."

"Is this your post?" Mia waves in the general direction of a phone. "Did you write this?" she asks me.

Slowly, blinking too fast, I say, "Yes. I did."

"Who the hell even ARE you?" she cries. "Why would you hack my account and ruin my feed?"

I shake my head frantically, words gone again. My eyes shift from Mia to my sister and back to Mia again. I will Mia to just shut up, just leave things be, just let us go and forget this ever happened. I will Jessica to understand.

"Why did you do this?" Mia asks me again. "I have spent years of my life creating this community," she tells me. "This is how I make my living. This is how I make a difference in the world. Why would you torpedo it like that? Just because you can? Because my password didn't have enough random numbers in it? Why would you take such advantage?"

I open my mouth to find something to say, anything, but Tucker cuts her off. "Mia," he says softly. "Maybe this is a good thing. Maybe this is your way out, if that's what you want."

"It's NOT what I want!" Mia whirls around on Tucker in distress. "I don't know how else to explain this to you: I am not just posting constant selfies because I'm some vain idiot. I have something to say! And this is the platform I've been given to say it in. Do you have any clue how lucky I am to have—to *have* had—half a million followers? Do you have any idea what a difficult accomplishment that was?" She turns back to me. "And do you?" she asks. "When I posted that I was going offline for a while, did you think that I actually meant, *Would a complete stranger please start impersonating me and then tell all my followers to, what, 'just get off social media for pity's sake'?*" She laughs an angry bark. "Because if so, in what universe would I ever use the phrase *for pity's sake*!?" She shakes her head angrily and then turns to my sister. "You said you're a longtime fan of mine. How could you not see that that post was fraudulent?"

"You're the one who's fraudulent," Jessica says, even as I try to pull her out of this fray. "You hired my sister knowing what she'd do. And then you paid her to post, knowing full well that she hated the very idea of influencers. Maybe you didn't directly tell her to write exactly this, but you knew what you were getting with her. You knew it would happen."

Mia, too, reaches out to my sister. Her face softens, and when she shows her kindness, my heart cracks in two. "Jessica, I'm sorry. I'm sorry for whatever you've been through. I can see it's been a lot. But I need you to understand: I never hired your sister. I don't know how she got my password. I do know she's committed a crime by hacking my account and probably cost me thousands of dollars in revenues too. I know that what she did could land her in jail."

Jessica shakes her head. "That's not true," she says. She turns to me, eyes full of tears. "Paige?"

I shake my head desperately. Trying to, what, deny this? I cannot. "Jessica," I beg. "I was going to tell you."

But she is inconsolable. "Why would you do this, Paige?" she cries. "Why would you tell me all these lies? Right now—when things have been so hard?"

"Please, Jessica. I didn't mean to hurt you," I say.

But Jessica, the loyal little sister who couldn't get me to stop spinning the merry-go-round, who I left behind to save myself, who had to learn on her own, because I did not teach her, about the place between the bridge and the water, has turned back to Mia. Her eyes are like little shiny points of fire. "I don't care what you say, Mia Bell. You *are* a fraud," she spits out angrily. "And you know it. You told everyone that you were married, to that guy," she shouts, pointing at Tucker. I wince at the loudness of her voice, the manic tone. "But I know for a fact," she goes on, "that he jilted you at the altar. And now I know why he did it! Because you're nothing but a liar and a fake."

In shock, I drop Jessica's arm. Mia's mouth falls open. I stammer around for what to say, hopelessly, but Jessica is already shoving past me in the opposite direction of the coffee shop, heading for the ski hill.

I look anxiously in the direction she moves, about to take off after her, but Mia points at me sharply. "Don't even think about moving an inch," she says, "or I'll call the police."

Tucker's eyes widen. "Mia, you don't need to call any police," he says. "This is probably all some big misunderstanding."

"I'll tell you the misunderstanding," I hear myself say. "I misunderstand how you could let people on your feed believe so many lies about you, lie after lie after lie, while they were desperately begging you for help. While their lives were in jeopardy. I misunderstand how you can stand here threatening me with jail time when any fool can see my sister is in danger."

I look at this woman, who has done nothing and everything at once, and sneer. "Why don't you go back with Tucker, Mia? Go back with him, go back to posting, go back into your make-believe world where everyone loves you and you're married and it was a beautiful ceremony—even though it never really happened. Enjoy yourself there. You don't deserve the real world." I turn on my heel. I scan the roads for Jessica and see her running up the stairs to the ski village. I don't know where she's going or why, but I know I must catch up to her, and quickly, while she is still safe. But even so, I look back over my shoulder and say as I go, "I know what I've done to you is wrong. But you've had hundreds of thousands of people looking to you for answers, and what you've given them instead, platitudes and sales pitches and lies—those things are far worse."

MIA

The real world.

I do deserve it, don't I?

Tears are rising up in my throat. Tears of anger, tears of frustration, tears of grief. Tears of regret.

In the moment, I turn to the person who has made my real-world life make sense: Dewey. I start to throw my arms around his shoulders for a hug, but he unpeels me and puts my arms at my sides.

"Mia," he says. His voice is flat. "Is this Tucker?"

Tucker nods. "And who exactly are you?"

Dewey doesn't answer, saying instead, "Does this phone belong to you?" He holds it out like he can't stand to hold it another second.

Tucker nods and takes it out of his hand.

"And did that Pictey account that was on screen belong to you?" he asks me.

I nod too.

"Then I think we need to talk."

"What's going on?" I ask. "Why are you talking to me like that?"

He shakes his head sadly. "You know how I feel about you. But you said that you had been jilted recently. You said that was why what we were doing here"—he gestures from me to him—"was just a friendship."

I look at him in shock. "I have. I was. Tell him, Tucker."

Tucker looks at Dewey. "Who the hell is this guy, Mia?" I notice at once that Dewey is six inches taller than Tucker and twice the man he ever was. I think of how I first imagined having a rebound fling with Dewey, and it seems ridiculous. I don't know much about basketball, but don't you only get two points on a rebound? Dewey is like one of those ridiculous halftime shots from the middle where you could win a million dollars.

"This is Dewey," I tell Tucker. "He's my friend. I met him after . . . we broke up."

"So you definitely did break up, then," says Dewey. "I guess that's something."

"Of course we did," I say. "Why would I lie about that?"

"Because you definitely *did* lie about that," he says. "To someone. A lot of someones. Azalea called me while I was walking over from the distillery. She told me you were some kind of internet star and your boyfriend was looking for you. She was confused and upset. I told her it had to be a misunderstanding."

For a moment I think he's talking about the hacked posts. I start to point to the hacker sister, but she's gone. Jessica, who seemed so fragile a moment ago, is gone, too, I realize, in some dim recess of my brain.

But Dewey's not talking about her anyway. "Just before you and I met on Mount Wyler, you posted that you got married," says Dewey. "Are you married, or aren't you?"

"I'm not married," I tell him urgently. "That post wasn't real. It was something I had to do in the moment." But I didn't have to do it at all, I think now. I told myself I had to, for money, for fear, for the pull of what had become my status quo. Those were all lies.

Dewey isn't fooled. "You *had* to tell half a million people you were married and then start something new with me?"

I try to say that I wasn't starting something with him. But that's stupid. Of course I was flirting; of course I knew he was flirting back. I may have said one thing about friendship and readiness, but we both knew something was happening, and neither one of us minded one bit. "I had a plan," I mumble, hearing the falseness in my own words. "A way to clear things up. I just needed time. There were financial considerations, and then there were all those people, with all their expectations." My voice feels thick as the truth cuts through. "Dewey, there were so many expectations. I didn't know what else to do."

"I had some expectations of you too," says Dewey. "Honesty, for one thing."

"I'm sorry. In the moment, I was so lost."

"So you lied," he says. He is looking down. I can see how disappointed he feels. I've lied and been hacked and screwed things up six ways from Sunday. And now Dewey won't look me in the eye.

"It was complicated," I say.

"Actually, it's not that complicated," interrupts Tucker. It startles me—I'd forgotten he was even here. "Let me break it down for you. Mia is an internet influencer. She makes her living making everything look better than it is. When life gives her lemons, she makes low-sugar pomegranate-lemon iced tea in a canning jar with a compostable spoon. And sorry to break it to you, but she probably was looking for someone to replace me with, and in a hurry too. I mean, here she is with you, some kind of mountain man, two weeks after quote-unquote marrying me. For all we know, she's about to post that she left *me* for *you*."

"I'm not going to do that," I try. "I would never do that." But no one hears. Tucker, scorned and now jealous, talks right over me.

"Soon she'll be grooming you to make sunset heart hands." Tucker holds his hands up to his heart in that stupid cliché and looks right at me, and the meanness in his eyes is a hot poker. "I just hope you see through it before you get in too deep."

Dewey looks from Tucker to me and back. I want to cover Dewey's eyes and his ears, like he's a child. It's all so ugly. It's not at all true. At least not this time.

Tucker looks Dewey up and down. "You're going to have to dress better. You need to know that before you get any more involved with her. You'll never get in front of a camera looking like that."

"Enough!" I shout, and then to Dewey I say, "There's nothing wrong with the way you dress. What he says isn't true. I don't want you to be part of all that. I don't want you to have to be on the feed. I don't want anything to do with that old life."

Tucker shakes his head. "Well then," he says. "Good luck with that, because without the feed, what are you? A washed-up yoga instructor with a dead dog."

Tears rise up in my eyes, and pain pierces the last bits of me that were still holding firm. "Why did you come here, Tucker? Why are you so dead set on hurting me?" I put my head in my hands, trying to hide my tears, but it doesn't do any good to hide from this.

"You know what? I don't know why I came here," he says. "I don't know why I thought you had changed at all. I don't know why I imagined that change would be possible."

"I did change," I say through a sob. I swivel around to Dewey, who is looking at me with sad eyes, lost. I am lost too. I don't know where I am anymore. I don't know which me is real.

There are a few people standing around staring at me, some taking my picture with their phones as waves of tears seem to spill down my face and drop off my chin. I reach for Dewey, but he shakes his head gently. "I'm sorry, Mia. I need to take this all in," he says. "I've fallen for you, you know that, but I can't take risks with my heart. Not when I share it with Lea."

My throat too tight to speak, I can only nod. Nod as he leans forward and wipes one of the droplets off my cheek. "Do what you need to do," he says in a lower voice so that only I can hear. He gestures to the crowd and to Tucker. "Figure out who you want to be."

With that, Dewey walks away. In silence I watch him until he is gone, knowing that Azalea will soon be out of my reach too. The hacker and her sister are both gone. And now I see Tucker is walking away, too, head shaking, anger coming off him in waves. "I did change," I say so loudly I hope they all can hear me, hear me on County AB and on the ski hill and at Pictey headquarters and from coast to goddamned coast. "I changed so much that I can never go back to who I was," I say, and as I do, I realize that it's actually the truth.

"I was going to quit it all and start again," I cry, and now I'm talking only to myself.

"But now," I say, softer, with no intended audience but my own battered heart, "I can't quit, can I? Now I have to go back. Now it's all I have left."

PAIGE

The likelihood of my going to prison for computer crimes is not as small as I would like. There are also some precedents in place that would not be in my favor in civil court. Nevertheless, I have bigger fish to fry. My sister has a long head start on me, and I'm going to have to break into a run. Luckily I am wearing running shoes.

The town of Copperidge is made up of a few larger commercial streets that run parallel to the front, and then the mountains rise up right out of the ski village, and my sister was last seen heading in that direction. I think of everything I know about mental illness as I run up the hill. The suicide rate in Colorado hovers around fourteen per hundred thousand people for young adults in Jessica's age bracket. Six out of every thousand people attempt suicide, with women being one and a half times more likely to attempt than men but more than a third less likely to die in the attempt. Of the behaviors indicative of suicidal ideation, Jessica has displayed several, including a previous attempt, withdrawal from normal friends and family, depression, anxiety, shame, anger, and, perversely, suddenly feeling better for a while.

Though I guess I took care of that last one today.

Common ways for young people to die intentionally include by firearm, poison, and hanging. Blood-loss deaths have reduced comparatively in recent years, probably because the most popular suicide-instruction websites list it as a high-pain method. I wonder what happens when a person tries to reopen previously cut veins. I wonder what tool Jessica could find to do such a thing. I wonder how I could have even let her out of my sight, even once, even for three minutes.

As I am running and considering Jessica's mind-set, weighing statistics and risk factors and opportunities, my own breathing is growing tight. Statistics aside, I am afraid for her. I am as afraid as I've ever been in my life. As afraid as I was when I was in Jessica's shoes and I thought one little surprise or disappointment could make me lose my own tenuous control. Afraid as I was when I once, at my uncle's house a week after the "accident," passed his gun safe and then returned to it later that night to try the handle, to see if it was really locked.

There's no way she could get a gun on a mountainside, is there? I wonder. There's no method she could find to hang herself before I get to her?

The typically automatic function of my air intake is starting to fail me. And also, the air, while always thin up here, has become empty, like a vacuum. My lungs draw in but don't expand. My heart gets nothing. I am still running, but instead of panting, I am only gasping occasionally, and the air I manage to push out seems unused. I force myself to exhale so I will inhale on the rebound, but the breaths are still coming back to me unusable.

I'm coming up on the last crossroad before the village now, and I'm trying to drag myself up the frontage road along the mountain. I see mountain bikers come down the hill, and they are plummeting at terrifying speeds. There is no question that without their pads and helmets, what they are doing would be just another way to orchestrate one's own death. Could Jessica do something like that? Because of my lies and omissions? Could she throw herself down a cliff on the back of a bike? Would she even need the bike, if she could somehow get to the top of the mountain?

Where the hell has she gone?

But then I see her. I see her ponytail, and then the rest of her, just out of the corner of my eye. She's maybe two hundred feet away. I shout for her, but there's something squeaky about my voice, and I realize now that I've been holding my breath for so long I can't speak. I've made so much fun of Karrin telling me to take deep breaths in every single moment of strife, but here I am, running after my sister, who may be planning to hurt herself, and she's in real danger, and for some idiotic reason I've stopped breathing myself. In the years since my own suicide attempt, I have turned down the volume on so many feelings, quieted my mind of any potentially upsetting uncertainty, blocked the potential for hurt or rejection or heartbreak from ever entering my life. But now, when I have broken my sister's heart, the thing that is going to do me in isn't feeling too much or crying too hard. It's going to be starving myself of the oxygen every human needs to survive.

I call again for my sister and try to pull my diaphragm down, try to drag some kind of wind into my lungs, but I can't seem to breathe in without breathing out harder, faster. Jessica is slowing, but I am too. She's standing in some sort of small line, maybe three people in front of her, waiting by a little building. I don't know what the little building is.

I am sinking to my knees. Maybe if I can get some air, I think, but now I am really falling. *Falling,* some part of my brain whispers to me. Falling. In the 8 percent of suicides not caused by guns or ropes or pills, there's blood loss, and there's that one too: falling. My knees hit the ground, then my right shoulder. My vision tightens so I lose the far edges and then the sides, and soon I am looking at one thing and one thing only. That thing is my sister. She is first in line. And now she is in front. She is waiting for something to come, looking behind her, just as though she might see me. Has she seen me? *Please, please, Jessica, look back and see me.*

But it's not me she's waiting for. It's something else. Something deadly. And as my vision blurs, I see her hop backward onto a swing, and the swing rises into the air, and then she is on the chairlift, moving high up into the sky, farther and farther up and away from me.

My last thought before everything goes dark is simply: *Falling*.

MIA

At first, in the echo of whatever just happened, I'm not sure what makes me walk toward the mountain. My car is parked a block away. I could get in it and drive back to Mom's and cry for a week.

But I don't get in my car. I feel like I'm not safe to drive. I'm shaking, after all, and my vision is blurry with tears. And I am angry—so incredibly angry—at the crazy hacker who just ruined everything, at Tucker, most of all at myself. If I had just told one truth two weeks ago, would things be different? What if I had told a thousand more truths, between when I lost Andy and when I lost Mike and today? Then maybe I wouldn't have also lost myself.

But that's not what I did, and now something has been set in motion. Something important, I realize as my heart rate begins to return to normal. I don't know what it is, but I saw it in the eyes of the girl with the bandages. I know I need to find her, make sure she is ok. I know it with the kind of certainty I've come to recognize, in the quiet of a campfire or a field of lupine or in the pleasure of an undisturbed walk up a hill, as my own intuition.

It is a four-block walk to the mountain from the street I'm on, and I decide I need to cover it quickly. As I jog, I glance down each side street, wondering if Jessica got in a car, if the sister—Paige Miller, I remember—has found her already and if I will ever see either woman again.

My stomach lurches. If I can't find them, then what?

I suppose I will just get a phone at one of the mall stores and delete all the things she posted. I could delete the dead-on impersonations of me along with the rant I myself have felt a million times but would never in a million years put up online. I could post that I came back from my honeymoon and found my account had been hacked and turn yet another underdog moment into a social media triumph.

It is, after all, entirely on-brand.

But to hell with my brand. I care about my mother, about Dewey and Azalea, and about camping and hammocks and dog bars and mountain sky. I care about fresh eggs with just-cut herbs and chèvre and the stories of beautiful births and running up Mount Wyler and walking back down. I care about someone I met once getting into a crow pose for the first time and the way a good deep breath in a loamy garden mends grieving hearts and microbiomes. I care about the people who followed me who are feeling hurt by what Paige posted, and I care about the people who felt seen by it too.

Most of all I care about the girl with the bandages.

I do not, in even the longest list of things to care about, have room to add "my brand" anymore.

When I realize this, I run faster.

And then I stutter to a sudden stop just moments before I trip.

On a body.

It is the body of the woman who hacked my account. I bend down in a panic and feel her wrist, warm and with a pulse, and shout for help. A man—a good-looking guy that I saw in front of the Sleepy Bear earlier with his bike—runs up to me and says, "I called 911 for Paige, but Jessica, her sister, is missing."

"Who are you?" I say.

"I'm Tim," he says. "I'm a follower. Well, I have been since one o'clock today."

I brush his comment away. "Never mind about Pictey. Is she ok?"

"Which one?" the stranger says. "Well, never mind, it doesn't matter, because I don't know if either one is ok. Paige, at least, has help on the way. The younger one, Jessica, she started a thread in your comments a couple weeks ago about taking her own life."

"I know," I tell him, heart in my throat. "I went looking because I was worried. I don't know what happened back there, between the two of them, but it was bad."

"I haven't seen her since she ran off," says Tim.

"Oh god," I say. "She wouldn't—I mean, not over an altercation between her hacker sister and an internet celebrity. Would she?"

Tim shrugs worriedly. "I'm not sure. I know she's a big fan of yours."

"Was," I say. "She knows I'm a fraud now."

He nods. "She's probably feeling like everyone's a fraud right about now," he says.

More tears rise up in my eyes. "Do you have any idea where she might have gone?" I ask.

He shakes his head. "Last seen heading toward the mountain. I was hoping you might know. I think I should stay here with Paige. I need to wait for help to come."

I look at this complete stranger and say, worry seeping through my words, "You'll take care of her?" I have forgotten my anger. It seems inconsequential now.

He nods. "I certainly will. But I'm not going to report her for what she did, if that's what you're thinking. She's very nice. She's a good sister, and she isn't a good fit for jail. No one even ever taught her how to ride a bike."

I look at him blankly, adding him to the list of things that don't make sense. "That is to say," he continues, "I haven't known her long, but it seems that for some reason her upbringing lacked key strategies for negotiating life's challenges, and as a result she has a set of coping skills that may to others seem slightly maladaptive."

It takes me two beats to figure out what he's trying to tell me. "So her coping skills involve hacking my social media account and then tanking it?" I say.

"Yes," he says. "Exactly."

"Because she blames me for her sister's . . ." I gesture to my own wrists, unsure how to refer to the bandages and what put them there.

"Yes," Tim says, sparing me.

"I blame me," I say. "I was useless when she asked for help. Less than useless." I feel the wave of hot shame come up the back of my throat. "I told her, what, to ride out her feelings and adopt a pet? Tim, what have I done?"

He shrugs. "The best you knew how, I have to guess."

Sullen, I nod. I know better now, but maybe it's too late. "How are we going to find her?"

He frowns. "I have no idea. The only place she could have gone from here is . . ." He points up.

I look around, up the mountain. I see the chairlifts. My hand slaps over my mouth in fear. "No," I say.

"You've got to find her," he says.

I clutch at my satchel in panic. There's no phone there. Who would I call anyway? "I'm going to go get my car and drive around the back way," I say. "Maybe she's just at the top, looking for her sister, or . . ." My voice drops off.

"Can you try her on Pictey? She might listen to you. Tell us where she's gone," says Tim.

I shake my head. "I have no phone. I threw it off a mountain because I lost my mind."

Tim frowns but then smacks his forehead. "Just take this," he says, and then he bends gently over Paige's prone body and removes a large cell phone from her hip pocket. "You can use it to call for help." He raises one of Paige's hands to the phone and uses her limp finger to turn off the lock setting.

He looks me in the eyes. "Now you have what you need to make things right."

I realize at once what he's saying. I have a way to fix my account or wreak vengeance on Paige's bank account or do any number of things with her unlocked phone. I only ask, "Can you call this phone when you get to the hospital?"

He nods. "I have her number from earlier."

"Thank you," I say.

He waves my thanks away. "Find Jessica."

"I'll find her," I say, though I have no idea how. "I promise."

And then, as a fire truck and ambulance arrive for Paige in a blare of sound, I think of something. Somewhere Jessica might be. I grab the phone, which feels so foreign in my hands after all this time without one, start calling the number last dialed, labeled *Jessica Odanz (mobile)*, and break out into a run.

PAIGE

I wake up in the back of a strange car. It's not a car. It's an ambulance. I wake up in an ambulance, and I shout, "JESSICA," but she's not the one on the stretcher. I am. I feel confused.

"She's with us," says one EMT to another. "She's trying to talk."

"Move the mask," says the other.

"What is it, Paige?"

"My sister is falling from the sky," I say.

The EMT puts an oxygen mask back over my face. She looks up at her partner. "Should we give her a sedative?" I hear her ask.

A sedative sounds incredibly appealing right now. I would like nothing more than to have a nice bit of Valium with a Xanax chaser. I nod emphatically. Then I remember what I must do, and I shake my head no.

"She seems agitated."

"I am agitated!" I say into the gummy plastic, and I pull the mask off myself this time. "My sister is in a chairlift."

"Ma'am," says the partner EMT, "your friend is riding in the front seat of the ambulance. He told us to tell you the police are searching for your sister on the mountain. And someone else."

"Mia Bell," says the lead.

I struggle to make this make sense. My heart is racing, my mouth dry. I had a panic attack, I piece together. I let down my sister, I ran after her, and then I saw her on the chairlift . . . "Is she dead?" I ask. I don't want to know the answer, but I'm done turning in the opposite direction of real life.

The two EMTs look at each other. One of them shrugs.

"He didn't say anything else."

I sit up in the gurney.

"Whoa there," says the woman. "Where do you think you're headed, ma'am?"

"Take me back to where you found me. Better still, take me to the top of that ski hill. I need to get as high as possible."

"You want us to drive to the top of Copperidge Mountain?" says the second EMT. He is amused. I feel anger build up in me. Raw and hot and scary. For the first time in years, I let it come.

"That's what I said," I say. "And that's what I want you to do."

"Ma'am," says the woman.

"Stop calling me ma'am!" I hear myself shout. "This is not a grocery store. This is an ambulance. I have a name. My name is Paige Miller, and I am extremely upset!"

"We have to take you to the hospital. We can't just drive you wherever you want to go."

"Why not?" I ask. I swing my legs over the side of the gurney. "No, really, why? I want you to tell me!" I hear my voice getting louder, angrier. "Have I been arrested? Have I been institutionalized? If not, I want you to take me back to where you found me."

"Lady," says the other, and I snarl.

"It's PAIGE MILLER."

"Fine. Paige Miller. You're going to the hospital. You gotta get your head checked. Your buddy says you were running and then stopped and went down hard. You might have had a heart attack. You might have a brain bleed."

I consider this. "If it's the former, then it's water under the bridge," I tell him. "If it's the latter, they'll just have to wait before they drill me open." I feel around my pocket. "Where's my phone?"

"That guy took it. He said to tell you he'll get it back to you."

"What guy? Tim?"

"Yes. Tim."

"He has a name too. Pull over and let me talk to Tim."

"You're going to the hospital," says the first EMT. "That's it."

"This is ridiculous. I'm being held against my will. This is tantamount to kidnapping."

"Oh boy, here we go," says the woman, who is putting the oxygen mask over my face and loading up a syringe.

"I hate the summer," says the guy. "I prefer the broken legs to the loonies."

That's it. I stand, grab onto a vinyl strap, and pound on the partition between us and the driver. "STOP!" I shout.

"I think we'd better do the sedative *now*," one of them says behind me.

I spin around. In any other universe, in any other lifetime, I would beg them to put me under. Anything to make this onslaught of anger and fear and guilt and panic stop. But I can't do that anymore. That may have kept me alive up to now, but it won't do a thing to help my sister. "Do not touch me," I say in the scariest voice I have.

"You can't be standing up in here, ma'am—Ms. Miller," says the lead EMT. "It's a fall risk."

The word *fall* focuses me, takes all those powerful emotions that want to drown me and channels them into something I can use. "Let me make myself clear," I tell them. "My sister is in danger. I am not going to the hospital until she is safe. You can take me back to where you found me, or you can let me out right here, but either way, I'm getting out of this ambulance."

The EMT's face bends into a grimace. He looks at his lead; she looks back.

"Maybe we should pull over," she says. "Tell Trina to pull over."

"That's easy for you to say," the second says. "I'm the one who has to chart this. What if we can't bill?"

I clear my throat. "WHAT IF I SUE?"

I am off that ambulance in under twenty-five seconds. Tim climbs down from the driver's cab with confusion and sympathy in his eyes. For a second I want to rail at him too—why would he call the ambulance? Doesn't he know what Jessica might do? Might have already done? But then tears are in my eyes, and I know he must have been frightened to see me lying there wherever I collapsed, not knowing just how many times I have shorted out my own brain in the face of crippling fear.

"I'm sorry, Tim," I say, when he is standing by the curb with me and the ambulance is pulling away. I realize, in that moment, I don't apologize very often. It would be too much to acknowledge where I have failed others, where I have failed myself. Now I can only pray I get a chance to apologize to Jessica. "I can't lie around in a narcotic haze while Jessica's out there somewhere."

He nods. "I understand completely," he says, and I can see from his eyes that this is true. "I don't know if you were awake at all before, but Mia was there too. She has your phone; she's calling your sister. She thought she might know where she could be. And the fire department came too. I asked them if they could stop the lifts. They got in the police and mountain patrol, had the lifts shut down in minutes. There's a lot of people out there looking now."

"What good does stopping a lift do if she's already on the lift?" I cry. I feel the weight of hopelessness throwing its heavy blanket on me, begging me to give up, to stop trying. I refuse. I am starting to wheeze again. I can feel my chest growing tight once more. I know I could go dark again, but I don't care.

Tim puts a hand on my arm. "I know you're worried," is all he says. "But are you sure you wouldn't be better off getting some medical help right now?"

I inhale with purpose. "Maybe I would be, Tim. But Jessica would not. We need to do whatever we can for her before it's too late."

"Ok, then," he says, and even in my panic, some little bubble of my brain tells me this: *You are angry, you are in trouble, but you somehow still aren't alone.* "Let's go find her."

MIA

Clutching Paige's phone for dear life, I understand, for the first time, what a cell phone is really *for*. This, this horrible frantic set of moments bleeding into moments, this is what people like my mom mean when they say they just keep a phone for an "emergency."

So I keep that phone from relocking like it is the difference between life and death, and maybe it is. When I am not looking up places I think I might find Jessica and navigating from one to the next, I am calling Jessica. First it rings for a while before I go to voice mail, and then, eventually, the immediate click of the computer recording tells me the phone is now off.

Tim texts me an update from the ski hill. He got the police to shut down all the lifts, and now they are searching for her on ATVs. They have Tim's number, and he says if he learns anything, he'll call. He hasn't called.

So I call Mom. She is the person who knows what to do in any situation, the person who has never failed me, not even once, the person who, I finally realize, never will, not so long as we are both in this world. I tell her as quickly as I can what's going on. I tell her about the girl who commented before my wedding, how I replied, how she disappeared, and how I found her again, got a second chance to help her, and somehow missed it again. I tell her, best as I can remember, exactly what I told Jessica weeks ago: I told her to find her own Mike. I remembered, in some small corner of my brain, that a best friend who truly knows how to do the job is all you need to get through even the hardest times. My best friends were Mike and Andy, and Mom's were Andy and me, and Azalea's was Maggie the kitchen chicken. Those friends, three legged, two footed, and winged, got us through the hard times. When our best friends left us, we weren't really the same.

I don't know who Jessica's friends were before her suicide attempt, but it's easy to see that her sister, Paige, took on the role after it. I suspect that Paige knew Jessica had posted her cry for help on my thread and thought I had let her down. And maybe in that moment I *did* let her down. Maybe anyone in my shoes would have been unable to change the circumstances. You can't save anyone through Pictey posts alone. But as a result of this, Paige was watching me as I faked the wedding, and she saw the opportunity when I signed off, and she took it. And though it's taken me some time to realize it, I benefited from it all, without even knowing what was going on, because I got away from that godforsaken app and everything associated with it. Even if it was only for a little while, it was the best little while I've had since Mike has been gone.

I tell Mom all of this, as quickly as humanly possible. She says, "Oh, of course!" because now that I say it out loud, it is so obvious. If you were my biggest fan—no, if you were @Mia&Mike's biggest fan—and you once believed in that feed unquestioningly and read every post with your heart wide open, and there was something hurting you so badly that you weren't sure if you wanted to even keep going, where would you go?

You'd go to the Humane Society.

Mom signs off so she can get out the phone book and start calling the county animal-rescue centers. When she gets a lead, she calls me back. I point the car from one place to another, but there are only so many spots to try, and the clock keeps turning numbers over and leaving me more and more fearful as it does.

Through it all, Mom calls me back, once, twice, four times, and each time she says, "We'll find her," and I pray she is right. If my hunch about what she has gone to do is wrong, then I have to believe it is probably too late. *Please, let me be right.*

And then, while looking in a place that is fruitless, I have a thought.

The tiniest, most far-reaching memory.

I point my car toward Black Diamond Baron's.

It was on a blackboard behind Dewey's head on that first night out, that not-a-date that he and I both wanted badly to be a date. It was written in chalk, in beautiful swirly script, and I remember being tempted. Terribly tempted, and then changing my mind because I couldn't stomach any more loss. Like with Dewey—someone who made my heart sing but who I kept at bay because of even the slightest chance at pain.

What an idiot I was. What was my plan for the rest of my life, exactly? I wonder. To orchestrate things so I lived only an online life and never had to lose anyone real again? To reduce my existence, my happinesses and sorrows, to the number of followers gained or lost on any given day? To sell strangers on a lifestyle that brought me absolutely no joy? To be nothing but a recipient of "likes"?

Here's what that blackboard said:

ADOPT-A-THON SATURDAY
Come by and meet your new best friend.
Dogs and cats available for adoption all day.
Save an animal and your next drink's on us.

I speed toward the restaurant while my mom stays on the line in silence. I pray. And at a stoplight, I send out a quick text.

And then there she is, on the sidewalk bench in front of the big open-air café that bustles with happy diners and their beloved dogs. I double-park and leap out of the car, still clutching her sister's phone.

Jessica is lying flat on her back on the bench, and her arms are hanging out by her sides. Her eyes are closed, and she is still. On her belly is a dog. A rough-looking black dog who is licking her face. My heart pounds, but my feet won't move.

But then she lifts up her arms to pet the dog, and the dog sits down right on her throat, and she says, "OOF!" And my whole body starts to shake with relief. I take as many deep breaths as I can between the car and the park bench, and then I come up to the bench and say, "Jessica, we haven't been properly introduced. My name is Mia Bell. May I sit down?"

She looks at me with her raw red eyes. She breathes out. She sits upright on the bench and moves the dog to her lap in a smooth motion that makes it seem like she's been a dog owner all her life. She gestures to the space she's made for me to sit down and says, without malice, "For all your bullshit, you were right about dogs."

"Did you adopt this dog?" I ask her.

"Yes. And it was crazy and probably wrong, and I may have to give her back, because I can't take care of her, but while I was doing it, it was the right thing to do, because it was better than my other idea, and it makes my other idea impossible. When you have to care for something, you have to live."

I feel the sensation of my heart tightening and hope and relief rushing through me in a mingled slurry. "It wasn't crazy," I say, my voice thick. "And it wasn't wrong. And you don't have to give her back."

"I have to go to the suicide rehab center," she says. "Until the meds work or I'm not crazy anymore, whichever comes first. Who is going to take care of her? My parents hate pets."

I shake my head at her needless worry. "I'll take her," I say without even thinking for a second. "I'd love to have her. I'll make sure she's safe and cared for so when you get home she's there waiting for you."

"But then she'll be yours," says Jessica.

"No. This is clearly your dog."

"You kind of do need a dog of your own," she points out. I look at this girl, who is right this second at the lowest moment that I hope her life will ever show her, and she is thinking about what I need.

I inhale deeply. Let it out. "Let me tell you about how I was when I adopted Mike," I say. "I was lost. I was trying to start a business that no one seemed to want, and my brother, the only person who understood me, had just died, and my mother, the person who didn't seem to understand anything, was left all alone far, far away. I couldn't face her because I was hurting so much, and I didn't know how we were supposed to work as a family without my brother to make us work. I knew I was being selfish to ignore my mom's sadness, and I started to feel worse every day. I started to feel terrible.

"The day before I got Mike, I couldn't get out of bed. I lay there, and I wasn't even crying anymore. I was just lying in bed and feeling absolutely nothing, which, it turns out, is worse than feeling sadness or grief. For a few hours, I thought I would never feel better than I felt right then. I believed that this was my life now, a loop of loneliness, guilt, and loss."

My eyes close. A single tear has gotten loose, even though that was all so long ago. I remember how awful it felt, and I hate that anyone else would ever have to feel that way. Especially this girl, too young to be despairing already. Maybe just a decade older than Azalea. But without even one loving chicken.

"So what did you do?" asks Jessica.

"I was driving to the store to buy something. I don't remember what. I was too sad to eat much, and I wasn't exactly taking care of myself. But I was driving to the store, because I couldn't figure out what else to do with myself, and I saw someone slow their car down right in front of me. And then they slowed down more, and I had to step on the brake hard, and I honked. Their driver-side window rolled down, and it being LA, I thought they were going to give me the finger. But instead I watched a whimpering dog being forced out the window in the intersection. They started to drive while the dog was half in and half out of the window. I saw the dog drop to the pavement and heard the most awful noise of his scream, and I'm not sure exactly what happened next, because it was a busy crossroads and tons of people stopped and the traffic was halted and it was all a blur. I just remember that somehow the dog was in my back seat bleeding and I was racing to the nearest animal hospital.

"That was Mike," I say, petting the little black hound mix with the long muzzle that has chosen Jessica. "Mike went through all that to come live with me. After the surgeries he needed constant care. He could never be alone. He was anxious and needy, and he shed everywhere. He was irreplaceable. I tried to replace him, with Tucker, with my followers, but no one, real or virtual, could compare to Mike.

"Losing Mike was hard," I tell her. "But not as hard as never having had him. Thanks to him," I say, thinking of Andy, Mom, Dewey, recalling the stricken look in Paige's eyes when she watched Jessica run away, "I know love when I see it.

"This dog," I tell Jessica, and I 100 percent believe what I am saying and wish only that I'd said it to her better the first time she asked, when she was only ones and zeros and not flesh and blood. "This dog will keep you alive. This dog will make you *glad* you are alive. If you go to therapy and take your meds and stay close with the people who love you and walk this dog twice a day, you will survive. And then, one day, you'll realize you feel better. All the way better."

She looks into my eyes. "Do you promise?" she asks.

I nod.

"Because I got thrown out of my college for cheating. And my only sister just came into my life for the first time, but it turns out she's, like, an identity thief." She grimaces. "Sorry about that. And my mom is kind of a handful. And I have no plans for the future and no idea what I'm going to do next. What do I do next?"

She looks at me for answers. Not @Mia&Mike. Just me. Mia Bell. I try to think about what I believe, really believe. Not what I'd post. What's in my heart. "You're going to pet the dog," I say at last. "And you're not going to hurt yourself. That's all you have to do next."

PAIGE

Somehow, Tim manages to bike at top speeds standing up while I teeter on the back of his bike all the way to the restaurant with the novelty straws.

I see Jessica and Mia on a bench, and my whole being erupts in tears of relief. Tim stops suddenly, and I fall off the back. When I get to my feet, Jessica and Mia are there to lift me up. I take Mia's hand and look her in the eyes.

"Thank you," I tell her, though I've been crying so hard some snot runs into my mouth.

She looks at me, takes me in. I'm the woman who ruined her feed. She's the person who saved my sister.

She keeps hold of my hand, though I am standing now, and says, "I think I know why you did what you did. Even so, I expect you to help me undo it."

I cry more. These are some of the first tears I've shed in almost twenty years, but apparently it's like riding a bike. Or falling off a bike, in my case.

Then I wrap my arms around my sister. She hugs back, and when the hug has lasted too long, she pulls back and clears her throat.

"I thought you were going to die. I saw you go on the chairlift, and I thought . . ." My voice trails off.

She nods. "Ever since I came back with you to the inn, I've been thinking about that chairlift," she admits. "Just thinking about it. I've been scared even knowing how close it is. I never said anything to you, because I know you've got the same thing I do. Major depression. Anxiety disorder. You did what I did when you were sixteen."

My mouth falls open.

"You attempted suicide?" Mia asks. I can't speak for shock, so I look at Jessica to answer on my behalf.

She nods. "She thought I don't know, but I do. She took a ton of pills, and my mom noticed they weren't in her purse and went straight home and called 911. My mom loves a good selection of psychopharmacology with her at all times. I was little, too young to remember, but we have gossipy neighbors who still talk about Paige all the time."

I look for words, stammer helplessly.

"I wish you'd just told me yourself," Jessica goes on, before I can think what to say. "Then we could have been more honest with each other, before we went through all this. I want to know how you got through, and I want to tell you what led up to my attempt. I want to make a plan for dealing with Mom and getting us both back on our feet."

I cover my mouth to keep in a sob. When I think I can speak, I say only, "Oh, Jessica, I'm so sorry. I'm so, so sorry. I wanted to help you, but I didn't know how to go back to that time."

Jessica nods. "I think I understand, actually. When you first walked into my hospital room, I thought: *Finally someone who will understand.* I thought you were sent by the universe to fix me." Her voice stutters for a moment around thick emotion. "But that's not fair; you can't fix me," says Jessica. "You're broken too."

Mia speaks up. "We're all a little bit broken, though, aren't we? Let's face it: I'm a tech addict. Paige is a hacker. My mom is a loner. You cheated on an exam. We're all just good people accidentally on purpose hurting ourselves."

"I guess . . . everyone is going to get broken at one time or other," Jessica adds. She looks at me, and I realize, with our matching wet eyes and tear-thickened voices, we have never seemed more alike.

I take both her hands in mine. "For the record, I did come here to fix you," I tell her. "I just didn't realize how much fixing I needed myself."

Jessica only shrugs and proves once again just how smart she can be by saying, "Then all we can do is try to help everyone fix each other."

I think of my panic attacks, of the Karrins and Tims who have set me back on my feet each time I've gone down. I think of Cary and Jessica and maybe even Mia and her followers too. I thought I depended on no one, but that's not true at all. And for the first time in a long time, I'm ok with that.

MIA

Dear friends of the @Mia&Mike feed,

A lot has happened on this feed in the last month.

Most of it is not true.

On June 4th when I posted several pictures of my wedding gown, I had recently learned that my engagement had been called off. I was disappointed and did not know how to handle the news. Rather than post about it or stay quiet, I decided to act as if the cancellation had never happened. I justified this by telling myself that you did not want to know about the bad things going on in my life and only wanted to see the happy, perfect, airbrushed version of Mia Bell at any given time.

But in fact, the truer motivations for my lies were that I was afraid of showing my imperfections and failings, and I wanted to honor contracts for sponsorships I couldn't afford to cancel. And I suppose I wanted to continue to live in my make-believe world a little longer, rather than face the difficult turn my life had taken.

As you may know, I lost my brother about six years ago in a car accident. As a way of coping with the grief, I adopted a dog named Mike and started posting his picture on Pictey on a regular basis. He and I enjoyed the experience enormously, and we grew to love our audience of distant viewers. Posting and sharing with you became my second-favorite thing, after doing yoga with Mike. The feed grew and grew, and in time became my main source of income. Sadly, it also became my main source of socialization, interaction, and human contact.

After Mike passed on last year, the joy of posting disappeared. But I was utterly dependent on my audience to prop me up. You supported me and empathized, and in time I started to feel as though the people on-screen were all the people I needed in the world. I also felt you needed me, and I had a responsibility to paint a picture of my life that was perfect, cheerful, and happy 100 percent of the time. That was the Mia Bell brand.

But that was not the Mia Bell reality. The reality was, I met a good-enough guy and rushed into things in order to fill the void that Mike had left, not just in my heart but also on my feed. I threw myself into wedding planning headlong, ignoring the reality of my actual relationship with my potential husband. When Tucker had the good sense to break up with me, I faked the entire wedding online rather than openly admit my disappointment and embarrassment. For that I am very sorry.

For the record, I am not married, nor am I dating anyone. I do not like lying and I didn't want to keep doing it, but also didn't quite know how to make things right. So I didn't try. Instead, a few days after my fake wedding, with the support of my family, I threw my phone off the side of a mountain and quit my digital addiction cold turkey. While I was offline, a new friend took over posting for me as a favor. A very weird favor.

Those of you who have recently rushed to my defense and said that the upsetting post about social media did not sound like me are correct. That post was not me, and I regret that it went up on my feed. But, upon reflection, I do feel that the poster has a point. My relationship with social media was way, way out of whack, and I will take the advice given from here on out.

The short time I lived without my phone was the most real and rewarding time of my life. I wish each of you the same happiness and freedom, even though I know it will end my career as an internet influencer. I'll miss you, but that's all I'll miss.

I wish you:

Long quiet walks where the wind is your podcast.

Lost wanderings where your instincts are your GPS.

Peaceful early mornings where you have your nose in a cup of coffee instead of an email inbox.

Yoga with a friend, not an app.

Family time with no "shares" and lots of sharing.

Mental selfies in the flat, calm reflection of a mountain lake.

Sponsorships of children and animals.

Quiet summer evenings where the stars are your backlight.

A phone that's used for calling someone you love.

Friends, I wish you joy. I wish you airplane mode.

Gratefully yours,

Mia

A special PS to Dewey and Azalea: If you're reading this, I'm sorry. If you want to try again, only for real this time, you know how to reach me. My mom's number is on your fridge.

PAIGE

In the end, the number of dogs we adopt is four.

One for Jessica, of course, the wee houndish thing who she names Ophelia, because she has a surprisingly dark sense of humor. Ophie has already made herself comfortable in Cary's kitchen at Jessica's feet, and though Cary is vowing he will bill us if he gets a health-code violation, he is also putting bacon fat on her kibble every morning when he thinks no one notices.

One for Mia's mother, Marla, who gets a big yippy three-month-old puppy, the kind of dog who will be a great deal of work and annoyance. I point this out to Marla when she comes to the Inn Evergreen to check on me and Jessica and partake in Cary's cooking. After the dog finishes his shots and comes home, she'll need to house-train it and walk it at least once, maybe twice each day. It will wake her up in the night to pee and never leave her alone during the day. She laughs at my protests and says, "Paige, honey. That's kind of the whole point."

One dog is for Mia herself. Since that horrible day when I almost lost Jessica, Mia has given me more kindness than I deserve and made me realize how vastly I misjudged her. She drove me to the ER to get my brain checked out despite what I did, and while I was held overnight, she and her mom hosted Jessica and kept her under close supervision. I realize there is nothing I can do to make what I did to Mia's Pictey account right, but that won't stop me from trying to ameliorate the situation. As a small step in that direction, I insisted on funding her adoption of a new pet, as she's a bit cash poor at the moment.

There is no replacing Mike, she says, so she didn't even try for a similar breed. Instead she looked around at seven different rescues and eventually got a toy-size mutt. It's some unhappy mix of Chihuahua and long-haired dachshund, and the mating process must have been truly something to see. It's missing an ear and is eight years old. I ask her if she knows what a dog's average life span is and understands what she's setting herself up for by adopting an older dog. She tells us, "In the course of our lives we are going to have to learn how to outlive several dogs. I will, hopefully, outlive this one by some fifty years. But he still needs a home for the next six or seven." She shrugs. "I will survive it somehow. Besides, this dog is smaller than a chicken, and that was my number one requirement."

Mia has told us, in what has become a regular breakfast meetup in Cary's kitchen since I was discharged after my panic attack, that she plans to stay here in the mountains and impose on her mother for a little longer. "I'm interested in a guy," she says. "And I'm going to have to chase him down, because he thinks I'm a liar and a fake."

"You are," I point out. Jessica chokes on her coffee, and I color. My prostrating skills need quick work if I hope to ever even the score.

"But only in certain situations," says Mia, just laughing at me. "None of which do I plan to be in again."

She has seen to that. Her follower number is down by two-thirds. She has gone from the top-twenty-influencers list on Pictey to the low thousands. Much of the loss was from a combination of our two posts—mine lambasting her followers, and hers blessing them and sending them on their way. But she's still losing people, because she's posting just once each day now, and for some of her oldest fans that's just a bridge too far. (Failed air force initiative of 1944. Great story for another day.)

The followers she has left, she says, are her *people*. So much so that she has deputized ten of them by providing them with the direct line of Consie, the Safety and Standards screener who saved my sister's life. She was all too happy to be their point of contact in case of another emergency like Jessica's. I just wish every Pictey user had a Consie.

Maybe someday.

I will not be a Consie. I finally have had to admit that as a sufferer of debilitating panic attacks, I may not be the right person to be dealing with a constant onslaught of psychological triggers for eight hours a day.

"What will you be doing instead?" Jessica asks Mia. "If you're not going to be @Mia&Mike anymore?"

"I'm just going to be Mia," she says. "I'm going to hang out with my mom and try to teach her how to have a verbal filter." Her mom shoves her, but she smiles and goes on. "I'm going to win Dewey back as a friend and then seduce him when his guard is down with sexy chicken talk and a steamy night in a hammock. I'm going to buy a yoga studio—maybe that studio I was supposed to teach in the night we all met. That owner seemed particularly vulnerable to the temptation of a financial windfall."

"Who is Dewey?" I ask. "And how could a hammock be seductive?"

"Dewey is the guy," she tells me. "*The* guy. The reason I got Renaldo instead of a normal-size dog."

Marla coughs. "Renaldo?"

"Look at him. He's such a romancer," she says. Renaldo is in her purse. Cary is pretending not to notice yet another beast in his kitchen but has also brought out a stack of paper towels and a lint roller and not subtly set them in the middle of the kitchen table.

"Your dog is not what comes to mind when one thinks of romance," I point out. "He's physically deformed and also lacking in some of the scientifically proven attributes that most humans find physically appealing. His face is crooked, and his eyes are beady."

"Don't listen to her, Renaldo," says Mia.

"Your dog can't understand me," I say. Jessica snorts.

"So Renaldo is another bid for Dewey, then," says her mom.

Mia nods. "In part. Renaldo is too small to be a danger to chickens. The chickens may be a danger to him."

"Is Dewey some kind of chicken aficionado?" I ask.

"You can say that," she says.

"If so, I recommend you avail yourself of the book *The Dinosaurs We Eat: On the Physiology and Phylogeny of Chickens as It Relates to the Saurischians of the Lower Jurassic*. It's quiet at times, but the last five hundred pages are riveting." Jessica laughs again. What she finds so funny, I'll never know. And as long as she doesn't ever stop laughing, I don't really care.

"Hm. Until things get truly desperate, I'm going to go a slightly more organic route," says Mia. "Like wearing cute tops and spending lots of quality time doing things we both enjoy."

I pause for a second. "I can also see the value of your plan."

"Jessica, do you have a plan?" asks Marla. "For after the clinic?"

Tomorrow a bed will be open in the psychiatric care center, and my sister will be able to get some time to heal—really heal, with experts and treatment. I understand that goes well beyond the traditional use of the word *healing*—in fact, her actual wounds are fading into shiny scars. She will also be getting progressive therapies and pharmacological support. And based on the brochures, she'll be painting *en plein air* and doing nature walks.

Whatever works.

Jessica bites her lip. "Paige and I were up late last night. We're going to work together to encourage our mom to get involved in my family therapy at the clinic. It's a long shot. But whether she does or not, I'm going to stay with Paige this summer, take a year away from school and work, and then try to be reinstated to finish my last few credits at Boulder."

"It would behoove her to have her college degree," I say. "In her future endeavors."

Jessica nods. "I wish to be behooved," she says. Last night I asked Jessica if she wanted me to hop into the records department at CU and do a little cleanup of her recent gaffe. She said no, and I was relieved. After this whole affair with Mia, I'm interested in avoiding such gray areas of technology use in the future. "And Paige will have her dog by then. So there is some hope for her too."

It's true. The fourth dog is for me.

I have time to have a dog now, because I'm not going back to Pictey. Or rather, I am, but in a new role and working remotely. With Karrin's blessing, I'll have a team of six offshore programmers and one local suicide specialist who are helping me code a new ideation recognition and aversion program for the US. The project is called IRA. Like Ira Flatow from public radio's *Science Friday*, my celebrity crush.

Though I do not enjoy change, the benefits of this one are many. I no longer have to go into an office, I no longer have to live in the valley, and I no longer have to lie on an anxiety self-report once a day. I also will be doing the bulk of my work in the evening when my offshore programming team gets to their desks, so I'll be able to be there for Jessica's sessions at the clinic and then drive her to appointments later, until she feels safe around a car again. And I'll have plenty of time to research best practices of canine ownership and care. I am on the waiting list for a very special sort of dog, and I take the responsibility very seriously.

My dog will be a service dog. The specialists at the hospital I was taken to have connected me to a reputable breeder and expert trainer. We will work together to raise a dog who can detect breathing abnormalities, signal for help, and even save my life in the event of a dangerous panic attack. And once I have that support in place, I won't have to spend every waking moment avoiding anything that could cause a panic attack. Anything like feelings.

"What will you name the dog?" asks Marla.

I think on this for a moment. "I suppose I could wait to see what sex I get, but as my dog will be fixed, he or she will probably not be strongly gender identifying. So," I go on. I have given this a lot of thought. "With Mia's permission, of course . . ."

She nods. A smile and a teardrop mingle on her face. "Mike," she says.

"Mike Two." I feel my chest tighten, but not in that scary airless way. This is something different. This is more like hope.

"I didn't mean to steal your life, Mia," I say carefully.

"I know that now," she says.

"But when I did, it was much harder than I thought it would be," I admit.

Marla puts her arm around her daughter. "Not everything hard is worthwhile," she says, and there is a smile in her voice.

"Just most things," replies my sister, and I realize that she is the hope I feel. "Like surviving."

MIA

The phone rings at my mom's house a couple weeks after Jessica goes to the clinic to get treatment. All three dogs lose their minds at the sound, as they've done over any number of other terrifying things like the blender, the mailman, and the sound it makes when I bump into the bed frame with my shin every night.

Renaldo runs to me as the scary phone attacks our house, and I pick him up in one arm. To my great satisfaction, he stops barking right away, and his one floppy ear rotates back into the relaxed position. Ophie is jealous and now starts running around my legs, trying to trip me, her yap yap yap louder than the phone, making it hard for me to find the handset. Mom's giant puppy, Bananas, hasn't started barking yet, and we just taught her not to jump up, but the energy has to go somewhere, and now when she gets too excited, she pees herself a little. She is crated when we're gone and very good in those situations, but she has to be contained in the kitchen when we're home, because the carpet-cleaning machine we ordered out of desperation won't arrive till next week, and if I have to try to soak out one more pee stain from the carpet while at the same time trying to keep the other two dogs from peeing two inches away from the first stain while they can still smell it, I'll probably just start peeing on the carpet myself.

So Ophie is yapping, Bananas is keeping four on the floor but having a little wee on the kitchen tile, and Renaldo is licking my face, and I think, *What on earth have we done?* but it is one of those happy thoughts, the same kind my mom expresses when both Bananas and Ophie want to sleep in her bed, the warm puppy at her feet and Jessica's dog repeatedly trying to rest her face on my mom's forehead before she falls asleep. As my mom says, "Don't tell Ophelia this, but I secretly love it. Still, it would be so much sweeter if she didn't drool quite so profusely."

The phone is still ringing, so I pick up Ophie too. She's too big for this kind of coddling, but needs must. I put Renaldo on my shoulder and grab for the phone and put it on speaker, because whoever is calling me needs to understand what I'm dealing with over here.

"Hello?" The moment I answer it, Bananas stops spazzing, and Ophie relaxes like nothing ever happened.

"Hello," says a young, high voice. "May I please speak to Mia Bell?"

It's Azalea. Ever since I got honest on my new, improved, and much less popular Pictey feed, she's been coming around with eggs and various other offerings, an unnecessary trade for puppy time. She strongly favors Bananas of all the dogs, but she'll take them all to our newly fenced dog yard and try to teach them manners, one at a time. I think they're the ones teaching her things, to be honest.

"Lea, hon, I keep telling you, just come down whenever you like. I'm here unless I'm at the studio, and if we're both gone, you can just let yourself in the back door and visit the dogs."

"Um, well," she says. "Yeah. Thank you. But actually . . ." Her voice drifts off. "I'm calling to ask if my dad can come over."

My heart gives a tilt, but I try to play it ever-so-slightly cool. "You're calling on behalf of your father?" I say. "Dewey? The grown man?"

"Yes," she says. "That one."

"Well, you tell him I said he can come down, but he should stop getting children to do his dirty work."

"Maybe could you tell him that?" she asks. "He's probably almost to your porch by now."

I look at the receiver in confusion. "He's here?" I look out the kitchen window. I see no one.

"He told me to wait fifteen minutes after he left the house before I called."

"Oh, for heaven's sake." I laugh. "What if I'd said no?"

"That's what I said," exclaims Azalea. "I said, 'Dad, you are so embarrassing.'"

"He really is," I say, and then because Lea still can't quite work sarcasm, I also add, "Actually, he's a very nice guy. I bet he's a great dad."

"Yeah, but he's goofy," she says.

Out of the corner of my eye, I spy him coming down the road approaching the house. There's a bounce to his step that matches the one rising up in my mood. "He's very goofy," I agree, taking note of our open front window. "Goofy can be a good thing. Did he say why he was coming?"

"He's going to tell you to stop calling the house to apologize," she says. I freeze up. Did I go too far with that last *When Harry Met Sally* impersonation? "And then he's going to see if you want to go to the Dillon fireworks with him."

"Really?" I ask, flooding with relief and happiness. I want to go to the fireworks with him very much, but I bet he knows that already.

"Yeah," she says. I watch him coming up the drive, his floppy hair, his relaxed walk, and his lips pursed in a whistle, all as warm and appealing as I remembered. "He says he likes where your head's at these days. I'm not really sure what that was supposed to mean."

"Azalea?" I ask as Ophie wriggles out of my grasp to go to the door; she senses a visitor, and visitors are always good news. Her entire hindquarters begin to shake. Finally the wag reaches her tail, and the whiplike curl starts flapping side to side, knocking into the leg of Mom's altar, where I'm embarrassed to remember she and I put a snapshot of Dewey in a wine-fueled moment of silly fun.

"Yes?" says the girl on the phone. I imagine her there on her land-line, standing in a kitchen looking out on a passel of chickens, and all at once I cannot wait to see her again.

"I'm going to say yes to the fireworks," I say. I watch Dewey turn up to the porch, run a hand through his unruly hair. Tucker was absolutely right. He's not social media–boyfriend material. He's much too good for that.

"You are?" she asks excitedly. "Does that mean you'll come visit us again?"

"I was thinking, actually, about coming to visit just you. Have you gotten your school supply list yet?"

A knock comes at the door. It's Dewey. Here to see me. Ready to forgive and move on and maybe even do this thing for real. I move away from the receiver and lean toward the open window. "Just a minute," I call. "Talking to a good friend!"

Azalea says, "Is he there?" and I say, "He is," and she says, "I just got my list on Monday."

"Would you like to go back-to-school shopping with me? We could go to lunch, too, girls only."

There's the tiniest moment of silence on the phone, and then she says, "Can we go clothes shopping? Dad is terrible at that."

Another knock comes at the door. Bananas is going, well, bananas. Renaldo is basically trying to retreat to the top of my head.

"I would love that, and in the meantime, could you do me a huge favor?" I ask.

"Yeah, sure!" she replies.

"Can you come play with the puppies for me, if you're not too busy? They might be lonely while your dad and I are at the lake."

"I'm coming right now!" she cries. "Tell Bananas I got him a new tennis ball!" The phone goes dead.

I grin. The smile comes from deep within me, like Ophie's wag, unstoppable, working its way up from my gut to my heart to my eyes. I walk to the front door, and with a quick flick of my free wrist, I slip the photo of Dewey behind a stack of tarot.

Then I breathe it all in. There are things you know you want in your life, that you know are good and right and true the moment you realize they exist. Things that you can only miss if you're not paying attention.

Usually, as far as I can tell, these things are dogs.

But sometimes they're people. People who run up mountains.

I open the door and let one of them in.

ACKNOWLEDGMENTS

Thanks go to my Lake Union Publishing team, starring Christopher Werner, Danielle Marshall, Jodi Warshaw, Alicia Clancy, Gabriella Dumpit, Jacqueline Smith, Hai-Yen Mura, Mikyla Bruder, Jeff Belle, Rosanna Brockley, Alexandra Levenberg, and so many others who row my books across the lake to waiting readers all over the world.

To Holly Root, your support is why I don't live in a cardboard box.

To my community of writers, the Tall Poppies, thank you for all the myriad ways you lift me up in this strange business that comes along with storytelling. Also for the laughs.

Thanks to my early brainstormers, helpers, and readers: Jennifer Sabet, Kelly O'Connor McNees, Caeli, Mandy Woods McGowan, Sara Naatz, Kris Adams, Abbie Foster Chaffee, Nancy and David Admire, Sally Harms, Roger and Kristine Harms, and Doug Harms.

My admiration to tech thinkers like Bill and Melinda Gates (who didn't give their kids phones till they turned fourteen), Steve Jobs, Cal Newport, and Tristan Harris, as well as to all my yoga teachers who chant mantras and quote Rumi.

To Griffin and Chris, thank you for sharing this wired life with me. I love you both!

To Scout, the best friend a girl could have, thank you for all the wags.

ABOUT THE AUTHOR

Photo © 2019 Kaia Calhoun Photography

@Kelly.Harms is the number one bestselling author of *The Overdue Life of Amy Byler* and other novels, and she's celebrating two decades working in the publishing business this year. Kelly lives in Madison, Wisconsin, with her excellent kid, her loving Irishman, and her fluffy dog. She enjoys hiking, sailing, beaching, and losing at euchre. She also loves talking to readers in person and virtually, and she can be found at www.kellyharms.com.